Praise for *A Casualty of War*

"Far more than simply a compelling mystery that moves from the field hospitals of World War I, telling of honor, duty, and loss, to the bereaved villages of England and the loves, envies, and rivalries that survive, and the compassion that forgives. I can hear the quiet voices of my own grandparents through it all, saying, 'Courage!' It is intensely personal, as all great stories should be."

—Anne Perry, internationally bestselling author

"*A Casualty of War* is another masterful work in this series, and I cannot recommend it enough." —Bookreporter.com

"*A Casualty of War* is [Charles] Todd's strongest war book."

—*Washington Times*

"Todd . . . illustrates the toll the war has taken on the battle-weary military as well as the nurses and doctors, the sacrifices of the residents, [and] the citizens' valiant struggle to maintain a sense of normalcy. . . . A vivid and personal look at WWI."

—SouthFlorida.com

"The latest Crawford mystery is rich in character and period detail, with a solidly constructed story that should keep readers immersed in the action." —*Booklist*

"Harsh period attitudes toward traumatic stress and the exhaustion of a long war add poignancy to Todd's satisfying puzzle of identity and inheritance." —*Publishers Weekly*

"Readers will love the heroine for her courage and determination."

—*Kirkus Reviews*

Praise for *The Shattered Tree*

"Admirable, courageous and occasionally reckless, Bess ranks among the best of fictional amateur sleuths. [Todd] again creates a thought-provoking novel that evokes the terrors and suspicions of war."

—*Richmond Times-Dispatch*

"*The Shattered Tree* is an enjoyable and quick read—well worth the time."

—New York Journal of Books

"*The Shattered Tree* is a true spellbinder. From spies to the brutal facts of war to Bess's unwavering determination to uncover the truth, author Charles Todd has penned yet another fantastic thriller."

—*Suspense Magazine*

"As always in this immensely satisfying series, Todd heightens the mystery by setting it within a war-shattered world of battered villages, barren farms, and broken people."

—Marilyn Stasio, *New York Times Book Review*

Praise for *A Bitter Truth*

"A superb whodunit—just when you think you have it figured out, Todd throws a curve—and a moving evocation of a world at war."

—*Richmond Times-Dispatch*

"Makes fine work of the brooding atmosphere."

—*New York Times Book Review*

"Outstanding."

—*Publishers Weekly* (starred review)

"Bess is a very strong series lead, the historical setting is as well-developed here as it is in the Rutledge books, and the mysteries are just as elegantly constructed. Readers who have yet to sample the Crawford series should be strongly encouraged to do so." —*Booklist*

A Casualty of War

Also by Charles Todd

The Ian Rutledge Mysteries

A Test of Wills

Wings of Fire

Search the Dark

Legacy of the Dead

Watchers of Time

A Fearsome Doubt

A Cold Treachery

A Long Shadow

A False Mirror

A Pale Horse

A Matter of Justice

The Red Door

A Lonely Death

The Confession

Proof of Guilt

Hunting Shadows

A Fine Summer's Day

No Shred of Evidence

Racing the Devil

The Gate Keeper

The Bess Crawford Mysteries

A Duty to the Dead

An Impartial Witness

A Bitter Truth

An Unmarked Grave

A Question of Honor

An Unwilling Accomplice

A Pattern of Lies

The Shattered Tree

Other Fiction

The Murder Stone

The Walnut Tree

A Casualty of War

A Bess Crawford Mystery

CHARLES TODD

wm WILLIAM MORROW *An Imprint of* HarperCollins*Publishers*

P.S.™ is a trademark of HarperCollins Publishers.

A CASUALTY OF WAR. Copyright © 2017 by Charles Todd. All rights reserved. Printed in the United States of America. No part of this book may be used or reproduced in any manner whatsoever without written permission except in the case of brief quotations embodied in critical articles and reviews. For information address Harper-Collins Publishers, 195 Broadway, New York, NY 10007.

HarperCollins books may be purchased for educational, business, or sales promotional use. For information please email the Special Markets Department at SPsales@harpercollins.com.

A hardcover edition of this book was published in 2017 by William Morrow, an imprint of HarperCollins Publishers.

FIRST WILLIAM MORROW PAPERBACK EDITION PUBLISHED 2018.

Library of Congress Cataloging-in-Publication Data has been applied for.

ISBN 978-0-06-267879-9

18 19 20 21 22   LSC   10 9 8 7 6 5 4 3 2 1

For "Wutinda Buggies," aka Lucinda, whose first two years of life were not happy ones. And then she found a loving home and lived to sixteen, giving back all that love, and more . . .

And for Goldie, who should have lived to a ripe old age, but for an ugly twist of fate. Rest in peace, dear one.

And not least, for nurses everywhere who, like Bess, stand between us and the dark with their skill, devotion, and warm hearts.

CHAPTER 1

FRANCE

Early Autumn, 1918

LIEUTENANT MORRISON DIED as dawn broke on that Friday morning, a casualty of war.

I wrote the date and the time in his record. I had sat with him for the last hours of his life—and stayed with him still for nearly a quarter of an hour afterward.

I hadn't known him, except as a patient. I couldn't have told anyone that he was a good man or that he liked sunsets or sailing or treacle tarts. He'd been unconscious since he came to us at the base hospital. But he belonged to someone. Parents, possibly brothers and sisters, perhaps even a sweetheart or wife. He belonged to his men, and they had come when they could to stand silently beside his bed or touch his hand.

We were so close to ending this wretched war. It was hard to watch men die when rumors promised safety and peace so near at hand.

I watched the stretcher bearers carry away his body, and later I would find the names of those he left behind and write to them.

Matron came to stand beside me and laid her hand briefly on my arm. After a moment she said briskly, "There are other men waiting for your care."

I turned and smiled as best I could, then went about my duties. Mourning was a luxury we couldn't afford, with so many wounded coming in.

Later that day, we were making the rounds with the medicine tray when Sister Walker came searching for me. I was just giving a Scots Captain his next dose of morphine—he had had surgery on his hip, and the pain had been more than he could bear, stoic though he was—and she waited patiently while I tended him. As I turned to go to the next patient, she took the tray from me.

"Matron has sent for you. I'll carry on here."

I thanked her and sought out Matron. She was in her small office, making notations in patient records. Looking up, she said, "Permission to sit down, Sister Crawford."

Oh, dear, I thought. Bad news from home? No, she didn't appear to be distressed for me. A reprimand? We were all pushed to our physical and emotional limits, and it would only be human to miss some important detail. A complaint? Lieutenant Booker was recuperating but irascible.

She seemed to be choosing her words with care, and that was even more worrying.

"Sister Belmont," she said finally. "Do you know her?"

"Not well," I replied blankly. "We worked together near Ypres, I think."

"Yes, I see. She was at the forward aid station with Dr. Weatherby. They just brought her in. Attempted suicide."

I drew in a breath of shock. In four years of war we had all seen more horror and more tragedy than seemed possible for a human being to endure. They kept us awake at night, and when we could sleep, they filled our dreams.

"One case in particular was more than she could bear. Face wound. A friend from her village. She and her brother had known him since childhood. The breaking point for her. She ran out of the tent, to her quarters, and found a pair of scissors."

"I'm so sorry."

"I shouldn't be telling you this, Sister Crawford. But they desperately need a replacement, you see, and the staff is understandably upset. I need a steady hand, someone who will take over Sister Belmont's duties and support Dr. Weatherby in every way."

I found myself wondering how I might feel if Simon, or someone I knew very well, like Sergeant Lassiter, had come in with such a wound. And it was shattering even to imagine.

"I will do my best, Matron," I managed to say.

"Yes, I know you will, Bess," she replied quietly. "That's why I've chosen you. The next ambulances should be in at two o'clock. See that you have turned over your patients to Sister Walker, and have your kit ready."

"Yes, Matron." I rose with a nod.

I had reached the door when she added, "Dr. Weatherby is very young. Help him to cope."

It had been difficult for her to give me so much personal information. It wasn't done. A warning, perhaps? Or a worry she couldn't quite bring herself to explain? Still, it would have been just as wrong to send anyone to the aid station without some knowledge of the problems there.

"I will do all I can, Matron."

She nodded as I shut her door.

I went back to my ward and informed Sister Walker of the change in my orders, then took her through details that she might not already know about the patients. When I'd finished, she said, "A wounded Sister has just been brought in. She's in her quarters;

we aren't to disturb her. She must be the one you're replacing. What happened?"

"I haven't seen her," I answered, telling the strict truth.

"Oh, I was hoping you'd know more than we do."

I smiled. "I apologize for disappointing you."

"Well, someone else might know," she said philosophically.

Another convoy of ambulances was just arriving. I heard the bustle as I left the ward, and I hurried out with the others to meet it and help bring in the wounded. A cheerful word was nearly as good as medical care for these men, already in pain and then jostled by the long journey across roads that resembled washboards, unsuitable for caissons, much less ambulances. I'd watched gun carriages bouncing over them like toys.

When they were all seen to, I went to my quarters, quickly stowed my belongings, then walked over to the canteen for a bowl of soup and a cup of tea. It might be hours until I next had time for a meal.

The long room was full, and I had to join a Captain at one of the many smaller tables. I asked permission to sit there, and he smiled. "Of course. Always a pleasure to have a pretty face across from me. Helps me forget the food."

I laughed. The food we were served was filling and nourishing, and that was about all that could be said for it. Everything had to be cooked in great vats, or in vast ovens, and it was either over- or underdone.

The Captain was a very attractive man—tall, fair hair, blue eyes. And quite healthy. He didn't appear to be one of our wounded, not even a recovery on his way back to his regiment.

And so, after starting my soup, I asked, "Are you being re- leased?"

"I wasn't a patient," he told me. "I'm trying to rejoin my

regiment. I was summoned to HQ to answer some questions about the situation at the Front, and I must make my own way back. An ambulance from Rouen brought me this far. I'm waiting for the next leg. I shouldn't be surprised to see an elephant or a hot air balloon. I seem to have traveled in every other conveyance out here."

"It might well be a camel, you know. Or a yak."

He grinned. "So it might be."

"Any news about the war?" I asked. After all, he'd been at HQ. It was a fair question.

"They were too busy asking for information to offer much in return. Sorry. A waste of time, actually. I disliked leaving my men. The front lines are changing so fast that I have no idea where they may be."

I was trying to place his accent. Proper English, educated, but not from a county I recognized. Nor from India or Canada. I was puzzling over that when he said, "What is it?"

I felt my face flushing. "Your accent. I don't know it."

"Not surprising. My family went out to the Lesser Antilles several generations ago. A younger son, having to make his way. The elder son inherited the estate in Suffolk. My great-grandfather received an inheritance from his mother and with it bought a plantation on Barbados. We've lived there ever since." He reached into an inner pocket and took out an oiled packet containing photographs.

The Lesser Antilles . . . the Caribbean Sea. Quite exotic to someone who had never been there.

Palms framing what looked like the clearest water edging white sand. A grassy square with blindingly white buildings around it, cool in the sun. A two-story wooden house with a long, wide veranda on the three sides that I could see, and a profusion of flowers in the gardens on either side of the path to the door. I'd lived in the tropics; I could imagine the riot of color. A market with all manner of fruits and goods filling the stalls, and people haggling over purchases or chatting in small groups. English and locals mingling together in the busy street. What appeared to be a cricket club, lawns as trim as any at Lord's in London.

Glancing up from the photographs, I saw his expression. He loved his home, and was happy to share it with someone. How many times had he looked at these same scenes on long night watches or waiting for the signal to go over the top?

"Is this where you live?" I pointed to the house.

"Yes. High ceilings to keep the rooms cool, and fans to keep the furniture from turning green in the rains. In the back of the house there's a wide courtyard with tables and a small pond. A number of large trees shade it from the heat of the day. We take our meals out there, if there aren't any guests. And to one side is the guesthouse, for visitors from England or from neighboring islands, like Saint Lucia or Martinique. Many of us keep a boat, to travel from one island to another."

"Martinique. That's where the terrible volcanic eruption was."

"May 1902. It killed twenty-eight thousand people, many of them our friends. My mother would go there to visit, and bring home bottles of the finest French perfumes and wines for all her friends on Barbados."

"Are your parents still living?" I asked, hearing the sadness in his voice.

"Sadly, no. Just as well, they'd be worried about me in this war."

Handing the photographs back to him, I asked, "And how do you like the winters in France?"

"Bloo— rather awful at first, of course. I'm used to them now.

I think it's the damp more often than the cold. It eats at one's bones."

"Do you visit your English relations when you're on leave? Barbados must seem very far away." German submarines roamed the Atlantic, torpedoing merchant vessels as well as naval ships, making any crossing a chancy business. The sinking of one of our ocean liners, RMS *Lusitania* in May of 1915, had helped persuade the Americans to enter the war two years later.

"My family hasn't kept in touch with the senior branch of the family. I know where they live, a little village in Suffolk. There are paintings of the house and the church that my great-grandfather took with him when he left. I've been to London, seen the sights, traveled to Oxford, where my great-grandfather was educated, and to Exeter, where my mother's family lived." He grimaced. "The cousin I met there died of his wounds a week after I saw him, and his mother died in the influenza epidemic. I don't think she wanted to live. Distant cousins own the house now. Sorry, I didn't mean to bore you with my family's history. What about you?"

And so I told him about growing up in India when my father was stationed there, and our other adventures following the regiment.

"Colonel Crawford's daughter? Small world! He attended the meeting I was summoned to at HQ."

"Did he, indeed?" Through these years of war I seldom knew where my father was sent by the Army. He'd retired from command of his regiment before 1914, coming home to Somerset as he'd always promised my mother he would. The man who had taken his place was competent and popular. And so, when war was declared, instead of recalling my father and giving him one of the new regiments so hastily organized, the War Office took advantage of his experience in other ways. I knew for a fact he'd been to France on any number of occasions—sightings had been reported to me from time to time—but what he was doing over here or why he'd also been sent to Scotland or Sandhurst or Salisbury Plain not even my mother knew. I had a suspicion that he'd helped oversee the training of the huge number of men who had volunteered in early August 1914, and he'd advised HQ on strategy and tactics. The pity was, too often HQ had gone its own way, to the cost of far too many lives.

I smiled. "How did he look?"

"Well enough. Tired. Everyone is."

"Armentières is back in Allied hands. And Cambrai has just fallen to the Canadians. Turkey is on the verge of collapse. That should lift spirits at HQ."

He glanced around, but the tables near us were no longer occupied, now that most of the staff had returned to their duties. Even so, he lowered his voice. "Cambrai is burning. Fires set by the retreating Germans to hold us up. They want an armistice with honor. The French and the Belgians aren't having it. They want the Germans to pull back to prewar lines. And to return all the captured rolling stock that was sent to Berlin: engines, carriages, and so on. Well, you can't blame the French, can you? After four years of hard fighting?" He shook his head. "It's going to be a different sort of battle, this one."

He shouldn't have been telling me any of this, but I could see that it was preying on his mind. After all, I was Colonel Crawford's daughter, and not expected to gossip. And he needed to do something about his own worry before he returned to the lines. There would be questions—and it was clear he had been given no answers to offer his men.

"But the Germans are already retreating," I said after a

moment. We had seen the hasty graves of their dead as we ourselves moved steadily north. "Surely that's raising the morale of the men fighting them."

"That's true. But we're tired, Sister. Beyond exhaustion, in fact. Food and water supplies aren't keeping up with us, and sometimes ammunition runs short. Every whisper of peace makes it harder to face dying. To ask men on the verge of collapse themselves to carry out one more assault or stop one more attack is cruel but has to be done. If the tanks don't arrive in time, we must clear out the German machine gunners ourselves, and those men don't surrender easily. When they finally do, it's hard to control my own men."

I found myself thinking that my father would approve of this officer: He put his men first, and cared about what happened to them. He understood what was going on and was trying to cope as best he could.

To shift the conversation back to less intense emotions, I asked, "What about Alsace-Lorraine? Surely the French will demand the return of both provinces?" They had lost them to Germany in the Franco-Prussian War a generation ago, and it was still a sore point.

"Of course that's a must." He toyed with his teacup. "We won't see peace for a while, you and I. Not until the French are satisfied or the Germans realize they're well and truly defeated. But I'm told Berlin has reserves on the Eastern Front. The Kaiser might bring them forward in a last-ditch effort to get better terms." His eyes were bleak. "The problem is, men will go on dying while governments argue. Such a waste."

I could hear a convoy of ambulances coming in and hastily finished my tea. "There's my own camel," I said. "I hope yours arrives in good time."

He rose. "It's been a pleasure, Sister Crawford. If ever you travel to Barbados, look up my family. Travis. Anyone can give you directions to find the house. You'll be welcomed. Tell them Alan persuaded you that you must see a corner of paradise for yourself."

"That's very kind, Captain Travis. Good luck."

I retrieved my kit and went out to help with the unloading of wounded, then said my good-byes as the empty ambulances were washed down. And then we followed the sounds of the guns— nearer and nearer to them—all the way to the forward aid station and Dr. Weatherby.

Once there, I assumed my duties without fuss and tried to bring a little cheer to the other two Sisters and the orderlies who were our staff. But it was going to take time for them to put the events surrounding Sister Belmont's removal from the station behind them.

Sister Brewer had started to drop things, her nerves on edge, and so I was given the task of assisting Dr. Weatherby while she was assigned to sorting the wounded as they came in. She seemed to be relieved by the change. Sister Williams dealt with the less serious cases, where drawing a splinter or dosing an early case of dysentery didn't require a doctor's attention.

I think Dr. Weatherby was happier to have a dependable nurse in surgery, and it didn't take me long to see that he had both skill and a willingness to take chances if they would save a life.

When I finally left the station, it was once more functioning smoothly and competently.

CHAPTER 2

1 November 1918

BACK FROM PARIS and recovered from my own wound, I was again assigned to Dr. Weatherby's forward aid station. But it was a very different Front now. Moving forward with the advancing British lines, we were often in what had once been the front lines of the German Army.

The landscape was heartbreaking. We'd been accustomed to the blackened, cratered, bloody expanse of No Man's Land, but now we were seeing what the German occupation had done to this part of France. Villages had been leveled, orchards cut down, garden walls turned to rubble, and the flowers that once had bloomed there had been churned into the earth. Under gray November skies, the sight was even more desolate. And often what couldn't be taken away had been burned. Even the church where Dr. Weatherby had set up his latest aid station was hardly more than a shell, and what was left of the walls and the altar was scarred. The window frames, without their stained glass, were stark outlines against the night sky, their Gothic glory skeletal.

Still, the crypt was habitable and dry, although the tombs

there had been damaged. With the November rain and cold winds, it offered a little shelter, and we had partitioned it to suit our needs.

I had been warned not to go into any other half-ruined house or shop in the village. The church had been swept by engineers and declared safe, but they had had no time to look elsewhere. The Germans had left traps behind, to make it hazardous to re-take territory.

Dr. Weatherby had greeted me effusively, delighted to have me back, and I was very glad to see that his staff—which earlier had been anxious and unsettled after Sister Belmont's attempted suicide—were as steady as they'd been when I had left them. And the doctor himself was a seasoned veteran now, competent and unflappable.

The level of noise from the nearby artillery companies was almost unbearable above ground, and even in the crypt we could feel the ground shaking with it. It had intensified, as if both sides were eager to use up their stockpiles of shells. The heavy bombardment left us with jangled nerves and raw throats from trying to speak over it. If they could hear these guns in Canterbury, England—and I knew that this had been so for most of the war—being so much nearer was painful.

We were seeing a wider variety of patients. With the colder weather, the Spanish flu had returned, almost as if it was deter-mined to kill those who had escaped its clutches in the last round of infections. We had even taken in a number of German soldiers too ill with the flu to be evacuated with their companies.

We also saw wounds from exploding traps. One Sergeant told me that in one of the villages they were clearing, his men discov-ered a baker's oven intact. One of them opened it to see if there were any loaves inside. He set off an explosion that killed him instantly and severely wounded the others who had gone in with him. Another soldier went into a garden looking for potatoes and was killed by a device hidden among the plants. Ingenious traps waiting for the unwary. It slowed the British advance, watching out for such surprises.

We'd also treated cases of poisoning, from drinking water from deliberately contaminated wells.

And there was still no word of an end to the fighting.

My second evening there, Dr. Weatherby and I had just finished a very delicate bit of surgery.

A piece of shrapnel had lodged near the spine in the patient's neck, but Dr. Weatherby feared that the jostling of the ambulance on the journey to a base hospital where there were more-experienced surgeons would leave the young Lieutenant paralyzed, and so he had decided to remove the shrapnel himself despite the risk.

"If I don't get it right," he said quietly to me, "it will be no worse than leaving it in."

He managed it somehow, and I'd marveled at his nerve and steady hand.

"There. He'll do. Orderly, handle him carefully. Tag him for Blighty."

I was bathing the patient's face as Dr. Weatherby spoke, and I saw the conflicting emotions there. Relief, yes, and a feeling of despair for leaving his men behind.

Trying to reassure him, I said lightly, "I shouldn't worry, Lieutenant. Base Hospital might overrule that."

He glanced up at me, a wry smile breaking through the haze of the drug we had administered.

We watched the Lieutenant being carried out, and then Dr. Weatherby washed his hands. He brushed them, still wet, across his eyes. "God, I'm tired. Will this killing never stop?"

I called to the orderly just outside. "Next."

He stuck his head inside the surgical area. "That's it for now, Sister. We've got four minor wounds, and Sister Harvey is taking care of them. There's time for a cuppa, if you like."

We did. A cup of tea was an elixir beyond price, I thought, even without sugar or milk. Hot, soothing, restorative. The kettle had just boiled when Sister Harvey came to join us, and she brought a tin of biscuits that had been tucked into her birthday packet. She shared them with us, and I took one gratefully. I could have devoured the entire tin, all at once realizing how hungry I was. How long had it been since lunch? I couldn't remember, because it was already dark, and impossible to judge the hour. And then one of the orderlies appeared, bearing a tray of sandwiches. They were dry but we ate them, and we were just balling up the papers they'd been wrapped in when the orderly returned to warn us that he'd spotted the first of the wounded from the fighting we could hear going on a mile or so ahead of us. Sister Harvey, tucking her precious biscuits aside, hurried away to assess them.

Dr. Weatherby got to his feet. "No rest for us, eh? Well, at least we enjoyed our tea." He stretched his shoulders, and we turned to climb the steps up to the nave, where Sister Harvey had shaded her lamp against the risk of snipers and was preparing for the new patients. We could hardly see the stretcher bearers and walking wounded coming toward us. Ghostly figures plodding slowly, silhouettes outlined by the artillery flashes, like summer lightning across the clouds, only noisier. And then we hurried below again.

We brought in the stretcher cases first, always the worst. The first man, a Sergeant, died even as we tried to stem the flow of blood from an artery in his leg. The second had a shattered arm, and so it went, until I lost track of everything but Dr. Weatherby's quiet voice, giving me orders.

I finished binding up a chest wound, then called, "Next," to the orderlies outside the canvas that separated the surgery from the lines of cots and stretchers.

And a new patient was brought in.

He was lying under a blanket, unconscious, his face such a bloody mask I couldn't at first judge where his wound was.

I dipped a cloth in a basin of water, then began to clean away the blood. Much of it had already dried across the lower part of his face, and I left that, concentrating on his forehead and then his hair, already stiff with it. I could see that the left shoulder of his tunic was black with blood as well. Head wounds always bled heavily. And then I found the long groove through his hair on the left side, deep enough that the skull was showing.

Dr. Weatherby began to probe the wound. "Bullet. Rifle, I should think, not machine gun. Close call, that. See how it bored a line along the bone? He's lucky it didn't penetrate to the brain. Only the barest fraction of an inch deeper, and we'd have had a very different story."

We set about cleaning the wound and binding up his head. We were just about to call for the orderlies to take him out when his lashes fluttered and his eyes opened. "Ah. An angel," he murmured, gazing straight at me. And then as full consciousness returned, he tried to sit up on the table. I realized I knew him. Captain Travis.

"I want that man arrested—" he shouted, pointing at the orderly standing by the partition opening. Breaking off, he looked wildly about the surgical area. "Where the hell am I?"

"Forward aid station—" Dr. Weatherby began, but the Captain cut in.

"Take me back to my command. *Now*. I saw him. It was *deliberate*."

Dr. Weatherby tried to restrain him. "What was deliberate?" he asked.

"He shot me. On purpose, damn it. He has to be stopped."

"Who shot you?" I asked, trying to soothe him by appearing to take him seriously.

"I don't know—yes, I do. It was an officer. The next sector. I don't know his name." His head must have begun to swim, because he put a hand up and closed his eyes. "Get me back there. I'll walk if I must."

"You'll go nowhere," Dr. Weatherby said firmly. "Not for a few hours."

"We'll see about that," Captain Travis said and swung his legs off the table, intending to leave. But the exertion and the anger were too much. His knees buckled as he tried to stand, and he went down. Dr. Weatherby and the orderly caught him before his head hit the ground, and another orderly came at my call to help put the Captain back on his stretcher. His head lolled, and I thought it just as well that he'd lost consciousness.

"Strap him down," the doctor instructed them. "I can't give him anything. Not with that wound. And keep him as quiet as you can."

They settled the unconscious man, covered him again with a blanket, and took him away as I called for the next patient.

It was well after midnight when we had dealt with the last of the wounded. An ambulance convoy had come and gone, taking away the most serious cases, but there had been no room for the Captain. A last-minute stomach wound had taken precedence.

I washed my hands, said good night to a weary Dr. Weatherby, and started for my own bed. The Sisters were in a corner of the crypt, set off from the wounded by canvas, so that we had a modicum of privacy, although conditions were rudimentary at best.

It was then I remembered Captain Travis. Sister Medford had night duty, charged with alerting Dr. Weatherby or me if a patient had difficulties or a serious wound was brought in, and as I looked for the Captain, intending to see how he had fared, she met me with a grimace.

"The man's mad," she said quietly, so that he wouldn't hear her. "See if you can do anything with him."

I went to kneel by his stretcher, and he glared at me.

"Take these straps away. I have work to do."

"Do you have a headache?" I asked, reaching out to take his pulse. It was pounding.

"I have a headache that would kill a horse," he said angrily. "What do you expect? I was shot in the bloo— in the head."

"You need to rest. In the morning we'll decide if you're fit to resume your duties."

"I'm fit now. I was shot *deliberately*. Do you understand me? By another officer. I have to do something about it."

I could feel the pent-up rage in him.

Thinking to let him talk, and perhaps calm him down, I said, "Why are you so certain it was deliberate? Were you retreating? It's always chaos then, hard to tell friend from foe." My tone was reasonable, inquiring, giving him the feeling that I believed him. The truth was, I didn't know if I did or not.

"Because he looked straight at me. For several seconds. We'd been caught in the open by machine gunners and were trying to get back to our own lines. It was orderly enough, but we'd been moving up in force, and the retreat was fast and bloody. My men, other companies, other officers shouting orders, and those in the rear trying to give us covering fire. The German troops we thought we'd pinned down led us into a trap. I was helping Sergeant Willard, whose leg was bleeding profusely. A

Lieutenant was just ahead of me, but he turned to say something to his men. He saw me then, stopped, stared at me with a frown, and then reached down for a rifle someone had dropped. He picked it up, pointed it directly at me. I shouted at him to keep going. Instead he fired. I remember thinking the Germans had followed us, that he was trying to stop them. Then I realized I'd been hit. And instead of looking shocked, he smiled. I saw his *face*, damn it. He intended to kill me. You don't mistake something like that."

"Did you know this man?"

"He must have been new to that sector. I could see his rank—Lieutenant—and I knew some companies had taken heavy casualties earlier. The odd thing was, I remembered thinking in that split second that he looked a little like my great-uncle. The photographs I remember seeing of him when he was young."

"Perhaps he's your cousin, your great-uncle's son."

"My great-uncle had two daughters," he said irritably. "They aren't likely to be serving in the British Army."

"No," I agreed, summoning a smile. Fatigue was hitting me like a blow. I could feel myself going down quickly. But he didn't give me an answering smile.

"You don't believe me," he said, closing his eyes, anguish in his face. Then he opened them again. "Why should I make up something like this?"

"You've had a serious head wound. You've been unconscious. There's the possibility of a concussion," I offered. "You might not be thinking clearly."

"A head wound isn't likely to make me imagine someone shooting me. And there's the wound to prove it." He tried to lift a hand to point to his bandages, and swore under his breath when the straps stopped him.

"Lieutenants carry revolvers," I reminded him. "Not rifles. Why didn't he simply raise his revolver and fire?"

"I don't know."

"Did the wounded Sergeant see this happening?"

"He might have done. I managed to get him back to our lines before I passed out." He turned his head. "He must be here. He must have been brought in at the same time I was. Ask him yourself, if you won't believe me."

But I was nearly sure it was his Sergeant who had died on the table. He'd been shot in the leg, and the bullet had nicked an artery in his thigh. He'd almost bled out by the time he reached us.

I didn't want to tell Captain Travis this. Instead, to keep him quiet, I said, "Your Sergeant? I think he was sent on to the base hospital."

He lay back, closing his eyes. "I'm telling the truth," he said quietly. "Whether you believe me or not, that's what happened."

"Well, look at it this way," I said, making my voice philosophical. "You'll be better able to do something about this Lieutenant tomorrow morning, when your headache subsides." I used my torch to examine his eyes, and I didn't like what I saw. "Just now you're more likely to collapse halfway back to your lines. And we can't spare anyone to lead you."

"I can make it. It's only a headache, after all," he said stubbornly.

"Possibly. I don't doubt your determination, Captain. But you'll need your wits about you, dealing with this Lieutenant. You can't go roaring in demanding his blood. Not with your only witness back in Base Hospital. You'll have to prove your case, and the last thing you want is to fall down flat on your face in the middle of your argument."

He could see the sense of that, although I could tell he didn't care for it.

"Do you have any other relations who might have joined the Army?" I asked, trying to distract him. "Perhaps on the Suffolk side of your family?"

His eyes focused on me, intent suddenly, but I could tell he was thinking of something else.

"Good God, I think you've hit on something," he answered finally. "I'm the only male of military age in my immediate family. But I've just remembered. I should have thought of it before this. It was in Paris. I was there on leave. 1917. Late April." He was frowning now. "I was just stepping out of the train at the Gare, and an officer was waiting to take my place in the same carriage. He looked at me, and I looked at him, and I had a feeling that I knew him. He must have felt the same way. He said, 'You aren't by any chance a Travis?' I told him I was. He said, 'We must be related.' And he held out his hand. 'James Travis, from Suffolk,' he said, and I answered as I took it, 'Alan Travis, from Barbados.' He laughed at that. 'The lost branch of the family? By God, I think you must be.' And I laughed too. 'Lost? Never. We know exactly where we are.' He said, 'Come to Suffolk when the war is over. Before you go home. I'd like that.' And I told him, 'I might even do that. It's not likely you'll ever find your way to the Caribbean.' Just then the whistle blew, and the train began to move. He leapt aboard, calling, 'Good luck, cousin.' I wished him the same."

The Captain was staring up at the undercroft ceiling, seeing another place, another time. After a long moment, he added, "I liked him. I wished we'd had time to know each other better. But there was no time, you see, the train was pulling out, and I never ran into him again. I hadn't thought about that encounter since."

He seemed quieter now. I was beginning to think I'd taken

his mind off his pressing need to get back to the lines. Perhaps we could both get a little sleep.

I was about to rise to my feet when he looked at me again. And this time he saw me, not the past.

"Why in God's name," he said, his voice so low I wasn't sure he was speaking to me, "why in God's name would James Travis want to kill me?"

I stayed where I was, trying to read his face in the dim light of the shaded lamp.

I'd succeeded in lancing the boiling rage that was consuming him. But inadvertently I'd also put a name to the man he was so certain had tried to kill him.

"Did James look at all like your great-uncle?" I asked, casting about for a distraction.

He closed his eyes, bringing back his memory of another time and place. "Yes. I think so. A little. That would explain why he seemed familiar today." He opened his eyes, and I could see his disbelief fighting with his certainty. "James Travis. I don't see how it could have been anyone else."

"I hardly think that side of the family would wish to kill you," I said, striving to divert him from his conviction. "Besides, if you didn't recognize him straightaway in that brief instant before he shot you, how can you be sure he knew who you were? After all, you said yourself it was a fleeting resemblance. And you haven't seen each other since Paris. That's long enough that you can't possibly be sure. And you'd liked each other then. If you want my opinion, when you go back to confront him, you'll discover that he's an entirely different person."

"You don't understand. I saw death staring me in the face, Sister. In that moment of clarity, I saw *him*. I'm not likely to be mistaken."

"Captain—"

"I appreciate your desire to help me, Sister. I'll wait until morning. But no longer than morning."

I said nothing for a moment, waiting for him to speak again. Instead he lay there looking at the stonework over his head. I rose to my feet.

I was just turning away when he said, "I'll find him. If it's the last thing I do. What if you're right, and he *is* different—if he's a danger to himself and everyone around him? Someone has to stop him before he kills again."

I hadn't meant it in that sense, when I said he might be a different person. But Captain Travis heard what he wanted to hear.

Chapter 3

I don't remember falling asleep. I had crawled into my cot and taken out my brush to comb my hair after long hours under my cap, and the next thing I knew, it was dawn and the brush was under my left shoulder, pressing into it. I retrieved it and set it on the makeshift table by my cot, and lay there for two or three minutes, summoning the energy to rise and dress. It was cold in my quarters—we had no fires or small stoves to keep us warm. It was a trial bathing and then putting on my uniform. Even my shoes were cold as I shoved my stockinged feet into them. I hurried through my breakfast but held the cup in my hands for several minutes for its warmth before I finished my tea.

I was just handing my tray to the orderly when I heard a commotion in the part of the crypt where we kept patients who were destined to go back to a base hospital. And there I found Captain Travis shouting at the night Sister, demanding to be released.

"What's this?" I asked, in no frame of mind to deal with his mood. There were four other men resting there, including one suspected appendicitis case we were watching and another with an arm wound that wasn't clotting properly. "You're waking up the Germans as well as all of us."

"You told me last night I'd be free to leave this morning."

"I did no such thing. I told you we'd reevaluate your condition in the morning."

I knelt by his cot to straighten out the blanket that he'd thrown aside as he struggled against the straps that held him down. When I pulled it up to his chin, I could feel the warmth of his body. An unnatural warmth. Moving my hand to his face, I realized that he was running a fever. We'd cleaned his wound very carefully, but it was deep, and infection was always a worry. Any temporary dressing that had been put on in the field to stop the bleeding couldn't have been as clean as ours, and men chasing the Germans through northern France had very little opportunity to bathe or change their clothing. The only thing keeping the lice population down, according to Dr. Weatherby, was the cold weather.

The Captain jerked his head away from my hand, but I had already identified the problem, and as an orderly brought another lamp for me, I could just see that my patient's blue eyes were far too bright.

"The doctor will have to decide whether you can go or not," I told the Captain, "and it will do no good shouting. So please be a little more considerate of your neighbors."

He lay back on the cot, his mouth a tight line of repressed anger. But he had quieted.

I looked at the other patients. The bleeding had stopped in the Sergeant's arm, the padding beneath his bandaging mostly dry save for the inner wad of cotton wool. Still, I didn't care for the look of the arm, and I thought it best to send him back to Base Hospital to be observed. The possible appendix case seemed much improved this morning, greeting me with a smile and no signs of fever or pain in his abdomen. Still, he too would go back. The remaining two, one with a long cut on his shoulder and the other with a sprained ankle, were much better as well, although the ankle had swollen more than I'd have liked during the night.

Leaving to find Dr. Weatherby, I discovered him shaving with cold water. Men at the Front shaved often, so that the gas masks they carried fit more tightly. My own mask lay on my cot, ready to catch up at any sign of that telltale mist. There had been an increase in gas attacks, another rearguard action.

"Sister Medford reported a quiet night," he said, "only the usual problems. How are our other patients?" His voice was muffled as he lifted his nose with one hand and shaved under it with sure strokes.

"The head wound is feverish. I think he should be sent back. And both the arm and the appendix as well."

I gave him the rest of my report, and he nodded. "Very well. Oh, damn."

The barrage of shelling from the German guns had stopped suddenly. That could only mean an assault was imminent. And in the sudden quiet, I could hear the approach of ambulances.

"They're early," Dr. Weatherby said, wiping off the remnants of shaving soap and reaching for his cap.

But there were only two ambulances, and we loaded our patients quickly, before the lines of new wounded started to appear.

Captain Travis was livid. "I tell you, I have to go back to my men. If he shot me, he'll shoot someone else. Damn it, they aren't expecting trouble. They didn't see him as I did. The bastard has to be mad. He's a danger to himself and everyone around him. Don't you understand? Get these straps off me, do you hear?"

I said, "Let Base Hospital have a look at that wound, and you'll be back before you know it. I promise you."

He turned to Sister Medford. "Can't you hear? Machine guns. Damn it, you aren't deaf! Get me back on my feet."

But he was safely stowed in the ambulance over his objections. I was settling the man across from him as Captain Travis continued to rail at me. But there was an overtone of feverishness now in his demands.

I could understand, I knew why he was so adamant. If he was right, if there was nothing personal between the two men, and the Lieutenant from the other sector had actually fired at him, as Captain Travis claimed he had done, then the man needed to be stopped. He was a threat to everyone around him. Fear alone could make a man fire at shadows, see an enemy where there was none. Men broke in different ways, and some recovered quickly. Others didn't. And the next man might not be as lucky as the Captain.

If it was true, that the other officer had picked up a rifle instead of using his revolver, that might well have saved the Captain's life. Officers weren't trained with rifles, and that unfamiliarity might have thrown off his aim. The next time it might be his revolver, and that could easily mean murder.

I turned back to Captain Travis. He was struggling against his straps and I was afraid he'd do himself a hurt long before he reached Base Hospital.

"Listen to me. If you will be quiet, I'll do what I can to send word back to your sector. Will that do?"

He couldn't reach my hand. But he clutched at my skirts. "Lieutenant James Travis. I'm sure of it. Find him, if you can. Don't let him shoot someone else."

Both of us could hear the drone of a reconnaissance aircraft coming nearer.

The driver was ready to close the rear doors. "Time to go, Sister."

"Yes, all right," I told him. Then, turning back to Captain Travis, I said, "I will do my best. I give you my word."

He nodded. "Colonel Crawford's daughter. Yes, all right, I believe you."

But I thought it was the exhaustion of fighting so hard to have his way and not my promise that caused him to close his eyes. As I turned to leave, he said, his eyes still shut, "On your head if someone else is killed."

The driver gave me a hand jumping down from the ambulance. "What's wrong with the head wound?"

"Fever," I said. "Tell them to watch him when he's put into a bed. He might walk."

The driver shut the doors and turned the handle to secure them. "Right you are, Sister."

And then he was climbing in his door, letting in the clutch, and starting on his journey.

I watched him out of sight, then hurried back to the tent where Dr. Weatherby was already examining a new patient.

I intended to keep my promise to Captain Travis. In all good conscience I had to try, whether he remembered events truly or was confused about how he was wounded. But how? Whether I believed him or not, it had to be done.

And then we were brought three patients from the Captain's company. One of them was severely wounded and would be sent back by ambulance. But the Corporal and the Private had shell splinters that needed cleaning and bandaging.

When I had a private moment with the Corporal while Dr. Weatherby looked for forceps, I asked if he'd carry a message to his Lieutenant for me.

"It's a matter that was on Captain Travis's mind just before he was sent back. He asked me to write it down for him and see that the Lieutenant got it as soon as possible." I'd done that myself, because it would carry more weight if this man believed it had come directly from his Captain.

"Yes, glad to, Sister." He took it from me—and turned in time to see what Dr. Weatherby was holding in his hand. "God help me," he breathed, and closed his eyes. But we got the fragment out without too much difficulty, and once bandaged and given a cup of tea, Corporal Meeker thanked us and started back.

I had worded the message with care.

Captain Travis had some concerns that he was unable to set down before the ambulance arrived to carry him back to Base Hospital Seven. He asked me to do this for him. In the retreat during which he was wounded, he was disturbed by the behavior of a Lieutenant Travis in the next sector. There was no time to look into this matter before he was carried to the aid station. He felt that Lieutenant Travis was exhausted and required rotation behind the lines to rest. Although the Lieutenant's courage is not in question, his level of fatigue could be a danger to himself and to his men, and he might not be the best judge of that.

Most of the men following the German retreat had had no time to rest, and to suggest that this officer had reached a point where he couldn't be trusted to carry out his duties to the best of his ability was merely an observation. If Captain Travis was wrong, no harm done. If he was right, this officer would be relieved and sent back for twenty-four to forty-eight hours. The Lieutenant might not like it, if he was innocent of any wrongdoing, but if he was guilty, it would take him out of the fray before someone was killed.

I felt a sense of relief, duty done to both men.

Some hours later, a casualty from the Captain's regiment brought me an answering message.

The Corporal bringing it had obviously been told what was in the message and to wait for a reply.

I opened it and read:

There is no Lieutenant Travis in the company in question. Lieutenant Anderson is a good man and steady. Are you sure you have the name right?

My surprise was evident.

The Corporal said, "I'd not heard of this man myself. Are you sure, Sister?"

"I don't know what to say. The Captain asked me to take down his message and be sure that it was sent." Thinking fast, I asked, "Were you there when the Captain was shot?"

"Indeed I was, Sister. If it weren't for him, there'd have been even more casualties. It was brilliant, how he managed. He's a good man, the Captain. I'm happy to serve under him."

Oh, dear.

I said, "Did you see who shot him?"

"It was utter chaos, Sister. I'd not be able to swear to that. The man next to me saw him stumble, but we thought it was the Sergeant's weight. And then we were diving headfirst into a ditch. The Captain came after me, with Willard, and I took the Sergeant's weight while Private Goode caught the Captain. I saw they were both hit and bleeding like a— like they'd bought it, and we dragged them back to the barn wall. We sent him and the Sergeant and three others back to an aid station, then began to sort ourselves out."

Oh, dear!

"We've been taking heavy casualties. We sorely miss the Captain. I'm to ask, is it likely he'll be back?"

"Yes, I should think so. You didn't see this Lieutenant Travis, then?"

"We were caught out, and it was every man for himself. It seemed like half the regiment was running with us. The Germans we were charging were front line troops, no old men or boys in that lot. They knew what they were about, and we didn't see the machine gun until it was too late. I'm not saying that this Lieutenant Travis wasn't present in the mêlée, mind you, but Haig himself could have been there, and we'd not have noticed. I could put out word you're looking for him."

And that would never do.

"I'm sure Captain Travis must have known where he came from, if he named him. Perhaps it was my mistake, writing that he was in the next sector." I smiled, making light of it. "I was asked to pass on a message, and that's what I've done. If the Lieutenant is at the point of extreme exhaustion, his own men will do something about it, don't you think?"

"We're all past that point, truth be told," he said with a grimace. "I can't remember when last I slept. Really slept."

I could see that in his face. Deep pouches under his eyes, lines around his mouth, and a blink that told me he was fighting to keep up a good front.

"This man Travis, the Lieutenant. Any relation to our Captain?" he went on.

"You'll have to ask him." That was a question the Captain ought to answer, I thought to myself. In case he was wrong about the connection. "It's not an unusual name."

"Aye, and the Captain's from Barbados. They make rum on his

plantation, and grow bananas and coconuts and sugarcane. I've seen a photograph. Well then, I'll be off, Sister, and tell our Lieutenant what you've told me."

"I wish I could be more helpful, Corporal. Captain Travis had a thundering headache from his wound. And he didn't want to go back to hospital. But it wasn't his choice."

"Aye, he doesn't give up easily. I'll say that for him."

And he was gone.

I stood there watching him go, grateful that I'd worded that original message with care.

Who then had shot Captain Travis? Or had it been a German rifle and not an English one that had brought him down?

A patient in the afternoon looked to be asleep on his feet, hardly aware of Dr. Weatherby sewing up the gash on his forearm.

I was speaking to him as we worked, as I often did with cases like this, where the wound wasn't as serious. I'd asked how his men were faring in their sector.

"We're all holding on as best we can," he said. "Silly to die before the end. I've got my eye on marching down to Buckingham Palace with flags flying and bands playing, to wave to the King. He won't see me in all that throng, but I'll see him."

I smiled and we sent him on his way, hoping he got his wish.

The rains came in the night, and we were hard-pressed to keep the wounded dry. Many of them were wet to the skin and shivering violently, but we couldn't risk a fire here in the undercroft with no real ventilation. We wrapped them in blankets and gave them bricks from the ruins above us, heated at a fire outside. Fevers were our worry now.

I was tending a case of trench foot when a shadow cast by the light of my shaded lamp made me look up.

"Bess," Simon said with a nod, as if he'd just seen me at tea, instead of days ago.

I excused myself to my patient, and we stepped a little apart. His uniform was muddy where it wasn't wet, and I put out a hand to brush some of the caked mud from his sleeve. "You wouldn't be allowed in the house, looking like this," I said teasingly, and he laughed.

"I've just been to the front lines with a message. Not that anyone is certain where that is now, it changes so rapidly. How are you? You look tired."

"It's only the lamplight," I said.

"It isn't that," he answered, reaching out to turn my chin toward him. "Your mother would be worried if she saw you now."

"Men are still dying."

"Yes, I know, but you'll be ill if you aren't careful. Get some rest, if you can. I must go. I only stopped because I saw the aid station and I was hoping I might find you here. Your father will be glad to know I've spoken to you."

"Give my love to everyone at home," I told him, and then as he was about to turn away, I said, "Simon—could you find out something for me? There's a Lieutenant Travis, first name James. English, from Suffolk, I'm told. I don't know his regiment—but it could be one of the Suffolk ones. What can you find out about him? I've been told—I can't say how true it is—that he's possibly breaking under fire. It could be a problem for those under him. You never know."

"I'll see what I can discover. The Suffolks aren't near here. I can tell you that much now."

Surprised, I asked, "Are you sure? I've been told that the fighting is so fluid that no one knows who his neighbor is."

"True enough—to some extent. But it isn't quite that mad out there."

"This is important, Simon. Could you get word back to me as soon as you discover where the Lieutenant is at the moment?"

"I'll do my best. Take care. This war is nearly finished. There's nothing left but the arguing over date and time and place. Stay safe."

"And you," I told him. "Tell everyone how much I miss them." I walked with him to the crypt stairs and climbed them with him. He was a brief breath of home, so far away just now. I suddenly felt a wave of homesickness.

Simon must have sensed what I was feeling, for as we stepped into the ruined nave, he turned and put an arm around my shoulders for a moment.

Then he was gone, vanishing into the night. I saw a party of six men materialize out of the darkness to join him as he disappeared. I turned back to my work, still feeling the emptiness even that brief a touch of home left behind.

Simon Brandon was all but a part of my family. I'd known him since I was very young, when he'd joined my father's regiment out in India, too young himself and rebellious and headstrong. The Colonel Sahib—only he wasn't yet a Colonel—had seen something in the raw recruit that he liked, and kept an eye on him by making him his batman, his military servant. There had been much hilarity over that, because the prevailing view was that he would find his new batman more trouble than the unruly tribes along the border with Afghanistan. But to everyone's surprise, even my father's, Simon settled down and became a proper soldier. He had gifts, that wild boy who had lied about his age to enlist, and these had made him rise in the ranks. Clearly well educated, he discovered an affinity for languages, and was often used in secret missions. In the end he'd become the youngest Regimental Sergeant-Major in the history of the Army. An honor conferred on few at any age. He'd also become a friend of my father's, he was devoted to my mother—and he was often assigned to keeping an eye on me. I still remembered any number of times when he'd helped me out of a scrape. He'd taught me to ride and to shoot and to fend for myself in a country where we were not always certain who was a friend and who was a foe.

I finished with the trench foot and went back to look in on a leg that would surely be amputated when the Sergeant was sent back in the next convoy of ambulances.

He had been shot in the knee by machine gun fire, and there was very little we could do besides keeping him comfortable. That meant morphine, and I could hear him calling out in drugged delirium as he tossed on his cot. I summoned an orderly and we strapped him down to keep him from doing more damage as he struggled with rising fever.

The next morning, the first run of ambulances brought back Captain Travis. He had a plaster on his head—it must have hurt abominably when he put on his cap—but he was free from fever. He claimed.

"I told you I was able to return to my men," he said briskly as I greeted him.

"A quick recovery," I agreed, smiling up at him. I could hear Sister Medford behind me, clearing her throat, wanting to speak to the handsome officer she'd tended through the night as his fever rose. He looked up and nodded to her, then turned back to me.

"Did you pass the word?"

I'd hoped that as his fever went down, his insistence on looking for Lieutenant Travis would fade. "Yes, through one of your Corporals. I must tell you that neither he nor his Lieutenant knew of an officer by the name of Travis. But it was so confused that day. Travis could have got separated from his own men. I'm told the Front is almost impossible to pin down at the moment, and your area has taken the brunt of the fighting for days." I took the note from my pocket and held it out to him. I'd kept it on the chance that he'd come back sooner than expected.

"Then Travis may well be new. It would explain why I hadn't seen him before he shot me."

"Lieutenant Anderson is the ranking officer in the sector next to yours, if you need to speak to him. I'm told he's steady."

"Yes, a good man from all reports. All right then, I've a walk ahead of me."

"Are you still quite certain that that's how you were wounded? By Lieutenant Travis?" I asked, keeping my voice diffident. "Head wounds are—difficult, sometimes."

"I'm neither mad nor imagining things," he said quietly. He touched his cap and left, striding back the way he'd come.

I watched him go, thinking that if determination could subdue a fever, the Captain had managed it somehow.

I went to find the ambulance driver, and I asked him what he'd been told about the officer he'd brought forward.

"Just that he'd been cleared to return to duty."

"No mention of concussion?"

"They didn't speak of it to me, Sister." He turned to look toward the shelling. "I thought he was all right. He sat next to me, not in the rear, and we talked."

"Then that's a good sign. Thank you for telling me."

"Did you know he's from an island out in the Caribbean Sea? Could have fooled me. I thought he was English."

I smiled. "And so he is. He just doesn't live in England."

The driver returned the smile. "I expect that's true."

I walked on to the section of the crypt where we held the more serious cases, most of them destined to go back. We had another possible amputation, the fifth in two days.

I opened the partition flap to find Sergeant Wilson half off his cot, lying in a pool of blood.

Hurrying to him, I could see that he'd ripped off his bandages and was trying to cut his wrists with a pocketknife.

"That will do, Sergeant," I said sternly, in the voice that Matron used to keep the wards in order.

He looked up at me, shocked and dazed. "It's no good, Sister. They'll take the leg, and I'll be no use to anyone."

"Nonsense. Pitying yourself is a waste of time. Your life matters, not your leg." It was not kind, but it had given me time to reach his side and take the knife before he realized what I was about to do. "Now let's see to that knee."

I could tell it was coming off, but I said nothing about that. "You're more likely to lose it to infection than to that bullet."

He reached out, intending to fight me for the pocketknife, just as one of the orderlies came in to fetch him for the ambulance.

"Here!" the orderly shouted and wrestled the Sergeant down again, cursing and struggling every inch of the way. But we managed to get him settled and give him enough morphine to keep him quiet until he reached the base hospital.

The next day, we left the church crypt to move forward again, this time to a cleared area behind what had been a farmhouse, built in the French fashion of a walled enclosure that included sheds and the barn. There wasn't much left, stones scattered here and there that were tripping hazards and one wall of the house, where we set up the cooking area. It was cold and far too open here—the wind swept through like a scythe, but we got the tents up and still dealt with the incoming wounded. We could build fires for hot water and tea in the lee of that house wall, to give patients a little warmth. A lorry moving forward in the wake of the Army brought us blankets and other supplies, including hot water bottles. But the ground was too hard and too cold for us to stay here long. Still, it saved lives, to stay close to the fighting.

An officer who came in with dysentery told us that we'd be moving up again soon, because the Germans were also on the move. "But it doesn't get much better forward. I saw an orchard cut down. Not for firewood, mind you, but to prevent anyone using it. Do you know how long it takes a fruit tree to reach the age where it bears well? Stupid, that's what they were. Bloody stupid."

An hour later, I watched Dr. Weatherby save the arm of a Lieutenant Barker, in a remarkable bit of surgery, in spite of the wind coursing through the broken walls and chilling us to the bone. I heard much later that he'd made a full recovery. Dr. Weatherby brought out his store of whisky and insisted that I have a little celebratory drink with him. "You need it, Bess. And so do I. God, I didn't think I could stop the bleeding, much less take out that bit of shrapnel." He downed his whisky in a gulp, then put the bottle safely away.

I was just washing my hands and hoping for a brief respite when a new line of wounded appeared.

We sorted the stretcher bearers and got the more seriously wounded under cover as quickly as we could. A man losing blood needed to be kept warm. I helped Dr. Weatherby with two shell wounds and another trench foot that was bleeding badly, and then we were told that an officer had been brought in with a life-threatening wound.

He was carried in next, facedown on his stretcher, a blanket over his body.

I said to one of the orderlies, "Spine?" And waited for the answer, dreading it.

"He was shot in the back. May've missed the vital bits, but nasty all the same."

I nodded, and we pulled away the blanket to examine the field dressings that had been put there when he was shot.

It didn't look good. I thought the shot had missed the ribs and lung on that side, and the major arteries, but how much internal bleeding there might be was another matter. I knelt to feel under him as Dr. Weatherby began to cut away his tunic and shirt.

"I think the bullet passed through," I said quietly. "Straight through, not at an angle."

"Are you very sure?" the doctor asked.

"See for yourself."

He put his hand where mine was and felt the exit wound. "Thank God," Dr. Weatherby whispered.

If the shot had angled through his body, we had no way of knowing what organs might have been compromised. The only X-ray machine that I knew of was in Rouen, a very long way away, and this man might well bleed to death before he reached the American Base Hospital in the former racetrack there.

It wasn't until we had dealt with the wound in his back and turned him over that I realized that this patient was Captain Travis. And this time he wasn't as fortunate. His wound might well end his war.

He was still unconscious when we put him with the other patients waiting for the ambulances to return. By the time they did, we'd lost two of our cases, the lung and the abdomen.

The driver who had brought the Captain back to the forward lines was in charge of this convoy, and as we were shifting his stretcher into place, he said, "I recognize that one. The man from the Caribbean Sea."

I smothered a smile, thinking of him swimming for dear life, like a turtle or a porpoise.

"Will he be all right, do you think?"

"I hope so. Infection is the worry now," I replied.

I was standing beside the first ambulance, giving final instructions to the lead driver, when Sister Medford called to me.

"It's the Captain. He's awake. I think we should give him a little morphine."

I went back to see to it, and Captain Travis's eyes were open, pain-filled but intense.

He recognized me as I came up to him, there in the ambulance, and he reached out to grip my arm.

"Sister Crawford."

"Yes, I'm here, Captain."

"It was the same man. Lieutenant Travis. *I saw him.*"

"You were shot in the back," I said as gently as I could. "How could you have seen him?"

"The shot. It spun me around, and as I went down, I saw him standing there."

"What did he do then?" I asked.

"He ran past me. Left me lying there. One of my men dragged me behind a wall. I asked him if he'd seen who shot me, but he hadn't. I had."

I was afraid this had become an obsession with Captain Travis. I said only, "I shouldn't say anything to Matron about this. Not until you have more proof. She'll think you mad."

"I'm not mad. It was Travis, I tell you."

His grip on my hand was hurting. I pulled it free and gave him the morphine. He didn't fight me. I think he was almost beyond coping with the pain he was in, and any attempt to return to his men and hunt down this Lieutenant was the furthest thing from his mind. Instead there was a determination to heal as fast as he could.

Through clenched teeth he murmured, "I wonder where I'll find you when I come back."

"We'll be moving again," I said. "But I'll look out for you."

He managed a crooked smile and then turned his face to the wall and patiently waited for the morphine to take effect.

As I made a final check of his comrades, I heard Captain Travis speak in a voice that quickly faded into a low rumble. Hardly intelligible.

"You're my witness. I need you."

I stepped out of the ambulance and watched as the convoy rolled away over the uneven ground, jostling the men as it gained speed only to encounter some sort of foundation half-hidden in the mud and bump raggedly over it.

I wished I knew what the truth was. I could speak for the Captain's wounds, but not for who had caused them.

The word *obsession* came back to me. I didn't know whether it was the right word or not.

CHAPTER 4

WITH THE DAWN, a new line of wounded appeared, most of them—thank God—ambulatory. And several of the men brought us copies of German newspapers left behind by the retreating Army.

A Lieutenant, Eric Mossby, who knew enough German to translate it for us, said, "If this isn't propaganda—if it isn't designed to make us believe Germany is about to change its tactics and halt the retreat—it appears that Ludendorff is out of favor in Berlin."

I'd been holding the tray as Dr. Weatherby probed the Lieutenant's forearm for shrapnel, and I nearly dropped it in my surprise.

I'd listened to my father and Simon discussing the German High Command, the role of General von Hindenburg and General Ludendorff in shaping the war, the brilliant strategies that had made General Ludendorff the hero of Liège for taking that supposedly impregnable city in the opening days of the war. Despite the courageous defense by the tiny Belgian Army.

"But who is taking his place?" The answer was so very important, this close to the end of the war. He might be replaced by a man who believed that it was time to sue for peace on the best terms available—or by a man who wanted to continue the fighting, whatever the cost in lives. We had sometimes found ourselves overwhelmed with German wounded, men too tired and dispirited to care about being taken prisoner.

Lieutenant Mossby said, resignation in his voice, "Who knows, Sister? I don't think Berlin has decided, much less made an announcement." He held up the newspaper in his good hand. "All of us look for these. I even read them to my men. It's just as well—" He broke off with a grunt, his mouth closed in a tight line of pain. When it had passed, he finished what he had been about to say. "It's just as well for them to know what's happening. I hope to heaven this means good news."

"And General von Hindenburg?"

"I gather he's still in charge, but someone is likely to be appointed in Ludendorff's place. And unfortunately, that's the worry. Better the devil you know than a cypher, someone we can't predict. It could change everything."

He was right.

Dr. Weatherby sewed up the wound in his arm and left me to bandage it.

He'd said nothing during the exchange, concentrating on his work. Now as the doctor washed his hands, he commented, "Medically I don't see how you go on. Day after day."

Lieutenant Mossby smiled grimly. "There's no choice, is there? If we stop pursuing the enemy, it will stop running. And once it stops, the German Army is likely to regroup and come at us while we're most vulnerable."

He thanked the doctor, nodded to me, and was gone, back to his men.

Both armies were using field guns, now that the Front was shifting so quickly. There was no time to unlimber and move the heavy artillery that had been such a factor in the early years of the war. But the number of shells being fired was overwhelming, and we were seeing their handiwork as well as machine gun wounds.

Later that day three very serious cases came in, two of them stomach wounds, and a third a chest. Dr. Weatherby did what he could, but as soon as the ambulances arrived, we sent them back.

"Go with them, Bess, if you will. I don't think they'll make it, otherwise."

I caught up my things—moving as much as I'd done, I kept my kit bag ready at a moment's notice to finish packing it—and went out to help load the three serious cases, along with three others awaiting their turn.

It was a harrowing journey. Holding on for dear life as the ambulance bounced and jerked and slid sideways, I stood up in the rear compartment where I could keep a close eye on the chest and stomach wounds. It wouldn't do for me to fall and be badly injured. But I'd collected a dozen new bruises before the base hospital was in sight.

The chest case gave me several minutes of real concern. I was afraid a lung would collapse, but Florence Nightingale must have been looking out for us. He was still alive when we pulled into the hospital forecourt, and half a dozen nurses and doctors came running. A lone ambulance usually meant trouble was arriving.

We got the men inside and settled in their cots, a doctor already examining the reports and the wounds.

Miraculously, the chest survived, but one of the stomachs died on the operating table.

With time on my hands after the exchange of reports and answering questions asked by the doctors about what we had done thus far, I went to inquire of Matron if there was anything we could take back with us in the matter of supplies. We needed blankets, with this colder weather, and one often wasn't enough out in the open, despite the tents.

I was just coming back from her office when one of the Sisters called to me in the passage.

"Sister Crawford?"

I turned to find Mary, one of my flatmates in London, hurrying to catch me up.

"Mary!" I exclaimed.

"Bess? I thought I heard your voice. Oh, how lovely to see you!"

She threw her arms around me, and I hugged her in return.

"How long has it been?" I asked.

"The better part of a year? At least." She stood back. "Let me look at you. Tired—aren't we all?—but well. I'll write to Diana and Lady Elspeth and Mrs. Hennessey to let them know we've met. Tell me, how is everything?"

We stood there in the passage, exchanging news and asking about friends we had in common.

It was very good to see Mary. At the start of the war, Mrs. Hennessey, a widow, had opened her London home to nursing staff looking for a London flat where we could live during our training and where we could come when our duties brought us back to London, sometimes only overnight, sometimes for a day or two when we wanted nothing more than to sleep.

It still wasn't considered proper for us to stay at hotels, and this was the perfect solution. And as Mrs. Hennessey lived downstairs, while we were upstairs, there was always someone to mind the door and retrieve the mail and keep us safe while we slept the world away. We'd all come to love her, and I knew for a certainty that my parents were fond of her too. She had rules, very stringent ones. No man was allowed to ascend the stairs unless he was related and carried a trunk and was accompanied by Mrs. Hennessey herself. That was true even of the Colonel Sahib. And RMS Simon Brandon was forbidden to climb the stairs at all, even though Mrs. Hennessey believed he'd saved her from an attacker.

"He's much too attractive, dear, and I must think about my young ladies and their reputations. He'll understand, won't he, dear? I trust him implicitly, you know that, but there are the other parents who depend on me to do what's best."

I had told Simon, who had chuckled with amusement. He liked her, and he abided by her rules with solemn courtesy. Which only made her admire him even more.

There were so many memories of these four years in her house, but Mary and I had only a moment before she was summoned to see to a patient.

"Before I go, Bess. Was it you who sent us that officer from Barbados?"

I steeled myself for bad news as I said, "Yes, I'm afraid so."

"We don't quite know what to do about him. Perhaps you should have a word with the ward Sister?"

And then she was gone to take charge in whatever emergency had arisen.

I'd been on my way to the canteen for soup and a cup of tea, but I turned back the way I'd come and quickly found the ward where Captain Travis was being cared for.

To my surprise, he wasn't in the officers' ward where recovering patients would heal or wait to be sent on to England for further care.

I said to the ward Sister, "I've been asked to look in on Captain Travis."

I was prepared for her to say that he'd left with the morning convoy for Calais. But Mary had spoken as if he was still in Base Hospital Seven.

The Sister looked down at her charts. "I'm afraid he's not here, Sister."

"Has he had more surgery? Is he in the Surgical Ward?"

"You must ask Matron, Sister. If you'll excuse me, I have a patient I must see to."

With a nod she hurried down the long aisle between beds, leaving me standing there.

I went instead to the Surgical Ward, but Captain Travis wasn't there. I looked into wards where other ranks and the influenza cases and the men in quarantine were kept. Childhood diseases like measles followed an army too.

I was about to give up and go to Matron as I had been told to do when I remembered that this hospital had a special ward for head wounds, shell shock, and other injuries that precluded putting men into wards with other cases.

Feeling a surging fear, I stopped a passing VAD, one of the nurses supplied by a different group from mine, volunteers who had varying amounts of training, to ask where to find it. She pointed the way.

I opened the door. The ward Sister was at the other end, trying with the aid of an orderly to calm a very distraught man. He was screaming, fighting the orderly and the Sister.

I'd seen such cases. His head was swathed with bandages, only his eyes, nose, and mouth visible so that he could see and breathe and eat. The back of his head bulged where there was extra padding, indicating where his wound was.

Ignoring them, I started down the aisle. Most of the patients looked at me with a vacant stare, and I knew they were drugged to keep them quiet. The shell shock cases lay staring at the ceiling, wary of meeting anyone's gaze. Other patients were strapped down to keep them from getting out of bed.

And one of these was Captain Travis.

He was a shadow of the man I'd had tea with in the hospital canteen in early autumn, when he'd told me about Barbados and we'd laughed over camels.

He had been shaved, but there were dark circles around his eyes, and they looked at the ceiling with a patience born of bleak despair. It hurt me to see it.

I went to his bedside.

"Captain Travis?"

He didn't answer, and I wondered if he too had been sedated.

"It's Sister Crawford, Captain."

Something changed in his eyes, and after a moment he turned toward me.

"Come to gloat?" he asked, his voice husky with disuse. "I've stopped screaming. But they still refuse to untie these straps."

I swallowed what I was about to say and instead asked, "I didn't know. Talk to me, Captain. What's happened?" For it was very clear something had. "Are you in pain?" I wondered if his wound had become septic. But if it had, why was he *here,* and not in a regular ward? Besides, I couldn't smell the telltale signs of rampant infection.

"They use my wound as an excuse. But it's healing cleanly. I can see that in the faces of the doctors who come to inspect it. I was beginning to lose my mind. What was left of it. I don't do well with laudanum. I never have. It drives me to madness. And they're sure that I'm there already."

"But what's wrong? Are they treating you for shell shock?"

"I don't know. They whisper in conferences. I can't hear what they're saying. And no one tells me. I think they're afraid to. I've got a handful of medals, you see. And I don't think they want to put down shell shock as a diagnosis."

"I don't understand."

"They blame it on the early head wound. They seem to think I shouldn't have been sent back to the Front so soon." The screaming had stopped at the far end of the ward. Captain Travis's glance strayed in that direction, then came back to me. "If I stay here long enough, I'll be as mad as the rest of them," he said bitterly.

I realized then what was wrong. While the wound in his back was healing, he must have fretted about being away from the fighting, and in the throes of fever, let it be known to anyone who would listen that he had to return to his men and stop a killer who had already sent him twice to hospital.

And no one believed him. If they had, he wouldn't have been strapped down or sedated.

Dear God.

"Do you still have headaches?"

"I'm not sure. The laudanum left me ill and confused. I've always had problems with it, even when I broke my arm as a boy. God knows what I've been saying. One of the Sisters reported that I was waiting for a camel to take me back to the Front."

I remembered our conversation back in the autumn. But anyone else would be disturbed by the reference.

We had purposely kept our voices low, and he was watching the ward Sister at the end of the room.

I said quickly, in the event we were interrupted, "Is it because you still believe that James Travis shot you? Is that why they sedate you, and keep you strapped down?"

"It's likely. But I say nothing about that anymore. I tell them it was the head wound that made me delusional. That I hadn't seen

Lieutenant Travis since we met briefly in Paris in the Gare du Nord. I tell them that he's a cousin, and I've been worried about him, hoping he was all right. That I was thinking about him when I was shot."

"And how do they answer you?"

He looked away, resignation in his face. It was thinner than I remembered it. "Apparently I was difficult when I arrived— well, to be truthful, I'd soon had enough of people telling me to be quiet and let the staff get on with it. I was impatient, angry. Twice now I've been shot by this one idiot, and I felt I had a right to be angry." Turning back to me, he said, "Then someone remembered how angry I was the first time I'd been shot. And they decided that it was something more than headaches and a new wound so soon after the first. And here I am."

He seemed to be telling me the truth. But he could also be using me, thinking I'd understand him and get him out of this ward and into another. For he was very persuasive.

"They're coming," he whispered. "You'd best go."

I turned to see that the ward Sister was walking our way with intent in her face.

I didn't answer him. I waited, and when the Sister was near enough, I greeted her cheerfully.

"Good day, Sister. I've stopped in to see how my patient is doing."

She gave me a suspicious look.

"I'm rather surprised to find him in this ward. What do the doctors say?" I moved away from Captain Travis's bedside and went to meet her, hoping she would give me a brief account of his condition. "How is the wound in his back?"

Instead she said, "You shouldn't be here, Sister. He's been quiet for several hours. We'd like to keep it that way."

I pressed. "But what is his diagnosis?"

"You'll have to speak to Matron, I'm afraid. But the general feeling is that he's suffered a brain injury."

Startled by that, I replied, "I saw the head wound when he was first brought in. The bullet hadn't reached the brain, it had only creased the skull."

Her mouth tightened. I'd questioned the doctors, and that wasn't done. Seeing that I was going to get nowhere with her, I said, "I'm leaving shortly. I'll say good-bye to the patient, if you don't mind."

And without waiting for an answer, I turned back to Captain Travis. In a voice that carried, I said, "Try to get well, Captain. You're in good hands. I'll look in the next time I'm here."

But what the ward Sister and the orderly coming up behind her couldn't see as I turned my back on them to speak to the Captain was what I was doing. I found his fingers under the sheet and gripped them. I saw the flare of surprise in his face, and then it closed down again. But his fingers turned under the sheet and gripped mine with a fierce strength.

He had found a lifeline, and he knew it.

A dangerous thing to do, if he *had* suffered an injury that we'd missed. But I couldn't leave him there, lost in a hopelessness that had no end but another ward just like this, in France or in England.

But I *would* look in again. To be sure.

I left then, and went to speak to Matron again.

She listened to me, then said, "You didn't see the Captain when he was brought in. You didn't hear him in his delirium, shouting at an imaginary cousin, calling him a killer, a traitor. You didn't watch him struggle against his straps, telling us he was healed and ought to be returned to duty. Whatever was driving this poor man, it was in his head, Sister, and we had to remove him from the ward he'd been taken to. He fought us, ill as he was, and we had to sedate him for his own sake, with that back wound. I believe you'd done the same when he was in the ambulance that brought him here. The driver had warned us that he was wild even then. You know as well as I do that a back wound doesn't behave like that. What's more, he aggravated his wound and we feared infection would set in." She shook her head. "Your concern does you honor, Sister, but given the facts as we have seen them, I think we have made the right decision for Captain Travis."

I could see that I was about to do more harm than good if I argued. But I said, "I think something happened during that earlier retreat that shook him rather badly. I hope you'll also take that into account."

"Are you telling me you believe that he's suffering from shell shock?"

Oh great heavens!

But I kept my wits about me with an effort. Frowning, as if considering the matter, I said, "I don't really know the answer to that, Matron. I saw the head wound when it was brought into the forward aid station. And I'm not convinced that it was severe enough to cause this aberrant behavior. In fact, he was returned to duty the next day."

"And that might well be the source of the problem, Sister. That he was released too soon. If we'd kept him longer, we might have seen these symptoms develop and dealt with them. He might have responded to treatment, early on. Still, I shall make a note on the Captain's chart, indicating your concern. Thank you, Sister Crawford, for your assistance in this matter."

Another Sister was tapping at her door, and I used that as my excuse for a hasty retreat. "I've kept you long enough. And my ambulance will be waiting. I must thank you for the supplies, on behalf of Dr. Weatherby. He will be grateful."

She nodded in dismissal and I got myself out of there without betraying the turmoil in my own mind.

Just as I closed the door behind the reporting Sister, I could hear the ambulance driver calling for me. I caught up my bag and hurried out to meet him. The hospital was far from shorthanded, I had no excuse to stay—and I might already have complicated matters.

I used fatigue as my excuse for sitting with my head back and my eyes closed. I hoped the ambulance driver would understand—he'd seen me on my feet all the way here, dealing with my three emergencies.

But what was going through my mind was what I had seen— and what I had done.

If Captain Travis was suffering from a brain injury, he was better off where he was, where he couldn't do himself or someone else a harm.

If I was honest with myself, I couldn't deny the frightening possibility that he had given the face of someone he'd met by chance to the man he believed had shot him twice. Even though it was far more likely that if it wasn't the Germans, he'd been shot accidentally in the chaos of battle. The question now was, would he go on insisting that he was right, go on looking for a man who might not even exist? And try to kill a stranger who was unlucky enough to resemble James Travis?

And yet I failed to convince myself that Captain Travis had invented a killer, that he believed himself to be invincible and needed to blame someone else when he discovered he was as vulnerable as any of his men.

What if, for the sake of argument, he was telling the absolute truth, that someone—even, as wild as it sounded, his cousin James Travis—had wanted to kill him? But the question then was *why*? If they had found themselves face-to-face in the midst of battle—which wasn't terribly far-fetched as the Germans retreated and the British Army was bringing every man it could muster to prevent a last stand—why had James Travis been so determined to see the Captain dead that he would try twice to kill him?

Stranger things had happened in war. Perhaps only James Travis knew the answer to that.

The unthinkable part of this whole dilemma was the chance that Captain Travis was telling the truth, no matter how unbelievable it might appear to be. And to abandon him in a world of madness would be unspeakably cruel.

I hadn't intended to raise the specter of shell shock, and I hoped Matron had brought it up only in an effort to find a realistic explanation for the Captain's condition. After all, I'd been present each time he'd been brought in to the aid station, and so I had firsthand knowledge of his case. Shell shock was believed by many to be arrant cowardice, not a medical matter at all. And if this diagnosis was confirmed, in Captain Travis's record for all to see, he would be shunned for the rest of his life.

It would be a very different nightmare from the one he was presently in.

There was really no one I could talk to about all this. Not here in France.

There was Mary. Could I turn to her? She'd told me to look in on Captain Travis in the first place. But why? A courtesy because he'd been my patient and I would want to know how he was faring? The fate of the men we'd tended mattered to us. Or because she thought I might be the best person to judge his condition?

It was too late to do anything about that now. But as soon as I reached the aid station, I quickly wrote a note to her, asking her as a favor to keep an eye on Captain Travis for me, and let me know how he did. Then I handed it to the patient driver waiting to go back to the base hospital.

As I watched the ambulance disappear down the rough track, I knew there was nothing more I could do now. I could only hope that the memory of the despair in Captain Travis's eyes wouldn't haunt me as I went on with my work here.

CHAPTER 5

THE NEXT MORNING early we left the ruined farmyard and moved forward. The medical corps had cleared another space for us, this time in the ruins of a blacksmith's shop on the outskirts of town.

Dr. Weatherby went to the nearest officer he could find and refused to set up his aid station there.

"There will be lockjaw present in the paddock behind the building. I refuse to operate in such conditions."

According to the account I heard, the Major was a city dweller and had thought only of the space we would have there and that the ambulances would be safe from artillery fire.

That meant a second move, this time to the far side of town in a brickyard.

Dr. Weatherby was still not pleased, but there was nothing we could do. He asked for the town hall, the *hôtel de ville,* which we could see was in fairly good condition, although the windows were broken.

We were told that this had been German headquarters for six months and it hadn't been cleared of traps.

Removing what we could of the shelled rubble surrounding us, we had the aid station set up in time for the first stretchers appearing down the road that led to the brickyard. Twelve hours later, we moved into the city hall, just as a patient brought more news, telling us there were rumors that Kaiser Wilhelm was abdicating. That the government had collapsed in Berlin.

We found it impossible to believe. The Kaiser was the grandson of Queen Victoria. But he had no love for the English, it was said, even though his mother was the Queen's eldest daughter. War with England had been an acceptable risk, in his view, when his troops invaded Belgium in 1914, on their way to the north of France. He had become the face of Germany in all the British recruiting posters, which showed him as a cruel, bloody invader. I simply couldn't imagine him walking away at this stage of the war.

And I couldn't help but wonder what the Colonel Sahib thought about this news—if it was true. He knew far more about such matters than I did, given his service to the Army since war was first declared.

Our next visitor was an unexpected surprise.

Sergeant Lassiter, who always seemed to find his way to me wherever I was posted, came by in the evening. Whatever grapevine the Australian forces had, he knew far more about what was going on than half the men serving in France, and if he couldn't find an answer to my questions, he found someone who did.

It was good to see him. Tall, rangy, and irrepressible, he was about to sweep me off my feet and swirl me around in midair, and just in the nick of time he happened to see Sister Medford in the shadows of the doorway. We'd both come out for air, but I was standing on the steps leading up to the door.

"Sister," he said plaintively, pulling off his hat—I thought for a terrified moment he was going to bow, right there in the middle of the village square—"this hand is bothering me again. Where you took out that bit of shrapnel. I fear it's festering."

He held it out, dangling from his wrist, as if it were about to fall off. A grimace of pain twisted his features.

A more pathetic act I'd never seen, and I had to hold in my smile.

"Yes, of course. Sergeant Lassiter, isn't it? Step inside and I'll have a look where the light is better."

He nodded to Sister Medford and followed me inside. He was far too attractive for his own good, and when I looked back, she was watching him with interest.

The central hall had several doors on either side, and one was the room where we examined incoming wounded. It was quiet at the moment, and I opened the door.

"In here, Sergeant," I said briskly, and closed the door after him.

He grinned broadly in the light of the lamp, his face tanned by the cold wind, his teeth very white by contrast. I thought of the Cheshire Cat.

"Bess," he said, keeping his voice low so that it didn't carry beyond the door, in case Sister Medford was nosy. "How are you, lass?"

"Well enough. And you look as if you're fit too." I backed against the examining table, suddenly aware that he had more on his mind than an old wound. "I'm happy to see it."

"The war's nearly over," he said. "And when it's finished, they'll be shipping us back to Sydney as soon as they can manage without us." He hadn't been home for four long, bloody, weary years. I knew how much this meant to him.

"Your family will be glad to see you," I offered.

There was silence for a moment.

"Bess." His voice was different now, the friendliness changed to something more personal. "Bess, I'd like to take you with me. As my wife."

I'd been afraid he'd come to say good-bye. I hadn't expected this. And yet I knew—I think I'd always known how he must feel.

I dearly loved Sergeant Lassiter. He had been friend and comrade and confidant, a trusted right arm when I needed it. But I wasn't in love with him. At least I didn't think I was. There had been no time to consider the future and how it might turn out for me.

He was earnest; this proposal had clearly been on his mind for a very long time. It was there in his face. I had never seen him so serious and determined.

What could I say, how could I answer? I struggled to find the right words.

I smiled, with affection. "I haven't yet drawn a breath to think about peace. There are still too many men dying. Too many in harm's way. I am honored, truly I am. And I thank you from the bottom of my heart. But I'm not ready . . ."

My voice trailed off.

He looked at me for a long moment. "Is it Simon Brandon?" he asked. "I'd rather know."

Shocked, I stumbled over my next words. "Simon? Good heavens—I-I don't think it's even possible—he's like a brother—a part of my family—"

He smiled. "Then there's hope, lass."

Without waiting for an answer, he turned to go, only to re-member the ruse that he'd used to see me privately.

With a rueful grin, he said, "You'd best put something on this hand."

I found a roll of bandaging and bound his hand quite effi-ciently, in spite of his closeness and his stare as I worked.

"There," I said, giving him back his hand. "It will do."

"A treat," he said, nodding in agreement. Then he touched my shoulder lightly. "I won't go home without you, lass. Not if I can help it."

And with that he was gone, leaving the door standing wide.

I closed the door, using the excuse of putting away the bandaging and the scissors to bring myself under control.

I should have known, I told myself. *I should have been more careful.* But it had been hard to keep someone as jolly as the Sergeant at arm's length. There had been times when I wasn't sure whether he was simply flirting with me—something the Australians were good at, ask any nursing Sister in France!—or was serious. There had never been time to consider what such a friendly alliance might mean to the Sergeant.

I liked him immensely. I always had. But how could I think about the future when so much remained to be done here?

More flustered than I cared to admit, I went briskly back to my ward and made the rounds. It had the effect of righting my sense of balance.

When the ambulances arrived late in the day, I saw that one of the drivers was the man I'd asked to carry my letter to Mary.

There was no chance to speak to him. As I was helping to load the serious cases into his ambulance, shelling began again just north of us, and one couldn't hear anything. I was about to turn away, to help with the next ambulance in line, when he touched my arm and handed me an envelope.

I was sure it must be from Mary, with news.

But as I was about to stuff it in my pocket to read later, I recognized my own handwriting.

I caught up with the driver just as he was climbing behind the wheel. Putting my mouth close to his ear, I asked, "What happened? Weren't you able to deliver this message?"

He shook his head and mouthed, "She'd gone."

"Gone? Where?"

He leaned closer. "They sent her to England with a convoy. Critically ill men, they needed an extra Sister."

It happened—I had done more than one unscheduled run myself.

"When?"

"Before I got there with my lot of patients."

My heart sank. I'd hoped she would be my eyes and ears, that she would look out for Captain Travis. Now I had no idea what was happening to him.

I nodded my thanks, and we got on with the loading. I could tell the British guns were shifting their aim a little and was worried they might be retreating rather than going forward. We needed these wounded well on their way. I'd even convinced Dr. Weatherby to send two more we had been worried about, just in case.

As we watched them out of sight, Dr. Weatherby called to us. More wounded were coming in. When at last, at the end of a very long day I reached the room I shared with the other Sisters, I took out my letter, opened it, and reread it.

Then I burned it. No need for anyone else to find it and wonder at my concern for Captain Travis.

With a sigh, I got myself ready for bed, falling asleep from sheer exhaustion.

The next morning we were moved again. The guns had fired all night, both German and British. We were roused from our cots at three in the morning to deal with the influx of wounded, friend and enemy alike. Some of the Germans were in a bad way, having been without care for days. One was hardly more than a boy, his arm infected and in need of surgery to clean the wound and remove the last bits of shrapnel. Another man's knee was already gangrenous, and so on and on. We worked until daybreak, a gray and chill morning. We had hardly sent the last patient on his way when the order came to leave.

I just had time for a cup of tea and a very dry sandwich. My kit was ready by the time the Army could spare a lorry to transport us forward.

The desolation was complete. The villages, mostly rubble, hadn't been cleared of the traps or the dead. It was a horrendous sight in the dull light of dawn. I saw several officers and men I knew, either from before the war or from treating them.

One of them, directing a company of men helping to clear the road, looked up, saw me, and shouted, "The next waltz."

Lawrence Mallory. I laughed and waved. I'd danced with him at a ball in late July 1914, just before war was declared. He'd asked for the next waltz too, but I'd already promised it to someone else.

He looked tired but fairly fit, although there was a filthy bandage around his lower arm. I would mention seeing him in my next letter home. My mother would let Captain Mallory's family know that he was alive and well.

The other Sisters were teasing me about him when our lorry went around a bend in the road and came to a lurching halt.

I could hear the driver cursing from his place behind the wheel, but I couldn't see what it was that had barred the road.

And then Dr. Weatherby got down and went to find out.

He came back almost at once.

"There's a column of German prisoners stopping to rest. Most of them must have been asleep on their feet. Haggard faces. A number have wounds. Bring what you need."

We gathered supplies and the driver was there to help us down from the back of our lorry.

Sister Medford stayed where she was, sitting on a crate of supplies. Her brother had died as a prisoner of the Germans. I said nothing to her, just turned to follow Dr. Weatherby.

We had come to a tiny square in a tiny village. What was left of the church was to my right, and to the left, what must have been the *hôtel de ville*, a more solid structure, what remained of it.

Seated in the rubble or lying on the cold ground, the Germans were not the fierce monsters of the recruiting posters. They were hungry as well as exhausted, and looked up at us with dead eyes, as if defeat had extinguished the last spark of life. We went among them, assessing their wounds. I followed Dr. Weatherby, who gave orders as he moved from man to man. They needed something warm to drink, most of them, but our own supply of tea was very low, and there were not enough cups or even teapots large enough to serve so many.

We cleaned cuts and more serious wounds as best we could, put on fresh bandages, and even found blankets for several men who were running fevers and shaking with chills.

They didn't speak to us, although their eyes followed us as they waited their turn, but offered no threat. The men guarding them stood at ease, some of them smoking. I saw one offer a cigarette to a stretcher case, and the man accepted it gratefully.

It occurred to me as I worked that these were simply tired, worried men a long way from home, and I found I couldn't hate them, even though so many of my friends had died at the hands of their comrades.

I had treated Germans before, men who still had hopes of victory. These knew only defeat.

By the time we'd finished, the road was cleared ahead and we moved on. My last glimpse of the prisoners was of a Sergeant ordering them to fall in for the next leg of their journey away from the fighting.

This time we found shelter from a cold rain in what had been a convent. The refectory was still fairly sturdy, although the rest of the buildings and outbuildings had been shelled beyond recovery or burned to the ground. Our voices echoed as we stepped inside the stone building with its wooden roof, but that changed as men walked or were carried inside, absorbing the sounds.

Sister Medford, suffering from a chest cold after the rains, was going back with the next convoy of ambulances, and I asked her to find out how Captain Travis was progressing.

It was quite late that night when a lone ambulance brought her back to us. I had nearly given up waiting for her to return, afraid Matron might keep her until she was better.

She climbed down from her seat beside the driver, her eyes red-rimmed with fatigue, and I hurried out to speak to her.

Coughing, she smiled at me in the light of my torch.

"How kind of you to wait up for me," she said. "I've brought supplies. Do you think the orderlies can unload them and see that they're stowed properly? I declare, I don't think I can take another step tonight."

I asked the sentry to see to it, and took her to the far corner of the refectory, where we had a small fire burning in the huge vat that the nuns had used to prepare porridge and soup for the convent. I set the kettle over it and began to make a pot of tea to warm her as she brought me up to date on the news.

"There's to be an Armistice, Bess. Word has gone around that all firing will cease on the eleventh hour of the eleventh day of November, at exactly eleven o'clock in the morning. It's peace, *finally.*"

That was only three days away. And yet the guns were firing with the same ferocity that had marked our nights for weeks.

"That's very good news," I said and smiled at her over the tea leaves I was spooning into the pot.

She said, "I can't believe it's really true." And she went on telling me all she had learned from the Sisters at the base hospital.

I listened as we drank our tea, and when I had collected both our cups and was preparing to wash them for tomorrow, I said, "Were you able to learn anything about Captain Travis?"

For a moment I thought she'd forgot to ask anyone about his condition. I was prepared to hear that he was despondent, or that he had been moved from the ward where the head cases were treated.

"I asked, Bess, just as you'd instructed me to. At first I couldn't find anyone who knew, which is always a bad sign. Or perhaps they didn't wish to tell me." Her face was drawn in the light from the single lamp we kept burning in the cooking area. "I finally screwed up my courage and spoke to Matron. Bess, I'm so sorry to have to tell you—"

My throat dry, I said it for her. "He's dead. By his own hand."

"No, no. They've sent him back to England. There was space in the next convoy after your friend Mary left. He's been assigned to a clinic in Wiltshire for the mentally disturbed."

I stared at her. "Are you certain?"

"Sadly, yes. I asked Matron why, and at first I didn't think she would answer me. But she remembered that you had been concerned about this patient. Bess, the staff had heard him when he was feverish, shouting at a man he believed had shot him, calling him by name. He'd beg to be cleared for duty, so that he could find the man and have him taken up for court martial. Even when his fever subsided, he still swore this man had tried twice to kill him. The doctors decided it was his head wound, that it had been more serious than anyone realized. After talking to you, Matron was concerned enough that she asked one of the officers coming through on an inspection tour to find out if this man

James Travis was a troublemaker, if he had a history of violence. And the Major did just that."

She hesitated.

"Well?" I said. "Where is he serving now?"

"That's just the trouble," she answered. "He was killed last year. At Passchendaele. The Major found someone who knew him, you see. Someone who had served with him earlier in the war. The man Captain Travis is so certain shot him couldn't have done it. He was already dead."

CHAPTER 6

I STARED AT her. Too stunned to say anything.

"Bess?" she said after a moment. "I'm so sorry. You weren't in love with this Captain Travis, were you?"

I collected myself. "No, I wasn't. I felt he'd been misdiagnosed. That's all. I was worried. Don't you remember him?"

She nodded. "He came in first with a head wound, and then later on with a wound in his back. Fair, quite attractive. And very angry. We had to strap him down. I recall something about one of his officers running amok. He was determined to stop the man. That would be the Lieutenant who was already dead. I don't know that I would have called him mad then, but now you do have to wonder."

"Thank you for going to so much trouble. I'm grateful," I answered, turning away to hang up the cloth I'd used to dry the cups. I was still trying to deal with the fact that James Travis was dead.

"Well, I'm sorry I couldn't bring you happier news. Are you all right?"

"Just saddened that it turned out this way. But I'd rather know than wonder what had happened to him. Go to bed. You're out on your feet. It won't help your cold."

"We've had too many sad cases," she agreed, coughing again. "Well, in a few days it will all be over. I'm not quite sure I believe it's true. But I'll be grateful if it is. I'll be glad when the killing and maiming stop for good. The answer to all our prayers."

"It is," I agreed and walked with her to our quarters. "Good night. Sleep well."

She thanked me, and I went on to the cubicle that was mine. I shut the door and went to sit on my cot in the dark.

I hadn't foreseen this ending to Captain Travis's story.

Perhaps he *was* deranged. Or the head wound had so confused him that he couldn't remember what had really happened. Somehow I couldn't bring myself to believe it.

I felt that in some way I'd been responsible for what had followed. For I had inadvertently given him a name to put to the face that haunted him. I hadn't meant to, I hadn't realized that he would find it so believable, or defend it with such ferocity. It would have been far better for the Captain if he hadn't been so sure, if he hadn't told everyone he could identify the man. A man who had been dead for a year. That had seemed to be the final proof that the Captain was delusional at best, or had a severe brain injury at worst. He might not have been sent to that hospital in Wiltshire if he'd never mentioned James Travis to anyone.

I remembered something I'd been told out in India when I was there as a child. That if you saved a person's life, you became responsible for that person. That in saving him, you took charge of his future.

I wondered what they would say about destroying someone's life, what responsibility one then bore for what happened afterward.

On that unhappy note, I lit my lamp and prepared for bed.

Only, I found it hard to sleep, and listened instead to the incessant bombardment not so very far from us.

I was not at my best the next morning, and we had nine very difficult cases in a row. Two of the men died on the table, in spite of all Dr. Weatherby could do, and I heard him curse the war when the second man died. He had lost both legs, and part of an arm. His heart hadn't been able to stand the shock of blood loss.

I couldn't openly offer a doctor comfort. It wasn't done. But I said, keeping my voice calmer than I felt, "He would have thanked you for trying. And afterward wished you hadn't."

Dr. Weatherby's reply was brusque. "I'll always keep trying." He squared his shoulders, waited a few seconds until his voice was steady, and called, "Next."

There was no respite, and we worked on for hours. Someone brought us tea, and we gulped it down, feeling the warmth and grateful for it. It was only afterward that I realized that a teaspoon or two of whisky had been added to our cups.

When we'd dealt with the last casualty, it was almost dark, the early sunsets of November. I found a place to sit down, and someone handed me a dish of sandwiches and a cup of soup. I didn't ask how we had come by it, but it was delicious, some sort of root vegetable, and bits of meat, chicken, I thought.

We had eaten dry sandwiches for so long. Not that I would complain, but the warmth of the tea and the soup sent me crawling into my cot, exhausted.

I was roused in the night by Sister Medford touching my shoulder.

"There's someone to see you," she said, smiling.

My hair was down, and I thought, *This is no time for Sergeant Lassiter to come and press his suit.*

Cross, I dressed hastily and went out to see who it was.

There was the Colonel Sahib, a dark shadow against the light of the small spirit lamp. I'd have known him anywhere, and I flew into his arms with a cry of delight. How long had it been since I last saw him?

He held me close, then at arm's length. I could see that he looked tired, and I could only imagine what he had been doing in these last weeks of negotiating for an end.

"I hesitated to wake you, my dear—I know how precious sleep is for you—"

I broke in. "All is well at home? Tell me, I need to know if it isn't."

"Well and looking forward to having you back with us again. I ought to be twenty miles from here, but I wanted to see you. Your mother sends her love, and so does Mrs. Hennessey. I don't know where Simon is at the moment, but when I last encountered him, he was looking rather pleased with himself. God knows what he'd been doing, he didn't say. I'll be happy when he's no longer at risk as well."

We talked for another ten minutes, and then his aide was there to let him know his time was up. I watched him walk out to the staff car that had brought him here and waved him out of sight before returning to my bed.

It had been a grave risk for my father to come so far forward. With the Front seesawing daily, he could have been caught in a collapsing pocket and taken prisoner. But he must have been given very good intelligence before setting out, for he was never one to put others in jeopardy.

In the morning, under a weak sun, we dealt with the wounded and with German prisoners, streaming south away from the Front. Most of them seemed glad that their war was over, men who had fought valiantly while they could, now facing the reality of defeat. Some of them spoke a little English, and were polite as we dressed their wounds. A few, eyes angry and sullen, still believed victory was possible.

The consensus was that Germany was collapsing, the war draining her of money and men and hope.

And still the guns fired, day and night.

Word came down that at the eleventh hour of the eleventh day of the eleventh month, all shooting would cease. It was real, then, this Armistice.

Eleven November, at eleven o'clock.

That was tomorrow.

I awoke to the guns, firing almost continually, the chatter of machine gun fire in the distance, and the cries of men who were hit and wounded.

In our quiet corner of this village where we worked, where there were no people or farm animals, not even birds singing overhead, sound traveled from the fighting to us.

We had mostly machine gun cases in the morning, legs shattered, in some instances unsalvageable. Dr. Weatherby did what he could but most were sent back in the long line of ambulances heading to hospitals.

At ten o'clock, I drank my tea as I sewed up a shoulder wound, and Dr. Weatherby was already dealing with a jaw from the shelling. Ten more men stood outside our tent, faces haggard. They had made it nearly to the end, and then their luck had run out.

At ten thirty, I was busy with a stomach wound, trying to stop the bleeding, and at ten forty-five, I was dealing with more machine gun knees.

Eleven o'clock came before I was aware of it.

We had just bandaged a head when Dr. Weatherby's pocket watch chimed the hour, the bell-like tones pure and sweet.

I stared at him.

In all the time I had worked with him, I had never heard it chime.

And we became aware of the silence.

We lifted our heads at the same time, listening.

In the distance I saw men falling to their knees, a column moving forward toward the fighting. Mercifully it had stopped.

I walked out of the convent. There was no mad cheering, just—blessed silence.

I realized that tears were rolling down my cheeks, and as I looked, I saw them glistening on the faces of those around me. Men who had endured so much for so long wept with me.

It was over. This bloody, wretched war was over. And in that moment I didn't care whether it was victory or armistice, I was just very grateful that the killing had finally come to an end.

Dr. Weatherby, standing beside me, put a hand on my shoulder, a comradely gesture of acknowledgment of what we were all feeling.

And then I walked back into the tent, for a line of wounded was still making its way toward us. The last casualties of this war.

CHAPTER 7

WE DIDN'T MOVE back straightaway. There were still patients to attend to, but as the week went by they were mostly German prisoners. The quiet was almost eerie.

Finally word was passed to Dr. Weatherby to prepare to move south, and he gave the order to us over breakfast on Thursday morning.

Ambulances came to take the last of the wounded, and there was room for all of us as well.

I stood by my door looking north, thinking about all the weeks and months and years we had moved toward this moment, and then I took my seat. Dr. Weatherby, in the last ambulance, gave the signal to start.

There were no shells to duck or aircraft to dodge, but the roads were still abominable, and the rains had done nothing to improve them.

It took us quite some time to cover the distance to Base Hospital, and I found changes there too.

Those who could be sent to England to recover were already being given their Blighty ticket, their permission to go home. And over the next week, as they were slowly ferried farther south to Calais, we discovered that there were empty beds—and no one waiting for them.

I wanted to ask for news of Captain Travis, but there had been many staff changes since the last time I was here. Most of the new Sisters had served in different sectors and wouldn't have any reason to know the Captain's history.

When I encountered Matron in the passage, I smiled. Some of the weariness had faded from her face, gone along with the desperate struggle to find beds for the dying men brought in by the next convoy of ambulances, only to see a new line making its way toward her and the struggle beginning all over again.

She still gave her orders with brisk efficiency, and we obeyed them just as quickly. But she seemed a little more approachable now. And so I stopped her to ask if there was news of Captain Travis.

Matron studied my face for a moment. "You are fond of this patient, aren't you, Sister Crawford? It's not wise, you know. Even with treatment his future will be bleak."

I stammered, "It's not— I was there from the beginning, you see, and— and it was an unusual case. I don't have any personal attachment. I did have some concerns, as you already know." It was rather a fierce defense to offer my superior, but I wanted to make it clear that I wasn't asking for news out of a misguided affection for him.

She nodded. "I hope you can continue to see him in that light. As for news, I'm afraid there's been none. Our task is sometimes made more difficult because we never know what becomes of the men in our care. But perhaps that's for the best. We're here to help now, in this moment, and we must leave what lies ahead of a patient in the hands of those who follow us."

I was reminded of Dr. Weatherby swearing when he lost a patient he'd fought to save. It hadn't been the future he was thinking about but the man slipping away under his hands, and knowing he didn't have the skill to do more.

"Thank you, Matron. I promise you, I'll keep that in mind."

She returned my smile then. "You're a credit to your family, Sister. As well as to your training." And she walked on.

Very soon we were left with those who were in no condition to make the journey. Some of them suffered from influenza or trench foot or wounds that hadn't healed sufficiently to risk the drive to Calais, the crossing to Dover or Folkestone, and the train to London. And because we had the space now, we could keep them a little longer. Base Hospital Seven had not finished its war. Not yet.

At week's end, I was just sitting down at a table in the canteen to eat my lunch when Sister Edgars came to find me.

"Bess? Matron would like to see you straightaway."

I frowned. "It's not the lung case, is it? Sergeant Melton?"

She shook her head. "I don't believe so. She asked you to come to her office, not the ward."

We'd fought hard for the Sergeant and his gassed lungs. Relieved, I quickly finished my meal and hurried to Matron's office.

She smiled as I came in, a reassurance that this had nothing to do with a critical patient. "Sister Crawford. Please, sit down."

I took the chair across from her and folded my hands in my lap.

"I'd like you to take the next convoy to London. Tomorrow morning. You can confer with Sister Walker meanwhile, so that she's fully informed about your patients."

I stared at her. This was completely unexpected.

"Matron—" I began.

"Yes?" She was surprised in her turn by my hesitation.

I asked the question that had popped into my head as she was informing me that I was to return to England. "Did my— Did Colonel Crawford arrange for me to be sent home?"

Her eyebrows went up. "Sister? Of course not." She held up several sheets of paper. "I have the rotation list here. All staff who spent more than the last month at the Front are being sent back as space becomes available. You'll have a fortnight of leave, and then be reassigned."

"But there's my work here. The war isn't finished for many of these patients."

"That's true. But we feel it's important for those of you who worked directly with the wounded in the field to have this opportunity."

"Is it likely that I'll be posted to France once more?"

"That's up to London, my dear. At this stage, you are scheduled to take this next convoy. That's an order."

I was trying to take it all in. I was a skilled surgical Sister. But there was less demand for those skills now. There were in fact enough of us that some of us could be spared.

Taking a deep breath, I said, "Yes, Matron, thank you."

Summoning a smile, I rose.

"You've been a very fine example of the best in nursing," she said as I opened the door. "It's been a pleasure to work with you, Sister Crawford."

It was another unexpected compliment. And this time it had a ring of farewell to it. I thanked her again and closed the door.

Home.

I'd looked forward to leaves all through the war. A brief opportunity to see my family and my friends. A way, really, to put the horrors I'd seen behind me for a bit and restore my courage and endurance.

Why should this be any different?

As I went to my quarters to begin packing, I remembered a story that my father had told us. There was a cavalry mount, taught to react to commands. He had been retired and sent to a farm not far from where he had been trained. The old farmer who had taken him in to live out his life in peace was disturbed by what he saw the first week the horse was there. He would do drills, there in the pasture, day after day, and the farmer thought the horse had run mad. He finally called the post and asked someone to come out and see what was happening. The Sergeant watched the horse for a few minutes, his smile growing broader and broader.

"There's no mystery here," the Sergeant told the farmer. "He can hear the bugles training the young horses. And he's obeying."

"I don't hear any bugles," the old man said.

"Ah, but he does," the Sergeant replied. "It's the only life he's known."

Nursing wasn't exactly the only life I'd known, but it had been my every waking and sleeping moment for four years. What I feared was being put out to pasture before I was ready to leave the Queen Alexandra's. I wanted to finish what I'd begun in 1914. Cases like Sergeant Melton didn't suddenly recover, stand up, and walk off just because the war had ended. Their suffering would go on long after the armies had gone home.

And then I smiled, hearing my father's deep voice again as he told that story to me at the age of ten. It would be good to see my parents. Tomorrow would have to take care of itself. Feeling a little better, I finished packing my belongings and then went to find my replacement and walk with her through the ward.

In spite of peace, Calais was still a madhouse of men and equipment. The convoy from the base hospital had wound its way down to the docks, and an officer of the *Sea Maid* was waiting to help us aboard.

I knew him from many crossings, and he greeted me warmly. It didn't take us long to unload the ambulances and carry my patients aboard. There were quite a few serious cases, but none of the critically wounded I'd often worried about through the rough voyage across the Channel. There was nothing worse than seasickness on top of great pain. At least today's transfer had gone smoothly, so far.

As we cast off, one of the crew members came to stand by the rail where I was watching preparations before going below to my charges.

"Seems odd, Sister," he said, "not to scan the approaches for signs of submarines. That was always the most dangerous part, before we were fully under way. Now I can stand idle as we slip out of the harbor."

I remembered, too well, the worry over submarines. If we'd been torpedoed, most of the wounded would have gone down with the ship, too ill to be saved or to save themselves. I'd been aboard *Britannic* when she went down, and the crew and the nursing staff had had a difficult enough time of it. We'd been grateful we were sailing empty.

From the bridge came voices, one with a familiar accent—I looked up to see that there was an Australian officer on board. I was reminded suddenly of Sergeant Lassiter and his proposal. I told myself I'd been right to say no. I wasn't ready to settle into a new life. Not yet. But I had been honored by it, and I knew I would always think of him with great affection. My only regret was that I couldn't love him as he must love me. The last thing I would have wanted was to hurt him in any way.

After a few more moments of watching Calais disappear from view, I turned and went below.

It was an uneventful crossing, and the landing in Dover

went well. We got the wounded on board the waiting train carriages, and I asked the First Officer of the *Sea Maid* if he would send a telegram to my parents in Somerset, telling them of my arrival.

"Are they on the telephone? Excellent. I'll do better than a telegram, I'll call them myself."

And so with some excitement I gave him the number.

One of the amputees was restless, and I thought that instead of soothing him, the clacking of the wheels had reminded him somehow of the war. I stood there and held his hand until he dropped into an uneasy sleep.

It was very late when we pulled into Victoria Station, the steam from the engine wreathing the lights and hiding some of the faces of those waiting for us. I saw to the unloading and signed papers describing each man's condition and his destination, and when at last the train was empty, the cleaning crew came on board to prepare it for its return to the ports in Kent.

Collecting my kit, I stepped off the train. The platform was nearly empty now, and I thought that my parents must not have received the telephone call from Dover in time to reach London. It was, after all, a very long way to London from Somerset.

I was just speaking to the stationmaster when I saw Simon Brandon striding toward me.

Turning, I smiled in greeting.

"Your mother is on her way," he said. "I'm to see you to Mrs. Hennessey's and stay with you until she arrives. I think she's afraid you'll vanish into thin air."

He took my hands in both of his and held me at arm's length. "You survived, Bess. We all did. I'm so very glad to see you safe."

And then he kissed me on the cheek.

"That's for your father. He's at Sandhurst at present, and

chafing at not being here to greet you. God knows what the staff
there is suffering as his patience runs out."

I laughed. "He'll leave the minute they've toasted the King."

He took my kit from me and gave me his arm. We walked out
of the station and down the street to where he'd left his motorcar.

London was quiet at this hour, and I stared around me at all
the lamps lit and the few motorcars on the road passing us with
headlamps bright. "It's so different," I said, accustomed to the
wartime precautions against the Zeppelin raids.

Simon handed me into the passenger's seat and went around
to turn the crank. "What will you do with yourself now? Stay in
London or go home with your mother to Somerset?"

"I've only been given a short leave. A fortnight. Then I'll be
reassigned."

He turned to look at me, surprised. "You aren't resigning from
the Queen Alexandra's?"

"Not yet. Not until the last of the wounded leave France. After
that—after that, I haven't decided."

He said nothing.

Changing the subject, I said, "While I'm here, will you help
me with something I need to do? There's an officer who was under my care. They've sent him back to England—some time ago.
And they've put him in a home with men suffering from shell
shock and head wounds. I want to see him. I want to know if
that's the right place for him."

"Bess. Your mother is going to expect you to come to Somerset.
At least for a bit."

"I will. But first I'd like to be sure that Captain Travis is safe.
After that I can rest. In a way I'm responsible for what's happened
to him."

"Tell me," he said simply. And I did.

In front of Mrs. Hennessey's house we sat in the dark in the motorcar for a quarter of an hour as I finished my account.

Simon hadn't interrupted. He'd heard me out before saying, "I'll do what I can. You know I will. If this man is so important to you. You asked me about this James Travis before. I sent a message."

"I never got it," I told him. "Sadly."

"Not surprising, as fast as events were moving out there."

"How would you feel, if you were shut away in a clinic and no one believed you? It would be a nightmare," I continued.

"The man the Captain has accused of shooting him is dead. The Army wouldn't make a mistake like that, Bess. If Lieutenant Travis was missing or a prisoner, it would have been reported."

I shook my head. "He's dead. Matron assured me of that. It still doesn't mean that the Captain was wrong. After all, it was a brief encounter in the heat of battle. He only said the man reminded him of his great-uncle. It was I who unwittingly gave him a name. And that's caused no end of trouble."

"It isn't your fault, Bess."

"Isn't it? If he'd told everyone it was a stranger whose name he didn't know, he might have been believed. But he felt so strongly that it had to be Lieutenant Travis. When it was established that James Travis was dead, had been for almost a year, no one would listen to him any longer. That's what worried me. Of course, there might have been more to the wound than Dr. Weatherby and I realized. I accept that. But it might also be some sort of terrible misunderstanding." I was weary, more weary than I'd realized. This was beginning to seem like an insurmountable task I'd set myself, especially here in the darkest hours of the night, when spirits were at their lowest anyway. I wished I'd had the courage to admit defeat too.

I leaned my head back against the seat. "Shall I wake up

Mrs. Hennessey, or will you? She thinks you saved her life. She might be happier finding you at the door." I didn't think I could move or get out of the motorcar.

"She'll be delighted to see you, Bess. As I was."

I took a deep breath of the cold night air, trying to rouse myself. "Will you help me, Simon? With Mother as well. I want her to understand, and not be disappointed."

He reached out and took my hand. He was a warm presence in the seat beside mine, his face hidden in shadow.

"Don't worry about it tonight. Don't tell her tonight. In the morning, it will seem much easier to deal with."

He was right.

And in the end it was Simon who went to knock at the door, and I climbed out of the motorcar in time to hear Mrs. Hennessey's cry of delight.

In her nightdress and robe, her hair down her back, and slippers on her feet, she ran out into the cold wind to meet me, her arms opened wide. Ignoring the fact that Simon, grinning, was standing there watching us.

And then I was being whisked into her sitting room, plied with tea, and told that it would only take her a moment to put fresh sheets on my bed. "Because they've been on there for several months now, and you must have new ones. And I'll make up Diana's bed for your mother. You just sit there by the fire and warm yourself, and I'll see to everything."

I was already drifting off to sleep as she closed the door. I realized that in the rush of her welcome, Simon hadn't told me when he would be back tomorrow morning—this morning, actually—as he wished us a good night.

I don't remember my mother arriving. And I never slept between those fresh sheets.

Someone—Mrs. Hennessey?—had put a pillow beneath my head and a warmed quilt over me, and I slept where I was, deeply and peacefully in Mrs. Hennessey's sitting room chair.

I woke the next morning to the sound of voices in another room.

I lay there, listening.

My mother's voice, and Mrs. Hennessey's. The deeper tones of my father's. But try as I would, I couldn't hear Simon's.

I had learned to live with the cold there in northern France. The winds that swept in from the sea, damp with rain, or the winds that seemed to blow straight from the Russian steppes, laden with ice, were just another hardship to be borne in silence. Here I was warm, the chair in which I had slept was soft and comfortable, a footstool drawn up to it, and the quilt over me smelled of lavender, not mildew or horses.

The only problem was the fact that I'd slept in my uniform.

The door to the dining room opened, and my mother's face peered through the crack.

When she saw that I was awake, she called to my father, and without waiting for him, she hurried across the room. I rose to meet her, and she flung her arms around me in undisguised happiness. Then my father was there, kissing me on the cheek and taking my hand in his. Mrs. Hennessey stood just behind them, beaming. I learned later that I was the first of her young ladies, as she called us, to return to London after the Armistice.

My parents had stood by me when I asked to join the Queen Alexandra's, encouraged me through my very difficult training, and offered me a haven when I came home on leave, never saying a word about their worry or their fears. I was their only daughter—their only child—and yet they had let me do what I felt I had to do.

It had changed my life in ways that I hadn't even begun to contemplate, but I knew what I owed them and why they were greeting me with such affection.

Afterward, in my crushed apron and muddy hems, I joined them at the breakfast table and listened to all their news.

Since last my mother had written to me, we'd lost more friends and members of my father's old regiment, men I knew all too well, but there had been happier events too. The village greengrocer's daughter had married her sweetheart, who had been invalided out of the Army last year after he lost a kidney to a sniper's bullet. There had been a huge wedding, all the village had been invited, and everyone had brought something for the bridal feast that followed. And Mrs. Dunning's cat had had kittens, three black and two gray—much to Mrs. Dunning's surprise, because for three years she had thought Biddle was a tom. The postmistress's twins were now learning to play the piano. They had had their first recital and performed brilliantly, according to everyone who had attended. I remembered that in one of her letters my mother had mentioned that a mysterious benefactor had found a piano for the girls. I had had a very strong suspicion that I knew that benefactor very well.

And then my mother glanced at the watch pinned to her jumper and said, "Look at the time! We should be starting out for Somerset if we're to be there for dinner."

"Mother—if you wouldn't mind—there's something I must do before going to Somerset. A patient—"

She looked at me for a moment, and then rose to the occasion like the Colonel's lady that she was. "Of course, darling. I understand."

I regarded her suspiciously. Had Simon already told them what I'd planned to do?

And then I realized that my mother probably did understand, far better than I'd expected, that her daughter wouldn't be coming back just yet. I could have hugged her for that, because her disappointment must have run deep. At least they knew I was safe, that no one would be shooting at me or shelling me, or taking me prisoner as the Front shifted back and forth between armies. She could wait a little longer to have me home again.

My father, on the other hand, frowned and said, "But I thought—" and broke off suddenly as my mother's foot must have found his under the table. He looked at her with raised eyebrows, then regrouped his forces and instead carried on. "But I'd thought you might wish to collect your motorcar and bring it down to London."

"I'm hoping Simon can help me find the information I'm looking for. There's a patient that I'm concerned about. I want to know where he was sent when the convoy brought him home from France."

"I'll help in any way I can," my father told me.

I smiled. "I'll save the big guns for reinforcements."

"Good."

We spent another hour just enjoying each other's company, and then the Colonel Sahib had to report to the War Office and my mother said briskly, "And I must be home before it's too late, or Iris will send out the cavalry."

We said our good-byes, and I was just seeing them out the door when Simon arrived. He greeted my father, and then turned to my mother with his usual deference. When I was a romantic girl of ten, I'd thought he must be in love with her, despite the difference in their ages, but as I grew older, I realized that there must have been a debt between them that he could never repay, and he would have done anything she asked of him without question. I asked my mother about that once, but she had only smiled and said, "You've been reading too many novels, Bess." And I had been wise enough to let the matter drop.

But my suspicions had been reinforced by our cousin Melinda Crawford some years later—unwittingly—when she was talking to my mother about India.

"I don't think Simon will ever go back," Melinda had said.

And my mother had agreed, replying sadly, "It would be too painful."

After that I hadn't probed further. Whatever it was in Simon's past that he didn't want to revisit was his affair and not mine. But I had often wondered if it had had anything to do with his joining the army so young. He'd sworn he was eighteen, and because he was tall and broad-shouldered for his age, no one had questioned it.

We saw them off, my father to HQ and my mother to Somerset.

Simon, watching them go, said, "It must have been a disappointment that you weren't going home."

"I think they understood."

"I've found out a little about this Captain Travis." We moved back into the shelter of Mrs. Hennessey's doorway, out of a sharp wind that chilled my hands and feet. "He's in Wiltshire. Not far from Salisbury. There's a clinic for head wounds."

"He's still there?" My spirits plunged. "I'd hoped that someone had come to his senses and moved the Captain. Do you think I'd be allowed to see him?"

After all, I wasn't related to him.

"Change your uniform, put on your best Matron air, and we'll see."

I left him sitting in Mrs. Hennessey's parlor and climbed the stairs to the flat I shared with my fellow nurses.

It was chilly, but oh so familiar, and I stood with my back to the doorway, thinking about Diana and Mary and Lady Elspeth.

I had already decided that I would keep the flat, although I hadn't said anything to Mrs. Hennessey. I wondered if they would as well. Diana was engaged and soon to be married, if she had anything to say about it, and she might well give up her room. Mary might stay. Lady Elspeth's home was in Scotland, and she might wish to keep a flat here, even one so cramped as ours.

And then I discovered that someone—Mrs. Hennessey or possibly my mother—had unpacked for me, and a fresh uniform was hanging from the hook on the door to my room.

I changed quickly, put up my hair with extra care, and looked at myself in the mirror. I could still see the shadows of tiredness around my eyes, and I was thinner, the uniform feeling a little loose, but that would change for the better with time. Catching up my coat, my gloves, and a scarf, I hurried downstairs.

Mrs. Hennessey was plying Simon with cakes from the bakery just around the corner and tea and her own views about the end of the war. He extricated himself with courtesy and followed me out to his motorcar.

"She likes you," I said. "It's a compliment. You should be honored."

He grinned. "The fact is, I like her as well." He closed my door and went to turn the crank. And then we were heading out of London toward Wiltshire.

It was later than I'd hoped. We stopped briefly for tea at an inn along the road and then moved on.

It was well after dark when we reached our destination, a village only three miles from Salisbury. There was an inn and Simon bespoke rooms for us.

Over a late dinner I was more than a little anxious about what I'd find in the morning. Simon, aware of it, said, "Bess. There's nothing you can do tonight. Let it rest."

I smiled, pushing my plate aside. "I feel guilty, that's all. And the doctors aren't always right."

After a brief silence, he said quietly, "Sadly, sometimes they are. Don't expect too much tomorrow. Don't set your expectations too high."

"I think that's just the problem. Nothing has gone right for Captain Travis since he was shot that first time. Very likely that hasn't changed. And I'm afraid that there's very little I can do about it."

He nodded. "I understand."

And I thought he did.

It rained in the night, with a touch of early December sleet in it, but the next morning was clear and bright.

The clinic was like so many I'd served in. A large house with many rooms commandeered for use by the Army for the care of wounded men. Many such clinics specialized. Broken bones, amputees, gas cases, burns, and so on. This one dealt with head wounds and other neurological issues.

When we turned through the gates and started up the drive there was a slight rise, and when the trees opened out onto gardens and fountains, I caught my breath at the beauty of the house before me.

Gray Cotswold stone faced in white; a long portico with white columns and wide steps leading up to a dark gray door. It was splendidly done, and I understood the name I'd seen on the gates: HIGH CLOUDS.

Simon, staring at it too, said simply, "Good God."

Someone had maintained the fountains and the gardens, and the paint around the door was bright and clean.

And then I saw the men being wheeled or walked through the

gardens, some of them shuffling and others with heads down, their view of their surroundings narrowed to the path beneath their feet. On a bench to one side sat two men, an orderly and a patient. The patient was listless, shoulders slumped, hands dangling over his knees.

Simon pulled the motorcar to one side and we went up to the door. There was a knocker in brass, but I could see that it wasn't necessary: the door was ajar.

As I stepped inside, the beauty continued. The entrance hall was almost two stories high, and there was a huge chandelier like a shower of glass above our heads. The flooring was black and white tiles, in a checkerboard pattern, and the walls were white with shallow niches where tall French vases added splashes of blue and gold. The handsome staircase rose before us, wide and imposing.

And there the beauty ended. Roughly painted partitions closed off the passages on either side of the stairs, and there was a pine table with a matching chair to one side of the door.

From above us up the stairs I could hear someone screaming. Not a frightened scream, but one that went on and on for a time, and then abruptly stopped.

A Sister came out of a room just across from the staircase. She was carrying a tray covered with a cloth. Seeing us, she came forward.

"I'm so sorry, Matron is with a patient at the moment. If you'd care to wait?"

She pointed to chairs along the far wall, chairs that looked as if they belonged in a dining room. "She'll be with you shortly."

We thanked her, and she went on about her duties.

As we waited, I could hear someone sobbing. I tried not to take any notice, but after a few minutes Simon got up to pace.

Finally Matron came down the stairs, a deep frown on her face. Then she saw us, and offered a smile of greeting.

I thought she must be in her late forties. Tall, slender, and fair with a kind face that showed signs of tiredness.

"I'm so sorry. The orderly who usually keeps the door has taken a chill, and we are rather shorthanded at the moment. Do you have a loved one here?"

"A friend. Captain Alan Travis. His family lives in Barbados, and they've asked me to let them know how he is."

"Yes, I've written to them, to inform them he's in our care. I don't know that he should have visitors at the moment." She opened the door to a room that had been partitioned into several smaller ones, leading us into the nearest and shutting the door. Above my head I could see part of an ornate plaster ceiling, and there was lovely parquetry on the floor.

After offering us seats and asking our names, she said, "I wouldn't speak of this ordinarily, but you're a nursing Sister, and I think it's only right that you should know. Captain Travis tried to take his own life two days ago, and we've kept him sedated for a time. Even a friend, seeing him in this state, could be detrimental. He would not wish for anyone to know what he's suffered."

Shocked, I made an effort to keep my wits about me. "All the more reason, I should think, for me to be allowed to see him." I could see a refusal forming on her lips, and I added hastily, "I happened to be the Sister who treated him when he was brought in with the head wound in question. My evaluation might be of use in judging how to proceed in future."

Matron was clearly surprised by my request, but she gave it fair consideration.

"He came to us after being treated in France for the wound in his back. It was slow to heal, and the attending doctor was worried about sepsis. And so by the time we had him, he was in a weakened state and very depressed. He told us over and over again that he was not ill, that he had been unfairly diagnosed. But we have a report that claims he saw a dead man shoot him, and that he was anxious to go and find this man, to stop him from killing again."

It was true—and yet a twisted truth.

I said, choosing my words carefully, "I saw the initial head wound, and while the skull had been creased, the brain wasn't exposed. It wasn't damaged."

"Physically, no, that may be quite true. But psychologically he's been confused and belligerent. We've had no choice but to restrain him at times."

I cast a despairing glance at Simon, who said then, "Sister Crawford had met Captain Travis before he was wounded. She can speak to his mental state then and now."

She sat there, observing us for a moment. And then she sighed. "I'm responsible for these men in my care, Sister. And it's at my door if one of them is made worse by unwise contact with those whose respect he cares about." She turned to me. "I must ask: Is there any emotional tie between you and Captain Travis?"

I could answer that one with a clear conscience. "Not at all. His family isn't able to come to England to look into his care, and there's no one else to act for them. He's been my patient twice, and I am in a position to understand what's being done for him."

That sounded rather pompous to my ears, but she must have believed me, for she rose. "I will allow you to see him, Sister. But not your escort, the Sergeant-Major. With respect, I think it's not wise to remind him too forcibly of the war."

"I have no objection to that decision, Matron," Simon said quietly.

And so it was that I was led up the stairs to a room down the passage. Matron hesitated outside the door, then took out a key and unlocked it. Signaling to me to wait, she stepped into the room. "Captain Travis? Are you awake? You have a visitor. Do you feel up to seeing someone?"

He murmured something I couldn't hear.

"No, not your family, I'm afraid. It's a Sister Crawford."

There was silence in the room, but then he must have nodded, for she turned to me. In a low voice, she said, "You may enter, Sister. I'll be just outside in the event you need me. You have only to call."

And so with a deep breath, I moved to the door and walked into that room with some trepidation.

My first thought was that Matron had shown me to the wrong patient.

Then the man strapped to the bed lifted his head and stared at me with an expression of pain and anguish and a deep, abiding dread.

CHAPTER 8

I DIDN'T RECOGNIZE him at first, but those deep blue eyes staring so fiercely at me I knew at once.

He was thin, too thin, and his face was marked by all he'd gone through, sallow and strained. Even his fair hair lay lank and lifeless on his pillow.

I walked to his bedside, reached out, and took his hand. He grasped my fingers in a grip that hurt.

"They say I'm mad. If I stay in this place much longer, I shall be. In the name of God, do something. Or give me something to end this nightmare."

Those expressive eyes were pleading now.

When I said nothing, my throat too constricted to speak, Captain Travis tightened his grip. "Please. I can't even lift my arms to tear up my sheets and hang myself. I've thought of nothing else for days. But they never forget to put the straps back before they leave me. Five minutes, that's all I need. *Please.*"

"You know I can't," I said gently. "But I will do all I can. I promise you. Hold on a little longer. Can you?"

He closed his eyes. "I don't know."

From the other side of the thin partition that divided what appeared to be a dressing room came screams, unintelligible at first, and then I could identify the words.

"No, no, no nononono. I can't go back there, I can't. For God's sake don't make me."

"Shell shock," the man on the bed said wearily. In a flash of memory I saw Captain Travis as I'd first met him, before he'd been wounded, on his way back to his sector after a summons to HQ. Now I was looking at a shell of that man. "He goes on like that most of the night, poor devil. I've tried to shut it out, but I can't."

I could hear the orderlies and a Sister trying to quiet their patient with soothing words, but from the depths of the dark well of pain the man was in, they couldn't reach him. And then blessedly there was silence as he was sedated.

"I'm not mad," Captain Travis said in a low voice. "But I've learned not to tell them what I feel or think or believe. Not now. I tell them what they need to hear. The staff. I try to convince them that it was only my concussion that made me believe my cousin shot at me. But I haven't been here long enough, they answer, to be properly evaluated. Then they'll decide what's to become of me. Dear *God*."

"Do you still believe it was James Travis?"

He gazed at me intently, trying to determine whether this was a test, whether I'd been brought in to find out what was really in his mind now. It was shocking to watch him fight for his sanity.

"No, don't answer that," I said quickly. "Forgive me for asking." I made a swift decision. "Instead, tell me where I can find your English branch of the family. Suffolk is a large county and I have only a short leave." Simon would be appalled—it was even against my better judgment, but how could I just walk away from here and do nothing? "Perhaps James was missing and thought to be dead, but he's still alive and his records haven't been brought up to date." I knew it was unlikely, but I'd have to begin somewhere. "Anything is better than this." With my free hand I gestured at the empty, lifeless little room, with nothing of hope or happiness in the plain walls. There was a chest to hold his belongings, and a chair for the Sister or the doctor.

I shivered. Not even a window. No view of the sky, of sunlight and clouds and stars. He had no way of judging the passage of time, whether it was morning or the middle of the night, save by the routine of the clinic. Nothing to occupy his mind or distract it from his own fears.

I had the feeling that he wondered, in some far corner of his mind where he didn't want to look too closely, if he was indeed mad and didn't know.

But before very long, I thought, he *would* lose his mind.

When he said nothing, still afraid to trust, I said, "Have you heard from your family? What have they been told?"

"I don't know. The Sisters don't tell me anything. I leave this room only to have a bath."

"No exercise? No fresh air?" I was dismayed.

"They aren't cruel. It's my fault. In the beginning I fought hard to make someone listen. They have a right to believe I'm dangerous." He looked away. "I tried to convince the staff that someone must look into what I was telling them, if only to prove me wrong. If I was mistaken about it being James Travis who shot me, it didn't change the fact that I had been shot twice, once in the back. Whoever had done that, he ought to be found and stopped. Men do go mad out there in the trenches and do crazed things. Did. I sometimes forget that the war is over. It hasn't seemed real to me." He hesitated, then took a deep breath. "I tried to make them understand that if he wasn't a career officer, he'd be mustered out soon, and sent back to England. And no one the wiser. But the thing is, once you learn to kill, and get over the shock of watching a man die at your hands, it can become easier. There's that to consider."

He didn't sound mad to me. Far from it. Cunning? Was he cunning instead?

I didn't think so. Watching that thin, exhausted face, expressive even as he tried not to show any emotion, I found it easier to believe him.

But then I'd known him, however briefly, before any of this had happened. And I'd had some measure of the man to judge him by now.

"I've lost faith in myself," he went on. "Lying here, going over and over and over what I saw, I begin to wonder if I imagined all of it. Then I try to lift my arms, and I remember."

He was still gripping my hand.

"Tell me where to find your English branch of the family," I asked again. "And I will discover what I can about James Travis. If he's dead, I'll try to find the man who shot you. But once I do, I won't lie to you. If I think that you are wrong, that you yourself broke out there in that retreat, I will not hide it from you." I couldn't bear to raise his hopes too high.

"Fair enough." He looked at me, those intense blue eyes scanning my face.

There was a tap at the door, and a Sister poked her head in the room. "I'm sorry, Sister. Matron would prefer it if you left the patient now. We try to keep him as calm as possible."

"Yes, of course." As he released my hand, I leaned forward. "Good-bye, Captain. I'll come and visit you again soon. You can depend upon it."

"Thank you," he said gruffly, and I turned away. But not before I'd heard his desperate whisper. "*Sinclair.*"

I walked out the door without looking back.

The Sister was saying, "How did you find him?"

"Quite calm, in fact. Although I would like to see him taken out in fine weather, and given a little exercise. It can't be good for his mental state to be left alone to dwell on what troubles him. Perhaps he's ready for a change of scene at this stage."

I spoke objectively, as if this man were one of my patients and I had been asked for my medical opinion.

"We can't put him in a ward, of course. Most of our patients have problems that disturb the others, one way or another, keeping everyone awake and agitated. You must have heard the poor man we were taking down to have the doctor look at his wounds. They were self-inflicted, you see. In France he was assigned to a burial detail. He can't forget what he saw. He was only nineteen; it was his first duty. Poor man," she said again, shaking her head.

We walked on, down to Reception, where Simon was waiting.

He had that particular glint in his eye that told me he'd spent his time well.

Thanking the Sister, asking her to thank Matron again for me, I said, "I'd like to come again. And give the Captain what comfort I can."

She smiled, but I had the feeling she believed it was not the best of ideas. I could understand. Many of these men were fragile, and families were not always helpful or encouraging—they hadn't been out there, they didn't know how or why their loved one had suffered.

Brace up! You're home now. The war is over.

As if the mind could cope on command, and put the darkness away.

I found that I didn't want to leave. On our way back to the motorcar, I walked over to an orderly sitting on a bench with an officer.

"How is he?" I asked, a visiting Sister inquiring about the patients.

"No trouble," the orderly said. He was of middle height, with dark hair and eyes. I recognized the Welsh rhythm in his voice. "He's too far gone to bring back. So they tell me. Poor sod—begging your pardon, Sister—poor soul."

"I'm told it's a fine hospital," I said, fishing for information.

"It is. Staff do their best. It can't be easy. Some of these men would be better off dead."

It sounded cruel, but looking at the patient beside him, I understood what he meant. A young Lieutenant, but there was no life in his eyes, no curiosity about me, no interest in the motorcar in the drive, probably no awareness of those around him.

"Where is the family who lived here? Are they still in residence?"

"I've never set eyes on them. I expect they left it all to the Army to deal with." The orderly went on, "When I first came here I'd never seen anything quite like this house. We'd had nothing like it in the valleys, everything black with coal dust, the cottages, the ground, the people. Depressed and depressing. Ma didn't hold with the fighting, you see, and I went to be an orderly. France wasn't much better. Men dying of wounds instead of coal dust and their lungs. What did it matter which killed them, I ask you? Dead was dead, wasn't it? Easy for me to leave the valleys. But I couldn't imagine anyone giving up living here. I look at the rooms and wonder what it was like, before the war. It makes my heart sing just to see it. They wanted to send me to a clinic closer to home, but I turned it down. I didn't want to leave."

"I came to see Captain Travis. Do you know him?"

"I've taken him down a time or two to be examined. He's quieter now. He'd rail at them in the beginning. Not like this one, unable to do anything without being told. The Captain, now, he'd shout that what he'd seen out there was real. But it wasn't. It was all in his head. And he couldn't understand that."

What would it be like, trying to convince someone that you were sane when they were sure you weren't? Convicted of madness by your own words?

I wished the orderly well, and walked back to the motorcar.

Simon turned the crank and got in beside me.

"Are you all right? What did you find out?"

"It was rather awful. I wish you'd been there. He's looking for ways to kill himself. If only for release."

"Does he hold to what he's claimed from the start? That he recognized the man who shot him?"

"He's very cagey about that now. He's learned that the doctors want to see improvement, and that to survive, to have any hope of being released, he must lie."

"I don't know that the medical staff always understands what's happening," Simon replied after a moment. "They try—but they sometimes feel the same as the civilian population does, that this is lack of moral fiber—cowardice."

I sighed. "He looks terrible, Simon. I hardly knew him."

"You've done your best. What more can you do?"

"I want to go to Suffolk. That's where the English branch of the family lives. They probably don't know the Captain is here, in England. Or what dire straits he's in. Apparently the two branches haven't kept in touch over the years. They might be able to do something to help him. I'd also like to find out more about James Travis. The Army can't have got it wrong, he must be dead. Still, there could be another brother—a cousin—who resembles him. If we could show that the Captain was mistaken, not mad, it could make such a difference. I don't know. But I have to do something. Will you drive me there?"

"Bess—your parents—"

"Please, Simon. There's something I must do. If I can."

He turned to look at me, something in his gaze that puzzled me. And then he said, "If that's what you want, Bess, I'll take you there."

I was so relieved I could have hugged him.

We found a telephone in the next large town and called my mother.

She hid her disappointment well. But I heard it in her voice.

"I'll have your kit packed when you get here," she told me. "Ask Simon if I can do anything for him."

I did, but he shook his head. He lived in a cottage just beyond the wood at the bottom of our garden. It would take him very little time to go there and choose what he needed.

And so we stopped at my home long enough for a meal. I owed my mother that. Then Simon put our cases into the motorcar and we set out for Suffolk. Darkness came so early at this time of year, and we drove until well after nightfall, making as many miles as we could. But it took us another day to reach Suffolk, and it wasn't until the dinner hour that we found ourselves in the small village of Sinclair.

The road coming into town from the south had twisted and turned like a corkscrew, hard driving in the early dark, but Simon knew what he was doing, and we got to our destination in one piece, having dodged hares and hedgehogs and once a startled pheasant asleep in the hedgerow at the side of the road.

We took two rooms in The George Inn and ordered our dinner. Over our tea afterward in the lounge, we decided not to say anything about the Travis family to anyone in the village until we had had a chance to have a look around.

We knew nothing about them, and we needed to know what questions we should be asking before giving our mission away.

I was so tired I slept without dreaming. To save time I'd spelled Simon at the wheel, and it was surprising I didn't have nightmares about the state of the roads. The cold and wretched rain showers that we'd passed through had overtaxed the motor-car's tiny heater, and puddles hid the worst of the ruts, making every bone ache from the constant jolting.

We met for breakfast the next morning. A pale sun had finally risen, and I had looked out my window to see a village green spreading out where the road curved. Indeed, I could see that the village was more or less strung along that road, most of the cottages and shops facing it as it turned and then followed the green in a long sweep.

I said to Simon as we waited to be served in a very pretty dining room that overlooked the street, "Where shall we begin?"

"The churchyard, I think. To see what names we will find on the stones there."

It was a very good idea. We finished our breakfast and walked over to the church. It was set well back, facing the upper part of the green, a grouping of thatched cottages between it and the High. Beyond it stood the plain brick Vicarage. We walked along the road, turned up a short lane that led between houses to the rear of the churchyard, and had our first really good look at the church itself.

A wool church, surely, a reflection of the prosperity of the county at the height of the wool trade, displayed for all to see.

It was quite long, with a well-defined clerestory and a checkerboard flint pattern along the nave and the apse. The windows were set in delicate stone tracery, and the tower was tall and square with an odd round enclosed staircase running up one side to the battlemented top.

We walked among the trees, looking at the gravestones. There were a number of Travis headstones here, mostly close by the church itself, going back to the 1700s. We were looking at names and dates, trying to connect the generations, when a woman, her arms filled with greenery for the altar vases, stopped. She was tall, slim, graying, with an air of competence and kindness.

Smiling, she said, "Looking for a family name? I'll help if I can." Then, deprecatingly, she added, "I'm the Vicar's wife."

"Hallo," I said, trying to conceal my surprise—I'd expected her to nod and walk on. We were not making much progress on our own, and so I added, "There seem to be any number of Travis graves here."

"There are more in the chancel. The family has been an important part of the parish for centuries. They've a house just beyond the village. Not the old one, of course—it burned in 1817, I think it was. Michael will be able to tell you. The Vicar. Are you related?"

"To the Travis family? No, sorry. But I do remember having nursed someone by that name. That's why it caught my attention. I don't know if he came from here or not."

"We lost a good many of our young men," she said, her face sad, as if she was speaking from a personal loss. "What was his Christian name?"

"James, I think." And then I added, prevaricating a little, "Or was it George? No, I believe it was James."

"Ah. That's our village hero. Lieutenant James Travis. He died last year, saving his men from a machine gun nest—he attacked it single-handedly and took it out, but died of his wounds by the time his men got him back to his own side. There was some discussion about a Victoria Cross. Of course, everyone in Sinclair felt he deserved it." She turned to Simon. "Were you in the war?"

"Yes," he said quietly, offering no other information. Simon's war had been no less dangerous but far more complicated than that of Lieutenant Travis.

"Then you'll understand what courage he displayed. And he was a reluctant soldier, you know. He didn't really want to go to war. But he was among the first to enlist. Duty and all that. His father had served in the Boer War, and his grandfather was in the Crimea. The Travises always served their country in its hour of need."

She turned back to me. "There's a memorial to him in the nave. He's buried in France, of course."

"Did he have brothers? Was he married?" I asked, since she was happy to talk to us.

"Sadly, no to both questions. His sister died in childhood, and he was the last of the direct line." She shifted the greenery. "He was to marry the nicest young woman from Long Melford. We all liked her. He said the war would be over by Christmas, and she was to plan for a Christmas wedding. But of course it wasn't, far from it, and she saw him only once after that, when he was wounded the first time."

"You mentioned a house. Who lives there now?"

"At present, only his mother. She's not well—I think James's death took the life out of her. He was her earth and sun and sky." Something in the way she spoke of Mrs. Travis's loss made me wonder if she'd lost someone she loved too.

"Did he have cousins who were close?"

"Sadly, no. Well, if I can help you any further, I'll be in the church. Do feel free to come and find me."

I thanked her, and she walked on. She went in the porch on our side of the church, and I heard the great wooden door scrape across the floor as it opened and then closed behind her.

"There seems to be little doubt that he's dead. James Travis."

Simon, still looking toward the church, said, "No. They wouldn't have made a mistake about that. There would have been too many men who witnessed what happened."

I moved on through the gravestones, looking at them so that I wouldn't have to look at Simon. Here was a newer one, dated 1915, with the name Hugh Travis. The size of the stone and the dates indicated he might have been James's father or uncle.

"Then Captain Travis couldn't have been shot by his cousin James."

"No," Simon said again. "It's not likely." He followed me among the stones. "What will you do now?"

I looked up at the fine slate roof of the church. "I hate the thought of going back and telling him that it couldn't have happened the way he claims it did. That James couldn't possibly have shot him. Either time. You didn't see him, Simon. It was rather awful."

"I understand. Do you want to go inside the church and look at the memorial to James?"

I shook my head. "Not yet. Perhaps later on in the afternoon."

There was no point in continuing to stroll through the gravestones. Not now. I walked on, to the lane that passed in front of the church and what appeared to be alms cottages close by the churchyard. The broad stretch of the green lay on the other side of the lane.

Several large trees grew there, standing well spaced across the greensward and spreading beautifully. Specimens, really. One was a maple, another an oak, I thought. The leaves had gone with the autumn, and the branches were like arms reaching into the watery sky.

"They must be beautiful in the summer," I said.

"Yes."

The green sloped down to the main road, the High, and we followed the lane to where it ended there.

I stood at the corner of the green, looking at the monument to the Great War that had been erected there. It was only in wood, and not weathered, the names apparently added as these men were reported dead, for there was no particular order, officers and other ranks given by the date of their deaths. Tall and slender, it rose above what looked liked the remains of pansies, planted there when it was dedicated and already touched by frost.

Pansies. For remembrance.

I took a deep breath.

Simon, beside me, asked quietly, "Are you in love with Captain Travis, Bess?"

Surprised, I turned to look at him. He was quite serious.

"I don't think so," I said slowly. Behind us, the church bells marked the hour. "It's mostly pity I feel. I met him when he was very different, and in a hurry to rejoin his men. We talked about our families, and the war. He was interesting, he had a fine sense of humor—we joked about camels—and I enjoyed that. Well, most of the men I saw were wounded, and they were in pain, their worlds shrunk to a single question, whether they were to live or die. Or they were doctors as tired and worried as I was. And there was Barbados. I knew so little about the island, except where to find it on a map. He had photographs of his home. In a way it was like talking to someone before the war. I expect that's why I tried to do something about his—his certainty that someone had tried to kill him."

Simon said nothing.

"I was being sent to a forward aid station, to replace a nurse who had tried to kill herself. Everyone was upset, unsettled by what had happened. It was my duty to do what I could to help them put it behind them. And so that short time in the canteen was in a way my escape from what was to come."

I had turned back to look at the memorial, and he came up behind me to put a hand on my shoulder. I could feel its warmth through my coat, and it was comforting.

"There's a shop just there that serves tea," he said after a moment. "I think we could both use a cup against the cold."

I looked across the road and saw it, very upright with long windows on the ground floor and shorter ones on the floor above. It was quiet and interesting and just what I needed.

And so we crossed the road after waiting for a farm cart to lumber by. I could see villagers near the other shops, doing their marketing, but we had this little island of peace to ourselves.

Simon opened the door for me, and above his head a bell tinkled musically. The shop was empty.

A woman stepped into the room and smiled. She had dark hair and a round face, with a round figure to match. "Choose any table you like. Tea, is it?"

"Yes, please," I said.

"I'll just put the kettle on," she replied. "It won't be a moment."

It was the oddest tearoom I'd ever been in. Many such establishments sold tea in bulk and teapots and cozies and the like. Instead, here there were other treasures. Among them were a tray of pins, most of them to decorate a woman's hat or to wear in her lapel, a sizable bronze elephant, a wooden model of an English tank, a set of silver goblets, and half a dozen quite pretty pictures of the seaside. A jar below them held a collection of thimbles, and there was a stack of crockery next to it, all in a pattern that looked very much like Spode.

I smiled and went to look at the various items on display while Simon took one of the small tables.

The woman came back, carrying a black lacquer tray with a white teapot, cups and saucers, a jug of milk, and a small jar of honey. Seeing me looking at her wares, she set the tray down in front of Simon, then said to me, "I'm like a magpie. Wherever I go, I find something to buy, and then I have no idea what to do with it. And so I put it out here, and hope that someone else will like it."

"And do they?" I asked as I came back to join Simon.

"Oh, yes. But then I find more. My husband says I should close the tea shop and simply sell my treasures. There are days when I agree with him. It's been difficult these past four years, with hardly anything to use for baking. Sugar was the first to go, then flour was in short supply. I ran out of sultanas and spices, but I was all right with eggs, because we kept hens. And I love to bake. Cakes and tarts and biscuits and breads. Oh well, the war is finished. In time, we'll have everything we need."

I hoped she was right, but my father had said that even with the war at sea ended, ships that had been converted to carry men and equipment must be retooled. It would be a while before the merchant fleet recovered.

We drank our tea, and I spotted the sweetest little owl, porcelain and quite nicely done. I bought it for Mrs. Hennessey, to set in the glass cabinet where she kept her favorite things.

We were just finishing when the shop owner asked, "What brings you to Sinclair? We don't see that many strangers."

"I'd heard about it from friends, and I thought it might be interesting to see. Can you tell me where to find the Travis manor house? We met the Vicar's wife in the churchyard, and she told us about it."

"It's not open," she warned us. "Mrs. Travis has become quite the recluse. But you can see it from the road. It's not very old, of course. I'm sure Mrs. Caldwell told you that."

"Yes, she was giving us a little local history, including that of the Travis family."

"So sad about James Travis. My daughter thought she was in love with him, when she was fifteen. That was before she met Archie, of course. She would race to the window to see James pass by. He cut quite a handsome figure on horseback, but the girls went mad when they saw him in uniform. As you'd expect." She smiled. "As a lad he'd come here to buy gypsy tarts for his mother. Such a nice little boy, well mannered and thoughtful."

It was Simon who asked the question.

"I understand he was an only child. How is the estate left, now that he's dead? Do you know?"

"It's rather a muddle. As you'd expect, James was his father's heir, but Mr. Travis insisted on leaving lifetime rights in The Hall to his wife, with an income to keep the house up. Of course, at her death, it would revert to James. There has been a great deal of speculation about James's will. And, I'm told, more than a little controversy. One rumor has it that the heir is serving in France. If that's true, he should be coming home now the war's finished. Another story making the rounds is that the heir is from an island somewhere in the Caribbean Sea, and he can't get to England because of the war. Miss Fredericks overheard Mrs. Travis swear that she'll burn down the house before he sets foot in it. There's said to be bad blood between this branch of the Travis family and the one out there."

"Is there indeed?" I asked, surprised.

"Oh, yes. The story my grandmother told me was that a younger son ran off with his brother's intended wife."

I stared at her. "Is this true?"

"I'm sure it must be," she said, nodding, her blue eyes quite serious. "To make matters worse, the younger brother went into trade. My grandmother said the elder brother forbade anyone to mention his brother's name in his presence ever again."

Simon commented, "He must have recovered enough to marry and continue the line."

"I expect he married a cousin. I doubt it was a love match, under the circumstances, but they had three sons and a daughter."

I tried not to smile. "Then I'm surprised that there aren't other heirs."

She shook her head. "The daughter died of the sweating sickness, and two of the boys were lost at sea before they were twenty. You can see the brass plaques in the church."

"But if Mrs. Travis refuses to accept this man, what becomes of the estate? Can she leave it elsewhere?"

"She says she will."

"But to whom?" Simon asked.

"Now that's a very good question. Nobody in Sinclair knows."

"I'm surprised," I said, "that the legal issues haven't been settled long ago. Whether Mrs. Travis agrees or not. A will must be probated, regardless of what the heirs might wish."

"Her solicitor is terrified of her." She grinned. "Everyone knows that."

The bell over the door announced a new customer, a slim woman with a little girl by the hand. "Good morning, Mrs. Horner," the woman said in greeting, and the shop's owner excused herself to speak to her.

Simon left the amount we owed on the table, and we thanked Mrs. Horner as we stepped out the door.

"What do you make of that?" Simon asked.

"I shouldn't think that could be anyone else but Captain Travis. Still, he never said anything about inheriting the estate here. He's never been to Sinclair. On the contrary, he seemed to be quite content to return to Barbados and take up his life again."

"Mrs. Travis may still have the solicitor too terrified to defy her."

"No wonder she's become a recluse," I said. "She must feel besieged."

"It's not our problem," Simon replied. "But I wonder if she's aware—or if the solicitor knows—that the possible Travis heir is now in hospital and considered to be a dangerous madman."

"Oh, great heavens," I said. "That might well be the case. The solicitor would make it his business to know. But that still doesn't explain why Captain Travis wasn't notified that he's the heir. Legally, whether Mrs. Travis allowed it or not, the solicitor would be required to carry out his responsibility to the estate." Another possibility occurred to me. "Do you suppose this heir in the Caribbean was someone else, and we've jumped to conclusions?"

"It could be that the heir serving in France and the heir in the islands are one and the same, but the gossips haven't realized that yet. I wonder when Lieutenant Travis's father died," Simon said thoughtfully as we walked back toward The George.

"I think I saw his grave in the churchyard—the large stone. If that was the right Travis, he died in 1915. His name was Hugh."

"Which means James would have been notified that he was the heir while he was still in France. And he'd have to make out a new will."

"I'm sure he must have done. It must be a sizable estate, not something left to chance. His family solicitor would have insisted on that." We had nearly reached The George, but we stood there in the road, talking, unwilling to discuss this inside. The wind whipped around my feet and tugged at my cap. I shivered.

"Yes. The question is, why did James choose his cousin in Barbados? If that's what he did. I expect the solicitor initially tried to find the heir in the islands, but the Captain was in France by that time. It might have taken a while to track the man down."

"We can't very well walk into the solicitor's chambers and ask him what he's done and what he hasn't. But I can tell you that when I first met the Captain, he said nothing about any change in his circumstances. I'll wager you he hadn't been told."

Simon looked back the way we'd come, toward the tea shop. "Did you see anything there among those items on display that you might want to consider as a gift for your mother?"

I blinked.

He laughed. "Any excuse to go back there this afternoon and resume our chat with Mrs. Horner."

"There was a lovely little rose pin. Yes. I think Mother might like that."

"Now let's get in out of this wind." And he went to open the door to The George.

CHAPTER 9

BUT THE TEA shop was closed when we returned.

Surprised, I said, "The notice in the window gives the hours as ten through five." Cupping my hand around my eyes, I peered through the glass. "It's tidy. Just as it was when we were there. I can't imagine she was taken ill."

Stepping back, I looked toward the empty green and then toward the row of shops across from The George, where one or two people were still on the street.

"The woman who came in had a child with her. Perhaps she was a friend and they went upstairs to visit."

I shook my head. "No, look, there she is, just going into the general store."

He followed my gaze. "You're right."

"Well. So much for Mrs. Horner. What shall we do now?"

"Have a look inside the church?"

A very good idea. We crossed the street, walked up the lane that ran between the houses and the green, and came to the churchyard. By the gate let into the flint and stone wall, we stopped to look at the notice board. It informed us that this was the Church of St. Mary the Virgin, and the Vicar was one Michael Caldwell. Below, the hours of services were indicated.

Tonight was Evensong.

The Vicar's wife had entered the church through the porch door, and we did the same, finding that it was unlocked.

It was quite lovely inside, open and airy. The ceiling soared above us, brightly lit by the tall clerestory. The slender columns were in clusters, and the west window above the altar was enormous. Above it arched a splendid barrel ceiling in wood.

I could see the greenery that Mrs. Caldwell had placed in tall vases by the altar. They were tastefully arranged, with branches trailing around them as if they were still living and spreading on their own.

A very ornate baptismal font stood in one corner.

In the stone floor of the nave, memorial brasses marked the resting place of generations of Travis men and sometimes their wives. Simon and I walked down them and looked at the dates. Here were Captain Travis's English ancestors, going back centuries. There were none of the tall standing Tudor tombs of the medieval period with their painted figures, but you couldn't come into this church without learning, very quickly, the name of the village's most prominent family.

Simon touched my arm and pointed.

On the wall of the aisle was a large brass plaque, the memorial to James Clifton Alan Talbot Travis, with his dates, his rank and regiment, and the battle in which he'd died.

One didn't put up such memorials unless the person was dead . . .

He had been only twenty-nine.

There would be no tomb in the stone floor for Lieutenant Travis.

The war had taken most of England's youth and buried them in foreign soil.

Just beyond, farther down the nave wall, I saw the plaques to the two Travis brothers who had been lost at sea. No tomb in the floor either, for Andrew and Richard.

I turned and walked back up the aisle, feeling depressed. There was no way on earth that Captain Travis had been shot by this cousin.

Simon followed me out into the churchyard.

After a moment, he said, "What do we do now?"

I think he expected me to tell him, *It's time to go home, back to Somerset.*

Instead, looking up at the bare overlapping branches of the trees, I said, "I don't know that Captain Travis would want this inheritance. You could tell he loved his home in Barbados. But he should at least have had a chance to make that choice for himself."

"There's not much you can do, Bess. You have no legal right to intervene."

"I realize that." I took a deep breath. "It just seems such a shame." I was avoiding facing facts, but I needed time to come to terms with them. Simon wouldn't let me have that luxury.

"Is he mad, Bess? You're trained to know what you're seeing."

"He truly believed that it was James Travis who turned on him and shot him. When he came to his senses as we were examining him, he was furious. Well, I could understand that, he'd met James in Paris, and even though it was quite a brief encounter, I think they liked each other. You can sometimes decide on the spot that you might like someone. Or, for that matter, heartily dislike him. Of course it's not always trustworthy, that feeling. But that's not what you asked me, is it?"

"No."

"Captain Travis told me in Wiltshire that even if he was mistaken about James Travis, he's certain it was an English officer, and that the man would kill again. I didn't know whether to believe him or not. It's one of the reasons I wanted to come to Sinclair. If James was truly dead, there might have been a relative of his who looked enough like James that in the split second as he fired, the resemblance registered. But there isn't a relative, is there? And there's no way for anyone to find that Lieutenant now. Which means that if Captain Travis is telling the truth, he has no hope of ever proving it. So it really doesn't matter what I think about his sanity. And I still haven't answered your question. But here's the problem, you see. When I met him in the canteen, he didn't strike me as a man on the verge of breaking. That's what I keep coming back to."

Simon was silent for a moment. Then he said, "I don't see a solution. But that doesn't mean there isn't one."

We turned toward the lane that led back to the inn, but when we got there, Simon asked, "Would you like to drive to the Travis house? Mrs. Horner told us it could be seen from the road."

I was grateful for the suggestion.

Those who built grand houses preferred not to be stared at by their neighbors, and so the house was often hidden by trees or at the end of a long, looping drive that offered privacy. Still, it wouldn't hurt to look.

We took the main road out of the village and soon saw ornate stone posts that heralded an estate, but the gates themselves were closed. A small lodge just inside them had an air of neglect, as if it hadn't been lived in for some time. Simon drove on, and then unexpectedly, through the trees, I could see the house. It was stone, in the shape of a B, and had at least three stories. There was a portico with pillars, and shutters at all the windows, even the tall ones.

Small as manors go—given the tombs in the church, I'd expected to see something far grander—but a handsome property all the same.

Simon found a place to reverse, and we drove back to the village.

He said, as we came to the outskirts, "I'll go on as far as the tea shop. It might be open now."

But it wasn't.

When we got to The George and started up the stairs to our rooms, the owner, a man in his late fifties, came out of the dining room and spoke to Simon.

"We're expecting guests tomorrow and will need the rooms you've booked. Are you leaving in the morning?"

I spoke up. "We booked them for three days. I expect we'll stay until then."

"But we're expecting other guests—"

Simon stepped in. "Then you must find other accommodations for them."

I had to smother a smile. Like my father, Simon had commanded men, and when he used that particular tone of voice, he got his way. This was no exception. The owner murmured an apology and disappeared into the nether regions.

We continued on our way, but outside my door, Simon said in a low voice meant for my ears only, "I have a feeling someone would be quite happy to see the back of us."

"The Vicar's wife was friendly enough, and Mrs. Horner was willing to speak to us. There was nothing then to indicate that Lieutenant Travis was a forbidden subject."

"The tea shop is closed. And the gates to The Hall. Now the rooms aren't available. Word must have got around," he answered.

"Which makes me wonder what there might be about the Lieutenant's life—or his death—that we mustn't find out."

We could hear someone else downstairs, just coming up. Simon opened my door and we both stepped inside, thinking it must be the owner rediscovering his courage.

We listened as whoever it was knocked at Simon's door. When there was no answer, he or she walked back down the stairs instead of trying my room.

Simon waited until we were certain that whoever it was had gone away.

"There has to be another way of finding out what's happening here," he said. "I'm open to any suggestions."

"I wish I knew. Possibly the best thing is to keep probing and see where it leads. I noticed a pub as we drove back into the village. Perhaps they're open for a late cup of tea?"

He opened the door and we went quietly down the stairs and out into the street. The wind was even colder now, whipping bare tree limbs and sending fallen leaves scudding down the High. We walked to The Five Bells and went inside.

It was low-ceilinged, cream plaster and dark oak beams, but the room was fairly large, and many of the tables were taken.

Heads turned as we stepped through the door. Because we were strangers? A nursing Sister and her escort in uniform? Or because we'd been asking questions? It was impossible to tell. We took a table near the window, and after a moment a very attractive young woman came to ask what we'd have.

I chose a pot of tea, while Simon had an ale. We talked, but only about trivial matters, while waiting to be served.

Looking around at the faces, avidly curious, I tried to find someone I might strike up a conversation with, but there wasn't the usual welcoming atmosphere one finds in village pubs. We might as well have dropped down from the moon.

Our order came, and I poured my tea.

"Surely not everyone in Sinclair is in a conspiracy against us," I said quietly, stirring in the honey and milk.

"Probably not. But you won't find them here, where anyone might see them being friendly."

I saw the woman who had come into the tea shop earlier, while we were there. The little girl was nibbling on a biscuit, smiling up at her mother over her treat. "I wonder if she knows whether someone came in after we left and asked Mrs. Horner to close down for the rest of the day."

"If she does, she's not likely to tell you." He finished his ale and, without waiting to be served, got up and went to the small bar to order the other half. There were two men in uniform there, and Simon spoke to them. One was a Private, the other a Corporal, and they exchanged comments for a bit before Simon brought his glass back to our table.

"They've just come home from France. They were in rotation and given leave. I could see from their badges that they were in the same regiment as Lieutenant Travis. And they knew him. Called him a fine officer, a gentleman. They were honored to have served under him. I asked if they were there when he died, and they told me they were in a different sector at the time, but word was that he'd done his best for his men, stopping the machine gunners from decimating them if they showed their heads. The nest had a very good location, able to sweep the field where Travis's company was supposed to be attacking. He got close enough to use a grenade, and then was shot by the only survivor, who fired as he lay dying."

I poured myself a second cup, making it last as long as I could. "That supports what we've been told."

"It does." He hadn't touched his second glass. "I asked if he had any brothers in France, and they told me he was an only son.

Then the Sergeant offered the fact that they were going to The Hall tomorrow to pay their respects to his mother. I made the proper comment, that such a loss must be hard for her to bear, and the Corporal said that his father had worked for her and called her a tough old bird. His words."

"Apparently the Corporal hasn't got the word that we aren't to be talked to."

Simon smiled. "I was hoping that might be true. I asked him who the heir was, and he didn't know, that Mrs. Travis had been left the estate for her lifetime, and so it wasn't important at the moment."

"I was watching, while pretending not to. The barkeep wasn't especially happy to see you speaking to those men. He kept his distance, but I expect he could hear every word, even so. As soon as your back was turned, coming to our table, he went over to have a word with them."

"Then they know now."

I didn't bother to finish my tea. Simon went to pay the reckoning. When he came back, we got up and left.

Huddling in my coat as we walked back to The George, I said, "We might as well leave in the morning."

"The devil we will," Simon replied shortly. "I'm beginning to dislike what's happening. If you're game, we'll stay on and, if we can, find out what this is all about."

I looked up at him. "What did the man have to say when you paid for our drinks?"

"He said nothing. He didn't have to. It was there in his face."

The next morning, as I opened my door to go down to breakfast, there was a square envelope just barely pushed under the edge. Of the best quality paper, I noticed, creamy and thick. I bent down to pick it up just as Simon came out his own door.

"What's that?" he asked.

I was looking at the crest embossed on the flap of the envelope.

"I think we've just been summoned to the palace." I broke the seal and read the short message.

"We have been invited to take tea with the Vicar and Mrs. Travis at four this afternoon."

"Have we indeed?" he asked with interest. "I have the feeling that our heads will be on poles by the dinner hour."

I laughed. "The Vicar won't approve, surely."

"That depends," Simon responded as we turned toward the stairs, "on whether or not he's under Mrs. Travis's thumb."

"Do you suppose someone saw us, driving out to find The Hall?"

"I wouldn't be at all surprised."

It was nearly four when we drove up to the gates of Travis Hall. They stood open now, if not particularly welcoming. Simon turned in through them and went up the long, looping drive to the house door. The Vicar's bicycle was already leaning against one of the pillars.

"We're expected," I said softly, and Simon got out to open my door.

We used the brass knocker in the shape of an ornate T.

A maid in crisp black, a white cap with black ribbons on her fair hair, opened the door to us, and we were escorted through the entry hall to the first door on our left.

It opened into a lovely room, longer than it was wide; at the end was a bow window with a great expanse of glass and a splendid view over a garden. I could see a sundial in a slightly raised mound surrounded by small boxwoods, and I could imagine tulips blooming in the spring at the foot of the pedestal, rose pink or perhaps even black.

There were two people waiting for us, one the Vicar, a man with prematurely white hair and a strong chin, and the other a very different woman from the one I'd expected.

Her dark hair, graying gracefully, was put up in an older style that was becoming to her face. Her features were patrician, her mouth firm, and her cool blue eyes were assessing us as we stepped into the room.

The maid gave our names, but of course Mrs. Travis already knew them.

"Sister Crawford. Sergeant-Major Brandon. Welcome to Travis Hall. And this is our Vicar, Mr. Caldwell. I believe you've already met his wife?"

Her spy system was the equal of Army Intelligence, I thought as I came forward to take her slim hand in greeting.

"Yes, we encountered her in the churchyard as we were admiring the Travis gravestones there."

"I do hope you found time to go inside and see the brass memorial to my son."

It was a statement, not a question.

"We did," I answered. "You must be very proud of him."

"I would rather have him alive and safe than dead and honored," she responded, "but then, he was my only son." Her gaze moved on to Simon. "You will forgive me, I'm sure, for feeling this way. I would have kept him out of the war if I could."

"I'm sure you aren't the only mother who feels that way," Simon replied. "The war took far too many lives, all of them precious to someone."

I saw the flicker of surprise in her eyes. I don't know what she'd expected, perhaps a very deferential man from the ranks, overawed at being invited to tea in this house. I could have told her that Simon was at home in far more elegant surroundings.

We were invited to sit, and the Vicar asked me where I had nursed the wounded. I told him, and he said, interested, "You've seen war firsthand. They didn't require my services, though I volunteered."

I wondered if Mrs. Travis might have had something to do with that. But I said only, "My father was a soldier, and while I couldn't follow in his footsteps, I could do something for the wounded and the dying."

"Did you perhaps attend Lieutenant Travis when he was wounded? Nineteen seventeen, that was."

"I wish I could tell you I had," I replied. "But I knew someone who met him in Paris, during a leave spent there. He must have been a fine officer."

"He was," Mrs. Travis said and picked up the little bell beside her. Ringing it, she said, "I enjoy having my tea in here. It's one of my favorite rooms in the house."

The maid entered with a tray.

A table had been set up beside where Mrs. Travis was sitting, with an immaculate white cloth and an array of cutlery and cups and saucers. The tray was set down there, and the maid proceeded to arrange the teapot, jug of cream, and a plate of little sandwiches.

Mrs. Travis poured, but the maid stayed to hand around cups and offer the sandwiches. There was egg and onion, ham and pickle, and egg and fresh cress. I thought perhaps there was a greenhouse somewhere on the estate.

As we were being served, the Vicar was recalling the elder Mr. Travis, telling us that he had enjoyed exploring The Hall's library with him. Mrs. Travis commented several times, and I gathered that her husband had been a man of parts, both a gentleman farmer and active in county affairs. I could also see that they had been very close, and that she revered his memory.

I found that intriguing, because we'd been told that she had become reclusive with the loss of her son. I thought perhaps it had begun with the loss of her husband. But she was no grieving widow, veiled in black, reclining on her couch in a darkened room, refusing to face life without him. Mrs. Travis's formidable personality showed through the gracious hostess role she was playing as she smoothly directed the conversation. I wondered how many people had been lulled into underestimating her.

Simon and I were asked where we were from, and we replied that both of us lived in Somerset.

There was a raised eyebrow at that, and I wasn't certain where she had imagined we were from. London, perhaps? Simon was wearing the insignia of my father's old regiment, but he didn't have the very distinctive Somerset accent, nor did I.

It wasn't until the maid had withdrawn that Mrs. Travis came to the point.

"If you didn't know my son at all, I'm surprised that you've shown such an interest in him."

Time to lay our cards on the figurative table.

"I'm sorry I didn't know him better," I answered with a pensive air. "The officer who remembered him from Paris was also a Travis. Imagine his surprise when he found himself sharing a train with someone of the same name." That wasn't precisely how the brief meeting had occurred, but I had my reasons for letting it appear that the encounter had lasted longer than it had. "Perhaps your son mentioned it in a letter?"

She smiled. "Travis is not an unusual name. I remember my husband telling me that there were unconnected branches in other parts of England. Gloucestershire, I believe, and Shropshire. Of course, there might have been a common ancestor. But we've lived here in Suffolk for generations."

Which didn't answer my question.

I'd been trying to work out why a woman like Mrs. Travis had decided to entertain two perfect strangers to tea, strangers she must not consider her social equals. I couldn't believe it had anything to do with our brief conversation with the Vicar's wife. But here the Vicar was, supporting her through this lovely tea.

Was she looking to find out what we knew about her son? Or was she hoping to throw us off the scent, so to speak, by appearing as a grieving mother eager to speak with anyone who had known her son during the war?

Similar thoughts must have been going through Simon's mind, for he said, "What brought your husband's family to Suffolk? The wool trade?"

"I have no idea. Hugh—my husband—could have told you their history without thinking about it twice." She smiled, turning to the Vicar. "When did the first Travis appear in church records?"

Caught off guard, he stammered, "Well—yes—um—as a matter of fact, I do recall the late Mr. Travis talking about that. He mentioned that his ancestors had a remarkable ability to choose the wrong side in any conflict. Three times they were given a title, and three times they lost it on the scaffold. Future generations appeared to take that lesson to heart and concentrated on making money. Which they did, in the wool trade. There was a Travis in this parish twenty years after the Black Death, recorded as a gentleman with twenty head of sheep and a house that stood on the corner of the present property nearest the village. The predecessor to this house burned in the early 1800s. I believe there's a drawing of it in Mr. Travis's study."

Money and prestige and a long history. Designed to impress us with its lineage. Did this have anything to do with the difficulties over James Travis's will?

All in all, it was the strangest tea I'd ever been a party to.

"This officer who shared a railway carriage with my son. Do you know him well?" Mrs. Travis was saying, and I had to bring my mind back to the present. Here finally was the main reason for our invitation.

"Not well. He was my patient on two occasions."

"Indeed. And he survived the war?"

"Yes. He has."

"And is he from Shropshire—or Gloucestershire?"

"From neither," I said. "He comes from Barbados."

There was consternation in Mrs. Travis's face, and Mr. Caldwell cleared his throat suddenly.

They hadn't expected my response. That was obvious.

Or was it that they hadn't expected us to be quite so forthright about Captain Travis?

All at once I realized what must be going on.

Had people thought Simon was a Travis, using one of his family names rather than his real surname? And that he had come here to find out more about the inheritance? A man of the ranks?

I wondered if this was the first time they'd had such suspicions about a stranger. It would explain why our conversations with Mrs. Caldwell and Mrs. Horner had brought us to Mrs. Travis's attention.

It would most certainly explain why she had invited a nursing Sister and a Sergeant-Major to *tea*.

And the Vicar was here as witness, to support Mrs. Travis's account when the police were summoned.

To my surprise, she rose abruptly. "I fear entertaining has been more tiring than I had expected. Please forgive me."

The Vicar rose as well, taking his cue from her words. He thanked her for tea and hoped to see her at St. Mary's when she was in better health.

We rose as well, thanked her in our turn, and found ourselves being ushered out by the Vicar, leaving Mrs. Travis standing there in her pretty drawing room.

As we emerged into a cloudy dusk, the Vicar apologized for having urgent business in the village. "I do try to come when she asks," he said, "however inconvenient the timing might be." He went to lift his bicycle from the post and prepared to mount it.

"I do wish I understood what this invitation was about," I said, trying to look offended by our sudden dismissal.

He hesitated. "Mrs. Travis is a very proud woman. I won't see her made unhappy by people who care only about her wealth."

Stung, I said, "I've asked nothing of her. You know that, you were present the entire time."

"Let it go, Bess," Simon told me. "It isn't worth discussing."

"But it is. Mrs. Travis *invited* us to come here. Your wife can tell you, sir, that we made no effort to persuade her to introduce us to Mrs. Travis."

"You questioned Mrs. Horner very thoroughly about the family and who the heir of Travis Hall may be."

"As I recall, we asked no favors of her, either. She simply gave us a little information about a family I'd already heard of and was curious about."

"Still, she acted rashly in telling you so much."

I shook my head. "I think Mrs. Travis is afraid that now the war has ended, the man who is next of kin will come to her door and ask to step into her son's shoes. I can't blame her. But that's not what brought us here. We didn't know about an inheritance, we wanted to—to see the plaque in St. Mary's. And learn something about James Travis. For personal reasons related to the war." The Vicar was looking skeptical. "I must return to my post in France in a few days. And Sergeant-Major Brandon will return to his duties. We don't pose any threat to Mrs. Travis."

He said only, "The conversation ended before either Mrs. Travis or I knew what you really intended by coming here."

I took a deep breath. There was nothing more that I could say or do. Simon was holding my door for me, and I could feel his disapproval.

"Sometimes our greatest fears are in our imaginations," I said and turned to step into the motorcar. Simon closed my door and saw to the crank before he came around to the far side and got in next to me.

The Vicar was still standing there with his hands on the handlebars of his bicycle, watching us as I looked back from the bend in the drive.

We rode in silence until we were outside the gates and turning toward the village.

"I wish I knew what was wrong here," I said finally. "Something is. Mrs. Travis struck me as far too intelligent a woman to deny that her son is dead. Emotionally, I mean, not in fact. Yet it's the only explanation I can think of for her to refuse to agree to James's heir."

"Some people, mothers in particular, find it hard to accept such a loss. She lives shut up in that house, seeing no one, seldom crossing the threshold, leaving her affairs to be dealt with by others. It's bound to matter who takes her son's place. She's already buried her entire family."

"I expect that's it," I said, and fell silent again.

We were pulling up in front of The George. Simon asked, "Should we leave tonight? Or wait until morning? You still have nine days of your leave."

"Tomorrow. I expect a good night's sleep will make everything look better than it does now." Somehow I didn't quite believe that. I turned to him. "We've finished what we came here to do. I don't know of any reason to stay." Staying wouldn't help Captain Travis prove he shouldn't be in that Wiltshire clinic.

Simon must have known what I was feeling. "The Germans were retreating. Every day was different, and men had to cope with that in any way they could, in spite of the fact they were exhausted, rations weren't keeping up with them, and they often didn't know precisely where the Front was. Whatever Travis thought he saw, in the chaos of the retreat, it might not have been true."

"It must have been."

"I don't mean it was a lie, Bess. The other officer might have been firing at someone behind Travis, at the same time that other man fired *at* him. Easy to misunderstand."

"Yes, I agree—or I would agree, if it hadn't happened a second time."

He pulled off his driving gloves. "There's that. On the other hand, what had the Captain done between the first and second wound? Had he been looking for the man he thought had shot him? And been unable to find him? Was he so convinced, so angry, he was prepared to believe that this officer had shot him again?"

"On the other hand," I echoed, "it could have happened just as he said it did, and a fellow officer tried to kill him. Just not James Travis."

"I know you'd prefer to believe that, Bess."

After a moment I said thoughtfully, "When a man is that sure—there must have been something to it."

"I'm not saying there wasn't. But getting at the truth won't be easy."

Simon got down and came around to give me a hand as I stepped out of the motorcar.

Just then the door of The George was flung open, light spilling into the darkness of the yard, and the owner stepped out, beckoning frantically.

"I thought I heard a motorcar. Sister? Could you come? There's been an accident. I was just about to go for the doctor."

I hurried inside to find a man with blood on his face lying at the foot of the stairs. I went to kneel beside him, and Simon, just behind me, said, "What do you need, Bess?"

"Water. Towels." I turned to the owner of The George. "What happened? Did he fall down the stairs?" I half heard the answer as I felt for a pulse and lifted one of the man's eyelids.

"I don't know. I heard something—crashing sounds, and when I came to see what the noise was about, there he was."

"Who is he?" Simon was back with what I needed, and I began to bathe the patient's face.

The owner, as pale as his shirt, said, "He just arrived—there was only the room under the eaves, but he was willing to take it."

I could see that he'd cut his forehead rather badly, and his chin. And he was unconscious, not a good sign.

Simon said quietly, "Bess." And when I turned, he pointed to a rapidly swelling ankle.

"He should see a doctor," I told the owner. "I'd rather not move him until I know what other injuries there are. You said you were about to go for him?"

"Um—yes—he's not far from St. Mary's. On the green."

Simon touched my shoulder as he went out to the motorcar.

I'd got the worst of the blood off the man's face, although both cuts were still bleeding. He looked to be in his mid-thirties, and healthy enough to heal if there were no other problems. One of the women who served in the dining room came down the stairs with a pillow for the man's head, and the owner started to object, then nodded. I raised his head a little and slipped the pillow in place, then turned my attention to the ankle. I couldn't be sure whether it was broken or badly sprained. If we were in France, I thought, we'd send him to Rouen for the X-ray machine.

I felt his arms and legs, but there was no indication of anything broken there.

He began to stir, then he moaned a little. After a moment his eyelids fluttered and he made an effort to focus his gaze.

"What happened?" His voice was strained, shocked. I didn't think he remembered falling.

"You took a tumble down the stairs," I said, smiling. "You'll be all right, I think, but we'll have the doctor look at you all the same."

My uniform bewildered him. "Am I in Casualty? I don't remember—"

"You're lying on the floor of Reception at The George Inn. I happened to be staying here. We've sent for the doctor."

"The George?" He started to lift his head to look round, and quickly stopped, alarm in his face. "My neck—shoulders—"

"I shouldn't be surprised that they're hurting. Lie down, please, until the doctor has a chance to look at your head. It's still bleeding quite a bit."

This time, the fog in his mind seemed to clear, for he grasped what I was saying. "Yes—The George—I was coming down to find out if dinner was still being served. If there was time to go out to—I forget."

"That's right," I said encouragingly. "The doctor will be here any minute. It's best not to move you until he's seen you."

He lay back and closed his eyes. Five minutes later, I heard Simon's motorcar pull up to the door again.

The owner had gone away to attend to dinner preparations and so I was alone with the patient.

The doors opened and a gray-haired man stepped into the room. He was tall and slender, and he walked with a limp as he crossed the floor to where I was kneeling beside the injured man.

"Dr. Harrison," he said, and took my place on the floor. "Hallo," he said to the patient, and then as the man opened his eyes, he repeated his name. "Let's see what we have here."

He set to work, and I stood to one side, watching as he slowly progressed down the man's body. When he came to the ankle, he glanced up at me. "We'll treat it as if it's broken," he said, "but it will hurt like the very devil either way." He looked at the stairs. "I take it his room is up there? Well, we'll have to find him another bed. He won't be climbing for a while. At any rate, not those stairs."

Simon had come in and was standing with his back to the door. The doctor turned to him. "I'm going to tape this ankle. When I've finished, we can try to get him into a chair."

"I'll help in any way I can," Simon answered.

We waited while the doctor closed the two cuts on the patient's face, then began to work on the ankle. As he was finishing, he asked, "What's your name, young man?"

"Thomas Spencer. It feels as if every bone in my body aches."

"Not surprising. I count—what? Fourteen steps? You fell down fourteen steps and landed on a very hard floor. Oak, I'll be bound. A thorough jarring. But if nothing comes of the blows to your head, and this ankle is only bruised, you'll be fine in no time."

He'd removed Mr. Spencer's shoe, taped the foot well, then

sat back on his haunches for a moment to admire his handiwork. "You won't be walking on that for a while," he said finally, "but I have a pair of crutches you can borrow. How did you come to Sinclair?"

"By train." Mr. Spencer seemed dazed still, his eyes moving around the walls and then coming back to the doctor, as if he wasn't quite sure yet where he was. But of course he'd only just arrived, he wasn't familiar with the inn.

Dr. Harrison nodded to Simon, and between them they lifted the patient and set him in the chair I pushed forward. He sat there, his head in his hands. I knew it must be thundering by now.

By this time the owner had returned, nodding to Dr. Harrison but staying by the doors into the dining room, as if distancing himself from all responsibility.

"We'll not get Spencer up those stairs," the doctor said, turning to him. "I don't suppose he could take over the back parlor?"

"There's no one to care for him. I can't spare any of the staff."

The doctor turned to me. "Sister?"

"I'm leaving in the morning."

"Well, then, it's the surgery," Dr. Harrison said with a sigh.

"I can't possibly walk—" Mr. Spencer began. Then, remembering, "And my valise is in my room."

"I'll drive you there," Simon told him, "but first let me get your luggage."

"Yes, all right—thanks."

Simon disappeared up the stairs, and Dr. Harrison was asking Mr. Spencer questions about his health as we waited.

The owner, relieved of responsibility, now tried to be helpful. "Is there anyone you'd care to notify?" he asked Mr. Spencer. "Any messages you'd like me to see to?"

Mr. Spencer thanked him but said, "It will be all right. My firm will send someone else."

"Where is your firm?" the doctor asked.

"London."

Simon returned, carrying a black leather valise, a hat, a coat, and an umbrella. He took them out to the motorcar, and I prepared to follow him. But the doctor was thanking me, adding that I'd handled the emergency well, and shrugging himself back into his coat.

They managed to carry Mr. Spencer out to the motorcar, but it was more difficult getting him into the passenger's seat. He grunted several times, and even cried out in pain once or twice, and I felt for him. I stood at the inn door, watching, knowing it was best if I stayed out of the way. When they finally had our patient settled and the door shut, I walked out to hand Dr. Harrison his bag. He thanked me again, climbed into the rear seat, and spoke to Simon.

Simon started slowly, gaining speed with care so as not to jar Mr. Spencer.

I took my coat and hat upstairs and sat by the window, waiting for Simon to return. It was a good half hour before I saw his headlamps turning out of the lane to the church and coming this way.

Another five minutes and he was knocking at my door. As I opened it, he was removing his coat. "All's well," he said, stepping into my room and closing the door behind him. "We got Spencer into the surgery, and I helped the doctor put him to bed. He's going to be very uncomfortable by morning. There were other bruises, the sort you'd expect from a fall, but no further injury that I could see. That foot is turning blue."

"Poor man, he's going to have a difficult time returning to London by train."

"Is that what he told you? That he'd come up from London by train?"

"Yes. The doctor asked him how he'd arrived."

"I can tell you he's not come from London. He arrived by omnibus. There was ticket and a timetable in his coat pocket with this afternoon's schedule marked. I took the liberty of looking in his valise before I brought it down. I suspect he must be from a solicitor's chambers in Bury St. Edmunds. He was carrying papers with their letterhead, and these reported that the solicitors have finally tracked down Captain Travis. That he's in Wiltshire, in a clinic for men with mental conditions. He must have been intending to take them to Mrs. Travis."

Chapter 10

I sat down, astonished. "That was clever of you."

He grinned as he took the other chair. "I've developed a very suspicious mind, following you into trouble."

"Why did Mr. Spencer lie about where he'd come from? I should think someone here in Sinclair would recognize him. I'm sure if the Travis family uses his firm, others in the village must have done. Still, we've learned that no one here knew where to find Captain Travis. Until now."

"Not too surprising, since he was wounded toward the end of the war and was no longer with his regiment. The real mystery is, what took them so long? James was killed in 1917. It's been well over a year. Unless of course someone did inform him that he was named in the will, and then lost touch."

"I'm sure he knew nothing about a will. He told me he'd never visited this branch of his family. The way he said it left me with the impression he wasn't interested in ever visiting them. He talked longingly about returning to Barbados, as if he wanted nothing more than to go home. I was a stranger, there was no reason for him to lie. It was the sort of conversation where he could easily have said that even after the war ended, there were affairs in England that would delay his sailing."

"He might not have told you for personal reasons. He'd only just met you."

"Then why did he swear it was James Travis who shot him, if he already knew James was dead?"

"I can't argue with that point," Simon agreed. "All right, the problem might have been at this end, a problem with the solicitors not knowing exactly who he was, or that he was in France. Until James named him in his will, there might have been no real reason to keep informed about a distant branch. There's even a chance that James might not have known anything more about him than his name and rank. I grant you, that's an odd way of choosing one's heir. But then James might not have thought it would matter. That he would survive. I rather think he might have made his own inquiries, and been killed before he could explain matters to his mother or the solicitors."

"You could be right. Mrs. Horner hinted at some confusion over who the heir was, which sounds to me as if no one was really certain. That points to the possibility that James didn't ask the family solicitors to draw up his will."

"There was no time to read anything but the first few paragraphs of the papers. Still, that was enough to tell me it had to do with Captain Travis and his present whereabouts."

"Did you see the name of the solicitors?"

"Yes. Ellis, Ellis and Whitman. Bury St. Edmunds."

I looked at the little watch pinned to my uniform. "It's too late to drive to Bury tonight. No one will be in at this hour. We could have used the excuse of letting them know about Mr. Spencer's fall."

"It's not too late to have dinner there, and afterward look for the address."

"That's a very good idea." I stood up and reached for my

coat. "I would give much to know if Mr. Spencer simply discovered where the Captain was and then came directly here to tell Mrs. Travis what he'd learned, or if he actually spoke to the Captain at the clinic and told him about the will. It might explain what he meant when he told us he'd come from London. Still, I really can't imagine Matron allowing them to talk. She might feel that learning he was the heir to the man he believed tried to kill him would upset the Captain too much. It's too bad I have no right to speak for Captain Travis. We would have a good reason to ask questions."

Simon was already putting on his own coat as he followed me down the stairs. The wind had dropped with sunset, but the evening was cold. "I expect you're right about Matron, Bess. But I'm just as glad you aren't more involved in this affair. Wills have a way of stirring up family resentments and causing no end of trouble."

I pulled up the collar of my coat and drew my gloves from my pocket. "It will be a day or so before Mr. Spencer can even consider carrying out his mission here. I can't imagine he would ask someone to take a message to Mrs. Travis, not while he's in such pain. And she isn't likely to call on him at Dr. Harrison's surgery, even if he did."

I remembered that Mr. Spencer had already refused an offer to send messages to anyone, including his own firm. That would have been the better course of action, asking someone else to finish his business here.

I said, "Do you suppose there's a telephone in the village that he could use? Or perhaps I could put through a call to my mother and ask her to go to Wiltshire for me. The Captain could tell her what I should do."

"I don't believe there's a telephone in Sinclair. Unless there's one at The Hall. Just as well, I don't think it's a good idea to draw your mother into this. Not yet."

Simon was right. Sending her to the clinic might do more harm than good just now. But I was feeling a sense of frustration that we could do so little.

The high beams of the headlamps picked out trees and barns, and we could see the lamps lit in farm and cottage windows. I could smell smoke drifting from chimneys, warm and comforting.

We came into Bury St. Edmunds and found a restaurant just across from the abbey ruins. It was still serving dinner. We went up the steps, walked inside. Simon spoke to the man who greeted us at the dining room door, and asked for a table.

One was available, and we were seated against a wall but could look out the windows at the dark shape of the tall abbey gates.

The meal was surprisingly good, and afterward we walked through the center of Bury, searching for the chambers of Ellis, Ellis and Whitman. On a lane that ran down to the High Street we found what we were looking for. The brass plate with the name of the firm was weathered, but the woodwork around the windows and doors was fresh, with what appeared to be, in this light, a dark blue paint.

Simon stepped back to look up at the building. "There's a lamp burning. I wonder if one of the partners is working late."

We were just turning away when a Constable came round the corner and hailed us. "Good evening, Sister. Sergeant-Major. Looking for someone?" he asked. He was portly, possibly in his forties, and had a belligerent chin. But his manner was mild as he spoke to us.

"An after-dinner stroll. How old is this building?" Simon asked.

But the Constable wasn't to be put off. "There was a breaking and entering here last evening."

"Here?" I asked, surprised into speaking before I thought.

"Yes, Sister. There's a senior clerk working in there just now, trying to determine what is missing." Lifting his truncheon, he gestured toward the light.

"Oh, dear. Was the man caught?" I stepped closer to Simon, taking his arm in apparent anxiety.

"Not to worry, Sister," the Constable said kindly, "but we are keeping an eye on passersby. Were you by any chance on this street last night? Walking along here?"

Simon answered for us. "We're staying in a village a few miles away. Sinclair. We decided to come to Bury for dinner, in the hope that the food would be different."

"Staying with family? Friends?"

"At The George," Simon replied easily.

"And what brings you to Suffolk?"

That was a much more difficult question to answer truthfully, given our reasons for coming here.

"One of the men I treated near the end of the war has connections in Sinclair. He's still in hospital. We thought perhaps his family might like to know more about his condition," I said. It sounded implausible even to my ears, but the Constable nodded.

"The Sister who nursed my son wrote to us until he was able to write on his own. We've never forgot her kindness."

I felt my face warming with embarrassment. I didn't intend to sound as if we were being kind.

Taking a chance, I asked, "There's a Mr. Spencer in Dr. Harrison's surgery in the village. He took a nasty spill coming down some stairs, and I assisted the doctor in treating his injuries. Do you know where his firm is located? I believe he's a solicitor here in Bury. I could leave a note for them."

I expected him to tell me that Mr. Spencer was a member of Ellis, Ellis and Whitman, and I could summon the clerk to take my message. It was the perfect entrée and would give me a few minutes' time with the man. I wasn't sure just how I'd manage asking about the Travis will, but I could at least mention having tea with Mrs. Travis and the Vicar, and see where that would take me. We might even be asked to carry a message back to Mr. Spencer. It wasn't much, but it was better than leaving Bury without learning anything.

Instead the Constable gave me a suspicious stare. "A solicitor, you say? I can't help you there, Sister. I'd walk on, back to The Angel, if I were you. There's an omnibus leaving within the hour. Heading in the direction of Sinclair."

"Thank you, Constable," I said, properly chastened.

"Good luck finding your thief," Simon added, and bidding the Constable good night, he took my arm and led me back the way we'd come.

Once out of sight of the Constable, I said in a low voice, "I wonder what that was all about? I thought it would be a simple enough matter to summon the clerk. For heaven's sake, you'd think he would be grateful to know about this latest catastrophe befalling the firm."

"For a moment there, I feared I'd have to explain to your father why we'd been taken up by the police."

"It did sound rather sinister. Here we were, showing an unfortunate interest in the scene of a crime, then mentioning one of the firm by name. But I do wonder why anyone would break in there. I should think any large sums of money would be deposited in the bank." I added, almost to myself, "If that happened last night, I wonder if Mr. Spencer knew about it? Surely he must."

"A good question, that."

"No use stopping by the surgery. We have no excuse to see him."

"I expect he's too uncomfortable to care." Simon hesitated. "Bess. If he lied about London, and he refused to contact his firm or even tell Dr. Harrison what he was, do you suppose it was connected to the break-in?"

"I can't think why," I said slowly. "Unless he was afraid it had something to do with his reasons for coming to Sinclair."

We had reached the motorcar, and Simon opened my door before turning to the crank.

As we drove out of Bury, we passed the same Constable. He stood there on the corner of the street and watched us pass. His expression wasn't friendly.

I was yawning by the time we reached The George, and we climbed the stairs in silence.

When I came down to breakfast the next morning, Simon was already there.

Joining him at the table against the wall, I said, "For a wonder, the sun is shining."

"So it is," he said, greeting me. "I've already walked outside. The wind has dropped as well."

I ordered my breakfast, thinking of the dry sandwiches I'd eaten so often at the Front. It was a pleasure to have porridge for a change. But I was still waking at dawn, listening for the sound of the guns. How long would it take to believe the war was over?

Not wanting to think about that, I said, "I think I should look in on Mr. Spencer."

"Surgery hours begin at nine. I saw the board last evening. Are you intending to tell him that you've been to Bury?"

"I can't think of a reason to bring it up. But that may change when we speak to him. Afterward, perhaps we could have tea at Mrs. Horner's. I wonder if she's intending to open the shop."

"I walked by there just now. I saw lamplight in the windows upstairs. Someone is at home."

It was a little after nine that we knocked at the surgery door.

An assistant admitted us and showed us into the waiting room.

A woman sitting in one of the chairs was wearing a uniform very similar to mine. I put her age at mid-thirties. A strong face, a pert nose, and gray eyes. She smiled when she saw me, and nodded. Professional courtesy.

"Good morning," I said, returning the smile.

"Where did you serve?" she asked, and I told her.

"I was mainly with the British regiments fighting in the mountains of Italy." The smile turned wry. "I lost three toes to frostbite. They sent me home."

"I'm so sorry to hear it," I said, and that was not just a polite reply. I meant it.

"I'd never seen high mountains before that—I'd never been to Wales or Westmorland. It was quite a shock, as you can imagine. And the cold was sometimes as bitter as any I'd ever felt. My fingers were always cold. But one couldn't wear gloves, you know. Not dealing with open wounds."

"When were you posted there?"

"My brother's regiment was pulled out of France just after the Third Battle of Passchendaele and sent to Italy. I wanted to be near him, and so I volunteered to go with the medical staff. He's still there, worst luck."

That had been a very different campaign. We had already been fighting in the Near East and in France, but when Italy decided to join the Allied cause, it opened up a new Front because of Italy's proximity to the Austrian border. Britain sent men to shore up the Italian Army.

We chatted on for several minutes, and then Dr. Harrison's assistant came to fetch the other Sister. As she reached for her cane, half-hidden behind her skirts, she said, "Sister Potter. Have you recently come to Sinclair?"

"Sister Crawford," I responded. "We're visiting in the village for a few days. One of my former patients had connections here."

"Come for tea, if you have time. Ask anyone, they'll tell you how to find me." She followed the assistant through the door.

"I was never part of that campaign," Simon commented, "although I trained a number of Berkshire officers who were later sent there."

The door opened again, and this time it was Dr. Harrison who came through it. "Sarah told me you were here. I expect you want news of Mr. Spencer."

"Yes, we were quite concerned about him."

"He had a most uncomfortable night. I'm still not convinced that the ankle is broken. But I did discover two cracked ribs. I'm keeping him for a few days. He's in no condition to travel."

I said, "Is there anyone he would like to notify—or reassure? I'll be happy to help, if I can. His firm, for one, might wish to know what's become of him. Or perhaps his family."

The doctor shook his head. "I can't give him anything for his pain until I'm sure the head injuries aren't as serious as they appear. I don't think you'll achieve much even if you speak to him. But I'll ask, as soon as I can. And if there's anything further you can do for him, I know where to reach you."

It was dismissal. A nursing Sister didn't contradict a doctor. It was not done. But we had other ways of putting our opinions across.

With a warm smile I said, "That's very kind of you, Doctor. Please tell Mr. Spencer we're concerned about him. And that we'll call again later."

He could hardly forbid me to appear on his doorstep.

After a moment, he returned the smile—wryly—and said, "To be sure, Sergeant-Major." He nodded to Simon and was gone.

When we were outside, safely out of hearing, I said, "I've never asked. Why did you search Mr. Spencer's belongings before bringing them down? And don't tell me you've grown suspicious of everyone after being in my company."

He laughed, that deep chest laugh that comes when a man is truly amused.

"I walked into the bedroom and realized that he must have only just arrived because his coat was across a chair, his hat on the table, and his valise on the bed. All I had to do was collect all three and bring them downstairs. I put his coat over one arm, picked up the hat in that hand, then reached for the valise with the other, thinking to lift it off the bed. But he must have gone into it for something, because one of the clasps hadn't caught when he reclosed it, and as I swung it off the bed, the remaining clasp snapped open as well. I caught the valise before it spilled everything onto the floor, and as I set it back on the bed to close it properly, I saw the papers. And the name at the top—Captain Alan Travis. I didn't have much time for a real search, but the doctor would assume I was repacking his belongings, and so I carefully looked through the valise and then his coat pockets, in case there was any identification there. That's when I discovered the omnibus ticket and schedule."

"We would never have known what had brought him here if you hadn't found those papers. And we wouldn't have known to go into Bury. We wouldn't have heard about the break-in. What could someone have been hoping to find, if not money? It doesn't make any sense, does it?" I stopped in midstride. "Simon. We've just *assumed* that Mr. Spencer is a solicitor—that he's a member of Ellis, Ellis and Whitman. What if he isn't?"

"Go on," Simon encouraged me, outlandish as the thought was.

"Well, all we really do know is that he was in possession of papers with that letterhead. Do you think that's why the Constable was suspicious? Because he knew there was no one by the name of Spencer in that firm? If that's the man's real name. Nobody at the inn recognized him, we'd already seen that. And I had the strongest feeling just now that Dr. Harrison was discouraging us from seeing Mr. Spencer. Do you think he told the doctor that he didn't wish to have any visitors?"

"Harrison did make it rather plain that you couldn't see his patient. Even though you were caring for the man before the doctor got there, and I helped settle him into his cot. So, yes, Spencer must have been the one who didn't want company."

"Unless it was Mrs. Travis who forbade us to see him," I said, walking on. "But unless gossip has already reached The Hall about what happened last evening, she probably doesn't know he's here."

Simon fell into step beside me. "What you're trying to decide is whether it was Mr. Spencer who broke into Ellis, Ellis and Whitman to look for those papers. What does he have to gain by that? For that matter, how did he even suspect they were there?"

I sighed. "You're right, it hardly makes sense. Still—blackmail comes to mind. What if he was there looking for something else, and he came across those papers? But that leads us back to what you were saying. How did he know that they mattered, that they were important?" I wasn't sure I really believed any of this. But what other explanation could there be?

"Those papers mean that Ellis, Ellis and Whitman had already discovered who and where Captain Travis might be. And Mrs. Travis would have been told where he was. What would Mr. Spencer have to gain? What's more, why was she so suspicious of us, when she already knew precisely where the Captain could be found? If she had any reason to think we were trying to take advantage of her, she would have had the Constable to take us into custody."

"We're going to find ourselves in gaol, one way or another, before this is finished," I told him bleakly. "There are only eight days left of my leave—it will have to be a light sentence. Surely she would have said something about Captain Travis being in a clinic in Wiltshire, if she'd known. If only to gloat. To tell us she couldn't be taken advantage of."

We had crossed the green.

"Whether she knew then or will be told shortly where Travis is, it will not make her very happy to hear that her son's heir is a deranged man. Spencer might think it's worth something to her to keep the rest of the world from hearing it."

"Pride," I agreed. "Everyone reveres James Travis so. But I expect she was against the Captain long before he was sent to Wiltshire."

"Strange as all this sounds, it could very well be true," Simon offered. We had reached the war memorial, and we stopped. Across the way, I could see that the tea shop sign read OPEN. "Proving any of it will be another matter entirely."

I glanced back the way we'd come. There was a woman just going into the doctor's surgery, and Mrs. Caldwell, the Vicar's wife, was crossing the churchyard. I wondered if we could learn anything by speaking to her, then rejected the idea. The Vicar would see to it that we didn't. He'd have warned his wife about us. "But what other choice does Mrs. Travis have? Is there anyone else she'd rather see inherit? Someone James overlooked? Or preferred not to leave the estate to? If it isn't entailed, he could leave it to the gardener or the gamekeeper, if he chose."

Before we could cross the road, a lorry lumbered by, and I waited until it had passed before saying, "We've overlooked something. Mr. Spencer's clothing wasn't that of a thief. He was soberly dressed too. I think that's why we assumed he was a solicitor."

"Back to where we started," Simon replied.

As we reached the far side of the road, I noticed a cottage set back from its neighbors. It boasted a dark blue door, and there were blue flower boxes at the windows, empty of plants this time of year. A plaque hung from a wrought-iron post halfway up the walk. It read THE POTTERY.

I pointed it out to Simon. "I wonder if that's where Sister Potter lives. She struck me as the sort of person who would probably call her house that."

"Yes, I think you're right." We walked on to the tea shop, several doors away. It was a bit early for elevenses, but I could always fuss over the gold pin with the red enameled rose.

But despite the sign, I found that the door was locked when I tried it.

"I hope whoever asked her to keep the shop closed is also willing to reimburse her for lost revenue," I said, disappointed, peering in the window.

Just then someone came down the stairs, more or less a moving shadow, and I stepped back. A moment later the door opened, and Mrs. Horner greeted us.

Her welcome wasn't as warm as it had been on our first visit, but I said cheerily, "I remembered a pin I saw when last we were here. I think my mother might like it."

Simon stood with me as I searched for the pin in the tray, found it, and picked it up.

"Yes, it's just the sort of thing she'd wear," Simon agreed as I showed it to him. I turned and handed it to Mrs. Horner, and then paid for it.

She took the pin and wrapped it neatly in a pretty paper, making a perfect little packet I could put into my kit. I thanked her, and then asked if she was serving tea.

"I am," she said, and we took the same table as we had yesterday. "I'm surprised you're still here," she added as she set about arranging a tray.

"I think it's a charming village," I said.

"Rumor has it you were invited to pay your respects to Her Majesty."

I was surprised—not so much by the fact that she'd know where we went, but because she actually mentioned it. And by the way she referred to Mrs. Travis. *Not much love lost there,* I thought. Then why did Mrs. Horner agree to closing her shop? If that was the reason it was closed.

"I expect she wanted to know who was exploring her village," I said lightly. "Even if she chooses to live a quieter life."

"She wasn't always this way," Mrs. Horner admitted. "Not when her husband was alive. For one thing, he'd have had a word with her about that. And for another, she was James's mother and wanted the village to love him as she did. Now she's neither wife nor mother, and all she has left is the Travis name."

"And did the village love James?" Simon asked.

"Of course they did. You couldn't help it. The Vicar and his wife were like a second family to him. And when he was a little boy, the shopkeepers always spoiled him shamelessly. I did my share, I must admit it. Miss Potter—Sister Potter as she is now—bound up his dog's foot when the poor thing had cut it on a stone. And it wasn't because James was from The Hall and we were currying favor with his parents. His death was such a tragedy to all of us. We felt like we'd lost our own." She looked out the window, the kettle whistling in the tiny kitchen behind her. "That's to be replaced by a stone. That wooden memorial. By next year, so Vicar says. Mrs. Travis has given a sum toward it, but the rest of us put up what we could. We lost so many men in Sinclair and the neighboring farms. And those who have already come back aren't well."

There was sadness in her voice.

When she brought the tray holding cups and saucers and the milk, I said, "Is the man who came to take a room in The George last night a frequent visitor to the village?"

"The one who fell down the stairs?" She shrugged as she set around the crockery and added a jar of honey. "The girl who does the dishes in the inn kitchen is claiming she didn't recognize him. I saw you come from the doctor's surgery just now. Is the man all right?"

"Cracked ribs and a badly sprained ankle. He'll heal in time, but he won't be leaving the surgery until he's able to manage crutches."

"Doctor will probably ask Sister Potter to nurse him, then," she replied, nodding. "She lives just up the way, and there are two bedrooms in the cottage."

"She's done this before?" Simon asked.

"It's convenient for Doctor and for her. We had three influenza cases this autumn, and she was asked to care for them. Mrs. Lacey and her daughters."

She disappeared into the back, then, and we drank our tea. Simon said in a low voice, "When we leave here, do you want to go back to Bury, to speak to the solicitor?"

"I'd thought it would be possible to use Mr. Spencer as my excuse for calling. But now I'm not so sure that's a good idea. What's more, the clerk would show us the door if we put a foot wrong." I hesitated. "Simon. There's one way. And it might do the Captain more good than anything we can accomplish here, now that we know James Travis is dead. I think we should take our chances with the solicitors."

"Then finish your tea and we'll be on our way."

It was just a little before noon when we lifted the brass knocker on the door of Ellis, Ellis and Whitman.

A clerk opened it and invited us inside, then asked how the firm could help us.

"Could you tell me which partner is handling the affairs of the Travis family in Sinclair?"

"There is only Mr. Ellis now. His father, the senior partner of that name, died the first Christmas of the war, and Mr. Whitman was killed during the second battle of the Somme."

"Then I expect it will be Mr. Ellis who can help me." I gave him the smile Matron used when she expected us to obey instructions without question.

The clerk hesitated. He was an older man, possibly nearing sixty, and schooled in the Victorian era, when one didn't contradict a lady, if there was a way around it.

"Let me ask if Mr. Ellis is free," he said with a slight bow and disappeared through the only other door in the room.

I liked what I saw here. The walls were paneled in dark wood below the chair rail, but linen fold in the old style above. Instead of the usual partner portraits or hunting prints, masculine and indicative of the firm's standing and longevity, there was a collection of lithographs of Cambridge in the early 1800s. Elegant carriages with handsome horses pulling them, women wearing bonnets that framed their faces, gowns with high waists and just showing tiny pointed-toe shoes. The backdrop, of course, was the colleges, beautifully drawn.

The door opened and Mr. Ellis himself appeared, giving his name and asking how he could assist us. I was sure he'd been curious but had every intention of sending us packing after he'd seen us.

He was a man slightly above medium height, fairly young—perhaps mid-thirties—with what in the old days would be called the look of a consumptive. Pale face, sunken chest, lank hair. I had no doubt he hadn't been fit for military service. And even as I was noting this, he coughed. It didn't sound very good.

"I've come about the care of Captain Alan Travis." If the papers Simon had seen were from this office, then Mr. Ellis would certainly know where the Captain was at present. "I have just visited him in hospital. They have done their best for him, but he needs personal attention from a physician trained to deal with head wounds. I have no way of reaching his family or his firm of solicitors in the islands. But as I am informed that he's heir to the estate of the late James Travis, I expect you are the person most likely to help him." I had used Matron's voice too, brooking no dissent, as if I believed I had every right to be here. And in many ways I did.

"And what is your relationship to Captain Travis?" he asked, glancing from me to Simon behind me, and then back to me again.

"I was the Sister who treated him when he was wounded, and while I've been on leave, I looked in on him at the clinic. I was appalled by what I saw."

"You'd better come back." He moved from the door and indicated that we were to follow him to his private office. The clerk, hovering in the shadows, closed the door behind us.

We walked into a room filled with papers, some in marbled boxes, others rolled and tied with ribbon. Every surface seemed to be covered with them. "I'm sorry," he said abruptly, coming in behind us. "There was an attempt to break in recently. I've been asked by the police to tell them what's missing."

I had no intention of telling him that Mr. Spencer might know something about that. I primly took the chair he emptied for me, and Simon sat in the only other uncluttered one. Mr. Ellis went behind his desk, coughed again, and sat down.

"Why do you feel that it's your duty to make other arrangements for Captain Travis?"

"Who else has done anything to better his treatment? I had had the good fortune to meet Captain Travis when he was rejoining his regiment after being called to HQ. We were both waiting for transport at the time, and I had an opportunity to observe him as a healthy man. What I see now is a man in despair, confined in a small room with neither exercise nor recreation of any kind. The clinic is shorthanded, they aren't cruel by intent. But something must be done before Captain Travis is made ill."

Mr. Ellis listened to me intently. "Mrs. Travis tells me that there is another branch of the family more closely related to her late husband than the branch in the islands. She has presented family records that support her belief. I am not certain that Captain Travis is our responsibility."

"Indeed," I said, genuinely angry now. I had expected to hear at least a promise to look into the Captain's situation and see what could be done. Mr. Ellis's callous dismissal of any duty toward a member of the family he served disturbed me. "Will you wait until there is a clear connection, or Mrs. Travis asks you to act on her behalf, before you do something for Alan Travis? He will hardly thank you, when he is well enough to take up his duties at The Hall."

"He hasn't requested our assistance. Nor has she." A fit of coughing caught him and he turned away.

I took a deep breath. "He's been told his cousin James is dead, but he has no idea that he could be the heir to his estate. He has no access to news."

"That's unfortunate. But I have no authority here until we have established who the legitimate heir may be."

"Do you even know where the Captain is at this moment?"

I could see that he did, even before he lowered his eyes to the file in front of him on the desk blotter. He had obviously seen and read the papers that Mr. Spencer now had in his possession.

"I'm afraid that's not pertinent to this conversation."

"It is," I said with a smile, "if you know and have done nothing to help him."

"You must forgive me, Sister, but I have another engagement. I am truly sorry that there is nothing I can do at present for Captain Travis. I suggest that you contact his solicitors and his family in the islands. They might be more successful."

He was rising as he spoke, and I had no choice but to do the same.

He escorted us to the inner door, where his clerk was waiting to see us out.

On the street outside his chambers, I turned to Simon.

"I didn't accomplish very much, did I? I thought—well, never mind. It was worth trying. Mrs. Travis won't hear us, and now Mr. Ellis has made it clear that he doesn't want to help."

"I saw his eyes before he turned away. He knows about those papers. I can't say whether he also knows if they're missing, or not."

"What part does Mr. Spencer play in all of this? The clerk just told us that there are no other partners or even junior partners in the firm. A good thing I didn't begin with their missing solicitor. Because he isn't."

We were walking back to the motorcar, and now that I realized I had nowhere else to turn, I was feeling rather depressed.

"I must go back to Wiltshire. I owe Captain Travis that much.

He deserves to know what we learned. As little as it is. Before I go back to France, I could write to his solicitors on Barbados."

"Bess. Ellis just mentioned another heir. You don't suppose that Spencer is representing *him*? It would be to his benefit to know what Ellis knows, and it would serve his client if it could be shown that Travis was mad and likely to be confined to a hospital or an asylum for the rest of his life."

"A solicitor doesn't go around stealing the files of his competitors," I said, but the idea was taking hold. "All the same, there's no doubt Spencer has the file, however he came by it. And he brought it with him when he came to Sinclair. After all, you saw it." I frowned. "He fell coming down the stairs, on his way to ask when dinner was being served. That tells me he was in a hurry. Not to have his dinner, perhaps, but to find out if he had time to go to The Hall either before or after. His next question would have been to ask for directions, and to see if there was any way to get there other than on foot."

We'd reached the motorcar, and Simon was holding my door as I stood there, trying to think through what I was saying to him.

"But now Spencer is in Dr. Harrison's surgery and unable to go anywhere. Not to The Hall. Nor back to wherever he came from," he said, picking up the thread of my thoughts.

"I can't believe he'd wish to speak to her in the surgery. There are too many people about—too many ears to hear and gossip later."

"There's the Vicar. What better go-between?"

"I don't know. Would the Vicar be a party to any of this? I think he came yesterday to protect Mrs. Travis from whatever it was she feared we might be doing here. After all, she's alone now." I got into the motorcar, and Simon shut my door. When he'd turned the crank and got behind the wheel, I said, "I wonder if, in so much pain, Mr. Spencer will ask for the Vicar, to give him the support of prayer? He would have to feel, wouldn't he, that the Vicar could be trusted?"

"Or he must wait until Mrs. Travis sends the Vicar to him."

But I kept going back to the main question. Did Mrs. Travis know why Mr. Spencer had come to Sinclair? Or had he traveled here on his own to represent his client, that different heir?

I turned to Simon, smiling ruefully. "It's rather like trying to diagnose what's wrong with a patient, when he's behind a screen and you can't look at him. We're missing too many bits of information to make a whole picture."

We traveled in silence back to Sinclair, and as we came into the village, we saw Sister Potter, leaning heavily on her stick, just coming out of the tea shop. She waved when she saw who it was passing in the motorcar.

"Simon. Do you think we might call on her? To see what she can tell us about this tangle of heirs? She must know as much about village life as Mrs. Horner, surely?"

"I'll set you down here, shall I? She might be more amenable to discussing the Travis family if you're alone."

"Good idea."

He slowed and I got down, walking back to meet Sister Potter before she reached her own door.

"How was your consultation with Dr. Harrison?" I began.

"Well enough." She made a wry face. "He wants me to take on that poor man who tumbled down the stairs at The George. Did you hear about that? You must have done, if you were staying there, and not at The Five Bells."

"Yes, I was first on the scene. I sent my friend, the Sergeant-Major, for the doctor, and dealt with Mr. Spencer until Dr. Harrison arrived."

"He's a good man, Harrison. A little brusque, but a good doctor. I didn't mind the Lacey family, they were people I knew. I'm not so certain I wish to take on a stranger, and a man at that. Not that I have anything against men!" She smiled. "I nursed enough of them. But that was different, it didn't seem to matter if you didn't know them, did it? You coped, and tried to save their limbs if not their lives. I know nothing about Mr. Spencer."

I could understand her reluctance to take him in. We'd been standing on the walk outside her door, and she added, "I've forgot my manners! Won't you come in? Smokie will be upset, but never mind."

Smokie was a small gray cat with green eyes. He met us at the door as Sister Potter opened it, then turned and stalked off as soon as he realized that I was about to come in with her.

The cottage was small but comfortable, and from the style of the furnishings, I gathered it must have belonged to her parents before her. There were family photographs on the table by the window, and on the pale blue walls hung small watercolors of the various sights of Sinclair. One of them was a rendering of the Travis house.

She saw me looking at them. "My mother insisted on framing them. She thought me quite clever. But of course I had sense enough to realize I had only a small talent. Still, I took my watercolors to France with me, and when I had time I painted." There was a sudden shadow of sadness in her face. "Not that there was much that was scenic. Blasted trees, ruined villages, and bloodred poppies. I'll never frame them. Still, it gave me something to do." Indicating a chair, she went on. "Would you care for tea?"

I'd seen her leaving the tea shop, and so I said, "Thank you, but Simon and I had our tea earlier."

She nodded. "Tell me more about where you served. I'd like to hear about it."

I gave her a brief account of my postings, and she nodded. "I knew one or two of those doctors. I was mostly at the base hospitals, but they sent me forward when there was a need for Sisters. Italy was so very different from France. I was appalled when I got there and saw where most of the fighting was taking place. Italy had just declared war on the Austro-Hungarians, and the border was a range of mountains. We had the devil's own trouble getting men back to proper care. I was with the British regiment, and I worried day and night that my next patient might be my brother. I'm ashamed to admit that I was so grateful when it turned out to be someone else's brother or son or husband."

We talked a little longer about the winter campaign, and then I said, "How long have you lived in Sinclair? All your life?"

"Yes, my father was the postmaster here. And we bred King Charles spaniels. Lovely little dogs. I enjoyed the puppies, and always hated it when someone came to claim them. But of course we'd have been overrun if I'd had my way and we'd kept them all," she ended, laughing. "I painted some of them—those are upstairs in my room."

"Did you know James Travis?"

"Everyone did. I was older than he was, worst luck, or he might have been my first love, instead of Geraldine's elder brother."

"Geraldine?"

"Sorry, one of my friends at school."

I had tried several times to bring Sister Potter around to Mrs. Travis. I finally asked outright. "Everyone speaks highly of him. He must have had fine parents."

"His father, Hugh, was a lovely man. I heard rumors of a wild youth, but according to my mother, once he married, he settled down and was all that a squire should be. He knew everything there was to know about every family in the parish, and if someone needed help, he was there to see to it."

"Was?"

"Yes, he died two years before James, for which I was grateful. I don't think he could have borne that loss too. James's sister died young, and it nearly broke his heart. She was such a pretty little thing, and as sweet as she was pretty."

"You haven't mentioned his mother?"

"She was a Cecil before she married. Not of the main branch of that family, but certainly a cut above the likes of Sinclair. I always thought she must have loved her husband very much to come to live at The Hall."

"It must have changed her, losing him as well as her children. I can't begin to imagine what that would be like."

"She's kept to herself since word came of James's death. But she knows everything that happens here. I'm not quite sure where she comes by all the news, much less the gossip and rumors."

I thought I knew. *The Vicar. Or his wife.*

As if it had just struck me, I asked, "But who is the heir?"

"I just got back to Sinclair fairly recently. But Mrs. Caldwell—the Vicar's wife—told me that there has been some difficulty over finding the next of kin. What with the war and all. James had to make out a new will while he was at the Front. It's up to the solicitors to hunt the heir down, whoever he is, but so far I've not seen him."

"That must be worrying to Mrs. Travis."

"I don't think it is, really. The house is hers as long as she lives. There's never been a dower house. At a guess, she would prefer not to have a stranger come in and upset everything."

And that was all I could learn. The talk moved on to what

would happen now the war was over and the Kaiser had abdicated. What's more, it was time I took my leave.

Rising, I thanked her, and she saw me to the door. "I don't know how long you're staying in the village," she said, "but do come again. No one else in Sinclair chose to train as a nursing Sister. I'm afraid I'm rather a fish out of water. It's pleasant to have someone to talk with."

I promised I'd call again, and then set off toward The George.

She hadn't said anything about a cousin from the Caribbean, and I wondered if she knew about Captain Alan Travis.

Back at the inn, I tapped on Simon's door to let him know I'd returned, and we compared notes.

After I'd told him about my visit with Sister Potter, he gave me an account of his conversation with the owner of the inn.

"I asked if Mr. Spencer had stayed here before, and I was told he hadn't. But the Vicar had come in this morning while we were in Bury, to inquire about the guest who'd come to grief. It seems that the daily at the Vicarage had brought the news of Spencer's fall when she came to work this morning. At any rate, the Vicar indicated that he would look in on the man and ask if there was anything he could do."

"That's kind of him," I said. "Unless he came not out of duty but to carry news to The Hall."

"A little of both, I think. Are you ready for lunch?"

I was, and we went down to the dining room.

Betty, the young woman who was serving today, took our order and asked if we'd heard anything more about poor Mr. Spencer.

While Simon told her what little we knew, I wondered if she was the one who had started the rumor mill buzzing this morning. The woman who did the dishes had already passed the news on to Mrs. Horner.

She lingered to hear all the details, and then went back to the kitchen to relay our order.

When she returned with our soup, she said quietly, glancing over her shoulder to be sure she wasn't overheard, "I hear you've been asking questions about James Travis."

I wasn't at all surprised that she had somehow discovered that. "I'd heard of him from a wounded officer I'd treated," I told her, wary of adding to her store of tales. "It must have been a shock when the news came of his death."

"It was. Tragedy seems to follow that family. My mother says it wasn't just this generation. Mr. James's father lost an older brother, and their father lost a sister and two brothers. It's as if the Travis name was doomed to die out."

Betty, I thought, had read too many romance novels.

"Hardly doomed," Simon replied, smiling.

"It's not to be taken lightly. There was a curse put on them. There was a terrible fight between brothers years before this generation, and the younger stormed out, swearing he'd never darken the door of The Hall again in his lifetime, nor his heirs after him, and he damned his brother and all his line before disappearing. Never to be heard of again."

With that final whisper, she turned away and disappeared in her turn—through the kitchen door.

"That was rather tangled," I said, "but if I followed her at all, it was Captain Travis's ancestor who stormed out and went to Barbados. That fits with what I was told by the Captain. Save for the curse, of course."

"Do you suppose there's any truth to what she was saying? That would explain why Mrs. Travis doesn't want the lost branch of the family turning up to inherit The Hall."

Using what came to hand, I sketched out the Travis genealogy as I understood it. "The salt cellar and the pepper are the two brothers who quarreled. Next came the brother who lost his sister and brothers. He's my fork. He had two sons—your teaspoon and mine. One of the teaspoons died—here, you can have yours back again—and the remaining teaspoon was James's father. I make that four generations, counting James."

Grinning, Simon looked at my handiwork. "I expect that's close enough."

"Which explains why Mrs. Travis is so adamant that the Captain must not inherit."

"She married into the family. I'm rather surprised that she should carry on the feud."

"She might feel that she's her husband's voice in this matter. We don't know how strongly he might have felt. If she adored her husband as I've been told she did, she might feel honor bound to uphold his views. Family histories can take on a life of their own."

Simon was silent, and I realized suddenly that he was looking inward. I'd never known anything about Simon's own family. He never spoke of them, and that seemed odd to me, a happy child with two loving parents. One day I'd asked my mother where *his* mother was—I must have been six or seven at the time, but I remember it clearly—and she had answered that some children were orphans and had no parents now. I'd pitied him for a very long time, and I was glad he'd found a family of sorts with us.

I concentrated on my soup, giving him time to recover.

After a moment he said, "Perhaps James never felt as strongly about past history. Or he saw something in the Captain that he liked, and the past didn't matter. The more I hear about James Travis, the more I like him."

A thought occurred to me.

When James went to war, he must have made a will. Most soldiers did. Even though his father was still alive at that time. Who had he named then? His father or his mother, most likely. But when he had to make a new one, he'd thought about the future. If he hadn't met the Captain that day in the Gare du Nord, if he hadn't realized at some point that this stranger was the cadet branch of his family, who would he have named instead?

The man who was now represented by Mr. Spencer?

CHAPTER 11

I FOUND I'D lost my appetite.

Pushing my plate away, the soup only half-finished, I looked out at the row of houses and shops across the way from where I sat with Simon.

Colorful, distinctive, a pretty village tucked away in a corner of the county, one of a string of others like it. But at the heart of Sinclair was loss and sadness. The wooden memorial stood out on the wintry green, starkly reminding everyone who could see it of the men who had gone to war and never come back.

I was beginning to understand what was happening in Mrs. Travis's mind. Her son was dead, and she would want to respect his last wishes and see that they were carried out. Only, how could she?

Had he written to her, mentioning Alan Travis, that look-alike cousin on a platform in the Gare du Nord in Paris? Or knowing the family's view of the cadet branch in Barbados, had he simply asked his solicitor or someone in London with the contacts to carry out his instructions, to find out more about this man? Perhaps he'd simply liked what he saw in that brief exchange and trusted to his intuition. He hadn't expected to die so soon.

Everyone called James Travis a very nice boy, a very nice man.

Perhaps he was just that, and thought the time had come to heal the breach in the past.

I turned to Simon. "What I don't understand," I said, almost continuing my thoughts aloud, "is where Mr. Spencer comes into this. Was he stealing those papers—assuming, of course, that he did steal them—to *show* to Mrs. Travis, or to make certain they were *never* shown to her? Which doesn't make sense, because the solicitor, Ellis, could simply replace them."

"I wonder what inheritance law has to say about dealing with someone who is diagnosed as mad?" Simon asked me.

"I think in general the question may be whether or not the estate is entailed. If it must go to the next legitimate heir, then there probably isn't much say in the matter. Unless of course if it can be shown that the madman isn't the next legitimate heir."

"Which is probably what Mrs. Travis is struggling to do. To find someone else."

I sighed. "A muddle, isn't it? And I don't know if Captain Travis would want the estate if he was handed it."

"Perhaps if Mrs. Travis knew that, she would be much happier."

"Now I understand why she's so particular about strangers here in Sinclair. Why she doesn't want anyone speculating about her son's will. I wish I could go to The Hall and talk to her."

"You can't, Bess. This is a problem you can't fix."

"I know. But before I leave England, I'll find a way to help Captain Travis. I can't go away and leave him in that empty, wretched room, with everyone thinking he's mad."

Simon gave me a wry smile. "Why am I not surprised."

We finished our meal, and I suggested we try again to see Mr. Spencer. "Although how I expect to ask him about those papers in his valise, I don't know."

I went up to my room to wash my hands and fetch my coat.

When I came down again, there were two Constables and an Inspector standing in Reception, speaking to the owner of The George.

They turned as one when I appeared.

The man not in uniform stared for a moment, then walked over to me.

"Good afternoon, Sister. My name is Howe. I'm an Inspector with the police in Bury St. Edmunds."

"Hallo," I said, trying to conceal my curiosity and at the same time appear to be perplexed.

"I understand you know a Captain Travis?"

I blinked in surprise. I'd expected to be asked about the mysterious Mr. Spencer. "Yes, I do," I answered after the briefest hesitation.

"I'm told by the clinic where he was being treated that you strongly recommended that he be allowed to exercise each day?"

"I didn't think it was necessary to keep him bound to his bed for twenty-four hours of the day."

I was feeling a surge of alarm now. What had Captain Travis done? Had he been given more freedom—and in despair, used it to try to kill himself?

Had he succeeded?

I kept my gaze on Inspector Howe's face, unwilling to ask.

"The clinic holds you responsible. Captain Travis was allowed to walk outside, in the company of an attendant. As soon as they were out of sight, he overpowered the man, took the orderly's clothing, and left the clinic grounds. A search has been made. He hasn't been found. That was three days ago."

I swallowed hard against the rising nausea I felt.

"Do they—do they believe he intends to do himself a harm?"

"The doctor in charge of his case feels that it's possible."

"What can I do?" And another thought struck me in the same moment. "How did you know I was here? In Sinclair?"

"There had been an inquiry at the clinic from a solicitor in Bury. Mr. Ellis. The clinic asked us to contact him, to see what he might know about Captain Travis. Mr. Ellis told us about your visit this morning, demanding better treatment for him."

I could see where this was going. I had complained at the clinic, I had complained to Mr. Ellis. Therefore I was responsible. Inspector Howe was right.

"I felt the Captain's condition didn't warrant keeping him strapped to his bed. I believed it wasn't madness that afflicted him, but something else. A confused state of mind possibly resulting from temporary shell shock."

There, I had said it.

And I saw the distaste on Inspector Howe's face, and in the faces of the two constables behind him.

"I understand he believes that Lieutenant James Travis tried to murder him," the Inspector said. I realized that he'd had quite a conversation with the clinic. And while *Travis* was just another name in Wiltshire, here in Suffolk, it had meaning. Here in Suffolk, it was known and respected.

"Mr. Ellis is mistaken there," I said, collecting my wits. "Captain Travis glimpsed the officer who shot him in the head, and afterward, as he tried to discover who it was, he somehow fixed on the name of James Travis. Of course unaware that Lieutenant Travis was in fact dead, and had been for months. Blows on the head are sometimes difficult. Often people who have suffered one don't have a clear memory of how it happened. They remember up to the moment—and then there is only a blank."

He wasn't satisfied. "Why should he have decided on James Travis?"

"The officer who shot him—in Captain Travis's account—resembled James. Or so he thought."

"But James was dead."

"Yes, but Captain Travis didn't know that. I've told you."

"Why should a British officer shoot the Captain in the first place? Was he trying to leave the field? Deserting?"

Shell shock. Lack of moral fiber. Cowardice . . .

"Of course not. There was a retreat, and retreats are often mad scrambles. Anything can happen. The Captain was attempting to rally his men."

"Was the Captain reported for leaving his post under fire?"

I held on to my temper. "He did not leave his post. The other officer, the one he believed shot him, was probably firing at the Germans, and Captain Travis mistakenly thought he was shooting at him. It's even possible that the shot fired by that officer did hit the wrong man—Captain Travis."

But they didn't believe me. I was, after all, a nursing Sister, not a trained Army officer. Never mind that I held an officer's rank in the Army, a system decided by the Services to give us the protection of rank.

I could almost see the thoughts running through the heads of the three policemen.

I wished for Simon, who at least could support my views. But he hadn't come down yet.

"This is beside the point," I went on. "What matters is that Captain Travis is ill. I hope he is found to be safe."

"What's his connection with the Travis family here in Sinclair? Would he try to reach Suffolk, to find the man he believes attempted to kill him?"

Far be it from me to tell them who Captain Travis was. Let

them find out for themselves that it was likely that he was James Travis's heir.

"I'm not even sure he understands that the war is over. He would want to return to his men. I can't think why he should come to Suffolk."

"You are here."

"Yes, with a friend. I have some few days of leave. I wanted to escape from the war for a little while."

"Odd that you should choose the village where the late James Travis lived."

Oh, for heaven's sake.

"What are you trying to tell me, Inspector? Am I to understand that you have come to Sinclair expressly to accuse me of some wrongdoing?"

"A Constable on the Bury force saw you loitering outside the Ellis chambers. After there had been a break-in."

I had to give Inspector Howe credit where it was due—he was thorough.

"Sergeant-Major Brandon and I had dinner in Bury that night and had gone for a walk. Hardly loitering!"

I could read his expression. What was I, a nursing Sister, doing in the company of a man in the ranks?

Suspicious indeed.

"If that's all, Inspector, I have other matters to attend to. Thank you for informing me of Captain Travis's escape from the clinic. I expect to be leaving shortly for my own home in Somerset. My father, Colonel Crawford, has asked Sergeant-Major Brandon to escort me there."

When he didn't respond, I walked to the inn door and went outside, pulling on my coat against the chill. I could feel my stomach churning. And I expected Inspector Howe to stop me at the door, or at least order me back into the inn.

A cab was standing next to Simon's motorcar, just beyond the door, but I walked past it and continued down the High, moving briskly—and aimlessly.

I'd seen the state that Captain Travis was in; I knew how desperate he was to escape the clinic. But where could he go? Certainly not to Suffolk, almost two hundred miles away. He had no money, unless there were a few pounds in the orderly's pocket. It wouldn't get him far. And he was physically in no condition to travel. That only reinforced my suspicion that he intended to kill himself.

I should have left well enough alone. I should never have gone to see him, or asked the staff to give him more freedom. I had thought to help. Instead I could very well have the Captain's blood on my hands.

A motorcar slowed behind me, and I turned quickly, thinking that Inspector Howe had finally decided to come after me.

But it was Simon. He pulled to the verge.

"Bess? What's wrong? Who were the policemen there in The George?"

I caught my breath on tears that wanted to fall, and kept my voice steady with an effort.

"It's Captain Travis. He's disappeared from the clinic. The staff remembered that Ellis, Ellis and Whitman had shown an interest in his whereabouts." I told him the rest, and why I had walked away.

I had stopped there on the street, and he got down to walk over to me.

"That's worrying. You believe he'll kill himself, don't you?"

"Yes." I looked up at the clouds over our heads. "It's likely, isn't it?"

"It's far more likely," he said bracingly, "that he's coming to find you—and James."

"He's not able to do that. It's not possible."

"From all you've told me, he's a determined man. He'll try. He *will* try."

I shook my head. "He has only his uniform and the clothing he took from an orderly. Where would he find the money to go anywhere? And he's been confined to his bed for weeks. With the best will in the world, his leg muscles are weak and won't support him for very long. And he won't turn back to the clinic. He'd rather die than let them take him back." My voice almost broke. "He *begged* me to help him tear up his sheets and give him enough time to end it. I don't think I told you that."

He put a hand on my shoulder and said gently, "I have never met Captain Travis. But I believe you're wrong about that. Now that he's free."

I didn't answer. I couldn't. I felt the responsibility of my actions. And I didn't think Simon, who always understood so much, could quite grasp that.

When I didn't say anything, he went on. "Get into the motorcar, Bess. You left without your gloves or a scarf. Your mother will have my head if I bring you home with pneumonia."

I smiled at that, as he'd intended, and finally got into the motorcar.

"At least," I said, leaning back against my seat, "the police don't know about Mr. Spencer. They would probably accuse me of shoving him down the stairs."

I was wrong about that too.

Simon drove on almost to the gates of Travis Hall before turning back to the village, to give the police time to leave The George.

But as we pulled into the space in front of the inn, I looked toward the doctor's surgery, intending to suggest that we go there while we were out, and saw that the cab from Bury that had been sitting by the inn's door was now stopped in front of the doctor's door.

"Do they think Mr. Spencer is Captain Travis?" I exclaimed.

"I wouldn't be surprised," Simon replied, looking in the same direction.

"He'll have a time proving he isn't," I said. "With a guilty conscience of his own."

"And sedated as well. You're right, he'll be dazed and not very convincing. Poor devil."

"What should we do?"

"Stay out of it."

I knew he was right, but I sat there for several minutes, waiting for the police to emerge from the surgery.

"What if they find those papers, Simon? If he's not really awake, they might ask to look through his belongings."

"It's possible. But not likely."

"No."

And still they didn't come out the doctor's door.

My feet were freezing, but I refused to take notice.

It seemed like hours, but it was only another ten minutes or so before we saw the door open—and the three policemen stepped out, still talking to someone I couldn't see. The doctor? It must be.

Then they turned toward the cab. The surgery door closed, and the local Constable stood there, speaking to Inspector Howe, then listening intently to what his superior had to say. Instructions? I was sure of it.

And then the second Constable got into the front of the cab. After a moment, Inspector Howe got into the rear seat.

"We shouldn't be seen sitting here, watching," I said urgently, and we left the motorcar and got ourselves through the inn door before the cab had come out of Church Lane and joined the main road.

From behind the curtains at the inn's window, we watched them drive out of sight.

"I don't think it's a very good idea to go to the surgery just now," Simon said quietly.

With a sigh I turned and began to climb the stairs.

The owner of the inn stepped out of the dining room. "May I ask? Are you leaving today?"

"Not today," Simon informed him curtly and followed me up the stairs.

I sat at my window, looking out toward the green and the tea shop and the bend in the road where the village houses began to straggle toward the outskirts, just beyond my line of sight.

I was torn about what to do. Return to Wiltshire and help in the search for Captain Travis? Stay here, even though my hands were tied? Or return to Somerset and wait for news? But at home I'd only fret.

I was fairly sure the Inspector had warned Dr. Harrison to be on the lookout for a man who might be in need of medical care by the time he reached Suffolk. How much more he'd told the doctor I couldn't guess. About Simon and me?

At least the cab had turned toward the Bury road, rather than continuing to The Hall.

An hour later, there was a tap at my door.

Thinking it was Simon, I said, "Yes, come in."

It opened, but Simon wasn't standing there on the threshold. The Vicar was.

Rising from my seat by the window, I found myself thinking

that news traveled in this village faster than it had ever done in the trenches of France, where it seemed to fly on the wind.

"Sister Crawford? May I come in?"

"Yes, please do."

"I shouldn't be speaking to you here in your bedroom. Forgive me. But if I'd asked for you to come down to the small parlor, we'd likely be overheard."

I thought of Betty, and wondered if he also knew she was a gossip.

"I understand. Please, be seated." I gestured toward the chair by the hearth.

"Thank you, Sister."

I went back to the window and stood there, waiting. I wasn't sure just what he wanted.

As the silence lengthened, he looked down at the hat in his hands and said, "Would you like to tell me what all this is about?"

"I'm not sure," I said slowly, "what you are asking me."

"To begin at the beginning, then. Are you, in fact, Sister Crawford? Or a Sister at all?"

Stung, I countered, "Why do you doubt that I am?"

"Because I cannot believe that Sister Potter would behave as you have done since you came to this village."

"I have done no harm."

"I'm not sure about that. And the young man with you? Is he in fact Captain Travis?"

"Good heavens, no." I was suddenly angry. "My father is Colonel Richard Crawford," I said, and gave him the name of the regiment he had commanded. "Sergeant-Major Brandon was asked to accompany me to Suffolk." I went to my kit and took out my identification, handing it to him.

He read it carefully, then gave it back to me. "I'm sorry. But

Mrs. Travis is alone in the world now, and I must act on her behalf if I feel that she is in some fashion being used by unscrupulous people."

"She is not precisely alone," I retorted. "There is Mr. Ellis."

His eyebrows went up in surprise. "You know who he is? Yes, of course you do, you would have worked out such details before coming here."

"I am not an 'unscrupulous person,' Vicar. Nor am I here to use Mrs. Travis. I left a man lying in his bed in a clinic, being told he is raving mad and being kept strapped down without exercise or even a book to read. I found that horrifying." It wasn't the whole truth, but this was not the time, I thought, to worry the Vicar even more by telling him that no one knew where Alan Travis was at this moment. For all I knew, he'd been found and returned to the clinic by this time. Or . . . found dead. "My concern is with him. I treated him in France. As the war drew to a close, we tried to do our best for the wounded, but sometimes even with the best of intentions, we miss a diagnosis. I strongly believe that is what we're dealing with in Captain Travis's case. I can't very well go to Barbados and speak to his family there. I came here, instead, hoping to find someone to speak for him." I crossed to the door and held it open. "I'd like you to leave, now, if you please."

He stayed seated. "I fear we've been at cross-purposes, Sister Crawford. Perhaps we should begin again. Will an apology convince you that I am trying to find my way through this morass, just as you are?"

I stood there, the door open, looking him in the eye.

Our voices must have reached Simon. He opened his door, saw me standing in mine, then his gaze went beyond me to the Vicar, by my hearth.

Closing his own door, he stepped into the passage.

"May I join you?" he asked quietly, as if talking about a tea party, but his voice was cold.

"Yes, please."

He came into my room then. It was getting crowded, I thought as I shut the door and went back to the window.

"Mr. Caldwell has come here on behalf of Mrs. Travis—"

He interrupted me. "May I clarify that? I am here because I am concerned about Mrs. Travis's welfare. She has not asked me to come; she isn't aware that I'm here. But I have been informed about the visit that an Inspector Howe paid to you and to Dr. Harrison's surgery." He turned to Simon. "I believed *you* were Captain Travis. But now I have been told that he had walked away from the clinic where he was being treated. I wanted to find out what was going on. And if you are a danger to Mrs. Travis."

We were indeed at cross-purposes.

I glanced at Simon, still standing by the door, a big presence in this room.

"I'll tell you what I know, if you will in turn tell me what is happening in Sinclair," I said before Simon could answer.

Mr. Caldwell gave that a moment's consideration, then nodded.

And so, with some trepidation, I explained what had happened to Captain Travis.

The Vicar frowned. "I had no idea. You say he's convinced that James, Lieutenant Travis, tried twice to kill him? But that's impossible. James has been dead for over a year."

"Which of course makes Captain Travis's claims appear to prove that he's not in his right mind."

"But what—*who*—did he actually see?"

"I don't know. Neither does he, you see. Head wounds can be difficult, Mr. Caldwell. I believe he saw someone turn and fire at him, and in that split second, he thought the man seemed familiar. Afterward, in casting about to remember who the shooter reminded him of, he became convinced it must be James Travis."

"Yes, it's possible. We all have look-alikes, they say. I was in school with two boys who might have passed for brothers, but they weren't." He amended wryly, "At least, we had no reason to believe they were."

"Your turn," Simon reminded him.

"Yes, all right," he said, reluctant even though he'd promised. "When her son was reported killed, Mrs. Travis was ill for some weeks. Not—physically ill. She grieved in her own way, sitting in her son's room, among his things, remembering. But I had asked the staff to tell those who came to offer their condolences that she was not well. Mr. Ellis had driven over from Bury several times, wishing to read James's will, as it was his duty to do. I don't believe Mrs. Travis could bear that so soon, and she put him off. It has a—final—ring to it, hearing a will."

I nodded, understanding. She had not been able to bury her son, to take comfort from the service and the sympathy of friends and neighbors. The truth was, she had no idea where his body had been buried. It would be easy to pretend that the telegram had been wrong, that some mistake had been made, and another would soon follow, listing him as missing or captured. But alive. She still had hope . . .

"When Mr. Ellis could be put off no longer, she received him and listened stoically as the will was read. I don't know, truthfully, what it was she expected her son to do. But when Mr. Ellis informed her that James had left everything to a distant cousin who lived in the Caribbean, she was shocked. Horrified. She knew nothing about that branch of the family, you see, except that they were anathema to her husband and his parents before him."

"I don't follow you. Why?"

"I had to refer to the Vicar at St. Mary's before me. He remembered being told by James's grandfather that the island branch of the family had left England in disgrace. There had been a falling-out over a woman—which brother was married to her, I can't tell you. Suffice it to say, there were hard feelings that were passed down through the family. I don't know if James himself was aware of the family history. His parents may not have told him. I don't know if he realized that this man you say James met in a railway carriage in Paris was related to him. I don't know if he made inquiries to find out. Certainly neither Mr. Ellis nor anyone in the firm had been asked to take on such a task. No one, not Mr. Ellis nor Mrs. Travis, understood her son's choice in the matter. You may not know, but his will came home in his belongings. Ellis never had a copy of it. For some weeks, there was a possibility he'd died intestate. When it did come, and his mother heard the contents, she claimed it was a forgery, even though it had been properly signed and witnessed by his commanding officer."

I could see that Mrs. Travis might have felt that this island cousin might well have taken advantage of her son's good nature. After all, she didn't know then how or when they had met.

"Mr. Ellis had no idea how to find this man. I don't believe he knew where that branch of the family had gone. And we were in the middle of a war, with military communications given priority. He was under the impression that they had immigrated to Australia. That inquiry went nowhere, of course. It took quite some time to discover that Alan Travis was from Barbados and a serving officer in the British Army, posted to France."

I wondered if Mrs. Travis had deliberately led Mr. Ellis astray, suggesting Australia to buy time. Time, perhaps, to learn that her son wasn't dead.

Perhaps James himself had never made inquiries of his own. Perhaps he believed in his own sound judgment of the man he'd met so briefly.

We'd probably never know.

Mr. Caldwell was saying, "When Mr. Ellis informed Mrs. Travis that he had located the heir, she forbade him to contact Captain Travis. She demanded instead that he do everything in his power to find someone with a closer English connection to the family."

"And did he?"

"Yes. He too was a serving officer in the British Army. A man by the name of Carlton Travis."

CHAPTER 12

I SAT THERE staring at Mr. Caldwell.

"But one can't simply change heirs in a will to suit a grieving mother."

"She refused to countenance Alan Travis as her son's heir. She felt her son had somehow been—persuaded—to do this by a man who saw his chance to avenge his own great-grandfather by taking over the English estate."

"Surely she doesn't believe that her son would do such a thing."

Simon shook his head. "She doesn't need to believe it, Bess. It's what she wants, and what she'll insist on."

"If Captain Travis is considered not to be in his right mind," the Vicar pointed out, "it would go far to convince a judge that James had been misguided."

"And when I came here, asking questions about James Travis and his will, alarm bells went off all over the village."

"I wouldn't say all over the village," the Vicar corrected me. "But word traveled back to Mrs. Travis, and she was not happy."

I turned and stared out the window, trying to sort out all that I'd just heard.

Behind me, Mr. Caldwell said to Simon, "What is your opinion of this man Captain Travis?"

"I haven't met him. When Sister Crawford went to the hospital in Wiltshire, they were reluctant to allow her to see their patient. When they finally agreed, I was asked to wait."

"And from what she has said, she barely knows him herself."

There was a note of hopefulness in the Vicar's voice. Perhaps I had also been taken in by this man . . .

I turned. "I expect you will find, if you have the opportunity to speak with him, that Captain Travis is not interested in being heir to The Hall."

"He may not be interested in keeping The Hall. His aim might well be to sell up and take the funds back to Barbados. I daresay he could live like a king there, with such an income."

"For a vicar," I said then, "you have a very poor view of your fellow man."

"It's not my view. Mrs. Travis has no one else to protect her. And so I must do my best to see that she doesn't find herself in the hands of a scoundrel."

I bit my tongue. But it did no good, I couldn't stop myself from answering that charge.

"You have never met Alan Travis. You have no right to judge him so harshly until you do."

"He has overpowered the man sent to accompany him on his walk."

"I expect any of us would consider doing that, given what the Captain knew he was going to return to in a quarter of an hour."

"What then is his view of his fellow man?"

I said, "Thank you for coming, Vicar. I can appreciate your concern for Mrs. Travis's welfare, but she is not *my* concern. My patient is."

"Former patient," he pointed out as he rose from his chair, and Simon stepped away from the door.

With a nod to me, Mr. Caldwell walked out of the room. Simon closed the door behind him.

"You can't fight their prejudices, Bess."

"No," I said, watching from my window as the Vicar strode toward the church. "But who is Mr. Spencer, and what is his role in all of this? And who is this Carlton Travis?"

"A very good question."

"We can't very well ask now to speak to Mr. Spencer. Not after the police have talked to the doctor—and possibly even to Mr. Spencer—about Captain Travis." I turned away from the window. "And there isn't time to drive all the way to London and look up the family genealogy in Somerset House in the hope of finding this Carlton. I'm not sure what we've got ourselves mixed up in. If I could reach a telephone, I'd ask Mother to go to Wiltshire and find out what's happening. I don't like being so completely in the dark." I wandered to the hearth and held out my hands to the fire. It was dying out, but I couldn't be sure whether the chill I felt was in the room or a part of my own worry.

"You think Travis is going to kill himself, rather than go back to that hell."

I looked up at Simon. "Wouldn't you? If you'd lost all hope."

"I think," he answered slowly, "I'd want to find out if I really was mad—or not. Then I'd know what to do."

"Should I go back to Wiltshire now? And help in the search?"

"Whatever is going to happen there has happened. I'd wait."

Easier said than done.

In the end we went back to Bury. Not to dine or to call on the firm of Ellis, Ellis and Whitman. Instead we walked in the abbey ruins, in spite of the wind that had picked up. My cheeks were cold and the tips of my fingers felt like they were half-frozen, and my feet were numb in my boots, but I didn't care.

We didn't speak, Simon or I. We strode side by side in a companionable silence, each of us busy with our own thoughts.

I couldn't read his expression. His eyes were distant, miles from here.

A few spits of rain sent us hurrying back to the motorcar, a little damp, but safely inside before the bottom fell out of the sky and the rain pounded on the roof.

We laughed at our close call—we'd have been soaked to the skin if we hadn't dashed the last few yards. I felt the better for the burst of activity.

"I don't suppose we could find a cup of tea," I said after a moment. The rain was still coming down too hard for Simon to get out and turn the crank.

"Not a bad thought. Shall I ring for it?"

"I wish you could."

The rain finally slowed, and a weak sun began to peer through the last of the clouds. We'd parked near The Angel, and I looked up to see Mr. Ellis stalking down the other side of the street, clearly in a foul mood. His face was grim, his mouth a tight line.

"I wonder if he knows now which papers are missing."

"Very likely he does," Simon responded, waiting until Mr. Ellis was out of sight before opening his door. He turned the crank, and we drove back to Sinclair without stopping for tea.

"Such a pretty village," I said as we came round the bend and could see the sweep of the green. "Oh, look, Mrs. Horner's sign is up. She's open."

He pulled to the verge, and I got down. "I'll see if she's still serving," I said, and skirting the puddles, I walked to the door.

"Come in," she called when she saw me standing outside. "The door is open."

I turned and beckoned to Simon. He left the motorcar where it was and came to join me.

"What's this I hear about the police from Bury coming to The George, and then crossing to the surgery? That poor man who fell down the stairs isn't in trouble, is he?"

She was eager to gossip. But I said truthfully, "I have no idea why they would wish to see him."

Disappointed, she kept talking about the police, speculating on their reasons for being in Sinclair. "They must have gone to The George first," she went on. "And discovered that he wasn't there, he'd had his accident. But they didn't take him into custody, did they? Quite a mystery."

"Ask Betty, at The George. She usually knows what is going on there."

Mrs. Horner made a face. "I would, but it's her afternoon off. Worst luck."

Her back was to us where we sat near the door, and I grinned at Simon.

And then her next words wiped the grin off my lips.

"I don't hold with the cards," she was saying as she worked with the tea things, "but Miss Fredericks likes them, and she knows how to read them. She says. What's uncanny is how the things she tells us actually happen. She'd warned us that a stranger would come to Sinclair. And he'd bring death in his wake. Now we've had three strangers, two of them men, and one of them fell down the stairs and could have killed himself. I don't know how to take all this."

After a moment, Simon asked, "And who is Miss Fredericks?"

"She's the daughter of Mrs. Travis's head groom. Well, he was head groom before the war, of course. He's retired, now, but he still lives on the estate in a grace-and-favor cottage."

I'd met Scots who firmly believed in The Sight. In knowing the future before it happened. But it wasn't usual in a village like Sinclair—Suffolk was progressive: railways, improvements in agriculture, close enough to London to understand town ways.

Still, sometimes the old superstitions lingered in small ways. Many people still tapped wood, tossed spilled salt over their shoulders, avoided black cats, wouldn't walk under ladders, feared setting shoes on the table, or took it to heart when a knife or fork fell to the floor—a warning that strangers were coming. The list was long and even varied by county.

"What does Mr. Caldwell have to say about the cards?"

Sensing our disbelief, Mrs. Horner said defensively, "I've never heard him speak against them. He tries to be fair-minded. But Miss Fredericks saw the baby. Before it came. She told us there was a right cradle and a wrong one, and to watch out. Even he couldn't say she was wrong there."

"What baby?" I asked, sipping my tea.

"That French girl, the one who came claiming she had James's child. Pretty little thing, the baby. A lovely smile. But Mrs. Travis looked into her, didn't she, and discovered the French girl had been living in London since before the war. Hardly the refugee she claimed she was. Nor any truth to her tale that James saved her from the Germans. I doubt she ever saw a German soldier. Mrs. Travis never discovered who put the girl up to it."

Small wonder Mrs. Travis was wary of strangers!

"What did she have to say about us? Miss Fredericks?"

"She told the Vicar that trouble came in many guises, and mercy was one of them."

Taken aback, I asked, "And do *you* believe everything Miss Fredericks has to say?"

"I don't know," Mrs. Horner replied honestly, setting aside the tray on which she'd brought our tea. "I ask myself how she could know such things, when what she tells us comes true."

"Has she ever been wrong?" Simon asked.

"I've never heard of it, if she has. You've probably seen her about. She comes to the inn sometimes to help if they're short-handed."

But I couldn't be sure I had.

She turned away, busying herself with cleaning the counter by the stairs. I thought she might be regretting that she had ever brought up the subject.

Here in this pleasant village, with its long street winding through a cluster of houses set facing the green, it was hard to imagine a Miss Fredericks, but on the other hand, I had never doubted that some people had gifts that we didn't understand. I had been there as a child when my mother had a premonition that the village my father had gone to visit was a trap. The visit had been set up as a reconciliation mission, trying to reestablish friendly relations after two of the villagers had shot an English soldier. My father had been very good at this sort of thing, and many of the village headmen respected him for his courage and his honesty, even when they were enemies of the Raj. She paced the floor all that night, her face pale, her mind following my father into the Khyber Pass. It wasn't until he and his men came riding in just after dawn that she relaxed.

And she had been right. It had been a trap. Only, my father had managed to spring it before he and his men were caught in it, and the village headman had claimed it was none of his doing. Whether that was true or not, my father was never sure.

For a very long time afterward, I remembered that look of anguish in her eyes, her helplessness in the face of danger to do anything to protect my father. Perhaps the Vicar thought that Miss Fredericks, in her own way, protected Mrs. Travis.

We finished our tea, and as Simon rose to pay for it, Mrs. Horner said, "It's nonsense, really. I shouldn't have passed it on."

"I'm glad you did," I told her. "I found it interesting." And I had, to see that from the first day we'd been under suspicion.

As we splashed our way back to the motorcar, the street a minefield of puddles filling the deeper ruts, Simon commented, "It's easy to foretell the future if you're vague enough. The Delphi Oracle was a master of that. 'Right cradle–wrong cradle' could mean anything, and so could 'the guise of mercy.'"

"It doesn't matter how we view it. It's how everyone else sees it. Even Mrs. Travis. She probably dismissed much of it as nonsense but still felt wary when that young French girl appeared. Or I came, in the uniform of the Queen Alexandra's Imperial Military Nursing Service."

We walked into The George to be met by the owner. He held out a telegram, and I saw that it was addressed to me.

Fearing something was wrong at home, I opened it quickly, and Simon, just behind me, leaned forward to read it over my shoulder. The telegram was from my mother, sent simply to "The Inn, Sinclair."

Bess. Someone from the Wiltshire clinic was here looking for Captain Travis. They are worried. It seems he has gone missing.

Captain Travis had known I came from Somerset—but not precisely where, and it isn't a small county. Nor could I believe he would waste time searching for me. For all he knew, I'd already returned to my duties in France.

I looked up at Simon, silently conferring with him.

"Not bad news, I hope," the owner of the inn asked. But his

tone of voice indicated that he would be just as glad to learn that this was a summons to go elsewhere. Anywhere but The George.

"Not at all," I said, folding the single sheet and stuffing it and the envelope into my pocket. With a smile, I turned toward the stairs, and Simon followed. When we were out of hearing in the passage above, I said, "What should I do?"

"There's nothing you can do. Except to go home to Somerset and put this business behind you."

"I don't know," I said. "It seems—it feels as if I'm giving up on Captain Travis."

"You've done what you could."

I had a headache that evening, and instead of going down to dinner, I went to bed with a cold cloth over my eyes. I seldom had headaches, and this one, I thought, was really the battle going on in my mind over what to do.

Simon brought me a pot of tea and a custard, and I managed to eat them.

Afterward I drifted from drowsiness to a light sleep, and then to a deeper one.

And dreamed that the war hadn't ended, and I was in the forward lines watching a blaze of fire from the German artillery. Knowing as I watched that the casualties would soon come in, ones and twos at first, then a longer line that soon doubled and then tripled. We were working as hard as we could to deal with all of the wounded, one broken body after another being gently lifted to the table where the doctor and I worked. There was blood everywhere; we only had time to wash our hands and our surgical pieces before the next soldier was brought in. I remembered brushing a hand across my forehead, pushing back the strands of hair that had escaped my cap. And the doctor leaned across with a pad in his hand to wipe off the streak of blood I'd left behind.

The next patient came in, and I saw to my horror that it was Captain Travis, and I knew without checking his vital signs that he was dying. His eyes were open, accusing, pleading, but even though we worked frantically we couldn't stop the bleeding. I watched helplessly as he died, and it was only then that I realized he had slit his wrists, it wasn't shrapnel that had killed him.

I turned away as the stretcher bearers, at a signal from the doctor, began to carry the body out of the tent.

And I began to cry, something I had never done in such circumstances. The doctor said to me, "Sister Belmont. Pull yourself together. Do you hear me? There are other men here."

But Sister Belmont was the Sister who had broken down, not me. I'd been sent out afterward to help the remaining staff at the aid station to cope.

I wanted to tell him that, but I couldn't stop crying, my shoulders shaking, and yet through my tears I could see the wounded outside the tent, waiting their turn, looking at me, at my weakness, as they died, one after the other.

It was all horribly, shockingly vivid.

And then someone was shaking me, calling my name, and I opened my eyes to the room in The George, in Sinclair, the firelight dim, shadows all around me, and Simon sitting on the edge of my bed, one hand on my shoulder.

I was crying, wracking sobs that came from somewhere deep inside me. He pulled me into his arms and said, "It's all right, Bess, you're safe. It's all right."

It was a while before I could get a grip on myself, though I tried hard. Finally I pulled away and began to apologize as he handed me a handkerchief.

"I heard you crying out," he said gently. "You've nothing to apologize for, Bess. I've seen strong men break. And be stronger afterward."

"The war—" I began, then stopped, unable to describe what I had seen in my dream. So much death all around me . . .

"I know. And it's over now. Finished."

He was a black silhouette against the fire's glow, and I couldn't see his face.

"But the wounded and the dead are still wounded and dead."

"I know." His voice was grim. "Their faces will stay with you for a very long time. All those you tried to save. They'll come back in dreams, or you'll glimpse someone crossing a street—passing in an omnibus—sitting at a table in a shop. And for an instant, you'll think you know who it is. But it isn't. And the hope that had flared will fade again. The dead are gone, except in your memory. There they are still young and whole and safe. Let them stay there. Until they're ready to leave."

I knew then that he too had dreams he couldn't escape, and perhaps my father as well. Anyone who had been to war and watched men die.

He sat there in the chair by the fire until I was calm enough to sleep again, and perhaps he stayed there for a while longer. He never said.

Chapter 13

The next morning, the swelling around my eyes required wet cloths dipped in the very cold water in the pitcher on my washstand and longer than I cared to remember before my efforts finally persuaded the puffiness and the redness to go away sufficiently that I could face the dining room and breakfast. The fire on the hearth had gone out, but I had to ignore it and dress quickly in the chilly room.

Simon was already there. He smiled but said nothing about what had happened last night, and I ate my porridge and toast, and drank my tea in a comfortable silence, knowing I'd never have to refer to it again.

And truth was, I felt better. I had never had time to mourn. For the war, for the wounded, for the dead. The war had ended almost as an anticlimax, blessed though it was that hostilities had ceased. There had been no glorious celebration, not where I was, for the stretcher bearers and the walking wounded were still coming in from the Front. The hospitals were still full. My duties had changed very little.

We were halfway through our meal when the village Constable walked into the dining room. An older man, he was graying and rather stout. He paused in the doorway, and after looking around, spotted us and crossed to our table.

"Good morning," I said when he stopped there.

"Morning, Sister, Sergeant-Major. If I could have a word?"

"Now? Could it wait until we've finished?" Simon asked.

"Now, if you please."

I put down my napkin and we followed him out to Reception, and from there into a small parlor that I hadn't seen before. It was dim, the curtains still drawn, no fire on the hearth, and no lamp lit. Even so, I could see that the Constable was all business, and that was worrying. I wondered if Inspector Howe had sent him.

His name, according to the small board above his pocket, was Simpson. J. R. Simpson.

He looked around, found a lamp, and proceeded to light it. We stood there, waiting.

Finally, taking out his notebook and wetting the end of his pencil with his lips, the Constable said, "Could you tell me where you were last night?"

I felt my face grow warm, but I said calmly, "I had a headache and missed my dinner."

"And you never left your room?"

"I did not."

"And you, sir?" He turned to Simon.

"I finished my dinner, stepped out to see the weather, and then went to my room. They can confirm in the dining room that I came down to my breakfast at seven thirty. A little after sunrise."

He had told the absolute truth, his voice as level as mine. But not all of the truth. He had left his room.

"What's this all about, Constable?" I asked. "My porridge is congealing as we speak."

"There was an attack on that man who fell down the stairs here at The George. Around two in the morning. The doctor's dog began barking, and the doctor came down at once, but someone had pulled Mr. Spencer off his cot and was trying to throttle him. The doctor got there, the dog at his heels, and after a struggle, the person got away. It was quite dark in the room, the lamp had been blown out, and neither Mr. Spencer nor Dr. Harrison got a good look at the assailant. All they could agree on was that he was not as tall as the doctor." His eyes flicked over Simon, as if measuring his height.

"Is Mr. Spencer all right?" I asked at once, remembering the ribs and the blow to the head.

"Doctor says he has a few bruises, but no harm done. Not from want of trying. I saw the marks around Mr. Spencer's throat when I got there. And assorted scrapes."

Simon asked, "How did he get away? This man?"

"Doctor was too worried about his patient to give chase. The dog followed whoever it was into the yard, but left off when he heard Doctor whistle for him."

"Did the dog bite the man?" I asked, hopefully. It would be one way of identifying him.

"Doctor doesn't know. And the dog isn't saying. But there was no blood in its jaws." Constable Simpson's expression was stern. "Mr. Spencer is a stranger. And so are you. There's no reason anyone in the village would wish to harm him, is there?"

Which pointedly left us as suspects.

"And no reason for us to harm him," I said firmly. "I attended him after his fall, before Dr. Harrison arrived."

I knew what he was about to ask. If we'd pushed Mr. Spencer down the stairs.

"The inn staff can tell you we were not here when Mr. Spencer fell."

"What is his business in the village?"

"You must ask Mr. Spencer that. He was in no condition to tell me more than where it hurt. He was asked if there was anyone we could notify, and he told us there was not. What does he say brought him here?"

"He was passing through, and as it was late, he decided to stop over at The George."

I didn't dare glance in Simon's direction.

Constable Simpson was a thorough man, but not one blessed with imagination. He wanted facts and proof. And so far there was nothing that connected us to Mr. Spencer.

After several more questions about our reasons for staying in the village, he closed his notebook, putting it away in the breast pocket of his tunic, along with the pencil. As he did, he cautioned, "I'd not be planning on leaving the village before the police have got to the bottom of this business. We've never had trouble of this kind here, and I'd like to keep it that way."

As he started for the door, I asked, "May I call on Mr. Spencer this morning? I'm worried about his ribs."

"Doctor is looking after him well enough, Sister."

"I'm sure he is, but Mr. Spencer was my patient before he was Dr. Harrison's, and that also counts for something."

Reluctantly he considered the point. "Very well," he said at last. "If Doctor agrees."

And he was gone. Simon and I looked at each other, and he was about to say something when I glimpsed the edge of a maid's skirts vanishing around the corner.

Betty was on duty this morning, although I hadn't seen her in the dining room.

I put my finger to my lips and walked out of the small parlor. She was nowhere in sight.

"Ears," I said to Simon, and we went back to finish our break-fast.

When we were sure that no one could overhear us, he asked, "This is an odd turn of events. Who would attack Spencer?"

"It would help if we knew what had brought him here."

"Is Ellis the same height as the doctor? What if he guessed Spencer had broken in and stolen the papers having to do with Travis? And came to retrieve them? We haven't told anyone what I saw in Spencer's valise. If someone was after the papers last night, it would have to be Ellis. He has the only reason I can think of to attack Spencer."

"But how did Mr. Ellis learn about Mr. Spencer?"

"Howe went to the surgery. He might have asked to see Dr. Harrison's patient. If he reported to Ellis when he got back to Bury and mentioned Spencer at all, Ellis might have recognized the name or a description. How many people outside of the village here knew that Spencer could be found in the surgery?"

"There's Mrs. Travis." I added quickly as Simon was about to object, "No, of course I don't think she came to the surgery herself. But if Betty is half the gossip she's said to be, Mrs. Travis was bound to hear about the other stranger in the village. If she had someone she trusted, she might have sent him to the surgery. But hardly to attack Mr. Spencer." I set my knife and fork across my plate, and rose. "Let's see how our patient is faring."

We walked in the cold air of morning to the surgery, feeling the wind as we crossed the upper reaches of the green. And then we were at the surgery and knocking at the door.

Dr. Harrison's assistant came to answer the summons. "Doctor's seeing a patient just now," she said. "You can sit in the waiting room if you like."

"We've really come to see Mr. Spencer, not the doctor," I said with a smile. "Constable Simpson has just called to tell us that there was a disturbance in the night here."

"I was that glad I was at home," she answered fervently, "and not on night duty. Doctor says he'll ask Sister Potter to sit with the patient tonight. He was expecting to send Mr. Spencer to her cottage for nursing, but his ribs are still worrying. It's a marvel that there was no new damage after last night."

"I doubt his assailant will come back," Simon assured her.

"You never know," she answered darkly, and turned to lead us back to the room where Mr. Spencer was lying on his cot, hugging his valise to his chest and looking thoroughly miserable. He had turned to the door, his eyes wide with alarm, when the doctor's assistant knocked before entering.

"What is it you want?" he asked, a worried frown on his face now.

"Just to see how you are," I said cheerfully, walking in as the assistant turned away. "Constable Simpson told us what happened."

"Oh God, it was awful. Bad enough to be laid up in this way, unable to put any weight on that foot, my ribs hurting every time I move. And then to be half killed by that madman. It's enough to give anyone a fright."

"But how did he get in? What did he want?" I asked.

"I don't know what he wanted," Mr. Spencer snapped. "As for getting in, Dr. Harrison told me afterward that the surgery door is always unlocked, and there's a bell that can be pushed in an emergency, to bring the doctor down. Anybody could have walked in. It's ridiculous. I told them to leave me the dog tonight."

Watching his face, I thought he was lying about not knowing what his attacker was after.

"Have you looked to see if any of your belongings are missing?" Simon asked. We could see a wallet, a handkerchief, and a small pile of coins sitting on the table next to the cot. In plain view.

"No. Nothing is missing." Then Mr. Spencer added quickly, "I don't have anything worth stealing." He nodded toward the valise. "Clothes, an extra pair of boots, a jumper. There's nothing anyone would want." But he avoided Simon's eyes as he answered, and I knew the papers he was carrying were still there in the valise.

"That must be terribly uncomfortable, at least for your ribs," I said gently. "Shall I put that under the cot for you?"

But he shook his head, unwilling to part with it.

"Where are you from, Mr. Spencer?" The English are a notoriously private people, not given to asking for personal information on such short acquaintance. But I tried to put a lightness in my voice, and use a conversational tone.

"I don't see why you should care," he answered curtly.

"As a nursing Sister, I am used to asking wounded men where they are from, and if there is anyone I could write to, to let the family know their son or brother or husband is all right, and expected to recover. Were you in the war, Mr. Spencer?"

"No. I was born with one kidney. They wouldn't have me."

"Do you have enemies? Someone who could have followed you here and decided the village is a likely enough place to be rid of you for good?" Simon asked. No one had mentioned attempted murder, but that got Mr. Spencer's attention.

He was suddenly agitated. "No. Why should I have enemies? I've done nothing wrong. And if you really wish me well, as you claim to do, you'll go and leave me in peace."

I had been looking down at a small white square on the floor, surely the edge of a calling card that must have fallen from the table where the contents of Mr. Spencer's pockets had been put. I bent down and picked it up. "I think this must be yours. Good day, Mr. Spencer." I set the card safely under his wallet.

And then we left.

"What did the card say?" Simon asked when we'd left the surgery and were walking back to the inn.

"Oddly enough, it had the name of Ellis, Ellis and Whitman scribbled in a corner."

"Good Lord," Simon said, surprised.

"But there was a firm's name printed on the other side. I only glimpsed it, but I thought it was Florian Agency. Something like that."

"What is it?"

"Your guess is as good as mine. A hiring service, for instance, for household staff? A secretarial service?" Those had become very popular in the past ten years. "It didn't give a location, though. Just the name. You'd think whoever gave out the card would have wanted people to find his place of business." I looked at the rows of houses across the High from us, and thought again how serene they appeared. Or those closest to the church, for that matter, and another cluster just up from The George. "Do you think the Vicar would set up another meeting with Mrs. Travis? I'd very much like to speak to her again. She may have had time to reconsider."

"It's worth a try."

Mr. Caldwell wasn't at the Vicarage. We found him in the church, selecting hymns for the morning service. He was humming bits of favorites as we came down the aisle, but when he looked up and saw who it was, he broke off.

"Is everything all right?" he asked, standing there by the pulpit, a hymnal in one hand and in the other the stack of brown and white numerals he was preparing to put on the board.

I said, smiling, "I'm so sorry we all seemed to get off on the wrong footing. We never meant to cause any harm here, or to worry Mrs. Travis. I came to help a friend, and even that didn't turn out well."

"No harm done, then," the Vicar said, but his smile was formal, not that of a kind shepherd speaking to his flock.

"Do you think we might call on Mrs. Travis once more? Just to reassure her that our intentions were good, even if our efforts were disturbing to her."

"I have no idea."

"Would you ask her? We're still at The George. I would take it as a favor, if you would intercede on our behalf."

He considered the question. "I will make no promises."

"We expect none."

Unbending a little, his voice less cold, he said, "Wouldn't it be best for you just to leave?"

"I've done no wrong. Disappearing into the night gives the appearance that I must have done."

"Yes, all right, I see that." He took a deep breath. "Let me finish what I've begun here. In an hour, then?"

We thanked him and left.

As we passed through the churchyard, I stopped at the stone belonging to Hugh Travis. "The memorials in the aisle floor are older members of the family. I wonder . . ."

I began to cast about, looking at dates. "Simon, here's an Alan. Hugh's father, I'd be willing to bet on it." He was looking at dates as well when I spotted another one. "Here's a Nicholas. If I'm right, he'd be James Travis's great-grandfather."

The stone was ornate, like those of Hugh and Alan. Henrietta, the wife of Alan, had an equally lovely one. A weeping tree, very popular in Victorian times, crowned it, and the lettering was deep.

"But look here—here's Charlotte. She must have been married to Nicholas, she's buried beside him. Her stone is quite ordinary."

No weeping willow, no ship on troubled seas, no lilies or roses. Just the name and date. Not even *Beloved Wife of.*

We were staring at it, our backs to the path. Someone spoke, and we started guiltily.

It was Mrs. Caldwell. "I see you've found the Travis family plot." Her voice wasn't as cordial as it had been that first morning. But she was polite.

"I'd just noticed. These must be Mrs. Travis's late husband, his father and mother, and his grandfather and grandmother."

"Yes, I believe that's right."

"But look here—that must be Nicholas's wife. Her stone is quite different."

"So it is," she said, and with a brief nod, she walked on toward the south porch.

We turned and went the other way, past The George, past three stone houses with gardens in front—gone to seed at this time of year, but it was possible to imagine how pretty they would be in high summer.

Back again to The George to wait for the Vicar to come. We sat in my room, beside the fire, burning comfortably now.

"I don't think she'll agree," Simon commented, looking at his watch for the third time.

"I'm afraid you're right."

I heard footsteps on the stairs and hurried to the door, but it was only Betty with an armload of fresh linen for the cupboard just beyond Simon's room.

The hour passed, finally, and there was no sign of the Vicar. I sighed, turned from the window where I'd been standing for the past quarter of an hour, and said, "If we go through London on the way home, I might be able to find out what this Florian Agency is. Mrs. Hennessey might know."

"That's a good possibility," he agreed. "But I'm not sure it has anything to do with the attack on Spencer. Another client, very likely."

"In which case, the Agency must know *him*."

Simon rose from his chair and walked to the window, his back to me. "I don't think we're going to solve this problem, Bess. I don't know why Spencer has those papers, but I can't see him telling us. And there's no one we can ask. If Ellis doesn't know about him, if we're wrong about that, we could do more harm than good by bringing Spencer to Ellis's attention. We can drive to Wiltshire and find out what has happened to Travis. With any luck, the clinic will find him in time. The Colonel will do what he can to see that the Captain is given better care. Or find a way to get a message to his family."

I sighed. "I wish I knew what to do. The longer we wait for news, the more worrying it is. He was so bent on suicide. A few minutes in that bleak little room listening to the screams on the other side of a thin partition was almost more than I could stand. Imagine hearing it day and night. I wish there was some way to save all of them."

"That's not a burden you can take on, Bess."

"I don't know. The war is over—but not for those men. It might never be. Not really." I stared into the heart of the fire. "In the euphoria of the war ending, I thought I could work one more miracle. We'd somehow saved so many, against worse odds. Captain Travis, the man I met in the canteen, didn't deserve to be locked up, even if the doctors believe they're doing it for his own good. Tilting at windmills, that's what I've been doing."

"I understand. But he can't be set free, either. Not in the state you saw him in."

"I'm not sure that's true. Given care and better surroundings, he might surprise all of us."

"Not if he still feels he must find this mysterious Lieutenant. That's impossible. The man could be anywhere by now. He could well have been killed in the last days of the fighting."

He broke off and turned toward the door as we heard footsteps on the stairs a second time. A measured tread. The Vicar.

I went to the door, standing there looking up at him as he reached the landing at the top of the steps and came toward me.

"Did you speak to her?" I asked.

"It took some persuasion, but she has agreed to a meeting. But not at the house. She's waiting in the church."

We caught up our coats and followed him down the stairs. Simon insisted on using the motorcar, and I think he reasoned that we might not wish to walk back to The George in the company of the Vicar or Mrs. Travis.

Getting down by the low wall around the churchyard, the three of us went to the porch door, opened it, and walked inside. As our footsteps echoed on the stone flooring, I looked for Mrs. Travis.

She was standing below the plaque to her late son, looking up at it with such sadness that my heart went out to her. Then, hearing us, she turned toward us, and her expression changed. It was cold and distant now.

"Mrs. Travis? Thank you for coming," I said, as if she had arrived at Mrs. Hennessey's for tea. Walking briskly, I managed to meet her while she was still there, close by the plaque. "He must have been an extraordinary man," I said, looking up at it. "Many good men died in France. I believe that Captain Alan Travis is a fine man too. Just now he's confused, and helpless to find answers that will help him sort out what happened to him. I know you don't care for that branch of your husband's family. But I don't believe that Alan Travis wants to inherit The Hall, only a chance to return to Barbados. I would think that's what you want as well."

To her credit, she listened to me politely, her face unreadable.

When I had finished, she glanced toward Simon, then turned back to me.

"Then how do you explain this?"

She reached into the pocket of her coat and took out a small envelope, the sort that my mother used when sending an invitation to a friend. It was of excellent quality, had come from a stationer's shop.

But the handwriting on the envelope wasn't of the same quality. It was an angry scrawl, heavy black ink, addressed to The Hall, Sinclair, Suffolk. It had been posted in Wiltshire. Yesterday.

I lifted the flap of the envelope, and with some trepidation pulled out the heavy square of fine paper. It was embossed with a frame, inside which the invitation would be written in elegant script by the hostess.

Instead the heavy black ink was dashed across the space, and I had no trouble reading it.

I have earned the right to know the truth.

I stared at it for a long moment. I had never seen the Captain's handwriting. But who else in Wiltshire could have sent such a message to her? I looked up into Mrs. Travis's face.

"Defend that, if you can," she said coldly.

I passed the square to Simon.

Captain Alan Travis was still alive.

I didn't know what to say.

"He bears no grudge against *you*," I said finally as Simon returned the message to her. "He wants to know why his own life has been made a misery. He feels he is owed some explanation. He may believe that the place to begin his search is here, in Suffolk." My excuses sounded lame even to me. Why hadn't he waited for me to come back to Wiltshire?

"I have no obligation to this man." I could find no compassion in her face or in her words. If I had lost my only son, could I be so callous about the fate of another woman's child? But then, she believed that Captain Travis was trying to take The Hall from her.

There could be no meeting of minds over that. I could protest, tell her that he didn't need her home, that he had his own on an island of warm breezes with the glint of the sea never far away. But I was not Alan Travis. And she would have no reason to believe me.

I said, "I didn't come here to hurt you. Or to disturb the peace of Sinclair. I needed to learn if your son was really dead—not missing, not a prisoner. Impossible to have shot at the Captain, because he himself was a casualty of this war. I'm returning to London. It's for the best now. Good-bye, Mrs. Travis, thank you for meeting me. And I am grateful, Vicar, for your help in arranging this."

Neither of them spoke. I turned away, had in fact taken half a dozen steps, when a thought occurred to me. Far-fetched, but it might tell me something I'd like very much to know before we left.

Turning, I asked, "Mrs. Travis. I wonder. Do you know a Mr. Spencer?"

Her expression remained unmoved. The name meant nothing to her.

"Do you have any idea what the Florian Agency is?"

The look of shock on her face then left me staring, trying to work out what it was I had said.

"How do you know about this Agency?" she demanded, taking a step in my direction. "*Tell me.*"

"I—it was on a card that I saw. The card was in possession of the man who recently fell down the stairs of The George. I called at the surgery to see how he was healing."

She glanced at the Vicar, who shook his head, and then she turned back to me. "Why should he have such a card?"

"I don't know. But scribbled in one corner was the name Ellis, Ellis and Whitman."

Her face paled. "And, pray, what do you know about this Agency?"

"Nothing. It meant nothing to me—I thought it might be an agency for hiring staff."

"It's a consulting firm," she said finally, and I could see that she was not at all pleased. "I have used it twice. Once to look into the background of a certain young person, and once to search for my husband's next of kin."

A *detective* agency? It was my turn to be surprised. "But surely your solicitor could have seen to that for you."

She was silent then, her lips a thin line. Mr. Caldwell shuffled uneasily.

Simon, just behind me, said, "You don't trust Mr. Ellis, do you?"

CHAPTER 14

When Mrs. Travis still didn't answer, Simon went on softly, "I wonder why."

Watching her, I saw her make the decision. Without consulting the Vicar, she said, "Did you bring your motorcar to this meeting?"

"I did, yes," Simon answered her.

"Mine is in the drive at the Vicarage. If you will follow me to The Hall, we can speak more comfortably there."

Turning on her heel, she walked back to the porch door and disappeared, Mr. Caldwell hurrying at her heels.

I said to Simon, "Do you think we should do as she asked?" I was still dealing with the fact that Captain Travis was alive. And I wasn't sure why she had suddenly invited us to The Hall.

"It might be enlightening."

"Then we'll go."

We waited in the lane for the motorcar belonging to Mrs. Travis to lumber out of the Vicarage drive and lead us to the main road and thence to The Hall. It was being driven by an older man, and I wondered if this was the intriguing Miss Fredericks's father. I wished she could look at her cards and tell me how to save Captain Travis.

Simon kept a bit of distance between his motorcar and theirs, giving Mrs. Travis time to arrive at our destination before us.

When we came up the drive, her motorcar was nowhere in sight, and The Hall's door was shut.

Getting out, I said, "You might want to leave the motor running."

Simon smiled. "I'd thought of that."

We went up the steps to the door and lifted the knocker. I half expected no one to answer. But almost at once a maid greeted us and showed us to a pretty morning room done up in shades of lavender and cream.

Mrs. Travis was waiting for us, standing in the center of the room. The Vicar was seated to one side. A lamp had been lit, deepening the lavender walls here, brightening them there. Outside the windows, there was an older man up a ladder, trimming a hedge.

"Please, be seated."

Simon and I took the chairs she indicated.

"I want to know more about this man who fell at The George."

"His name is Spencer. He claimed he'd come up from London, but there was an omnibus ticket and schedule in his coat pocket, not a railway ticket." I hesitated, uncertain how much to reveal.

"We had just returned to The George," Simon added. "When I went up to the injured man's room to bring down his coat and valise while Dr. Harrison was preparing to take him to the surgery, the valise fell open. In it were papers to do with Captain Travis. The letter was on stationery belonging to a Bury solicitor, Ellis, Ellis and Whitman. We learned later that evening about a break-in there."

She regarded him for a moment. "A break-in? I hadn't heard. But yes, Ellis, Ellis and Whitman were my husband's solicitors, and therefore are mine. I'm afraid I don't much care for the present partner. He's—more modern. That's why, when word came that my son had been killed, I wrote to a family friend in the War Office, to ask that this dreadful news be verified. I refused to believe—I was convinced there had been some mistake. But it was true." She turned to watch the man working in the garden. "There was a memorial service, and afterward I agreed to hear my son's will." Mrs. Travis faced us again. "It's somehow so final, you know. A will. You can imagine my astonishment and horror. I couldn't believe James had left me to the mercy of *that* branch of the family."

"He hadn't confided in you what he intended to do?" I asked.

"James was in France, at the Front. I trusted him to make the proper dispositions. His father's death had been distressing for both of us, and James knew his duty. Or so I thought. It makes no sense, what he did."

"Who would you have had him choose?" It was Simon who spoke then.

"I don't know." She got up and walked across the room, straightening a frame that was already perfect. "There was a distant cousin. Carlton Travis. He was killed some months ago. And of course there was the boy at Eton with James. Oliver Masters, from Cheshire. It seems his mother was a Travis. At any rate, he called James 'cousin,' and James went to visit the family in Chester. There must be some connection, although my husband was never certain just how far into the past it was. James saw Oliver again in France. He told his father about it in one of his letters. I would have been happy enough if my son had decided to name Oliver as his heir. The connection is slight, but I could have accepted that. It would have kept The Hall in the family, tenuous though the bloodlines are."

But people change. War changed men. James must have seen

something in the grown Oliver that put him off. It was the best reason I could think of, if the two boys had once been friends.

"Did Oliver come to Suffolk?" I asked. "Did you meet him?"

"He was invited, of course, but his mother was ill, and I expect he knew her time was short. She died soon after he left Eton. James and his father went to the service for her."

"Where is Oliver Masters now?" Simon asked.

"Still in France, surely? I've asked Mr. Ellis to find him, but he's made any number of excuses. He tells me he's tried, but I think he believes that nothing can be done about Alan Travis inheriting."

The will would have to be set aside.

"And the Florian Agency?" I asked.

"Ah. There was a young Frenchwoman who came to my door. She had a child with her, and she told me the little girl was James's daughter. I didn't believe her. James would have said something. And I thought the child a little too young. The mother claimed she was small for her years. Mr. Ellis was inclined to believe her, but I went to London and applied to the Florian Agency. They discovered the mother had left France at the start of the war. And so she couldn't have been at Ypres in April of 1915, when she claimed James had rescued her from the Germans."

"But who put her up to such a thing?" I asked.

"Florian couldn't discover that. The young woman herself finally confessed that she had been given fifty pounds to come here, but she didn't know who had found her in the first place, or paid her the money. It had all been arranged by post. Someone went to a great deal of trouble to seek out a Frenchwoman of the right age who had a small child and was presentable enough to make me believe my son had had a liaison with her and intended to marry her. The Agency informed me that such schemes are sadly common with so many men dead, and so many grieving families willing to believe."

"It was a nasty trick to play," I agreed. "And a dangerous one. You could have had her taken up for what she did."

"Not with the child, I couldn't have done that," she said, in the first sign of softness she had shown. I was beginning to see that she was a remarkable woman, one who took matters into her own hands when her family was being threatened. She wasn't a Travis herself, but she was prepared to defend their heritage in the only way she believed she could.

She was saying, "And I have used Florian to find out what they could about Alan Travis. There has to be some explanation for his hold over my son. He has to be another of these schemers, who saw his main chance. I'm determined he'll never set foot in this house. Not while I live."

"Have they found out anything so far?"

"Now that the war is over, they've agreed to send someone to Barbados."

I said, "This brings us back to Mr. Spencer. Have you visited him, Vicar?"

He started, not prepared to be called on. "I had no reason to, before this. I inquired of Dr. Harrison, of course, if the poor man wished for spiritual comfort or if I could do anything for him. I was told that Mr. Spencer was not well enough to receive visitors, even from the clergy."

Mr. Spencer was afraid. And with good reason, if he'd been attacked.

"It's odd that he hasn't made any effort to contact me," Mrs. Travis commented. "The Florian is discreet, but if he's so badly injured, surely he would inform the London office and they would send someone else. And why does he have papers belonging to Mr. Ellis regarding Captain Travis?" She turned to the Vicar, worry dawning in her face. "What if he's a solicitor representing the Captain? The war is over—that man might have hired someone to present his claim while he's in hospital. But why should he have Florian's card?"

"It's more likely he's up to some mischief," Mr. Caldwell agreed. "He might have called on them to see what they knew about you. They're a very well known firm. They would have turned him away, but he would still have their card."

But when would the Captain have found a solicitor? He'd been wounded—had come home to go directly to the clinic, and he'd been there ever since. Besides, he believed James was still alive . . .

Someone pretending to represent him? *He's in hospital, Mrs. Travis, and I am authorized to handle this matter for him . . .*

"I can't believe he knows the Captain," I said slowly. "If he's not from Florian, then he's another charlatan looking to take advantage of you."

Mrs. Travis turned toward a table with photographs and for a moment looked at them with affection and longing.

"When my husband died, the *Times* carried a tribute to him from a friend. He was interested in stamps, you know. Philately. And he owned some of the finest early examples. He left his collection to the British Museum. They were very pleased to have it." She turned back to me. "We received a number of letters after that. Asking us to support good causes. Or to help those in need. I turned them over to Mr. Ellis. He said all but three were frauds."

"Did he help those who weren't?"

"With my permission, yes. And—anonymously. I didn't care to find myself deluged with new requests. It isn't a matter of charity. These were strangers. There are more than enough people needing my support here in Suffolk."

"I'm sorry that our presence has made your circumstances more painful," I said, preparing to leave. "I never intended that to happen."

She rose, and I thought she was about to see us out, an unexpected courtesy.

But she crossed to the bell and pulled it, then turned to us. "I think we need something more than tea."

A maid came to the door almost at once. "The drinks tray from the drawing room," Mrs. Travis said. "Thank you, Annie."

When it came, Simon accepted a whisky, and I chose a sherry, as did the Vicar. Mrs. Travis, to my surprise, preferred gin.

"Tell me about Captain Travis," she said as she handed me my glass.

"There's very little to tell. Is that a photograph of James—in the silver frame?" I added, pointing to it on the table. "There's a fleeting resemblance, surprisingly. Around the eyes, I expect."

"How does he sound?"

"Sound? His accent is no different from yours."

"He grew up in the islands. What about his education?"

"I don't know," I replied, thinking hard. "He never mentioned it. He isn't—ignorant," I added. "Nor stupid. He's as well spoken as anyone who has been to university." I wanted to add that he could hold his own with her and Mr. Caldwell, but I refrained.

It seemed that she might be relenting in her attitude toward her son's decision, but then she said, "You can speak freely, Sister."

"I have tried," I told her. "I have no desire to tell you lies. What I do feel is that someone must find a way to help the Captain before it's too late. An act of kindness. After all, he *is* related to you; he's not a stranger asking for charity."

"And what about you? What will you gain from this fierce support of a man you hardly know and I have never met?"

"Peace of mind. I became a nurse in an effort to do something about the suffering in this war. Just because Alan Travis isn't on the table with a gaping wound in his body, it doesn't mean that he isn't in anguish."

"There's a problem, Sister. If he is in this clinic, being treated for head wounds, I will have a better chance of convincing a court that he can't inherit. And I will see to it that he never leaves that clinic."

Stunned, I stared at her. Finding my voice at last, I said, "Wouldn't it be simpler for him to refuse to accept this inheritance?"

Mrs. Travis shook her head. "People don't walk away from such a fortune. He will see the good he can do with it in the islands. Or he may sell it, lock, stock, and barrel, and walk away. This land has been in my husband's family for generations. I won't preside over its dissolution."

"Vicar?" I asked, pleading.

"My hands are tied," he said quietly.

I set down my glass and glanced at Simon. Whatever he read in my face, he rose too. "Thank you for your hospitality, Mrs. Travis. I've taken up enough of your time." I started for the door.

"What are you intending to do?" she asked in alarm. "What do you want from me? What will you take to drop your support of this man and go back to your nursing? There are other wounded who need you. He's not the only one."

It was so insulting that I didn't dignify her proposition with an answer. I simply walked out of the room, Simon behind me. Our coats were lying over a chair by the outer door, and I took up mine, not even stopping to put it on.

The cold hit me as I stepped into the motorcar, and I shivered. Simon turned the crank, then got in beside me.

"Bess?" he said quietly.

"I had such high hopes," I replied, not looking at him for fear I might cry.

"I know."

"Take me back to Wiltshire. I'll find Captain Travis, if he's still alive, and ask the Colonel Sahib to intervene somehow. It's all I can think of to do, just now."

"It's for the best," he agreed. And then, as if he couldn't stop himself, he added, "Damn the woman!" under his breath.

It was early—we'd decided to go down to dinner straightaway and use the evening to pack. There was only one other party in the dining room, celebrating a birthday. I counted twelve in the family. Grandparents, what appeared to be aunts and uncles, and a pretty little girl of three in a child's chair, watched over by beaming parents. I thought perhaps this was the father's first chance to share his daughter's birthday, for he was wearing a corporal's uniform, and one arm was still in a sling. He had very little use of it, but no one minded. There was much laughter, and once I saw the young wife touch her husband, as if to make certain he was really seated next to her. Watching them lifted my spirits. Heaven knows they were in the depths.

I hadn't been hungry, but Simon reminded me that what had happened wasn't my fault. To please him, I ate a little.

"This would have played out in exactly the same way if you had stayed in Somerset. Mrs. Travis has made up her mind, and Mr. Caldwell isn't a strong enough man to tell her she's wrong. Whatever part the solicitor and this man Spencer have in this affair, it's nothing to do with you. You came here to find out what had become of James Travis, and now you know."

"I wanted to do something about the Captain's situation too.

Even that's beyond me now. He's taken matters into his own hands." I hesitated, and then confessed, "I was angry enough at The Hall to feel that Mrs. Travis deserved to be cheated, if someone foists a counterfeit heir on her in the Captain's place. And she could easily be cheated, Simon. She's so eager to find some way around her son's choice."

"I wonder why he chose Captain Travis in the first place," Simon answered.

"Possibly he couldn't think of anyone else. It could be that he didn't care much for this cousin Oliver, when he met him again. Otherwise why wouldn't he have named him instead? On the other hand, he must have seen something in Captain Travis that he liked, even in that brief encounter. Possibly liked well enough to find out more about him. We'll never know."

"You don't suppose Oliver Masters is behind Mr. Spencer's appearance here? Assuming, that is, that Oliver survived the war and saw his own chance to benefit from James's death?"

"Anything is possible," I said. "I don't know that Mrs. Travis would really care."

The door to the dining room opened, and Mr. Caldwell came through, pausing there on the threshold.

The family called to him, and the Corporal rose, pulling over an extra chair for him, telling him that he was just in time for the cake to be brought in.

I had the strongest impression that the Vicar hadn't come to join them, that he'd wanted to speak to us, but he grinned and walked over to their table, warmly shaking the Corporal's good hand and asking about the arm.

Watching the happiness at that table, I felt a surge of homesickness.

And then the cake was brought in by the beaming staff,

wishing the awed little girl a happy birthday. It was not the usual birthday cake, decorations on top. But there were three candles, and everyone was coaxing her to blow hard and snuff all three out.

She was so excited that the first puff hardly moved the flames, and then she took a deep breath, and with much encouragement, blew them out—with a little help from her father. There was much clapping and laughter.

I turned back to Simon, smiling. "Mr. Caldwell will have cake whether he wishes it or not," I said in a low voice.

Simon chuckled.

By the time we had finished our meal and were waiting for fresh tea to be brought to us, the Vicar had extricated himself from the happy family, and he came across to our table.

"May I join you for a moment?" he asked politely, and we could hardly say no.

He took the extra chair, cast a glance toward the family, busy with one another, and said quietly, "I am so sorry about this afternoon. But you must understand. Mrs. Travis is not well, and this business with James's will has upset her terribly."

"Everyone says she isn't well," I said. "What's wrong?"

"Dr. Harrison hasn't found anything specific. But she's become a recluse in her despair. And in the end, that will make her ill. Even his will has brought her pain. I was as surprised as you are when she first told me that she wouldn't allow Captain Travis across her threshold. She says it's because of the family history, but if you want to know what I think, she is unprepared for someone else—anyone else—to come into that house and make it his own. A final blow, the final reminder that her son will never come back again. As long as she puts off the truth, as long as Captain Travis doesn't appear, she can live in the past."

"But surely Mr. Ellis contacted the Captain. He was legally bound to do so."

"I don't know why he's accomplished so little. Out of pity for her, I expect, although she doesn't appreciate him as she should. And of course there was the war. You must ask him." He glanced over his shoulder again as another burst of laughter filled the room, and said, "After you left The Hall, I tried to persuade her at least to look into the situation at the clinic and conditions there. But she wouldn't hear of it. She's not a cruel or hateful person, Sister Crawford. It's just that she isn't able to cope with any of this."

I found myself thinking that as long as everyone danced around her grief, and let it go on and on like this, she would never come to terms with anything. She was probably one of the solicitor's wealthiest clients, and she was probably the largest supporter of the church here in the village, the person everyone turned to when they needed money for a good cause. And so they couldn't bring themselves to tell her the truth. It was sad . . .

Simon was asking the Vicar, "What do you know about the Florian Agency? If the Agency is as trustworthy as Mrs. Travis believes, and Mr. Spencer is employed by them, why has he failed to contact her?"

"He's made it plain he doesn't wish to have visitors. I stopped by the surgery before coming here, thinking I might act as intermediary. But he refuses to see me as well."

"Someone attacked him. We've wondered if it could have been Ellis," Simon commented.

Mr. Caldwell stared at him, shocked. "Surely you aren't serious? Mr. Ellis is well respected here and in Bury."

"But Spencer was carrying reports written on the firm's stationery," I said.

"Have you considered that he contacted Mr. Ellis and

arranged to have these sent to him? Especially if he does represent Captain Travis, he would have a right to ask for information concerning the inheritance," the Vicar countered.

But if he represented Captain Travis, he would *know* where his client was. He wouldn't need to steal papers relating to his whereabouts . . .

An imposter might need to find out where the Captain was, if he was about to claim he represented him.

"Mrs. Travis could find herself making wrong decisions—trusting the wrong people," I said. "You and her solicitor must keep watch."

"I know, I've already spoken to Ellis about that."

He prepared to leave. "I would help the Captain myself, but I have no authority to speak for him. I can write to his family, passing on the need for someone to do something," he offered.

But that might well be far too little, too late.

He nodded to us. "Sergeant-Major. Sister." With a final wave to the family party, he left the dining room.

As soon as we'd finished our dinner, Simon and I drove to Bury to look for a telephone. And after some difficulty finding the number through the switchboard, I put through a call to the Florian Agency, hoping that there would be someone in the office even at this hour.

And I was right, there was.

When a male voice answered the call, formal and quite distant, I identified myself as Miss Crawford and asked to speak to one of their employees, a Mr. Spencer.

The voice didn't hesitate. "We have no employee by that name," it said, and disconnected.

Simon, listening at my shoulder, said, "If they are the sort of firm Mrs. Travis has told us they are, they wouldn't tell you who was employed there. Unless they knew you as a client. Still, it was worth a try."

"I should have claimed to be Mrs. Travis. They must have some way of being contacted by clients." But it was too late now. Another call, on the heels of the first, would only arouse more suspicion. "We could stop in London on our way south and call in person."

"Then we should make an early start in the morning."

I hesitated. "Should I try to reach the clinic in Wiltshire?"

"I doubt they're on the telephone."

"We could try."

Our luck held, although it was several minutes before the number could be found, and then several more before I could be put through to Matron's office. To my relief, another Sister answered, and I said, "This is Sister Brandon. I'm telephoning in regard to a Captain Travis, who has gone missing. I need to finish an official report on the situation. Have you located him yet?"

I expected her to question me closely and discover that I had no business asking for information about the Captain. The last thing the clinic would want in such circumstances was an uproar over losing a dangerous patient.

But she said, sounding more than a little harried, "A body has been found in a stream five miles from here. We don't know if it's Captain Travis or not. Matron is talking to the police just now."

"Then I'll wait for further developments. Thank you, Sister." And I rang off.

Simon was watching my face. "Bad news." It wasn't a question.

"Yes. The police have just told Matron that there's a body in a stream some miles away. They're still talking to her."

"I'm sorry."

As we left the little room where the hotel's telephone had been installed, I said wearily, "So am I."

We drove back to Sinclair, and I packed everything but what I'd need in the morning, turned down my lamp, and went to my window for a last look as the moon rose and the village was bathed in a frosty glow. From somewhere there came the sound of laughter, and I saw a young man with a girl on his arm walking past the inn. Their heads were close together, and while I couldn't hear their voices from my perch, their laughter rang out.

They disappeared into one of the houses beyond the tea shop, and a silence fell.

I wasn't sleepy. On the contrary, I was restless, my thoughts going round and round, reliving the conversations with Mrs. Travis, with the Vicar, and even with the Sister's harried voice on the telephone. I wondered if Simon was asleep by now or if he sat by his own window, as wide awake as I was.

Another hour went by, and I wrapped the coverlet around me, for it was growing cold by the window. I heard the church clock marking midnight, and still I sat there, thinking of the long drive home. And then it struck one.

A movement in the far corner of the green, under the trees, caught my eye. At first I thought it was a dog following a scent trail, because it moved erratically. Whatever it was, it clung to the shadows.

Even the room was chill now as the fire died to a small blue flame that barely lit the hearth. I shivered and got up. The bed would be warmer.

I took a last look at the moonlight, thinking that no one in France need fear snipers tonight, or a stealthy attack across No Man's Land. The war was over, and while the dying would go on for a while, there would be no new convoys of wounded making their way back to a base hospital, and where there had been forward aid stations, all would be quiet.

The distant figure moved out of the shadows. I could just see it, like some large crab, scuttling for the trunk of the next tree, wary and watchful.

Who was it? It appeared he'd come from the direction of the surgery, but I couldn't be sure.

I could hear whistling as someone left the bar and made his way down the High. The figure stopped close to the trunk of a tree, waiting until he'd passed. And then it moved on, this time struggling to walk.

Could it be someone on crutches? But what would Mr. Spencer be doing out at this hour? With damaged ribs and a swollen ankle, it was foolish. If he stumbled and fell, he could hurt himself badly. Was he secretly testing his ability to use the crutches?

Riveted now, I sat down again and watched, wishing for my father's field glasses, to see better. At this distance, details were difficult to make out.

But the figure didn't move from the tree trunk, even when the way was clear.

I waited by the window. Another five minutes. Another ten.

What if he'd overtaxed his strength, what if he'd thought he was well enough to slip away unseen—only to find that he couldn't make it beyond the green? And if he couldn't go forward, he most certainly would be too weak to go back.

I waited another five minutes, listening to the church clock chime. And then I dressed quickly, found my coat and boots and a scarf with only the firelight to guide me, and caught up a blanket.

Whoever was out there would be feeling the night's dropping

temperatures too. He couldn't wait until morning when someone noticed him and got help.

It never occurred to me that I shouldn't go out and investigate. I'd served in all kinds of conditions in France, and the call to duty was still strong.

I opened my door, listening for a moment outside Simon's. But I couldn't tell whether he was asleep. The room appeared to be dark, except for the faint flicker of firelight under the door.

I turned and made my way down the stairs, wincing as first one tread and then another creaked under my boots. I moved to the outer edges, and the stairs were silent.

Reception was dark as well. I felt my way across the floor, wishing for a torch, but as my eyes grew accustomed to the ambient light, I found the door, lifted the latch, and let myself out into the cold air.

I stayed where I was for a moment, letting my eyes adjust again as the moon lit the scene before me. And in that instant, I realized that it wouldn't be wise to go directly to that tree. Whoever was there, he'd see me crossing the open green long before I could reach him. I turned left out of The George and found my way down the High to a side lane that went up between houses to the church. I walked as quietly as I could, so as not to give anyone a reason to look out a window, and soon came to the gate into the churchyard. I started to push it open, caught it before the squeak became a roar in the silence, and stepped over the low wall instead.

The gravestones were dark shapes, and I kept to the path rather than risk tripping over the footstones or the small square posts that marked family plots.

I could see the green now, quite clearly, bathed in moonlight. Another ten feet and I'd also be able to see the tree where the figure had stopped.

Intent on moving to a point where I could watch but not be seen, I was paying no attention to my surroundings. After all, except for rabbits and foxes or a hunting cat, a graveyard held no fears for me, and the church, soaring to my right, was half-lit, the upper parts bright in the moonlight, the lower walls and the church door deep in darkness.

I took another step, hoping for a clear view to the tree, when something moved in the darkness just behind me, a scrape of a boot against a stone, and dropping the blanket in my arms, I whirled to meet whatever was coming toward me from the blackness I'd just passed through.

CHAPTER 15

I COULDN'T SEE anything but a shapeless mass, and my first thought was, should I speak—or scream, just in case?

That gave me courage.

"Who's there? Speak up, or I'll call for help."

Silence.

Then, "I mean you no harm." The voice was low, hardly audible.

"Who are you?" I repeated sternly, in my best imitation of Matron's voice.

"I was looking for a place to shelter."

Taking a chance, I said, keeping my own voice low, "Mr. Spencer? Why did you leave the surgery? It was foolish, you haven't the strength to go anywhere. Let me summon the doctor. Or help you make your way back."

Silence again.

"You'll do serious damage to that ankle. And if you fall, your ribs could puncture a lung."

"I'm not this man Spencer. Whoever he is. I'm—looking for work. But it was a longer walk than I expected to find a village."

The voice had changed. Now it sounded like a man from the ranks, London perhaps. Not at all like Mr. Spencer.

"Are you an ex-soldier?" I wasn't sure now just who I'd cornered.

"Yes. Just—go away. I'll be all right. But I'll take that blanket you dropped—*no!*—leave it." And then, weariness creeping in, "Is the church open? I'll be all right in there." He appeared to be leaning on a gravestone.

"I can't very well walk away and leave you like this," I said.

"Don't be a busybody," he said roughly. "Let it go."

I was beginning to wonder if it was Mr. Spencer after all, when suddenly a torch flashed on, blinding me with the unexpected brightness, and I heard the figure swear.

"*Who did you bring with you?*" The roughness in his voice had vanished.

Before I could answer, Simon's voice came out of the darkness, brooking no argument. "Whoever you are, stand up and face the light. Or I'll take you to the police myself."

There was a heavy sigh. Then the figure straightened up and said, "Let me go. I'll leave the village. No harm done."

But Simon turned the torch so that it lit the man well enough for me to see who it was.

I gasped, looking into a face I knew. Only it was barely recognizable. Far too thin, lined with exhaustion and pain. Only the intensely blue eyes alive with feeling.

"Captain Travis?" I asked, unable to hide my disbelief and shock. *He wasn't dead, he hadn't killed himself.* "It's Bess—Sister Crawford."

He said nothing at first, staring at me. And I realized that with the scarf instead of my usual cap, he couldn't be sure I was who I claimed to be. I don't think he'd ever seen me with my hair uncovered.

I opened my coat, the light from the torch catching the whiteness of my apron.

"Good God," he said blankly, leaning heavily on a gravestone again. "Bess?"

Simon lowered the light.

"What are you doing in Sinclair?" I asked, but I had already guessed.

"The same thing that must have brought you here."

"But how—?"

"I had enough money from the orderly's pockets to take an omnibus going to Reading. I got rid of his uniform as soon as I could, and put on my own again. No one asked any awkward questions of an officer they believed had just been released from hospital to go home on leave. After that, Shanks's pony, and lorries. I don't remember how many. Five? Six? The last one put me down just below Clare, and I walked the rest of the way here."

He'd managed to travel nearly two hundred miles.

Simon spoke. "It isn't safe to be talking out here."

But we couldn't take him into the pub. If anyone saw us, there would be no end of questions.

I said, "Can you walk as far as the church? There's something you should see."

"Yes." The single word was abrupt, denying his exhaustion.

Simon killed his torch, but not before I'd found the blanket again and put it over my arm.

He set out toward the south door. But the Captain was moving on will alone now. I could tell. I'd seen too many officers and men who swore they were well enough to return to the Front, when the truth was, they were close to dropping where they stood.

Halfway there, the Captain stumbled over a footstone, and Simon stepped forward to offer him an arm. At first I thought he would refuse, but with a curt nod, he took it. Once we'd reached the safety of the deeper shadows in the porch, the next problem was the door. Careful as we were, the scraping sound echoed as we eased it open. I prayed that Mr. Caldwell and his wife were heavy sleepers. We left it ajar and stepped into the nave.

Moonlight from the windows gave it an eerie feeling. A gray and grayer palette that was ghostly, the darkness soaring overhead, silent and mysterious, the wooden ceiling pitch-black.

I paused, then started down the aisle, my footsteps echoing in the stillness, the sound hollow and without reality. The two men followed.

When I came to the memorial to James Travis, I stopped to one side of it and pointed. Simon, moving away from the Captain, carefully shielded the torch light so that it shone on the brass but not toward the windows.

Captain Travis frowned, glanced at me, and then turned to look.

I watched his face as he read each line, the truth dawning on him slowly and crushingly. He'd done his best to accept the fact that James was dead, but there must have been a corner of his mind where he still believed what had seemed to be the evidence of his own eyes. Here was final, undeniable proof.

He read the lines again, as if doubting what he'd seen. And then he looked at me.

"They must be right." He drew in a breath. "I must be mad."

And he started slowly toward the church door.

I caught him up, took his arm, led him to one of the pews.

"You saw something. Someone," I amended. "Whoever it was, he reminded you of your family. That doesn't mean you weren't shot by a British officer. It just means that the resemblance was all you had to go on in trying to identify him."

Standing behind him, Simon shook his head slightly. I knew what he was trying to tell me. *Don't give this man false hope . . .*

Was I? I looked up at Simon, then back at Captain Travis.

I'd somehow misled him once before, drawing his attention to the man he'd met so briefly in a railway station in Paris. Was I doing the same thing again? Trying to offer him the consolation of an officer he'd never be able to put a name to, when I should be trying to convince him it was all the creation of an exhausted mind on the verge of breaking? Add to that the head wound, and it was understandable that he couldn't really be certain what had happened to him.

What should I do? What *could* I do?

He said nothing for a while, staring toward the altar but not seeing it. His gaze was inward, reliving the heat of battle, the shock and realization that he'd been wounded, the face yards from him, the rifle raised.

Even in this gray light, I saw him wince, as if he felt the bullet striking home.

"I didn't imagine it," he said, his voice low, talking to himself and not to us. "I can't have done. Withering machine gun fire caught us charging across open ground. It was a trap, and I shouted to my men, calling them back, urging them toward the nearest shelter, which was what was left of a barn. I saw Willard fall, he reached out to me, and I turned back for him. Other companies were mixed with ours, heading for the wall and a ditch in front of it. I dragged Sergeant Willard with me, still looking over my shoulder to see if any of my men were behind me. To this point my men gave the same account of the action. I asked them afterward. Just then I saw a Lieutenant I didn't know, but he was one of ours. He was firing his revolver. And then the machine gun stopped firing. I expect they were conserving ammunition. That's when he dropped his revolver and picked up an abandoned rifle. I remember the revolver swinging from his lanyard as he brought the rifle up. My first thought was that he was firing at the machine gun nest, that he'd seen a head come up, but he turned, looked directly at me, and fired. I saw him smile just as I felt the bullet strike, but I thought it had caught my cap, and I swore at him as I nearly lost my grip on Willard. Then I was going down, and my last coherent thought was, What the hell is my great-uncle doing in France? They told me afterward that Willard and I went headfirst into the ditch, and my men came out and pulled us to safety."

His voice trailed off.

We said nothing for several minutes. Then Simon asked, "If he had his revolver in his hand, why did he use a rifle?"

"I've thought about that. Gone over and over it. Two possibilities. The chamber was empty, or I was just out of revolver range and he wanted to make sure of his shot. We'd been firing steadily, trying to force the Germans to keep their heads down and give us time to get our men back. He could easily have run out, and there was no time to reload."

"What did he do next?" It was Simon who asked.

"I don't know. My knees were buckling, everything was going black, and then I came to as one of my men was trying to clean the wound and bandage it. I remember asking how many made it back, and he answered me, but I was already losing consciousness again. The next thing I remember was seeing someone wearing a veil bending over me. But of course it wasn't a veil, I was just going in and out of consciousness and couldn't see clearly."

"When you went back to your sector, did you look for this man?"

"Yes, of course I did," he said, irritated by the question. "But no one knew who I was talking about. I was searching for a Lieutenant Travis." He gestured tiredly in the direction of the plaque.

"I know now why no one knew who he was. How could they have known? His regiment wasn't in that sector—and he was already dead."

His hand was shaking. "No wonder they stared at me. I thought someone was covering for him. That they *knew*, but didn't want to tell me. Afraid of what I might do if I found him. Why else would they have been so unhelpful?" He shook his head. "It didn't make sense, and I felt betrayed and angry. I went to the next sector, when we were drawn back for two days. They swore they'd never heard of James Travis. Of course they hadn't. How could they have?"

"It never occurred to you that you might be wrong?" Simon asked.

"All the facts I had pointed to James. God forgive me, I didn't want to be pawned off with lies when I knew what I'd seen. I even asked if he'd been wounded, if that was why he wasn't there. And then I saw him again. And I knew that I'd been right and everyone else had been wrong. It was a bitter realization. Bitter. It was worse in hospital, when they refused to listen to me. I remembered then how much I'd liked James Travis when I saw him in Paris, and it occurred to me that everyone else liked him too, those who knew him far better than I did, and they didn't want to believe he was a murderer. I thought that it must be James who had run mad, not me, and because he was who he was, it was being covered up."

"In the beginning, did you never ask yourself why he should want to kill you?" I asked.

"More than once. God knows. The only thing I could think about was the quarrel between our great-grandfathers. That he'd remembered it after we'd met. But that was generations ago, hardly a reason to kill *me*. I'd never been to England until the war. And he hadn't been angry in Paris. But perhaps he hadn't been told everything about the strained relations between our families. That's why I hadn't traveled to Suffolk while I was in London. I wasn't sure what sort of welcome I'd have."

Above our heads the church clock struck the hour, and we all jumped.

"We can't worry about that tonight," I said, trying to think what to do with Captain Travis. "But we can't take you to the inn. Everyone in this village knows the Travis family—there would be talk, and someone might be worried enough to contact the hospital. And they would come for you—they're searching the south of England for you now." I looked across at Simon. "What should we do?"

"We've already told The George that we're leaving in the morning. If we go before the sun is up, we can stop here at the church and take the Captain with us."

He was suddenly wary. "Where will you take me?"

"I don't know," I told him truthfully. "They've already come to my home in Somerset looking for you. Somewhere we can talk and make plans. You'll have to trust us. But it means you must spend the night in here."

It was cold in the nave. In spite of the sun during the day, the interior would never be really warm. And the benches were hard. Not the best place for a weary, footsore man.

"Leave me the blanket you have there. I've got this one. I'll use one of the kneeling cushions for a pillow."

I was torn. If we left him—would he still be here in the morning?

The Captain must have sensed my hesitation.

"I've nowhere else to go," he said, his voice despondent. "Except home. To Barbados. If I don't straighten this out soon, I won't be allowed to leave England."

I almost told him then that he was the heir to James Travis. But a little voice in my head kept me from doing it. *He doesn't need to know that. Not yet.*

I heeded the warning. Instead, I said, "Then we'll come for you. And I'll ask the kitchen to put up sandwiches and a thermos of tea, for the journey."

"Bless you. I don't remember when I last ate. I'd run out of funds."

Simon spoke then. "The village has a constable. I expect he's already made his rounds. There's no reason for him to come into the church, even if he hasn't. But be aware of that. Sir."

The Captain nodded. "I don't think we've been introduced, Sergeant-Major. But thank you."

"Brandon. Sir."

I could think of no reason for staying here. My feet were cold through my boots, and my hands were chilled as well, even shoved into my coat pockets.

"You'll be all right?"

"Not to worry. I've slept rougher than this, in France."

We left then, inching the porch door shut behind us so that the sound wouldn't attract any notice.

We made our way across the dark churchyard to the darker lane. Simon took my arm to guide me through the maze of gravestones, and from there to the street. When we were well out of hearing from the church or the houses overlooking the lane, I said, "How did you know where to find me?"

"I wasn't asleep. I heard you pause outside my door, and I expected you to knock. When you didn't, I listened, and heard the outer door close. And so I came after you. What in the name of God took you out into the night like that?"

I told him what I'd seen from my window. "I thought it was

Mr. Spencer, and I couldn't fathom why he was leaving the surgery in such a stealthy fashion. I wanted to know what he was doing."

He said, exasperated, "You could have got yourself into trouble."

"I think I have," I said slowly. "Do you believe him, Simon?"

He said nothing until we had nearly reached the door of The George. "The account he gave was consistent enough. I'll reserve judgment until I hear more."

"But what are we to do with him?"

He grinned at me, his smile white in the moonlight. "I was wondering when you were going to face that." The smile went away. "He can't stay here. If word reached Mrs. Travis, you're right, she would contact the clinic straightaway. We can't take him to Mrs. Hennessey's, she'd never allow him up the stairs. And if we go to Somerset, we'll involve your parents. There's my cottage, but your mother will expect you to spend most of your time at the house."

"We might not have to cross that bridge," I said. "He might have already left St. Mary's, as soon as our backs were turned."

We stood there in silence.

"If he's not there," Simon replied finally, "then you're well out of it. It means he's probably mad."

We let ourselves in the door and made our way up the stairs to our rooms. I went inside mine, shut the door, and crossed to the window without lighting a lamp.

But there was no one out there on the green or moving along the High.

I undressed and crawled into bed, thinking that if I were Captain Travis, I'd wait until I was absolutely certain that the two of us were in bed and hopefully even asleep before leaving the church.

But that meant I didn't trust the Captain. Or really believe him.

The fact was, I wanted to believe him. I wanted him to be well. But my time was running out here in England, and I wasn't sure I could rely on Simon to see this through if I went back to France. He too was still at the beck and call of the Army, and that would have to come first.

Well, there was always my mother, as a last resort.

With a sigh I rolled over, watching the moonlight cross my ceiling until I fell asleep.

It was still dark outside my window when I woke to Simon's tap at my door, and the soft "Bess? Are you awake?"

I realized that the moon had set and we must be close to dawn.

The church—and Captain Travis.

"Yes, thank you, Simon. I'll be right down."

I dressed quickly, for the room was very cold, put my hair up in my cap, and set my kit by the door, where Simon could find it and bring it down.

In the dining room, a sleepy woman brought us our breakfast and agreed that it was indeed possible to order sandwiches and tea for our journey. "And we have nice apples, as well as eggs for the sandwiches, and I wouldn't be surprised if there wasn't a bit of roast chicken left over from the party last night."

We told her that that would be lovely. She yawned as she turned away and disappeared through the kitchen door. Simon went up to fetch our things and take them out to the motorcar. I heard voices in Reception and realized that someone must have spoken to him, and he was settling our account.

They would be glad to see the back of us, I thought as he came through to the dining room just as our breakfast platters were being brought from the kitchen.

We ate quickly, then paid for the sandwiches and tea that the woman brought out to us. "Where is Betty?" I asked as we rose to leave.

"She's coming in for lunch. No need for her, with only the two of you staying over."

We were just going out to the motorcar when I looked up to see a woman coming toward us from the High.

She had a scarf over her head, and I thought at first it must be Betty, confused about her schedule. And then I realized that it wasn't.

She stopped just short of the motorcar. I could only see part of her face, fair and strong-featured, her hair a butter yellow.

"Sister Crawford?"

"Yes. Who are you?"

"You don't know me. My name is Lucy Fredericks. I live in one of the cottages at The Hall."

But I did know her—of her—though we'd never met.

"Did Mrs. Travis send you?"

She shook her head. "She doesn't know I've come. It's something else." She hesitated. "The man who attacked that Mr. Spencer, the one being kept in Dr. Harrison's surgery. I know who he is."

Frowning, I said, "But you should tell the Constable. He's the proper person to deal with this." I wasn't sure I quite believed her. And all we needed now was five more minutes, and we'd be out of Sinclair and safe.

"I can't go to him," she said. "I saw this in a dream. I thought someone ought to know."

"In a dream?" Simon had come around from turning the crank. "Are you sure?"

"They always come true," she said, looking up at him. "I don't know why."

"I'd heard," I said, "that you use the cards."

She smiled, shaking her head. "I tell people that. They'd laugh if I told them I'd dreamed what I was telling them."

"Who did you see in your dream?"

"It looked like James Travis. I know that sounds odd. He's dead. But it did, it looked very like him, the way I remember him from before the war. I thought someone ought to know. I couldn't speak of this to Mrs. Travis. It would upset her terribly."

That was an understatement.

"How did you know we were leaving early?" I asked. "Did you dream that as well?"

She smiled. "No. I came early hoping to catch you at breakfast. I have to hurry back to cook my father's." And without warning, she turned and walked away, her head down, her pace brisk.

I said to Simon, keeping my voice low, "What did you make of that?"

"I don't know," he said grimly, "but if Captain Travis is still at the church, we should get him out of here as fast as possible."

We hurried to get into the car, and without turning on our headlamps, we set out for the church.

"How much does Captain Travis resemble James? Do you know?"

"I saw his photograph," I answered. "That is, James's. At The Hall. There's a resemblance. Not strong, mind you, but it's there. Mostly around the eyes, I think. And possibly the chin. If Mrs. Travis hadn't had such strong objections to him as heir, she might have drawn some comfort from that resemblance."

He didn't answer, but I knew what he was thinking. How long had Captain Travis been in Sinclair? Had he been hiding here when Mr. Spencer was attacked?

We pulled up in front of the church. Around the village, lamps were being lit in cottage windows as people started their day. And in the east, there was the very smallest hint of a brightening in the sky. Across the green, lamps were being lit in the surgery too. And that worried me, because the surgery looked out toward the church.

Simon had hardly put on the brake when a shadow detached itself from the deeper shadows of the stair tower and moved toward us.

Captain Travis said, "I couldn't sleep," and got in behind me.

Simon let in the clutch, turned the motorcar around, and headed for the High. We passed The Pottery and the tea shop, and then reached the bend in the road.

Sinclair disappeared from our view.

I passed the sandwiches and the thermos to the Captain, and realized he still had the blanket belonging to The George.

He thanked me and uncapped the thermos, drinking the hot tea. "There was frost this morning when I first came out. If my great-grandfather hadn't left England when he did, I would have left myself. This climate and I are not suited."

"Would you stay here, if you had the chance?" I asked. "If you had property here or investments?"

"Very likely not. I'd sell up and go home."

Ten minutes later, he was asleep in one corner of the rear seat, and I thought, looking at him, that this must be the first real sleep he'd had for a very long time. His face was slack, his body relaxed, and the jolting over the abysmal roads didn't disturb him. Like the soldier he was, he'd learned the knack of sleeping when he could, in any conditions, and that was serving him well now.

We hadn't solved the question of what to do with Captain Travis, Simon and I. I was hoping that he might stay asleep and give us a chance to talk. But he woke several times, on edge, asking, "Where are we going?"

"I don't know yet," I answered the first time. "We've got to work that out."

And the second time, Simon asked, "Where would you go?"

"I've no idea. I don't have the sort of friends here where I could drop in and expect to stay for a time."

As the dawn broke, and finally the first brightness reached the motorcar, I looked back.

The Captain hadn't shaved for days, his hair unkempt, his uniform rumpled. He looked like an ex-soldier searching for work, and his face was haggard as well. I said to Simon, "We need a place where he can shave while we find some new clothes for him. But how are we going to manage that?"

"Leave it to me."

And so I did.

As we came into Cambridge, Simon pointed to a small hotel on the edge of town. It had seen better days, but it appeared to be respectable still. I watched as a young couple came out the door, smiling, holding hands. He was in uniform, a Sergeant in a Yorkshire regiment. She was wearing a jaunty hat, a sprig of violets on the lapel of her coat. They were silk, but quite pretty.

"Newlyweds," I said, watching them as they laughed and stayed close to each other as they walked up the street.

"Now let's find a place where I can purchase what we need."

A little farther along there was a shop, and Simon pulled in front of it. Twenty minutes later, he came back with a sack. In the next street was a men's shop with what appeared to be second-hand clothing in the window.

Simon was gone longer this time, and he returned with a small valise.

We drove back to the hotel we had seen earlier, and Simon went inside while the Captain and I waited a third time.

When Simon returned to the motorcar, he gave me a slight nod.

"I have rooms," he said as he came to my door. "One for you and the other for the two of us. Your mother wouldn't approve, but the rooms are clean and the clientele is respectable enough. I don't think there will be any trouble." He turned to the Captain. "You, sir, are my commanding officer, and you got quite drunk when you learned your wife had left you. We found you, and I've brought you and your sister here to make you presentable enough to return to your regiment. We're on our way to Kent, where you're posted."

Captain Travis started to speak, then thought better of it. "I expect it will throw anyone looking for me off the scent," he said in resignation and prepared to open the rear door.

Simon opened my door. "Leave the cases, I'll bring them in."

We went in to Reception, the woman behind the desk staring at the Captain, an expression of pity on her face. I smiled at her and followed Simon up the stairs.

My room was clean, papered in a floral pattern with chintz slips on the only chair and matching curtains at the window. It looked out at the side of the building across a narrow alley. Simon and the Captain were in the room next to mine. Simon brought up my kit and said, "I don't expect to stay more than a night. It would look—suspicious—if we left before that. Do you have everything you need?"

"Yes. I'm fine. What did you buy?"

"A razor, a shirt—no one will notice under his tunic that it isn't military issue. And a cane. If he can manage a credible limp, it will help. An officer recovering from a leg wound and accompanied by a nurse won't remind anyone of the troubled man who walked away from a Wiltshire clinic. Other clinics might have been notified, in the event he was brought into one. Thank God he kept his own uniform. He ought to have a fresh one, Bess, but I'll ask them in the kitchen if they can do something about his. The problem is, what will we do with him once he's presentable? He can't go back to Barbados without his papers. And he can't hide forever."

"I know," I said with a sigh. "At least they won't shoot him for leaving the clinic without permission. But his own regiment might consider him a deserter, if he's not accounted for. And soon."

"Let's see how he looks when we've cleaned him up. I've sent for hot water for shaving, and he can have a bath as well. I bought scissors to trim his hair. I'll polish his shoes. They've seen rough weather and a good deal of walking, but I'll do my best."

"I didn't intend to put this on you, Simon," I said contritely. "If any trouble comes of this, you can blame me."

"Hardly," he said with a smile. "But the Colonel Sahib might need to come to our rescue before this is over."

"God forbid," I said, with a pretend grimace.

We had hoped to go down to dinner as soon as the dining room opened, before it became crowded.

Simon came to collect me at six, and I was thunderstruck when I saw the Captain in the passage.

He was still haggard, and far too thin, but he looked like the officer I remembered seeing in the canteen at the base hospital—it seemed like years ago. His uniform, sponged and pressed in the kitchen, didn't fit quite as it once had, but he carried himself well, a clean-shaven English officer who bore no resemblance to the wretched figure in the churchyard of St. Mary's, or the desperate man on the cot in the clinic. Simon had even helped him trim his hair. He would pass inspection, I thought, if the search for him widened. Still, there was a more noticeable resemblance now to the photograph I'd seen of James Travis. If someone looked hard enough.

We had very little to say to one another as we ate our dinner. The things we wanted to say we dared not, for fear that someone might overhear. But there was a tiny parlor to one side of Reception, and we took our tea there afterward. No one else had come in, and we could speak freely, though we kept our voices low.

Captain Travis was worried about his future, and I could see that we might well have to turn to the Colonel Sahib to get us out of this predicament.

"I can't go back to the clinic," he said, staring into the heart of the fire that was struggling to take the evening chill from the room. "I won't. I can't face it again."

"But until you are properly discharged from there, you can't return to your regiment," Simon pointed out. "Nor can you leave the country without proper papers."

"There's my cousin—James's mother. Would she speak up for me? That might carry some weight. Or her doctor might declare me fit again."

I knew how these cases worked. I didn't think the clinic would dismiss Captain Travis quite so easily, not until they were convinced he was "cured" of his strange obsession.

I said, "They would insist that you return to be evaluated. And that could take time."

"Does Mrs. Travis have a solicitor? He might help me."

"Or he might turn you in. There's a problem, Captain, that you aren't aware of. After his father's death, James Travis drew up a new will and made you his heir. I don't think he expected to die so soon after his father, you see, and he must have remembered his meeting with you."

He was startled. "This is the first I've heard of an inheritance.

Are you sure of this? All the more reason, then, that they might help me."

"That's not quite—there are extenuating circumstances, you see. Mrs. Travis wasn't aware that you and her son had met. And she feels very strongly that the estate ought not to go to your branch of the family, because of the unpleasantness at the time your great-grandfather chose to leave England."

With some trepidation I tried to explain what was happening in Suffolk, and he listened intently.

"And so the first thing she would do, if you arrived on her doorstep, would be to summon the Constable to take you into custody."

"But—I'm grateful to James, it was a gesture of respect to trust me to take over the estate and care for his mother. Still, I have property of my own in Barbados, I like it there, and I prefer the climate. What would I do with The Hall?"

"There's no one else. At least, that appears to be the case."

He got up to pace. I could see that the wound in his back was still bothering him, for he moved stiffly. Sleeping in an awkward position, first in the cold church and then in Simon's motorcar, hadn't helped.

"Look," he said finally. "I'll go to Mrs. Travis, tell her I have no interest in the estate, and if she'll help me escape that clinic, I'll sign everything over to her."

"I don't know that you can. And what will happen when she dies? Who will she leave the estate to then?"

"Oh, good Lord. Then I need to speak to her solicitor."

I took a deep breath. "I'm sorry, Captain. I don't think you'll have much joy there either. I don't know that you understand just how strong their feelings are. You've become—they think the worst of you. And her solicitor seems to be afraid to press her to accept the terms of her son's will. To be fair, Mr. Ellis isn't well enough to fight her. Even the local Vicar is afraid to speak up. Have you received any letters from Mr. Ellis, informing you that you're James's heir?"

"I've received no correspondence at all."

"Oh, dear. He must be afraid of losing her as a client. She's very influential."

"The estate has to be settled sooner or later. One way or another." He turned to look toward Reception, where we could hear voices, then said, "I came to England to fight for King and Country. I brought letters from my bank in Barbados to a bank in London, to ensure that I had the funds I needed, but I have no other connections here. As soon as I finished my training, we were given a few days' leave, and then met our train to Folkestone. I know Paris better than I know London. Perhaps the best course open to me is to speak to this man Ellis. At least as the Travis heir, I will have more standing in England than I do now. It might be the only way I can get clear of my own problems. I don't see any other option. Could you take me back to call on this Ellis? And vouch for me? It might work."

Before I could answer him, the door opened, and the couple I'd seen earlier in the day came in, smiling and greeting us as they chose the two chairs in the corner.

And any answer I might have given Captain Travis would have to wait.

CHAPTER 16

CAPTAIN TRAVIS WAS still very tired, and he went up to bed after our dinner. That gave me an opportunity to speak to Simon privately.

We walked for some distance along the street outside the hotel, shop windows lighting our way where they were still open and patches of shadow falling across our path where they were not. Ahead of us, a church tower loomed against the night sky. People were making their way home or stopping at the last minute to make purchases for their tea. They paid no attention to a soldier and a Sister in their midst.

After several minutes, Simon broke the companionable silence between us. "Travis has a point, Bess. He can't hide forever. But I think he's looking in the wrong direction, if he expects help in Suffolk. You could ask the Colonel Sahib—or even Melinda Crawford—to straighten out this business with the Army and clinic. I'd afraid you won't have time to finish what you've started. Your leave is up in less than a week."

I could imagine Cousin Melinda going to war for Captain Travis. She had a soft spot for those in trouble, and for a moment I considered traveling on to Kent to ask her for help. As for my father, I had no idea where he was—for all I knew he could be in

France, involved with the negotiations going on there. Time was our enemy just now, and Captain Travis's as well. While he was a fugitive, regarded as dangerous, he was still a serving officer. Eventually the Army would find him and might well consider him a deserter.

"I don't think he realizes just how passionate Mrs. Travis is about this matter. And then there's Ellis, and heaven only knows where he stands," I answered slowly. "Captain Travis could have made this wretched journey from Wiltshire for nothing. I'm still astonished that he did such a thing. It must have taken enormous determination."

"He has to face his situation sometime." Then Simon grinned down at me. "Shall we toss a penny and see whether it's Melinda or the Colonel Sahib?"

"Convincing the Captain to trust Melinda might be a problem. He doesn't know her the way we do. He's so certain he can reason with Mrs. Travis or Mr. Ellis."

We turned and walked back to the hotel. Its tiny pub was busy, but the dining room was nearly empty. We climbed the stairs without speaking.

As it happened, I was right. Captain Travis was a man accustomed to ruling his own life in the islands and commanding men in battle, and the prospect of letting others fight for him instead of taking charge himself was as foreign to him as it would be to Simon or my father. As I listened to his decision the next morning, I couldn't help but think that men sometimes preferred to meet trouble head-on, while women looked for an easier way.

In the end, of course, Simon and I could only agree to try, despite our trepidation.

"You realize, sir, that if you're taken up by the Army, it will make it all that much harder to get you clear of the clinic?" Simon asked.

"Yes, Sergeant-Major, and I know it seems to be the wrong course of action to go to Sinclair before I'm free of it, but if this man Ellis will help, that should go faster. He's legally bound to abide by the terms of James's will, and whether he likes me or not, he will have to represent me. I'm not in Wiltshire now, where he can ignore my existence. I'll be in Suffolk."

That settled, after our breakfast we set out for Bury St. Edmunds, where we could find Mr. Ellis.

But when we got there, late in the afternoon, we discovered that he'd left only an hour earlier for Sinclair and The Hall.

"Well," Captain Travis said philosophically, "I expect we'll have to beard the lioness in her den."

"I don't know that that's the right strategy," I told him.

"Bess, I shall have to face her sooner or later. And it forces Ellis, whatever his personal feelings might be, to choose between us. I'm his client now. He knows I could take my business elsewhere. Will he risk that?"

Only half-convinced, Simon set out for Sinclair. And when we came up the drive to the house, we saw what must be the solicitor's motorcar already in front of the door.

Simon pulled up a little behind the other vehicle, and we got down, walking without speaking to lift the knocker and wait to be greeted.

The maid who answered our knock stared at the three of us on the threshold, and then started to close the door in our faces, her own face a picture of shock.

Simon caught the door before she could swing it more than halfway, and he said gently, "It's rather important that we speak to Mrs. Travis. We mean her no harm."

But she was staring at Captain Travis, and I realized that she must know, just looking at him, who he must be: the man her mistress refused to accept as the new owner of the estate. The resemblance to Lieutenant Travis was slight, but there would have been gossip below stairs about the cousin from Barbados, and Mrs. Travis's quarrel with us over the heir.

"I can't announce you," she said, finding her voice, looking up at Simon with pleading eyes. "She'll be that angry, I'll lose my place."

"Then we'll announce ourselves," Simon told her, and he set her aside. We followed him into the handsome foyer.

Captain Travis was staring in his turn, looking around with surprise and some respect. "I hadn't realized . . ." I heard him say under his breath.

Hadn't realized what he was giving up?

Fine as the house in Barbados must be, with its wide veranda and bright gardens, The Hall was elegant. And his own great-grandfather had walked away from here to make his own way.

I could hear voices coming from the drawing room. Taking a deep breath, I walked ahead and tapped lightly on the door. When I heard Mrs. Travis impatiently call, "Come!" I swung it open.

Her shock was ten times stronger than the maid's.

Her gaze on Captain Travis's face, she rose from her chair and stood there, staring at him as if she'd seen a ghost. Tall, fair, blue eyes—he must have reminded her of her son, if only for an instant. And then, collecting herself with an effort, she said, "What is the meaning of this?"

The thin figure closer to the hearth rose as well, and I recognized Mr. Ellis. He stepped at once toward the bell pull and said, "Let me deal with this, Mrs. Travis."

But the Captain was already speaking.

"Mrs. Travis? I met your son only briefly. I'm sorry I never had the opportunity to know him better."

I thought he was going to step forward to offer her his hand, and she must have believed the same thing, for she moved back quickly, almost stumbling over the chair she had just vacated and in her shock had forgot was even there.

"*Murderer,*" she exclaimed, finding her voice at last. "How dare you come here, how dare you face me down in my own house!"

Mr. Ellis, his hand on the bellpull, stopped in midmotion. "Murderer?" he repeated, and then exclaimed, "My God!"

Behind us in the doorway, the maid was hovering, uncertain what to do. Simon moved to close the door, shutting her out.

"I'm not afraid of you," Mrs. Travis declared fiercely. "And I remind you that I have a house full of servants. You won't get away with killing me."

Caught completely unprepared for that, we stood there in confusion.

My first thought was that she was trying to accuse Captain Travis of killing her son, however unlikely that was, but in her grief over her loss, over the stressful knowledge that her home now belonged to this man, she was lashing out at him in the only way she could think of.

And then I realized that she was speaking literally.

I said quickly, "What do you mean, murderer?"

Looking past the Captain, she spat the words at me. "He was murdered. That poor man you were on about the last time you were here. With that Agency in London."

Struggling to take that in, I said, "But he was recovering well, I thought."

"Yes, and all the more reason to get rid of him. He was carrying papers—papers that showed that this man"—she pointed a shaking finger in the direction of the Captain—"is a dangerous madman, capable of anything. *Anything.* The police and

Dr. Harrison found them in his valise. Papers he'd stolen from Mr. Ellis, that he'd intended to bring to me to show me what sort of person had been named as my son's heir." She took a step forward, and I thought she would have liked to attack me physically. "You told me he was suffering in some clinic in the south of England, and you *lied*. He was here all along, waiting while you played on my sympathies and worked to convince me to see him."

Ignoring her accusations, I wanted to know more about Mr. Spencer. "But I don't understand—when was he killed?"

"Of course you know. Night before last, when you slipped out of the village like a thief."

"Hardly like a thief. Ask the staff at The George, where we had breakfast," Simon told her, visibly annoyed with her.

But I remembered something else—something she couldn't have known: that we'd left Captain Travis alone in the church until we could come for him while it was still dark enough for us to stop at St. Mary's. I felt cold. Rallying, I said, "Someone attacked Mr. Spencer earlier. You're telling me that it happened again, and now Mr. Spencer is dead?"

It was Ellis who answered me. And all this while, Captain Travis had said nothing.

"Are you being deliberately dense? Dr. Harrison came down to look in on Mr. Spencer before bringing him his breakfast. He found him dead. Choked to death while he lay helpless. His killer searched the cupboard and the doctor's own office. Fortunately Dr. Harrison had persuaded Mr. Spencer to allow him to lock his valise in a storeroom."

I remembered how he'd clung to it, despite his ribs.

Simon spoke now. "We've been in Cambridge. We can prove that if necessary. If your solicitor already had these papers, why hadn't he shown them to you? I don't see that killing Spencer had to do with those papers. Or Captain Travis."

But Mr. Ellis and Mrs. Travis weren't interested in reason.

Mr. Ellis reached again for the bellpull and this time gave it an angry jerk. "Sister Crawford, Dr. Harrison told the Constable that you and the Sergeant-Major had come several times, demanding to be allowed to see Mr. Spencer, and he'd turned you away. Before and after your first attempt on his life had failed."

"That's nonsense, and you know it. And what," I added, "were you doing, going through that valise with Dr. Harrison? Where was Inspector Howe while all of this was happening? Or Constable Simpson?"

Mr. Ellis said, "I'd come to speak to Mrs. Travis. It was still quite early when I got to Sinclair, and I stopped at The George for my breakfast before driving on to The Hall. When the alarm went up, I went at once to see what it was all about. It was Dr. Harrison who insisted on going through the valise, to find out what we could about where Spencer was from, who should be notified. He insisted on a witness. Someone had already gone for Inspector Howe, and Constable Simpson was searching the grounds."

The door opened and the maid, looking frightened, said, "Yes, Ma'am?"

Ellis answered her. "Send someone for Constable Simpson. Now. At once. Tell him it's urgent."

I said, "No, that won't be necessary. We're leaving."

Captain Travis said to Mr. Ellis, "I've come about my cousin's will. Will you meet with me later?"

The solicitor turned to Mrs. Travis. "You were right. He will take this house without a qualm of conscience. Even if he must commit murder. I should have listened to you."

I was reminded of an opera I'd seen once in London, where

the principals were all singing at once, voices rising and falling, intertwined, reaching a crescendo in the end. But this wasn't *Lucia di Lammermoor*. And we needed to be away before the Constable reached The Hall.

I said, "Whatever papers Mr. Spencer carried, it doesn't matter. We'd already asked you to intercede on the Captain's behalf—"

"Captain Travis wasn't wasting away in a clinic, was he?" Mrs. Travis demanded viciously. "Mad he may be, but pathetic he is not. Well, I've already found the man my son should have named in his will, and would have done if he hadn't been shamed into naming *you*."

Anger flared in the Captain's blue eyes.

Before he could answer her, I turned to Simon, and he reached out to lay a warning hand on the Captain's arm. After the briefest hesitation, Captain Travis nodded grimly and moved to follow him toward the doorway, where the maid was still standing, uncertain what her mistress expected of her. I was the last to go, fighting a rearguard action.

"You've got it all wrong," I told Mrs. Travis. "But perhaps it's for the best that this should go to court, and be settled once and for all there."

Mr. Ellis was about to speak, thought better of it, and smartly closed his mouth.

Mrs. Travis looked suddenly horrified. I thought the prospect of having to deal with all this so publicly, to have everyone know she was calling into question her own son's wisdom in choosing a stranger, was more than she was willing to face. But as I watched, she gathered herself together with a visible effort and said, "It won't matter, will it? A man who commits a murder for gain will be hanged, and he won't be allowed to keep what he killed for.

Wait and see. It can't have turned out any better, in my opinion. While I'm sorry for Mr. Spencer, I didn't know him, did I? And if his death frees me of this man, it won't have been in vain."

I could still hear her shrill, angry voice as I reached the outer door and stepped into pale sunlight trying to find its way through the clouds.

Simon was already turning the crank, and I was urging the Captain into the motorcar.

He said, looking back at the house he'd just left, "I had no idea . . ."

I couldn't be sure what he was starting to say.

Then he shook himself, as if waking from a bad dream, and added, "This was a mistake. I should have listened to you. I can't believe that hateful woman is James Travis's mother."

He climbed in beside Simon, and I took the rear seat.

"Where to?" Simon asked, glancing toward me over his shoulder.

"Just drive," I said as Ellis came to the door and stared balefully after us.

As we reached the outskirts of the village, I said to Simon, "Look, drop me at The Pottery. I might be able to find out something from Sister Potter. Come back in a quarter of an hour. I'll be waiting."

"It's too grave a risk," Simon told me, shaking his head. "If Mrs. Travis believes we're guilty in Spencer's death, the police will want to speak to us."

"But we need to know—we can't fight this in the dark."

"She's right," Captain Travis said.

"It's not a risk I'm willing to take. Sir."

"But I am. Please, Simon? It's the only thing I can think of," I pleaded.

And in the end, I got my way. He set me down in front of the little cottage across from the green and drove on, disappearing around the bend, where the shops were. *The butcher, the baker, the candlestick maker,* I thought, watching him out of sight, only it was the butcher, the baker, the greengrocer, the tobacconist, and all the rest.

Then I hurried up the path, praying that Sister Potter was at home.

She came to the door almost at once after I'd knocked.

"Sister Crawford," she said.

"Could I come in? Something's happened, I need your help rather badly."

She looked up and down the High, then reached out for me. "Come in. Quickly now."

And I stepped inside her cottage.

I hadn't planned what I was going to say to her. I wasn't even sure why I trusted her. Because she was a Sister, and had served the wounded?

Smokie wound himself around my ankles as I closed the outer door behind me.

Sister Potter seemed a little flustered by my appearance, but she was all courtesy.

"Let me put the kettle on," she said.

The British answer to any awkward situation, I thought, and shook my head. "There isn't time, but thank you for offering. I've just heard—about Mr. Spencer. It's quite awful. What happened?"

"You've been away," she began, leading me into the front room and offering me a seat. I chose the chair by the window, where I could watch for Simon.

"Yes, in Cambridge. We were there just overnight, really. When we got back, we were met with the tragic news."

"And 'tragic' is the right word," she agreed, taking the chair across from me. "It was a shock to all of us. I mean, *murder*. What's more, I'd spent some time with him the day before, because Dr. Harrison had asked me to take over Mr. Spencer's care." She shook her head. "Someone walking into a doctor's surgery and killing a patient? I ask you."

"Then it really was murder? Not a medical issue?"

"Oh, yes, there's no doubt about that."

"Dr. Harrison mentioned that you might take over the patient's care when he was a little stronger. What if he'd been here—in the cottage? You wouldn't have been in another wing of the house. It's too small."

"Yes, I'd thought about that. I wondered what I would have done. And then I wondered what *he* would have done, whoever it was. Frankly, I was reluctant to take Mr. Spencer on, anyway. Not to speak ill of the dead, but he wasn't the best of patients, and Dr. Harrison had already asked me once before to sit with him. I wondered if there was something on his mind, something worrying him. Well, he was in pain, of course, and he was impatient to leave as soon as possible, but I was told he'd fret at night, then be feverish by morning. The doctor couldn't watch him, nor could his assistant, much less his wife. She's expecting a child, you know. Their first."

I hadn't known.

I said, "But there was an earlier attempt on his life, as I recall."

"Dr. Harrison didn't think it was as serious as the Constable made it out to be. There's Billy Ryan, you see. He lives on a farm some two miles away on the other side of the church, and he became addicted to laudanum while recovering from his wounds.

Doctor has been trying to reduce his dependency, and he thought Billy broke into the surgery to find what he needed—and discovered someone was there. Frightened, he'd attacked Mr. Spencer."

I hadn't heard this account. "And he came back? Even knowing Mr. Spencer was still there?"

"Billy must have been desperate."

"Have the police arrested him?"

"That first time," she said evasively, "Mr. Spencer couldn't identify him with any certainty—well, he doesn't live in the village, he wouldn't have known who Billy is. And when Constable Simpson went to speak to Billy, he denied it." She shrugged. "That didn't surprise the Constable, and it didn't surprise me."

I said, "I heard that the doctor's dog might have bitten the intruder. Was there evidence of that?"

"That was the odd thing, there wasn't a mark on Billy." She turned to look out toward the green.

"Then perhaps Billy Ryan was telling the truth. He wasn't the intruder."

"Constable Simpson was satisfied, and Dr. Harrison felt that he must have been mistaken about the dog bite. Billy got off with a warning then, because it would have killed his mother to see him taken up." Her voice was neutral. I couldn't tell whether she was sympathetic to Billy Ryan or disagreed with the Constable.

"Were there any drugs taken? Does Constable Simpson believe that Billy Ryan came back, and this time killed Mr. Spencer?"

She still didn't answer me directly. "Inspector Howe has apparently taken over the inquiry. I'm told that whoever he was, the murderer had time to rifle through Mr. Spencer's belongings but never took anything from Dr. Harrison's medicine cabinet. It's locked, you see. And the lock was still in place. And so there's some—confusion."

It wouldn't do for Inspector Howe to learn what Mrs. Travis thought about the guilty party. I wouldn't put it past Mr. Ellis to tell him as soon as possible. Or did he already suspect us, strangers in the village? Did Sister Potter know more than she felt comfortable telling me?

The silence lengthened. I wished Simon would come back for me, and we could be on our way to Kent and Cousin Melinda's house.

Finally, with a slight frown, Sister Potter broke it. "You and the Sergeant-Major left early that morning. I had risen early myself. There was much to do, to prepare for Mr. Spencer. I'd done most of it the day before, but there were still some things to see to. I saw your motorcar there by the church, before first light."

I was caught off guard. But I looked her in the eye and, avoiding any reference to the Captain, said, "Simon and I had no reason to kill Mr. Spencer. Why should we? I'd done what I could for him when he fell down the stairs at The George."

"Yes, I remember that as well." She took a handkerchief from her pocket, then shoved it back again. "What is going on, Sister Crawford?"

"I wish I knew. But I might as well tell you that Mrs. Travis believes that it was Captain Travis who killed Mr. Spencer. The man her son chose as his heir. Alan Travis is actually here in Sinclair at the moment. And you must know—she's convinced we're accomplices."

"*Was* it this man? The Captain?" Her voice was level, but her gaze held mine, demanding the truth.

"I can't believe it had anything to do with the Captain." For one thing, how would he have found out who Spencer was—or where he was?

Unless he had already known Spencer would be here, and why.

But that too was impossible. He hadn't been allowed visitors in the clinic.

And then, forced by her gaze, I added, "Mr. Spencer's murder might have had something to do with James Travis's will. But I can't quite see how." I debated with myself before telling her more. "When Dr. Harrison decided to move his patient to the surgery, Simon—Sergeant-Major Brandon—went up to Mr. Spencer's room to bring down his valise. The latch hadn't caught properly. He prevented it from spilling everything, but he couldn't help but see. There were papers in there, on Mr. Ellis's stationery, regarding Captain Travis's treatment in a clinic in Wiltshire. What's more, there was a break-in at Mr. Ellis's in Bury. I was never told if anything was missing, or what the thief must have come there to find. I don't even know if the two events are connected."

I took a deep breath, then launched into what had happened to Captain Travis. After all, Mrs. Travis knew, Mr. Ellis knew. It would do no harm to tell Sister Potter the truth.

She listened. Nurses are good listeners; they have to be. When I'd finished, she said, "I must tell you frankly, I'd have worried about his state of mind, if the Captain had been my patient. Of course I might not have met him, as you did, before he was wounded. But what I don't understand is, why should he have thought James shot him? You say they'd liked each other in Paris. What if that isn't the full story? They might have spent more time together than we've been told, and quarreled."

It was something I'd never considered. That there was more to that meeting in Paris than Captain Travis had admitted to me. It would explain why he was so ready to believe his cousin wanted to kill him. Would it have made a difference if he'd said to me, "We quarreled. We ended as enemies"?

I wouldn't have felt quite so guilty for helping him recall James Travis . . .

"I can only answer that as the other officer fired at him, Captain Travis thought he saw a resemblance to a great-uncle. But there's no male relative from Barbados serving in France. There *is* a slight resemblance between James and Alan Travis. But perhaps it wasn't that. Perhaps James looks more like that great-uncle."

Sister Potter smiled. "My mother was a Kerr. From Scotland. And they were noted for being left-handed. So was she. Traits can come down the family tree. Cleft chins, for instance. Baldness. Nearsightedness." The smile faded. "Have you spoken to Mrs. Caldwell? The Vicar's wife?"

"I met her in the churchyard my first day in the village, and spoke to her once after that. She was the one who suggested I look at the memorial in the church."

Nodding, she said, "I'm not surprised. She had a son, you know. He and young James were inseparable as children, in and out of The Hall and the Vicarage. Young Nigel died at ten of a virulent fever. Nothing Dr. Harrison could do stopped its progress. Mrs. Caldwell watched James grow into manhood, thinking, 'Nigel would have done that—Nigel would have enjoyed that—Nigel would have felt like that.' A yardstick, you see, of what she had missed in her own child's lost years. I think she came to love James too. When he was reported killed, it nearly killed her as well. She would have felt that Nigel would have joined the Army too, that he would have been as brave as James, that he might have died in the same way. A terrible blow. I wasn't here, of course, but she wrote to me, long letters talking about her grief, and how she had hoped to see James home again, to wed and have children of his own. She told me she would have wanted to be godmother to one of them, to have a share in something she herself would never have. It was terribly sad. I wrote to her, tried to offer what comfort I could. And she's a strong woman, in the end she put aside her grief and went on living. The Vicar was at a loss how to comfort her. He didn't understand, he'd mourned his son in a very different way. Men often do."

I could understand. I'd never had children, but I had read so many letters from the families of the men I'd taken care of. I tried to write to all those whose names I knew. Some of the men died with *Unknown* on their records, too badly wounded for me to learn any more about them. I'd felt I'd let them down somehow. But if the Army couldn't identify them, how could I?

Sister Potter was looking out the window. "I think your Sergeant-Major has come for you. And is that Captain Travis with him? Ask them to come in —I'll make a fresh pot of tea."

She saw my hesitation. "I won't eat him, much less turn him over to the police. But I'd like to form my own opinion, if you don't mind."

What could I do but go to her door and ask Simon to come in and bring the Captain?

I could see that he was reluctant, quietly saying something to Simon about staying in the motorcar, but I smiled. "It's all right. Please, do come."

And by the time she'd brought in the fresh pot of tea, two large men were sitting in her small parlor, their uneasiness writ large in their eyes, in spite of my assurances.

She walked in, summed up the situation at a glance, and said, "Captain Travis? It's a pleasure to meet you, sir. And to see you again, Sergeant-Major. It quite makes me feel as if I'm back in Trieste for a few days' leave. The hotel was always full of British officers and other ranks."

They smiled, and the next ten minutes were taken up with military matters, questions about the war there, and her views on the strength of the Italian Army and its officers, as well as the political situation now that there was an Armistice.

When we finally came back to England and the problems at hand, she said as bluntly to the Captain as she'd spoken to me, "Even if he were alive, James would never have tried to kill you."

He cast a questioning glance in my direction, then answered, "I know that now. But you have to remember, in the midst of a withdrawal, the machine gunners finding their mark, I wasn't expecting to be attacked by my own side. Just before the Lieutenant brought the rifle to bear, I saw his face, set and determined. He knew what he was doing; he wasn't frightened and shooting at anything, friend or foe. I watched him smile when he saw he'd hit his mark. And then I don't remember much after that."

"And you thought he resembled a great-uncle?"

"That was what ran through my mind as I was facing him. It wasn't until later that I remembered James. It was hard to believe—but I had the evidence of my own eyes. James looked more like my great-uncle than I do. I wanted to know why he should turn on me. And if I had been the only one he shot."

"And were you?"

"In the chaos of that withdrawal, no one even saw me getting shot. Or knew what had become of the other officer. Still, I tried to find him, and I was almost convinced I'd imagined him. Until it happened a second time."

"Were you expecting to be shot a second time—by the same man?" Sister Potter asked. "Were you looking for him to find you again?"

"Good God, I wasn't expecting to be shot by anyone. Not if I could help it."

Satisfied, she nodded. "You have my sympathies, Captain. But you must also remember that mistakes are made in the heat of battles."

"I've had more than enough time to think. You weren't in that small, poorly lit, empty room in the clinic for days, listening to other men scream or beg for mercy or just go on and on and on until you thought you'd run mad just from listening to them. You don't sleep during those nights, and you can't sleep during the day, even if those men are too exhausted to go on screaming. Not with the Sisters and orderlies and doctors looking in on you every half hour to be sure you haven't found a way to kill yourself."

Something in his voice as he spoke reached Sister Potter, and she said, "I have nursed such men. I still hear their cries in my sleep."

They looked at each other, and I thought, *I'm so glad she demanded that he come into the cottage.* For it was one thing for me to believe in him, because I had been there just after he was shot. I knew, firsthand, what the Captain had felt. And whatever reservations Simon might have had he'd kept to himself. But Sister Potter had no reason to believe a word. She could have sided with the doctors and the clinic. And so her opinion mattered. Especially on the heels of Mrs. Travis's tirades.

I said, "We must go. The longer we stay here in the village, the more likely it will be that Constable Simpson will be told we're here."

"I wish you would wait and speak to Mrs. Caldwell. I think it would be good for her as well. If no one else has, I'm sure her husband has told her about Captain Travis. She cared so, it will have hurt her to think someone believed James could have done such a thing."

"I'm afraid to stay any longer," I said. "But if you could tell her what we've told you? It might help."

"What about the will?"

The Captain spoke for himself. "I have a home in Barbados. It's all I want."

Sister Potter sighed. "I understand. Yes, you must go before there's more trouble. I'm sorry you've had such a sad introduction to Sinclair. Godspeed, Captain."

She was ushering us toward the door when there came a thudding knock on the wooden panels, and we froze where we were, like figures in a pantomime. But this wasn't acting. This was fear.

CHAPTER 17

SISTER POTTER SAID at once, "I don't like the sound of that. You must go. Out the kitchen door. Quickly!"

"There's the motorcar," I said. "It's in front of the cottage, for all to see."

The thudding came again.

Simon stepped forward and opened the door.

Constable Simpson stood there, and Mr. Ellis was just behind him, watching anxiously.

"I've been given evidence that indicates Captain Travis"— the Constable peered into the shadows behind Simon—"has information relevant to the suspicious death of Mr. Spencer, in Dr. Harrison's surgery. I've been asked to take him into custody and see that he's taken to Bury St. Edmunds to Inspector Howe, who is charged with looking into this murder."

Listening, I thought it sounded as if he'd been prompted by Mr. Ellis.

Simon stood his ground. "Has Inspector Howe ordered his arrest? What evidence is there, beyond Mr. Ellis's claims, that Captain Travis is even a suspect?"

When Simon was in command, men listened.

Constable Simpson glanced quickly over his shoulder,

looking for reassurance from Mr. Ellis. The man nodded, and the Constable turned back to us. "We are actively searching for Mr. Spencer's killer. We believe the Captain can help us with our inquiries."

Behind me, I heard Sister Potter respond quietly for my ears only, "It's true. The police have knocked on every door. Including mine this morning." Dropping her voice to a whisper, she said to Captain Travis, still in the front room, "Go through to the kitchen. Quickly! Let me deal with the Constable."

She stepped past Simon. "You've already questioned me. The motorcar belongs to the Sergeant-Major here. You must ask him where the Captain is. Sister Crawford came to my house without him. I will swear to that in a courtroom."

It was her own Matron's voice, firm, authoritative, confident, and it was persuasive. Yet she'd told the truth. So far as it went. Constable Simpson was confused. Once more I saw him turn to Mr. Ellis for help.

Frustrated, Mr. Ellis said, "I demand that you search her house."

The Constable, frowning, said, "I can't. I don't have a warrant."

No one so far had questioned Simon. I moved forward. "I came to say good-bye to Sister Potter. We are on our way back to London. If you want to speak to Captain Travis, I suggest you look in the church." And I sent up a silent prayer that none of the neighbors looking out a window or someone in the street had seen Captain Travis come through Sister Potter's door.

Constable Simpson was in a quandary, and he wasn't possessed of a strong enough character to withstand Mr. Ellis.

The solicitor was saying, "I'll stay here while you bring back Inspector Howe. There's my motorcar. Can you manage it? Yes? Then drive to Bury as fast as you can, and bring Inspector Howe—and a warrant—back with you as soon as possible."

"He could walk right by you," the Constable protested. "You can't arrest him."

"He won't get by me," Mr. Ellis answered him roundly. "And if he tries, I'll follow him."

"What about the Sister and the Sergeant-Major? They'll spirit him out of the cottage somehow while I'm away."

I thanked Sister Potter for tea, said good-bye, and walked past Simon, past the Constable, and past Mr. Ellis, who eyed me sourly. He'd have stopped me if he could, but he wanted Captain Travis more than he wanted me. After the briefest hesitation, Simon followed me. I had no idea where Captain Travis had got to, but my greatest fear was that he would feel he'd caused enough trouble for everyone and gallantly give himself up.

But he kept his head. We reached the motorcar without looking back, and then Sister Potter called, "Don't forget—you promised to say good-bye to Mrs. Caldwell before you leave the village. She'll be very upset if you don't. I'd like very much to come with you, but I don't trust these men not to invade my house while my back is turned, and I refuse to have them turn it upside down hunting for someone who isn't even here." And with that she shut her door with such firmness it sounded like a slam, right in Constable Simpson's face.

As Simon bent to turn the crank, I saw the Constable's frustration as he moved away from the door and said something to the solicitor.

And then we were pulling away. I tried to look as if I weren't worried about the situation at the cottage. For all I knew, Sister Potter had already smuggled the Captain out the kitchen door, but where would he go? And what about the neighbors who might see him leaving in such an odd fashion while the village Constable was standing outside the other door? They were sure to take notice.

But there was nothing I could do.

As if he'd heard my worry, Simon commented, "We can't help him if we're taken up with him."

That was true. Comforting—but not erasing all of my worry.

"Where do we go? The rectory?"

I gave it some thought. "Let's try the church first."

He drove up the lane and stopped in front of St. Mary's. I got down and he joined me as we walked across the churchyard to the south porch. I was reminded again that I'd left the Captain here for much of the night, and the figure I'd seen walking in the shadows had—so I thought then—just come from the surgery. In fact, I'd thought it might well be Spencer himself . . .

We had just reached the porch when I heard a motorcar and looked back the way we'd come. Constable Simpson had been persuaded to go fetch Inspector Howe. Mr. Ellis was still there by Sister Potter's door.

The south door creaked on its hinges as I walked into the nave. It was bright now, but I still remembered it in the dark, with only moonlight and Simon's torch letting us find our way.

I heard something and looked toward the altar. Mrs. Caldwell came out from behind the pulpit, an empty vase in her hands.

"Oh," she said, seeing who it was. "I thought it might be my husband. Have you come for him?"

"I spoke to you a few days ago. About James Travis," I began, walking toward her. "Perhaps you remember telling me about the plaque?"

Her gaze strayed toward it. "Yes, I do," she said, a note of sadness in her voice, and then she added briskly, "I'm told you've been upsetting his mother. Mrs. Travis."

I stopped midway down the aisle. "Not on purpose—well, I did want her to help someone, but she refused."

"The heir? James's heir?" She turned to put the vase down, looked at her hands, dusted them together, and then said, "I have wondered . . . what sort of person he might be."

Then Mr. Caldwell hadn't told her yet about the confrontation at The Hall.

"He's from an island in the Caribbean. Barbados. I met him before he was wounded. And I liked him. Very much. I also happened to be in the forward aid station close by his regiment. He was wounded. Twice." I was choosing my words carefully. "He's been in a clinic in Wiltshire, recovering."

"Oh. How sad."

I had a feeling she meant it.

"I don't think Mrs. Travis cared much for him, even before she met him. And the meeting didn't go well. She's accused him of all sorts of things. I expect she hopes that by doing so she can set him aside as heir."

Mrs. Caldwell's mouth tightened. "I think her grief has turned her mind. A little. It's—I've said nothing, my husband's living is in her hands. But if James made this man his heir, then he wanted him to inherit The Hall." She looked again toward the brass plaque. "It was a great tragedy that he was killed," she went on quietly. "I know that every man who died belonged to someone, and his loss was felt deeply. But this was James, and his mother had suffered enough heartache. Sometimes God is cruel. I don't know why. People tell me that it only makes you stronger, to face loss and survive. I don't believe they know what they're saying. It doesn't make you stronger, it simply breaks you in ways you can't recover from."

I realized all at once that she was talking about herself and her own loss. About the young man who had taken her son's place, in some obscure fashion, and given her something to cling to after the unimaginable sorrow of a child dying young. Just as Sister Potter had told us.

"Captain Travis needs help," I said, after giving her a moment. "Let me explain."

And I did, as concisely as possible. Simon was standing at the south porch door, watching The Pottery. Time was running away with every tick of the clock in the tower.

She listened without interrupting me, then when I'd finished, she said resolutely, "Tell me what I can do."

I was surprised. I'd only come because Sister Potter had insisted, and because we didn't dare leave the village without Captain Travis. Mrs. Caldwell was an unlikely ally, but I was grateful for her willingness to help someone in need.

"He's trapped in the cottage with Sister Potter, and the door is being guarded by Mr. Ellis while Constable Simpson goes to Bury to bring back Inspector Howe."

"This is a sanctuary church. Did you know? Perhaps Sister Potter remembered. If we can get him this far, the police can't touch him. The question is, how can we accomplish that?"

Behind me, Simon stirred. "If I remember correctly, sanctuary was abolished by James the First."

"Was it indeed?" She seemed surprised. "Well, we'll just have to think of another way." Glancing up at the light from the windows, she went on. "It's getting dark. I can find my way to the kitchen door of Sister Potter's house, and guide this Captain Travis to meet you at an appointed place. By the time Inspector Howe reaches the village, he'll be gone and Sister Potter won't find herself in trouble for harboring him."

I realized that she wanted to see this man James Travis had made his heir. Very badly. I knew then I could trust her.

It was the best solution we could come up with, to allow her to guide him, and we agreed, after much debate, that we would meet her—and the Captain—at The Swan in Clare, the village just down the road from this one. "It's rather a long walk," she told us anxiously. "Can he manage it?"

"Yes, I believe so," I told her.

"Then I'll see you at The Swan. You can't miss it. And no one will think it odd if we meet there. This village might just as well be on the moon, as far as Clare is concerned."

She left her shears, the vase, and the rest of the holly branches she had been trimming, then took off her apron. She was wearing her coat against the chill in the church, and she pulled her gloves from a pocket, along with a woolen cap.

We hurried back to the motorcar, and Mrs. Caldwell got quickly into the rear while I watched Mr. Ellis. His back to us, he was staring at the door of The Pottery as if he could see through the wood. Mrs. Caldwell ducked out of sight as we drove down Church Lane and turned toward the outskirts of the village. Mr. Ellis, hearing us, turned quickly to peer at the motorcar, expecting to see Captain Travis with us. We ignored him and drove on.

When we were beyond the last house in the village, Simon pulled to the verge and Mrs. Caldwell got out. We sat there, watching her disappear in the gathering dusk, for the sun had dropped behind a bank of clouds.

As we waited, I said to Simon, "How on earth did you know when sanctuary had been canceled?"

He was watching her walk on, and didn't turn. "An odd fact that somehow was fixed in my mind."

I didn't believe him, but this was no time to be pressing him for details. I still didn't know exactly what he thought about the Captain, but he'd done his best to help.

After a few minutes, when we were fairly certain that she wasn't coming back, we drove on to Clare and quickly found the black-and-white Tudor inn with its sign above the door: THE SWAN.

Inside, Simon asked for two rooms, and then we settled down to wait. I ordered tea, more to warm myself than out of hunger, and Simon asked for sandwiches for himself and a bowl of soup for me.

"We might have to move quickly," he said. "Just as well to eat while we can."

And then there was nothing we could do but be patient.

The tea trade had come and gone. I'd seen them in the pretty room to one side of where we sat in a nook just off the bar. There was a fire on the hearth beside us as well as one in the little tea-room, and I watched one of the girls who had been serving bring in more scuttles of coal for the dinner trade. Meanwhile, the bar was filling up, men talking and laughing, occasionally casting curious glances in our direction. The serious drinking wouldn't begin until later, but already the talk was growing louder as the taps were kept busy.

I looked at my little watch for the seventh or eighth time. The hour hand seemed to be moving faster now. It was already close on six, and even on foot two people walking to Clare should have arrived by now.

"What has gone wrong?" I asked Simon in a low voice.

"Give them time. They might not have been able to come directly here. Much will depend on when Howe arrives from Bury."

The church clock struck six. And then the quarter past, the half, and still no sign of them.

"We can't leave. It would be our luck that they arrived by a less direct route, just after we drove back to search for them."

"It will be all right. Be patient."

But that was growing more and more difficult. During a lull in the conversation at the bar, as men went home to their dinners and before the post-dinner drinkers arrived, I heard the church clock strike seven.

By seven thirty, I knew something was wrong—had known it, truth be told, since we set Mrs. Caldwell down to go after the Captain.

"They could have had to hide, if a search was going on," Simon told me, forestalling my next question.

"I don't think so. Mrs. Caldwell was so certain she could do this."

He was silent. Seven thirty. We'd got here a little past four thirty.

I reached for my coat. "I can't sit here any longer. Something has happened, and we need to *know*."

Simon, whose chair had a better view of the door, said, "Bess." It was a warning, and I turned quickly to see a very worried Vicar step through the door and search the bar.

Simon rose, and Mr. Caldwell, only a little relieved, hurried over to where we were now standing.

"What is it?" I asked before he could even draw breath to speak.

"My wife has sent me. She's in Bury. The dogs in the house next but one to Mrs. Horner's tea shop began to bark. Ill-trained little terriers, but it's a sharp bark, and it drew the attention of Inspector Howe, who had just arrived. Travis was already out the kitchen door, and he was moving so quietly that Vera missed him somehow in the dark. Howe found him first, and Vera reached them just afterward. Needless to say, Inspector Howe has taken the Captain into custody." He looked from Simon to me. "How did you drag my poor wife into this? Did you tell her that this was what James would have wanted? What have you done? I can't bear to see her *cry*."

Distraught as he was, it took us a quarter of an hour to calm him enough to ask him questions. Apparently Mrs. Caldwell had insisted on being taken to Bury as well, and Inspector Howe, in no mood to deal with what he thought was a troublesome woman, not only took her to Bury but put her in another cell for aiding and abetting the escape of a murderer.

Sister Potter had gone to find the Vicar, met him on his way back from The Hall, and told him what had happened. He went directly to Bury, and his wife told him where to find us.

"But surely they won't keep her," I said. "And what about Sister Potter, have they dragged her into this as well?"

He sighed. "They couldn't prove that Travis had come from her house. They had no grounds to hold her. That had already angered Howe, and by the time he encountered Vera—my wife—he was in no mood to show anyone any mercy. Look, you've got to do *something*. You got her into this, you must go to Inspector Howe and tell him that she was misguided and just trying to *help*."

He looked to be at his wits' end. Dusty from traveling from the village to Bury and then to The Swan, exhausted, worried, and afraid for his wife, he was beyond reasoning with.

I said, "Of course we'll go at once to see that she's set free. I'm so sorry, it shouldn't have ended this way." It was sheer bad luck, but he didn't want to hear that. "But first, would you like a sherry—tea? It will help."

"No, no, I couldn't swallow anything, not with Vera in a cell. It smells, it's filthy. It's no place for my *wife*."

Simon helped me on with my coat, took up his own, and said, "The motorcar's just outside. But I must settle our account. Go on, and I'll follow."

I urged Mr. Caldwell to come with me, and after a moment's uncertainty, he did. I got him in the rear seat and went to turn the crank. Then I climbed into the driver's seat.

The Vicar was craning his neck, trying to see through the windows, looking for Simon.

"We took rooms. We thought we were on our way to Kent. He'll have to deal with that as well as our tea," I said, resisting the temptation to peer through the windows as well.

And still no sign of Simon.

The Vicar already had his door open and was about to get down when Simon finally appeared, his face grim.

He gestured for me to move over, but I shook my head. I'd driven his motorcar before and I was going to drive it now. His mouth tightened into a thin line, but he didn't argue. He picked up the vicar's bicycle, leaning against one of the flower boxes by the windows, found rope in the boot, and quickly lashed it in place. Another man had come out of The Swan just behind him, setting off at a trot in the opposite direction. I started to say something to Simon about him, worried that he might be on his way to the police. There was no reason to think he was, but by this time I was truly worried. Anyone could have overheard the Vicar and taken it into his head to go for help.

Simon stepped into the motorcar, I dealt with the clutch and the brake, and we were moving at a good clip past the church and to the turning for Sinclair.

After a moment, Simon asked me, "Do you remember Major Inglis?"

I blinked. It was unexpected, and it took me several seconds to realize what Simon was telling me.

Major Inglis had been in command of a troop of cavalry that my father had sent for to help put down a rising in one of the villages near the Khyber Pass.

I smiled, realizing that Simon had just told me that he'd sent for the cavalry. I didn't know how he'd managed it, but then I remembered. This village had a train station, and there must be a telegraph office as well.

"What does Major Inglis have to do with this matter?" the Vicar asked, suspicious.

"Nothing," I said. "Except that he was a very brave man, and the Sergeant-Major is trying to keep my spirits up."

I drove with speed, but also with care. Once, I heard the Vicar start to say something and then think better of it as we rounded a bend in the road a little too fast. It was a dangerous stretch, I remembered that too, and slowed a bit.

We reached the outskirts of Bury, coming up the hill and around buildings that jutted out in our way, making it necessary to swing around them. And finally I saw the police station.

I didn't draw up in front but went past and around the corner. There I pulled over and said, "We can walk back."

We stepped through the door of the station and saw a Sergeant just coming out of a door on our left.

It was the Vicar who spoke first. "My wife. I'm here to see her."

"Yes, sir, if you'll just come this way." He glanced at us, and I knew that Inspector Howe hadn't expected us to come here. The Sergeant hadn't been forewarned.

I said, "And I should like to see Captain Travis, if you please. I'm the Sister assigned to his care."

"And the Sergeant-Major?" the Sergeant asked.

"He's here to see that I come to no harm."

The Sergeant went away and came back with a ring of keys, then led us toward the rear of the station.

There were only three cells beyond the locked door we had just passed through. And two were occupied. Mrs. Caldwell started to speak. Just then her husband came through the door after Simon, and she turned to him.

Captain Travis had the makings of a very nasty black eye, and there was a scrape on his chin.

"My goodness, Captain, whatever shall I tell Matron?" I said, before he could greet us.

Wary now, he said only, "They took exception to my efforts to escape."

"I shall make a note of that. Matron will not be happy—"

Behind me I heard the Sergeant close the outer door—and although I listened carefully, I didn't hear him turn the key.

Relieved, I said softly, "And how are you?"

"Well enough. I almost made it, that was the damnable thing. But the dogs belonging to one of the houses I was passing heard me and set up a racket. I tried to move away, but there was a locked gate in the next back garden, and I had to go around. The pity is, I saw Mrs. Caldwell coming from the other direction, and I thought she must be one of the pursuers. I was moving away from her when the police caught sight of me and gave chase. I don't know how the Inspector got there so quickly. He must have been on his way, and Constable Simpson intercepted him."

Mrs. Caldwell had soothed her husband, and she called to us. "I wanted to be sure they didn't strike him again. The Inspector can't keep me. I have asked to see the local Vicar, claiming I was arrested under false pretenses. He'll speak to the police."

"How did you explain being out there?" I asked.

"I was searching for my cat. She was frightened by a passing lorry, and she hasn't come home." Her eyes twinkled. "Fortunately they didn't search the rectory, or they would have found her asleep on the hearth rug."

Mr. Caldwell told her that it was wrong to lie, and she said, impatient with him now, "Yes, I understand, my dear, but surely you wouldn't wish my little escapade to reach Mrs. Travis's ears. It's all a very sad misunderstanding." She glanced toward the door, as if half expecting the Sergeant to be listening on the other side. Lowering her voice, she said, "They haven't discovered that Mr. Spencer had come to Sinclair to see me. I hired him to find out about Captain Travis. But he refused to send for the Vicar, and so I had no idea that he was in the village to make his report. I thought—well, I thought he must be passing through on other business. I'd never met him, you see, and his wasn't the name I'd dealt with when I contacted the Florian Agency in London."

"Vera—" the Vicar protested.

"Yes, well, Margaret Travis was refusing to do anything, and that man Ellis was too weak to face her down. And so I did what I could." Tears filled her eyes suddenly. "How would you feel if it were Nigel's last wishes, and someone refused to address them, much less carry them out?"

"Nigel is dead, my dear," he said, infinite sadness in his voice. "He never went to war, and I thank God every day that he was spared that horror. James isn't your son, he never was."

"Of course he wasn't," she said, her voice thick with tears, "I always knew that. But he was a measure, you see. A measure by which I could remember Nigel, and think, 'He'd be as tall as James . . . He would be good at cricket like James . . . He would stop and admire my garden, just as James often did.' It was a comfort to me. You had your God, and I had James." She buried her face in her hands then, her shoulders shaking, and the Vicar couldn't reach her to console her.

The door opened and Inspector Howe strode in. "Quite a gathering, I see," he said. "Good evening, Sister Crawford.

Sergeant-Major. Tell me why I shouldn't unlock these and put you inside as well."

"I should like to hear the charges," I said before Simon could come to my defense.

"I'm sure you would. Interference with the police in pursuing their duties, to start with."

"Did you find Captain Travis in Sister Potter's house?"

"I did not, but it was clear he'd just left it."

"Can you prove that he was in Sister Potter's cottage? Did you find any evidence to show that he had come from there or was headed there?"

"No, but he wasn't far from it."

"Nor was he far from Mrs. Horner's tea shop and several other dwellings. Mrs. Caldwell tells me she was close by where you found the Captain, but if you ask her, she will give you her word that she had never met Captain Travis until you found her searching for her cat at the same time you were searching for him. When I stopped to say good-bye to her, she was in the church, arranging greenery for services. If you don't care to believe me, go there and look for yourself. The holly is only half-trimmed."

"Sister," Mr. Caldwell warned, his tone indicating that it wasn't my place to challenge Inspector Howe.

I wanted to tell him to speak up for his wife rather than criticize me, but there was too much at stake to upset him.

"Is this true, Mrs. Caldwell? That until the encounter in the Brentwoods' back garden you had never met or spoken with the Captain before?"

"I give you my solemn word, I had not."

So far we had spoken only the truth, if not the entire truth, except for the matter of the cat.

And then Mr. Caldwell said reluctantly, "The cat does roam.

Mrs. Brentwood has a female from the same litter, and they are friends."

Faced with such corroboration, Inspector Howe gave up. I don't think he particularly cared to have a Vicar's wife in custody. He called to his Sergeant and had the door to Mrs. Caldwell's cell unlocked. She cast a grateful glance my way as she stepped across the threshold and said firmly, "Thank you, Inspector Howe. I am happy to see that justice prevails."

But there was nothing I could do for the Captain. Not yet. I heard Simon offering to drive the Vicar and his wife back to Sinclair, and for a moment I thought Mr. Caldwell was about to refuse him. It was late, and cold, and his bicycle was not comfortable for two. Finally he said, "I thank you, sir," as if he'd just been offered his choice of poisons.

As they started through the door, I had an opportunity to speak quickly to Captain Travis. "Don't worry."

But I could see his face clearly, and behind the exhaustion lurked the very real worry that before I could do anything to help him, he would be brought up on a charge of murder and sent back to the clinic in chains.

The four of us drove in an uncomfortable silence back toward the village. It had begun to rain, a chill and penetrating rain, and as it beat against the windscreen, I thought about what lay ahead. For me, for Captain Travis.

The two men were riding in the front, staring straight ahead. In the darkness of the rear seat, Mrs. Caldwell reached out a hand and clasped mine. Her fingers were cold—I don't know what had become of her gloves—and I put both of mine over hers to warm them a little.

And then, as if she'd found courage in the touch, she said to her husband, "You must know, if the police in Bury charge Captain Travis with the murder of that poor man in Dr. Harrison's surgery, I shall expect you to do your very best to see that he's set free."

"Vera. I can't do that. Mrs. Travis will be furious with me if I even try. Our son is buried in the churchyard of St. Mary's. I don't want to be forced to leave this church. Please understand. It would be more than I could bear." He turned his head a little, to look toward her in the dimness of the rear seat. "What is this man to you? You swore you'd never met him. Was that a lie?"

"It was not," she said firmly.

"Then why do you care so much?"

"I have mourned Nigel in my own way."

"Yes, with this unhealthy obsession with James Travis."

"What is unhealthy about watching my son's best friend grow up, and wishing I could have seen Nigel at the same age? His life didn't stop for me when we lowered his casket into the ground. The little boy I lost would have been a man now, and now the only mirror I had of what might have been, of what he might have done, if he'd lived, has been taken from me. This is a mother's grief, my dear, not obsession."

"Yes, very well," he said, goaded, "but you have no reason I can think of to support this Captain Travis. I won't allow it, do you understand?"

"Very well. You leave me no choice. If the police charge Captain Travis with the murder of Mr. Spencer, I will go to Bury if I have to walk there, and I will tell them that they have arrested the wrong person. That I killed Mr. Spencer myself. After all, I had hired him. And *that* I can prove."

CHAPTER 18

THERE WAS AN electric silence in the motorcar. It was as if the world beyond our headlamps didn't exist, as if the farms and cottages along the road, an uneven pattern of squares of light in the darkness, were only a backdrop to the misery in our midst.

I thought Mrs. Caldwell was crying softly, and I found a handkerchief to offer her. The Vicar seemed to be struggling with his shock, his duty to Mrs. Travis, and a wife who had suddenly become a person he no longer knew.

"I fail to understand you, Vera. To go behind my back and interfere in Mrs. Travis's affairs is unconscionable. I still can't believe you contacted the Florian Agency. This just isn't like you." His throat was tight, and his voice came through the constriction with a harshness that must have cut his wife to the quick.

She sighed. "It would have been all right, if he'd just told you who he was looking for. But then you never got to speak to him, did you? He refused to see the local Vicar, unaware that you were Mr. Caldwell. I had no idea who he was, everyone thought he was just passing through the village. I expected something by post, I didn't know the Agency had sent someone to speak to me in person. And so I never got his report."

"Vera, in God's name, what possessed you to do such a mad thing?"

"I was sick of the way Mrs. Travis and Mr. Ellis ignored James's will. It was *his* will, you see, not yours or theirs. It was the disposition *he* wished to make of *his* estate, and he provided for his mother and for all the staff and the church, and the poor. *His* estate, Michael. What would you say to him, if by some miracle it was discovered that he hadn't been killed, that he was a prisoner of the Germans or some such, and the Army had made a mistake? What would you have said to him, when he came home at last, only to find that his will had been set aside? How would you have justified supporting his mother instead of seeing that right was done?"

"He's dead, Vera. He won't be coming back." It was almost a cry.

"You don't know that. The war has just ended, there hasn't been an accounting. You are putting your own comfort ahead of what is *right*."

We were just coming into the village now. The streets were empty, save for a single figure hurrying homeward under his black umbrella. Lamps were lit in the houses and cottages, but the shops were dark. It was well past the dinner hour, and people were snug in their homes.

We had nearly arrived at The George when Mrs. Caldwell reached out to touch Simon's shoulder. "Sergeant-Major, will you stop at the inn, please. I don't feel that I can go home tonight. Perhaps in the morning, when I am stronger."

Her husband began to protest, but she stood firm. "Tomorrow we will talk. Tonight I need silence."

Simon did as he was told, and she got down, turning to me and saying, "Shall I ask for a room for you? You've no place to stay."

It was Simon who answered. "Yes, please. I'll be in directly, as soon as I've taken the Vicar home."

"Yes, do that, please." And she turned resolutely and walked through the rain to the inn door, opening and closing it without looking back.

Mr. Caldwell, distressed and embarrassed that we had been witnesses to his confrontation with his wife, said, "That was wrong of you, sir."

Simon answered him. "She made her wishes known. If you disagree, you can come down to The George and reason with her."

We drove on to the Vicarage, and Simon left the motor running as he got down to unlash the bicycle from the boot. Mr. Caldwell took it from him, gave him a curt nod, and disappeared up the walk to his door.

It would be a cold homecoming, I thought.

I didn't know the right or wrong of their disagreement, but I could understand both sides of the issue, to some extent. The Vicar was beholden to Mrs. Travis for his livelihood. And Mrs. Caldwell was emotionally tied to James Travis, because he was her son's friend, his surrogate.

As Simon pulled away from the Vicarage, I said, "Should we stay here? Or return to The Swan?"

"Here, I think. It's closer to Bury. And I don't think we should leave Mrs. Caldwell alone."

We had settled into our former rooms and were dressing for a late dinner when there was a commotion on the stairs. I hurried to my door to see what it was about. My first thought was that Mr. Caldwell, finding his courage, had come back to demand his wife's return to the Vicarage.

But when I opened my door, it wasn't the Vicar coming up the stairs, it was Mrs. Travis, followed by the inn's owner, remonstrating with her.

"She's here, I have been informed that she is here. I *will* speak to her."

Mrs. Travis saw me, and her face flushed. "*You*. I should have known you were behind this."

I said nothing, and she arrived in the passage in almost a frenzy. "I will not have you or anyone else interfere in the affairs of my family. Mr. Ellis tells me that the Vicar's wife was taken into custody for trying to keep the police from arresting that madman. It was your doing. She would never have crossed me like that if you hadn't put her up to it." I flinched at the fury in her face.

Simon had come to his door, standing staunchly behind me, and she stepped back to the top of the stairs.

"I have been tormented by people since my son's death," she said, her anger crumbling into anguish. "I wish it would end. I have tried to do what my husband asked of me. I have *tried*."

Fearful that Mrs. Caldwell would feel it was necessary to come out of her room and face Mrs. Travis, I reached out and took her arm. "This is no place to talk. You don't wish the staff to hear you." Opening the door to my room, over her protests I gently led her in to the chair by the fire, and Simon followed us, closing the door.

She stared into the fire, lost in a past I couldn't know.

And then she straightened. "You don't understand how it was," she said finally. "It was my husband's grandmother who was at the heart of this quarrel. She was still alive when he was a boy, he knew what had happened. I never learned the whole of it, but she loved both brothers, you see, and had to choose. She married my husband's grandfather, but they were never really happy. The shadow of the brother who left England was always between them, and Hugh told me his grandfather was never sure whether it was The Hall that weighed in his favor, or if she truly loved him best. Hugh's father had an unhappy childhood, even though Nicholas, his grandfather, had prayed for a son. Always a son. And when James was born, you would have thought I'd delivered a prince of the realm, because it meant that the line continued. James knew this, he understood that his duty was to provide the next heir. And if this God-bereft war hadn't started, he might well have done just that. I would have given anything to be spared his loss."

I remembered Captain Travis telling me about his great-grandfather leaving England to settle in the islands. I hadn't got the impression that the same sort of black cloud had hung over his family for generations. Of course he might not have mentioned it to a stranger, but still, the way he spoke of the past never hinted at anything like this.

Still, it was true that the winner in such a quarrel often found it hard to believe in his good fortune. Or found it harder still to believe he deserved to win.

I wished I could see a portrait of the woman who had loved two brothers, to see for myself whether she'd suffered from her husband's suspicions. Then it occurred to me that it was her husband, the man she had chosen, whose likeness might tell me more. Instead I had only Mrs. Travis's version of events.

But there was that plain stone in the churchyard . . .

This branch of the Travis family must have suffered more than the one that had made its way to a Caribbean island. Easier for them to forget a house in far-off England.

There was no comfort I could offer.

She sat there, wrapped in her misery, refusing to break down, and yet at the end of her strength to fight battles that had never been hers but had been forced on her.

It was Simon who broke the silence.

"If not your son—if not Captain Travis, who should inherit the estate? Who would you be satisfied to see in your son's place?"

"I don't know," she said, her voice infinitely sad. "There is no one. Oliver Masters, perhaps. I can't even be sure that the connection is real. Hugh never found a common ancestor. And I haven't seen Oliver since he was a boy. I've tried to keep up the pretense that there was someone else."

She drew her dignity around her like a shield and rose. "Did Captain Travis kill that man? The one in Dr. Harrison's surgery? Rumor says he's been taken up by the police."

I hesitated a second too long before answering her.

Simon moved away from the door, where he'd been standing. "I think Inspector Howe was relieved to find a suspect. *Any* suspect. And Mr. Ellis was certain that the Captain was guilty. I wonder why."

Mrs. Travis shook her head, weary now. "He knows how strongly I've felt about Alan Travis inheriting. He's given me his support from the start. As he should—his family has served ours for generations." She walked out like a queen going to the guillotine, back straight, chin high.

Concerned about her, I caught up my coat and followed her to the door, walking down the stairs with her to see her to her motorcar.

Miss Fredericks was standing beside it, her face anxious, a bicycle by her side.

"They've sent me from the house to find you, Mrs. Travis. There's an officer, just arrived. He's asking for you."

Mrs. Travis turned to me. "Dear God. They've set Captain Travis free," she said. "I don't want to see him again, I can't bear it. Not now, not tonight."

"I'll ride with you, and ask him to leave," I told her, striving to conceal my relief that Inspector Howe had come to his senses and let the Captain go. I could take him to Melinda in Kent now, and let her deal with the clinic. I heard footsteps behind me. "Simon, will you drive out? You can bring me back to The George."

He was already moving toward his own motorcar.

I got in beside Mrs. Travis while the heavyset chauffeur dealt with the bicycle as if it were a child's toy, and Miss Fredericks got in next to him.

I was very tired now, and I only wanted this to be finished.

We rode in silence, Mrs. Travis picking at her gloves, her face tight with something I couldn't read in the dimness.

It wasn't a very great distance back to The Hall. I could hear Miss Fredericks speaking to the chauffeur in a low voice, but I couldn't make out the words.

We turned in through the gates and followed the drive to the door. A cab from Bury was already there, the driver obviously told to wait.

Mrs. Travis got down, moved reluctantly to the door, and took a deep breath as it opened and one of her maids, an older woman I hadn't seen before, stood there.

"Madame," she said, and something else that I didn't hear.

Miss Fredericks had touched my arm just as Mrs. Travis had turned her back. Standing on tiptoe, she leaned toward me. "There's something wrong. I'm frightened."

And then she was gone, taking her bicycle from the chauffeur and disappearing around the side of the house.

That galvanized me, and I hurried to the door before the maid could shut it after Mrs. Travis. In the hall, we gave up our coats and prepared to go into the drawing room. Simon, arriving on our heels, opened the outer door in time to join us.

Mrs. Travis stopped in midstride and turned away. "No, I won't do this. I won't see him. Just—take him away. Please." And she moved swiftly to the stairs and began to climb them, leaving us to stare after her.

The maid, confused, said to me, "He wished to see Madame. He told me she knew him."

"Yes, I understand," I told her, finding a smile. "But she's given me instructions. It will be all right."

I could see the doubt in her eyes, but she led us to the drawing room door and opened it for us.

Only one lamp had been lit, although a fire was blazing merrily on the hearth. I could hear the crackle of the flames as I came through the door. He was standing in the shadows by the long windows, his back to us, looking out into the darkness.

His name was on my tongue, I was already preparing to ask him please to go back to The George with us, when I realized that it wasn't Captain Travis.

The two men were similar in height and coloring, and I could see only the back of his uniform, not his rank or regiment.

He turned in the same instant. "Mrs. Travis? I'm so sorry about James—" He broke off with a frown. I was clearly not the mistress of the house. "My apologies," he said at once.

"Lieutenant?" I asked, noting his rank. "I'm Sister Crawford."

The frown deepened. "Have we met?" He looked beyond me. "Sergeant-Major. I was expecting to speak to Mrs. Travis. Don't tell me—she's not ill, surely." He moved forward, into the fire's glow, holding out his hand. "My name is Martin Bonham."

It was my turn to be surprised. My first thought as he'd faced us was that this must be Oliver Masters. Mrs. Travis and I had just been talking about him, and this man was telling us he'd known James. My second was the fleeting feeling that he'd been a patient of mine. But it was gone in an instant, and I wasn't even sure I'd seen it.

Behind me, Simon stirred.

"Lieutenant," I said again, trying to recover. "It's my turn to apologize. Mrs. Travis has just come in, and she went to her room to rest. Perhaps I can take a message to her for you?"

"I didn't intend to disturb her," he said contritely, with a smile. "I served with James, you see. I wrote to his mother after he was killed, and we've corresponded a time or two since then. She wanted to know everything I could tell her about him. I'd like to think it brought her some comfort. I'm home on compassionate leave—my favorite aunt has been ill. I felt I should come and speak to Mrs. Travis in person. I liked James very much. He was a good friend."

Oh, dear, I thought. *She'll wish to see this visitor.*

"Let me go up and speak to her—to see if she feels like coming down. The maid only told us that someone had come to speak to her. We didn't know who it was."

"Please, if she's resting, I don't want to disturb her."

"We'll see," I told him.

I left them together, Lieutenant Bonham and Simon, and went to find the maid. That took me downstairs to the kitchen, where what was left of the staff had just finished their dinner. The maid rose at once, a questioning look on her face, and the other women stared. The only man was the chauffeur, and in the brightness of the servants' hall, without his cap, I could see that he must be close to sixty. He rose too.

"Please, could you show me to Mrs. Travis's room?" I asked. "I must relay a message to her."

The maid came forward as the chauffeur asked, "Will she be needing me again this evening, Sister?"

"I don't know. I shouldn't think so."

And the maid and I went back to the hall, climbed the main staircase, and came to a halt outside a room that must be above the drawing room, with the same floor-to-ceiling windows.

I knocked and called, "Mrs. Travis, may I come in?"

After a moment, she said, "Come," in a cold voice, and I opened the door.

It was a beautiful room, although it was lit only by the fire's brightness. The walls were a pale lavender, trimmed in white, and there were slightly darker lavender drapes pulled across the windows. There was a rose coverlet over the bed, and the chair in which she was sitting was also covered in a rose fabric. All very feminine.

"What is it, Sister?" she asked, anxious. "Is he refusing to leave? Please ask the Sergeant-Major to make him go."

"Your visitor isn't Captain Travis," I said. "It's Lieutenant Bonham. He's in England on compassionate leave from his regiment. His aunt has been ill. He's come to see you."

Her face brightened in a way I had never seen, happiness erasing lines of grief and anger. I thought, *This is the woman who loved her son, who had been mistress of The Hall before her world came to an end.*

"How thoughtful of him," she said, rising. "Oh, dear, I must look a fright. Will you light that lamp over there, Sister? Maddie," she went on to the maid, "you must help me with my hair."

It took ten minutes to satisfy her that she looked well enough to receive her guest. And her step was light as she crossed to the door and walked down the passage to the stairs.

I couldn't help but think about the contrast between her happiness over this visitor and her harshness toward Captain Travis, still in that cold and empty cell, so like the cold and empty room in the clinic.

Her head was held high as she crossed to the door of the drawing room and reached out to open it. "My dear," she said, walking in and greeting Lieutenant Bonham. "How very kind of you to come and see me. Have you dined? And you must stay the night. It's a long drive back to London."

Someone had lit two more lamps, and the room was bright. The Lieutenant came to greet her, holding out his hands and taking hers in a warm clasp.

"I am so glad to meet James's mother at long last," he said, smiling. "I couldn't go back to France without seeing you. It was late to call, but I couldn't have got here any sooner."

"Sister Crawford told me your aunt has been ill, that that's why you're in England. How is she?"

"Much better, I'm happy to say. She has a weak heart, and any prolonged illness is difficult for her. We feared pneumonia, but she appears to be herself again."

"I'm glad. You must tell her how much it means, your coming all this way to see me. She's kind to spare you."

It was as if we didn't exist, Simon and I. The Lieutenant led her to the chairs by the hearth, still talking about his aunt and then asking after *her* health, mentioning that I'd told him she had had a tiring day.

"It was, but all the better for your being here."

I was reminded suddenly of Mrs. Caldwell, who had found in James a surrogate for her dead child. Was this man a surrogate for James? Someone from the war who had known him, fought beside him, and could tell her about the son who had gone where she couldn't follow, the son she'd not been able to hold as he died?

So many mothers had said much the same thing to me in

letters. That their greatest sorrow was not being there to bring comfort to their boy at the end. However old he might be, he was still their boy . . .

And how many young men had called for their mothers as they lay dying?

I turned away, caught Simon's eye, and sent him a silent message. He'd been standing near the door, and he quietly opened it. We left without either the Lieutenant or Mrs. Travis noticing.

I took a deep breath as he closed the door behind us and led the way to the outer door.

"I felt like an intruder in there," I said as we walked out into the rainy night. "It would have been wrong to stay."

"Yes." He opened the door of the motorcar, and I got in, shivering after the warmth of the house. He turned the crank and got in beside me. The cab from Bury was still there, waiting. I thought someone ought to have asked the driver to go to the servants' hall for a hot drink. But he'd been forgotten, and it was not my place to suggest it.

As our headlamps swept over his motorcar I could see him huddled in his seat, a rug pulled up to his chin.

Simon was silent until we'd passed through the gates and turned toward the village.

"I think," he said slowly as we drove through the night, "that that man is the one who shot Captain Travis."

Lost in my own thoughts, I sat up and turned to stare at Simon. "Are you quite serious?"

"Never more so. I brought the conversation around to the last days of the war. Bess, he served in the same sector as Alan Travis. He had no idea I knew the Captain. He described that retreat in detail. I've spoken to the Captain about it. I know where it was. The machine gun, the ditch, the barn wall. From what I could tell,

Bonham was in the same action where Travis had been shot in the head."

"But he doesn't look anything like James," I protested. And yet, standing there with his back to me, I had thought he was Captain Travis . . . and I'd never met James.

Simon would know the questions to ask, would recognize where on the war map both men were, and he would have found a way to put the pieces together.

I was still uncertain. "It doesn't mean that this man shot the Captain. He wasn't the only officer in that mêlée."

"He told me he'd got separated from his men."

I remembered something else. Captain Travis had gone back to his sector, had asked everyone if they'd seen Lieutenant James Travis. And of course they hadn't. Because he hadn't known the right name . . . What if he'd known to ask for Bonham instead?

"There's only one way to be sure, you know that. We must find a way to bring these two face-to-face."

"Not very likely, with Travis in Bury gaol, and Bonham on his way back to London."

"Then we must pray he stays the night at The Hall."

I'd had no appetite for dinner. I asked for a bowl of soup to be sent up to my room with a pot of tea, and as I ate, I sat by the window from which I'd seen the figure on the green the night I'd found Captain Travis in the churchyard. The rain was still coming down.

It wasn't that I didn't believe Simon. If he told me that it was Lieutenant Bonham who had tried to kill the Captain, then chances were that he was right.

But why? If the two men had never met, if there was no other connection between them beyond the common factor of knowing James Travis, what could possess the Lieutenant to shoot the Captain? Surely neither realized the other's connection to Lieutenant Travis. They hadn't even spoken before the shot was fired.

I worried that, like a dog with a soup bone, trying to think it through. But nothing made sense. And the man I'd just seen with Mrs. Travis hadn't given me any reason to think he could be a killer. It wasn't unusual for men who had served together to take the time to visit the families of their comrades. Especially when one had been killed in action. I'd seen it myself, in my father's regiment. It was what one did for a fallen friend.

Simon had trained men, he had learned long ago to find their strengths and their weaknesses very quickly. Young as he was, he understood how they would face enemy fire, and which ones would need a word before the fighting began, to bolster their courage or to calm them down before they did something rash. I'd watched him manage men.

Unsettled still, I set my tray outside my door—and saw the lamp still burning in Simon's room, the line of brightness under his door a telltale sign. I nearly tapped on the paneling, to see if he was awake, to ask him to explain what it was that had made him question Lieutenant Bonham. But I lowered my hand instead, went back into my room, and closed my door as quietly as I could, so as not to alert him that I too was still awake.

Banking the fire so that it would keep the room reasonably warm until I was asleep, I went to bed.

My dreams were mixed.

I woke to a gray dawn, rivulets of water running down the High, tree limbs and eaves dripping heavily past my window. I remembered such days in the forward aid stations, mud everywhere, the tents and canvas sagging as rain weighed them down, trying to keep my hands warm so that I could bandage a wound without fumbling or hold another one together while the doctor sewed. Worrying about having enough blankets when men shook with fever or keeping them dry on the way to an ambulance.

It hadn't dawned on me fully that the war was over . . .

I built up the fire and dressed quickly in the little warmth it offered, but there had seldom been fires in many of my quarters at the Front.

Shaking off this mood as best I could, I put my hair up beneath my cap, found a shawl to throw over my shoulders, and went down to breakfast.

Simon was already there, looking tired, and I recalled seeing the light under his door when I put my tray out.

"Good morning," he said as he held my chair for me.

"Another fine day," I agreed, and gave my order to Betty. Her hair was still damp, straggling about her ears, but she was full of news.

"Such goings-on," she said brightly. "The Vicar's wife, Mrs. Caldwell, taken up by the police. A murderous fugitive caught in Mrs. Brentwood's back garden. And that poor man killed in a pool of his own blood right there in the doctor's surgery."

I said, "Mrs. Caldwell is at the Vicarage." I'd tapped at her door before coming down the stairs, but the room was empty, the bed tidily made when I looked in. "She was merely helping the police with their inquiries. I saw her myself, last evening."

Chagrined that one of her best bits of gossip was not true, she took herself off to bring us our tea.

Simon watched her pass through the door into the kitchen, then said, "The town crier."

I smiled. "I wonder what they've been saying about our return to the village."

Then soberly, I asked, "What are we to do, Simon? Where is the cavalry you sent for? I'm a QAIMNS nursing Sister, you're a Regimental Sergeant-Major, and between us we have no particular authority to demand Captain Travis's release. He's no better off where he is, and if he's tried and convicted, he faces the hangman."

"I've wondered about the cavalry myself. The evidence against Travis is circumstantial, but a local jury might find it compelling." He broke off as Betty came back with the tea tray. When she had gone, he continued, "It strikes me that the real question here is not what we're to do about the Captain. Let's view it a different way. If Travis had never escaped from the clinic—or if he had, but only went to London to find his banker, shall we say—would Spencer have lived, or died?"

I nodded, seeing where he was leading. "If the murder had to do with the papers he was carrying, yes, he would have died anyway. The problem is, the murderer didn't take them with him. And those papers weren't all that damaging—in fact, Mrs. Travis might have been delighted to discover a very good reason to contest the will. Captain Travis might want to conceal any reference to Wiltshire, but if he killed Mr. Spencer to keep those papers from becoming public knowledge, he'd have had to kill Mr. Ellis as well—after all, the information was on his letterhead." I smiled wryly. "That doesn't leave us with many suspects."

"We'd told Mr. Ellis and Mrs. Travis about the Wiltshire clinic. And so this would only have been news to Mrs. Caldwell."

I gave that some thought. "What have we overlooked? There must be something we haven't considered."

"There's this: It would be difficult to kill Mrs. Caldwell, to stop her from doing what her conscience might convince her was right. Better to kill Spencer, the stranger in the village, before he could tell her what he'd discovered."

"Still, what could she do, even if she learned that the Captain was in Wiltshire? She might have decided to visit him, might even have tried to make his conditions better, but the Vicar wouldn't have allowed her to confront Mrs. Travis or tell her she was foolish to stand in the Captain's way." I put down my teacup. "The Vicar. He owes his living to Mrs. Travis. This is the church he wants to keep at all costs. If he'd found out about the Florian Agency, he might not have intended to kill Spencer, he might have only wanted to stop him from involving his wife in Mrs. Travis's obsession about Captain Travis and the will."

"And things got out of hand—or Spencer tried to call Dr. Harrison, and the Vicar panicked." Simon thought about it. "Caldwell is a weak man, a follower. Sometimes they're all the more dangerous because of that. Especially when something they care about is threatened." Then he shook his head. "Still, I find it hard to believe that he'd try twice to kill Spencer."

I had to agree. I could see him screwing up his courage to face Spencer once, but not twice.

"And Mr. Ellis," Simon went on, "isn't a likely candidate for murderer. He could have had Mr. Spencer up on charges of theft if Spencer had broken into his chambers and stolen that report. He needn't kill the man."

"Yes, there's the question of the break-in. We can't overlook that." Our food had come and I waited until Betty had served us and gone away again.

Looking after her as she went back into the kitchen, Simon commented, "Too bad we can't ask her opinion. I'm sure she has one."

"Or Miss Fredericks, who sees answers in dreams." I was

dipping my spoon into my porridge when a thought struck me. "Simon. Do you really think Mr. Spencer took those papers from Mr. Ellis's office?"

"The only other possibility is that Ellis gave them to him, through a request from the Florian Agency for information about Captain Travis. But given the timing of Spencer's arrival here and the break-in in Bury, I'd say it was worth considering. After all, he lied about the train, didn't he?"

"What if—what if it wasn't the papers he took that mattered? What if there was something else in that file or on Mr. Ellis's desk or in the clerk's office that he shouldn't have seen? What if we've been so worried about the Captain and Mrs. Travis and that will, that we just *assumed* the break-in had to do with their affairs? When, in fact, it had to do with something else entirely? If Mr. Spencer was an investigator, he might have realized the importance of what he saw. And the only reason he hadn't done anything about it was that fall down the stairs."

I didn't feel like eating.

Simon, watching me, said, "Bess."

I smiled wryly. "I know. Mother has always told me that a good breakfast is a good start to the day." I turned to my porridge and ate as much as I could. It settled like a lump of coal in my stomach.

"Do you think my father is in France? There's been no word from him."

"I sent telegrams to his club and to Somerset." Seeing my alarm, he grinned. "And no, there was nothing in the telegram to alarm your mother."

"A telegram from you will be alarm enough."

He laughed, then was serious again. "What are we to do about Bonham?"

"There's nothing we can do. I could stop in at the Vicarage

and tell Mrs. Caldwell that the Lieutenant is visiting at The Hall. And that we aren't sure what his motives are for coming. For that matter, that's all I *can* say to her. I can't tell her that you believe he tried to kill Captain Travis. But if he did, why is he here? Do you think he's looking for the Captain?"

"I don't see how he could have discovered where Travis is. I think he told the truth, that he came to see Mrs. Travis for her son's sake. What happens when she tells him the Captain is here?"

"That could become a problem."

We finished our breakfast, went upstairs to fetch our coats, and drove to the Vicarage. Neither Mr. Caldwell nor his wife was at home. I tried the church next, but it was empty, although I called to her several times.

We were just getting back into the motorcar when I said, "Simon. I want to stop by the surgery. Mr. Spencer's things are there, unless the police took them along with the papers that came from Mr. Ellis. Has anyone notified his firm? Has anyone thought to find out if he's got a family in London, wondering what's become of him?"

"Bess, it's not your responsibility."

"Possibly not. But there might be something in his valise that the police overlooked, thinking it wasn't pertinent to their case."

Reluctantly he agreed, and we drove on to Dr. Harrison's surgery, at the top of the green.

We had nearly reached the house when the door opened and Mrs. Caldwell stepped out, saying something to a woman we couldn't quite see from where we were.

And clutched in her arms she had a man's coat, hat, umbrella—and valise.

CHAPTER 19

I WAS ABOUT to call out to Mrs. Caldwell, but she gave me a tiny shake of the head.

"Drive on," I told Simon, and he did as he was asked, leaving her to carry Mr. Spencer's belongings all the way to the churchyard, juggling her umbrella and the valise.

We circled the green, and as we were coming back up the High, I saw that Mrs. Caldwell wasn't carrying her burdens to the Vicarage, as I'd expected, but through the churchyard toward the south porch doorway.

"That's odd," Simon commented.

"We should leave the motorcar at The George and walk up the back lane," I said quickly.

He tucked the motorcar into a space on the far side of the inn, then got the umbrella out of the boot, and we started toward the lane. Walking up it, we let ourselves into the churchyard through the back gate, then made our way through the wet grass to the porch door, keeping close to the apse wall. I wasn't sure why it was necessary to be so careful, but Mrs. Caldwell had felt it was. That was enough for me.

Simon left his umbrella by the porch door, and we stepped into the damp chill of the nave, looking around for Mrs. Caldwell. I was just about to call to her when I saw her, half-hidden by the tall pulpit.

We hurried toward her, and she gave us a smile of greeting. "It occurred to me last night that it would be charitable of me to take this problem off the good doctor's hands and see that poor Mr. Spencer's belongings are returned to his family. Really, it was Constable Simpson's responsibility, I think, but never mind. This at least gives me a chance to look through them."

"Very clever," I said, but she shook her head.

"Mrs. Harrison was glad to be rid of them. She didn't even ask the doctor. So, here we are. All that's left of Mr. Spencer—at least here in Sinclair."

She searched his coat pockets as we watched and found the omnibus schedule and ticket, just as Simon had done. Then she opened his valise.

Boots fell out, and she looked at them. They seemed somehow forlorn as she set them aside. I noticed that one sole was more worn, as if the owner dragged that foot. Of course, I'd never seen him walk, but it was likely that foot had also caused Mr. Spencer to trip on the inn stairs.

Taking out the layers of clothing one at a time, Mrs. Caldwell inspected each item, refolded it, and set it aside. So far there was nothing of interest. Shirts, trousers, braces, stockings, underclothes, ties, handkerchief. Enough for a brief stay in the country, calling on his client.

"You had the same thought we did," I said as we folded another shirt and carefully put it back into the valise.

"Yes, I'd hoped there might be something here. I expect the police are finished with these things and have already contacted the Agency, if they know about it. If they haven't, someone in London ought to be told. I feel responsible, somehow."

I remembered Mr. Spencer clutching his valise to his chest, in spite of his pain, afraid that someone would take it from him. And then . . . then it hadn't been in the room with him when he was killed . . .

Why had he been fearful of letting it out of his sight at one stage, but let it be set aside later?

I reached for his extra pair of trousers and felt in the pockets. Nothing. I took out his boots again and felt inside. The first one was empty. The second one had something stuffed into the toe. I reached down, fingers probing, and came up with a stocking. That, I thought, was curious—the others were neatly folded. I reached down again and this time pulled out a small notebook, the sort that would fit comfortably in the palm of my hand.

"Ah!" Mrs. Caldwell exclaimed and reached for it. I let her have it.

Even so, I could see it was a diary, a collection of names and addresses and sometimes notations beside them.

"Here's my name," she said, turning the diary to show me. "And Captain Travis's, with a question mark beside it. Oh, and here is Mr. Ellis's firm." She peered at the entry, then gave up. "Such tiny print," she said, passing the book to me.

I looked at the tiny writing, all capitals. "There's Mr. Ellis's name too. Then the Captain's name a second time, with another question mark next to it." I glanced at Simon. "I expect he hadn't had time to make any new entries before he fell. And here's James Travis. What's that below the name?" I peered at it. "Just one word. *Ledgers*." I looked up at Mrs. Caldwell. "Did you also ask him to look into James Travis's will?"

"No, of course not, I had no right to pry into that. But the firm of Ellis, Ellis and Whitman has always been above reproach. Most of the village use them for any legal matters. Well, to be perfectly honest, I don't care much for this Mr. Ellis. His father was a much more approachable man, kind and avuncular. You could tell him anything and not feel a fool. This one takes after his mother. I have always felt that it must have been a love match, for she was the opposite of her husband. Blunt, no charm, and lent little to the firm's social life." She shrugged ruefully. "The Vicar's wife should have no opinions about people, much less speak ill of the dead. But I'm afraid I can't help it when it comes to the late Mrs. Ellis. I was always glad she lived in Bury and not here."

There was nothing else in the diary of interest to us, although I was sure Mr. Spencer's firm would recognize other names, other clients whose work the Agency had handled or Spencer himself had dealt with. Just looking at the entries, I couldn't make head nor tail of them, but there were cryptic remarks after most names.

Reluctant to stop looking, I went through the pages again, and this time I found Mrs. Travis's name. She had used the Florian Agency once, and here the notation was. But it offered no more information than I already knew: *False heirs*.

With a sigh I handed it back to Vera Caldwell and she restored it to the boot, adding the stocking to help conceal it once more.

"A waste of time," she said, her voice sad. "But I'll contact the Agency, ask them what to do with these belongings."

"What were you hoping to find?" Simon asked me.

I shook my head. "I don't know. Whatever it was that Mr. Spencer saw in the solicitor's? I expect he thought he had time to write it down. Little did he know."

Mrs. Caldwell looked from Simon to me. "Do you really believe Mr. Spencer would break into a solicitor's office?"

"Mr. Ellis doesn't look well," I said, pulling my gloves on

again. Sitting still here on the cold pews had let the chill creep up from my toes to my hands. "Perhaps he's worried, or there's something weighing on his mind."

"He's overworked. He's not been able to replace his father. I expect that now the war's over and men will be coming home, he'll find someone suitable to bring into the firm."

But I thought it was more than overwork that afflicted Mr. Ellis. Tuberculosis, for one thing, especially if he'd been wearing himself down trying to cope with clients on his own.

I said to Mrs. Caldwell, "Thank you for this. We were on our way to the surgery ourselves, and it was better that you approached them. Any request on our part might have seemed unpleasant curiosity."

"Poor man," she said, closing the valise and snapping the latches. "Thank you for freeing me from that awful cell last night. I could hardly sleep, remembering how it smelled. I'm sorry the Captain had to stay there. Can you do nothing for him?"

"I don't know," I said, giving her the truth.

"I think I can see why James liked him," she said with a sigh. "He was very angry about getting caught. But he was even more worried about me. I found that very touching." She picked up Mr. Spencer's coat and hat, then reached for the valise.

"I'll take that for you," Simon offered, but she shook her head.

"No, it's best that I take it to the Vicarage myself. Michael has one of his headaches this morning, and I don't want to distress him. But thank you."

Still, he reached for it and carried it as far as the porch door, opening her umbrella and handing that to her before giving her the valise as well. She walked out into the rain without looking back, and I wondered if she was wishing she had never hired Mr. Spencer.

Simon put up our umbrella, and we walked back down the lane toward The George.

Halfway there, I said, "I just remembered something. When we were working with Mr. Spencer while he was lying there on the floor at the foot of the stairs, do you remember what he said?"

Simon frowned, thinking back to that evening. "He was on his way down to ask what time dinner was served."

"Then he said something about to see if there was time to go out—and then he stopped, and said, 'I forget.' But that's why I always assumed he was on his way out to The Hall, to see Mrs. Travis. With the church almost next door to the inn—and large enough to be seen as Mr. Spencer was coming into town—he wouldn't have said 'out to the Vicarage.' He would have said 'up to' or 'across to.' And yet it was Mrs. Caldwell who'd hired him, not Mrs. Travis."

"Mrs. Travis had dealt with the Florian Agency before. He knew that."

"What made him lie about how he'd reached Sinclair? And why would he be on his way to Mrs. Travis?"

"He knew something that he believed she ought to be told." Simon looked down at me. "Now all we have to do is find out what that is."

"And Mr. Spencer is dead, and can't tell us."

We reached the inn and went up the stairs. When I opened the door to my room, the cavalry rose from a chair by the fire, where he must have been waiting patiently for me to come back.

"I didn't know you were here," I said, hurrying across the room to greet my father. "And what have you done with your motorcar? I didn't see it out front."

"It's in Bury, with a fellow officer," the Colonel Sahib said, bending down to kiss me. "He dropped me here to wait for you. You look tired, Bess. Sit down and tell me, please, why you needed my help?"

"I didn't send for you," I said, laughing, "but I'm very glad to see you." I hurried to the door and went across the passage to fetch Simon, and he greeted my father with some relief.

"We've hit an obstacle where we needed the big guns," he said, propping himself on the windowsill. "Nothing less would do. And time is running out." Then, together, Simon and I told my father about Captain Travis.

He listened as he always did, interrupting only to clarify a point or to ask for more information.

When we'd finished, he looked from Simon to me, then said, "Well. It's a very good thing I brought Major Davison of the Medical Board with me. Your mother told me the Wiltshire clinic had come to the house looking for Captain Travis. I wasn't quite sure how he could have reached Suffolk from Wiltshire, but on the off chance, I came prepared. I expect we can deal with the issue of his head injuries, but murder could be beyond even my abilities."

I smiled. The cavalry indeed.

"Do you think this man is in need of medical care in a clinic?" my father asked, serious now. "Is he delusional still, thinking he's seen a dead man trying to kill him?"

"I don't believe he is delusional. He saw what he thought was the truth, that James had tried to kill him, not once but twice. Put yourself in the Captain's place. He hadn't been told that James was dead. And there seemed to be a conspiracy of silence when he tried to discover what sector James was in. Everyone told him there was no such person. Even when he described James, they shook their heads. They couldn't see the likeness he'd seen. He refused to believe the medical staff when they tried to tell him

James was already dead. He thought *they* were lying to him too. It must have seemed that everyone was protecting James for some reason."

The Colonel Sahib turned to Simon. "What do you make of him?"

"I wasn't certain at first, sir. But I've come round to Bess's way of thinking. It's likely that the Captain was already beginning to face the truth about Lieutenant Travis, but the memorial in the church was the final evidence. And that speaks well for his sanity."

"But he still thinks he was singled out and shot," my father said.

"He gave me an account of both attempts. I couldn't find fault with them."

My father nodded. "Then I expect our first step is to see that he isn't dragged back to Wiltshire. Or that threatening to send him back can't be used to coerce him into pleading guilty to murder. We'll worry about the charges against him later."

We collected our coats. As we came down the stairs to go out to the motorcar, Betty was peering from the dining room door. My father was an impressive figure in his uniform, tall, remarkably attractive, his dark hair just touched with silver, and with that air of command that comes from handling men for most of his adult life.

I could imagine the tale she would carry round the village. And our standing in her eyes must have soared. I hid my smile. It would do us no harm if she told everyone that someone from the King's own staff had come to Sinclair.

As my father turned the crank and Simon got behind the wheel after opening the rear door for me, the bells at St. Mary's struck the hour.

We were silent most of the way to Bury. We found Major Davison just coming out of a pub, speaking to several men who wore the uniform of the wounded. He hailed us and got into the rear with me.

A slight man with a long face and fair, wavy hair, he greeted me warmly and said, "Your father sang your praises all the way to Suffolk. But he needn't have done so. I've known a few of the doctors you've served with. They were always pleased to have you working with them." Turning to Simon, he added, "And how is the shoulder, Sergeant-Major?"

"It's fine, sir. I've had no problems with it."

"Happy to hear that."

Simon had been seriously wounded at one point, and this must have been the doctor who had cleared him to return to duty.

We stopped in front of the police station, and the Colonel Sahib gave the Major a brief account of what had happened.

"Shell shock is the very devil to treat," he said, nodding. "Can't fault the staff, but you can see their view of the case. Well, we'll soon have the Captain out of their clutches and back in the field."

We got out, and my father led the way into the station, striding in as if this were a field command and he'd been sent by HQ to have a look.

The Sergeant at the desk rose, staring.

"Good day, Sergeant," the Colonel Sahib said briskly. "I've come from London with one of my medical officers. I wish to see Captain Travis, if you please."

The Sergeant frowned. "Sir. He's not called for a doctor," he said, trying his best to take charge of the situation.

"He's an Army officer, he's been wounded in the line of duty, and I have the authority to determine whether he's fit to return to his regiment or if he's still convalescing. Which way?"

I could see the choices running through the Sergeant's head. Should he find his own superior, or allow the Army to see the prisoner? I realized this must mean that Inspector Howe wasn't in—a piece of luck for us.

"Well? I haven't all day. I'm expected back in London tonight."

A Colonel with a full entourage standing in front of him barking orders won the day.

The Sergeant reached for his keys and said, "This way, sir."

He led us back to the cells, and I saw, when we got there, that the Captain hadn't been allowed to shave. For fear of cutting his own throat or someone else's?

My father held out his hands for the keys. "The Major can hardly examine him from here." The Sergeant was a brave man. He stood his ground for all of a handful of seconds, then passed them over. "Thank you, Sergeant, you have your own duties to attend to. I'll have the Sergeant-Major call you when we're ready to leave."

With all of us crowding in, it was already tight quarters in this small space where a turnkey could sit and guard his prisoners. And at this point, there was nothing more the Sergeant could do. He turned to go, shutting the outer door to the cells behind him.

Captain Travis was standing there, and I could see the alarm in his eyes. He thought the clinic had discovered where he was. And then he recognized my father.

I stepped forward, keeping my voice low. "Hallo," I said. "I've brought my father and someone from the Medical Board to see if they can help you."

Some of the tension drained out of the Captain's face as the Major, receiving the keys from my father, opened the cell door. "Step out here and let me have a look at you."

After the briefest hesitation, Captain Travis said, "Sir," and did as he was told.

Talking to him about his war, Major Davison proceeded to examine the prisoner, and I waited outside while he looked at the wound in his back. When I returned, a general air of satisfaction greeted me.

"That back needs several more weeks to heal properly," the Major was saying to my father. "I won't say he's damaged it since leaving the clinic, but it hasn't been well served. As for the head injury, in my opinion it has healed nicely, and any problems that might have been caused by it have been resolved."

Captain Travis was listening closely.

The Major turned to him and added, grinning, "If they don't hang you, you'll live to a good old age. When you're out of here, I'll send you to a clinic in Surrey that does wonders with wounds like yours. Meanwhile, I'll write to Wiltshire and tell them I've examined you and find you are neither mad nor delusional, and no longer assigned to their care. Will that do?"

"Yes, sir, it will do very well. Thank you, sir."

"Now, tell me about Barbados. I've never been to the islands, but my brother-in-law was posted in the Bahamas for a time."

Captain Travis glanced at me, then turned back to the Major. "I had photographs of my home. They were taken from me in Wiltshire. But I can tell you it's truly a bit of paradise, unless Atlantic storms roll in. And then it can be a struggle to survive. Our house is more or less sheltered, and we've been fortunate." He went on describing his life there, and Major Davison asked questions about how rum was made.

Clearly enjoying the conversation, he suddenly remembered where we were and said, "Well. Thank you, Captain. I found that interesting. When I write to the clinic, I'll ask for the return of your belongings, and in particular those photographs. Bloody-minded fools."

Simon and my father had been standing to one side, their arms folded, like a pair of bookends. I'd thought, more than once, that Simon was the son my father had never had. Two tall men who had made the Army their lives, and seen the best and the worst that such a career could offer. They had been marked by it, bore the scars to show for it, and yet had never lost their humanity.

We were just turning to go when the door thundered back on its hinges, and Inspector Howe came striding in.

He found three men in uniform, a nursing Sister, and a prisoner who had just stepped back into the confines of his cell. But the door was still open.

"What the hell is going on here?" the Inspector demanded. And this time it was the Major who addressed him.

"The Colonel and I have been examining my patient. He's still recovering from a serious wound, and he's still an officer in the British Army. If you have any objections to me doing my duty, you can take it up with the War Office. Good day, Inspector." And he handed the keys to Simon, then marched past the Inspector and his Sergeant, who was standing just behind him in the passage.

Simon was closing the cell door and turning the key in the lock.

Inspector Howe turned on me. "This is your doing. You're lucky I haven't locked you up with him, you interfering—"

He got no further. My father had stepped in front of me, his face like a thundercloud, and Inspector Howe's red face began to pale.

"Whatever you have to say, you say to me. Sister Crawford is an officer in the British Army, and I'll have you reduced to constable if you forget that again." And then he ushered me past the astounded Inspector, and Simon, as angry as my father, walked by him, fists clenched.

Inspector Howe hurried after us but kept his distance, and said only, "I have a duty as well, to see that justice is done for a man found dead in Sinclair. And this woman has frustrated me at every turn."

My father turned, and Inspector Howe stepped quickly out of reach.

"Then perhaps you should rethink your case, Inspector. If it's this fragile, it will never stand up in court."

And then we were out of the police station, and I heard my father clear his throat. I knew he was making an attempt to control his anger.

Turning to Major Davison, he said, "Where have you left the motorcar?"

"By The Angel," he replied blandly, as if nothing had happened. "I've missed my lunch. We might as well dine there, don't you think? I want to hear more about this dead man."

Chapter 20

I FOUND MYSELF repeating what we'd told my father, but a shorter version.

We were sitting at a table in a side room commandeered by my father, and so Simon and I could speak freely.

"Yes, well, it seems to me that this murder has nothing to do with Captain Travis. Not the man I saw earlier."

"But from the point of view of the Inspector, both the Captain and the victim are strangers. The village will be happier with that solution too. No one has connected Mr. Spencer with the break-in at the solicitor's, and Mr. Ellis won't cross Mrs. Travis by support-ing the Captain. She won't either, and after Inspector Howe had to take the Vicar's wife into custody, even if only temporarily, the Vicar will side with Mrs. Travis. If the Inspector needed more proof, there are the papers that Mr. Spencer was carrying. They seem to give the Captain a very strong motive, to protect his in-heritance."

"Reminds me of my time in Africa," the Major said musingly. "I saw people who were told they'd been cursed, and no amount of reason could save them. I doubt you'll be able to reason with these people either, or change their minds. Well, I wish the Cap-tain the best. I'm just sorry I couldn't do more."

I said to my father, "I have to return to France, and I'm sure you don't have time to stay here and make certain the Captain has a fair trial. I was wondering if Cousin Melinda could be persuaded to help?"

The Major's eyebrows went up. "Melinda Crawford? Is she related to your family? Good God. Half the General Staff knows her. I heard General Haig claim that if Mrs. Crawford had stayed with Gordon in Khartoum, it wouldn't have been such a debacle."

My father nearly choked on his wine, claiming it had gone down the wrong way. Simon busied himself with his knife and fork.

I barely managed to keep a straight face, saying only, "Let's hope she's as successful with the Captain."

We had lingered over our meal. I was enjoying my father's company, especially knowing that in all likelihood I'd have to go directly to London from Suffolk and leave for France without returning to Somerset. I could only wish my mother were here as well. The three men had turned the conversation to the last days of the war. Our silverware, the salt cellar, and the sugar bowl were pressed into service, and then our cups and glasses formed divisions and reserves. I was the Belgian border and Simon was the Channel coast.

We were deep into discussions of the political situation in Germany when I looked up to see that the restaurant was nearly empty, the woman who had served us waiting patiently for us to finish talking.

I called a truce while she cleared away the battlefield, and I took the opportunity to ask my father to find out what he could about Lieutenant Martin Bonham.

"What does he have to do with this matter?" Major Davison asked, frowning.

Neither Simon nor I had mentioned him in the course of our account. We hadn't wanted to muddy the waters by bringing up the issue of who had actually shot the Captain.

"He's presently visiting Mrs. Travis," Simon answered for me. "Back from France on compassionate leave. His aunt has been ill. He'd served with James and took the opportunity to call on Mrs. Travis. She's had several imposters trying to take advantage of her circumstances. He might be another. Or not. I haven't served with him, sir, I don't know anything about him except what he's told us."

Major Davison commented, "I don't recognize the name either."

My father made a note. "I'll see what I can discover."

Ten minutes later, we had settled our account and were walking out the door. Simon held my coat for me, and I was glad of its warmth as we stepped out into the evening wind. My father was driving with the Major back to London, and he promised to put in a call to Melinda as soon as he reached the city.

"She will know the best person to represent him, someone who isn't from Suffolk, I should think," he was saying.

It went against the grain to leave a task unfinished. But I was wise enough to know that I had done all I could. I would still be here when Melinda arrived, and that would give me a chance to tell her what Simon and I had discovered. I could also introduce her to Mrs. Caldwell and Sister Potter.

We had just reached our motorcars when a man stepped out of the shadows from the side of another vehicle left there.

I drew in a breath before I recognized him, and I felt Simon tense at my side.

It was Inspector Howe.

We stopped, and my father moved forward.

"Inspector," he said coldly.

"I'm glad I caught you," he replied, sarcasm heavy in his voice. "Captain Travis has just attempted to murder Mrs. Travis."

"That's impossible. He's in a cell in your police station."

The Inspector relished what he was about to say. I could see it in his face, even in the dimly lit square where we were standing.

"But he's not. I released him an hour after you left the station. And the first thing he did was to seek out Mrs. Travis. Dr. Harrison is with her now."

He held out his palm. In it was a spent bullet from a revolver.

CHAPTER 21

WE STOOD THERE, appalled.

I was the first to recover. "But why? Why did you release him? You were convinced of his *guilt*."

"That was before Mr. Ellis went to speak to Mrs. Caldwell earlier today. He felt responsible for her having been swept up in the Captain's capture, and he went to apologize. She told him it was she that Mr. Spencer had come to see, that he was bringing her information regarding Captain Travis, most of which she'd already learned elsewhere by that time, and she showed him a little notebook that was filled with other cases that might have been responsible for the man's death. Then she confessed that she was afraid a trial would only serve to embarrass Mrs. Travis and herself when the Captain was exonerated."

"That's a likely outcome," the Colonel Sahib agreed. "Go on."

"And so he sent a telegram to this Florian Agency asking about Mr. Spencer's clients. He got a reply, saying that Mr. Spencer had been involved in a very nasty black market case just before taking up Mrs. Caldwell's request. There had been threats against Mr. Spencer; it was one of the reasons he was sent to Suffolk, to get him out of London." There was bitterness in his voice. "Ellis was a fool."

Still in shock, I said nothing. We hadn't known any of this. When I rang Florian, the voice on the telephone refused to help me. Had the Agency feared that an unknown caller might somehow be connected to the death threats and was trying to find him?

"I told Mr. Ellis in no uncertain terms that the Captain must not leave Bury until the inquest, but Mr. Ellis insisted that he would be safer in The George under your eye. But you weren't there, were you?"

We stood there in the cold air, taking all this in.

"Get on with it, man. How did Travis attack Mrs. Travis?" my father asked.

"Ellis and Mrs. Travis were in the parlor, the room with those long windows. She was a perfect target, lit by the lamps. So Ellis told me. And someone fired from just outside, not ten feet away. The shot went through the sleeve of her gown, just grazing her. By the time Ellis and a houseguest who had heard the shot went out to look, Travis had gone. They drove directly to The George, but he wasn't there—because he'd gone to The Hall the minute Ellis turned his back on him."

My heart sank. "But where could he have found a revolver?" I asked. Simon had his own in his valise.

"It belonged to Henry Douglas." When we stared blankly at him, he added, "The owner of The George. It was his father's. He fought in the Boer War."

"But how did Captain Travis know it was there?"

"Apparently while the staff was preparing dinner, he ransacked Douglas's rooms."

I wanted to ask why Captain Travis would have taken such a risk when there was a service weapon ready to hand. It made no sense. But someone had known about Henry Douglas's souvenir.

"Where is Captain Travis now?" my father asked.

"The village is being searched. I've already spoken to Mrs. Caldwell, and she was shocked at the allegations that Travis had tried to shoot Mrs. Travis. She refused to believe it. But she gave me leave to search the Vicarage—which told me he wasn't there. Nor was he at Sister Potter's. She was cooking her dinner."

"I intend to look into this," my father said, turning toward his motorcar. Simon and I hurried to his, and Inspector Howe stepped forward, begging a lift to Sinclair.

With the Inspector's presence in the rear seat, I couldn't talk freely with Simon. But in the glow of the headlamps, I could see his face, set in angry lines.

A thought kept running through my mind. A revolver was accurate at that distance. Captain Travis had been in the trenches, he must have been a better shot—he would have hit his target, and Mrs. Travis would be dead by now. And his way to the inheritance cleared . . . I didn't want to think about that.

"Where was Lieutenant Bonham when the shot was fired?" I asked the Inspector, and he leaned forward to answer me.

"Dressing for dinner. His shirt wasn't even buttoned, according to Ellis, when they encountered each other in the entrance hall. Bonham was just running down the steps."

I wondered if Simon was thinking the same thing I was. Had the Lieutenant just run *up* the steps before Ellis came bursting out of the parlor? For of course he'd have assured himself that his client was all right before leaving her. She might have been more seriously wounded than he knew.

But that was idle speculation. There was no reason to suspect a collusion between Ellis and the Lieutenant. It was just that I didn't trust Ellis, or his reasons for seeing to it that Captain Travis was released and returned to Sinclair. Vera Caldwell had meant well, but now the police had a far more solid case against the Captain.

I wanted very badly to ask Inspector Howe about that break-in at Ellis, Ellis and Whitman. And whether Mr. Spencer had been involved. If Mr. Spencer was dead, and Captain Travis was hanged, the whole matter would be tidily resolved, wouldn't it? And anything that Mr. Spencer might have seen in the solicitor's office would be safe forever.

But the Inspector was in no mood to think about anything else, and I was worried about Captain Travis. Where could he hide? He hardly knew the village!

I sat back. Behind us my father's headlamps cut the early winter darkness. Simon reached over and briefly put a hand over mine where they were clasped in my lap.

His was warm, while my fingers were cold. I'd forgot to put on my gloves. I reached into my pocket to find them, slowly drawing them on.

"Is Mrs. Travis all right?" I asked. "What does Dr. Harrison have to say?"

"I've had men out looking for Travis. I wasn't there when the doctor arrived. And I haven't been back to The Hall. I was searching for you by that time. Your belongings were still in your rooms. I came back to Bury."

Both motorcars, Simon's and my father's, had been standing outside The Angel while we lingered over our dinner. Hadn't anybody noticed? Hadn't anyone even looked, before the Captain was released?

It didn't matter now.

We were coming into the outskirts of the village, and my father pulled ahead of us before we reached the inn. The Inspector barely waited for us to stop before he was out of the motorcar and hurrying inside. Simon went after him. Both men were back before we had gathered outside the door. One look at the Inspector's face told us the Captain wasn't in either room.

But behind the Inspector's back, I saw my father raise an eyebrow, and Simon give the slightest nod. A question and an answer had passed silently between them: Simon's weapon was still there and hadn't been fired.

My father made the decision. "Simon, go to The Hall, find out what you can. The Major and I will wait here, in the event Travis comes back. Or we find out where he is."

"Sir," Simon responded and was back behind the wheel almost at once.

"A waste of time," Inspector Howe said. "The doctor is with Mrs. Travis. We need to find the Captain."

"Then stay here," Simon told him shortly. But it was clear that Howe didn't trust Simon, and he got in as well, shutting his door smartly as Simon reversed and turned toward The Hall.

I called, "Wait!" and Simon stopped. I ran to join them.

Silence followed us all the way to the gates and up to the door of the house. There was nothing Simon and I could say with the Inspector there, and he was busy with his own thoughts.

There seemed to be lights on all over the house. Dr. Harrison's carriage was still there, and when I got down and hurried to the door before Inspector Howe could reach it, I found it ajar.

Pushing it wide enough for me to enter, I stood for a moment at the foot of the stairs, but I couldn't hear voices anywhere. I turned and walked into the drawing room. A maid I'd seen before was trying on her own to drape a sheet over the shattered panes, and I went to help her. Startled, she nearly dropped the sheet. But I smiled and took up one end, and she finally picked up her corner again. Simon crossed the room to help secure it. As he did, I said, "I've come to see how Mrs. Travis is. I'm worried about her."

"It was terrible. We heard the commotion downstairs and we ran up to see what it was. There was the outer door standing wide, and someone moaning, and I dashed in here to see who it was. Mrs. Travis was lying back in that chair, just by the window, and there was blood all over her gown. I felt ever so faint, thinking she was dying, but then she spoke to me, and I hurried over to see her. It was her arm, bleeding like nothing I'd ever seen before, and she asked me to summon Dr. Harrison. I didn't know where Mr. Ellis had got to, and him with a motorcar, to get to the doctor's surgery all the quicker, but he'd gone. That's what I truly thought, and I went to the door, and there was Mr. Ellis, pale as could be, and that Lieutenant beside him, his shirttail untucked and his feet bare."

She had a sense of drama, and it brought the scene vividly alive for us.

The Inspector was standing in the doorway. "Where is your mistress now?"

"In her room. Mr. Ellis and the Lieutenant must be with her. And the doctor as well."

"Where is it?" the Inspector asked, and she told him. He started for the stairs, and after the briefest hesitation, I followed, Simon on my heels.

The Inspector tapped lightly on the door, and we heard a man's voice say impatiently, "Come in."

And the three of us did.

Mrs. Travis was lying wanly on a chaise longue by the window, the drapes already drawn to shut out the darkness and whoever had been out there. One of her sleeves had been cut away, and a bandage had been wrapped around her arm.

The doctor was mixing something in a glass of water, a powder that swirled in a cloud and then seemed to vanish. "I won't have you disturbing my patient," he said sharply.

Mrs. Travis lifted a hand. "I don't know why he's running free—he nearly killed me." I came forward and took the glass from the doctor.

"It must have been rather awful for you," I said gently and held out the glass. I was the only woman in a room full of men, and I thought I could help. "Can you drink some of this? It will help calm you."

"I won't be calm ever again—he's ruined my peace of mind. I'll never walk into that room again without hearing glass breaking and feeling pain in my arm."

I managed to coax her to take a little of the sedative.

Inspector Howe came forward. "Did you see him? Was there anything you remember that might help us find him?"

"Nothing, I saw *nothing*. There was suddenly a loud report, the glass breaking—"

She was running that moment over and over again in her mind, upsetting herself afresh, and very close to hysteria. A woman like Mrs. Travis would never be able to forgive herself for having made a scene.

"I understand. I was shot once," I said quietly. "I know how horrid it is."

"You were?" she asked, turning to me as if really seeing me for the first time. Her eyes were wide with surprise.

"Yes, and it was quite some time before I got over it," I assured her. "But in the end, I did. You are so very lucky it was only your arm, and Dr. Harrison came so quickly. I required surgery." I got a little more of the sedative into her, and I was beginning to see some of the tension fade from her face. Turning, I glanced at the men gathered around her and nodded toward the door. Mr. Ellis and the

Lieutenant moved reluctantly toward it. Inspector Howe was on the point of refusing to leave, but Simon was behind him. In the end, Simon closed the door after them. Dr. Harrison had stayed.

"Would you like me to call your maid?" I asked. "I'll be happy to help you get into your bed, if you'd prefer that."

"I couldn't sleep," she said, slurring her words just a little. "I'm more conf—comfortable here." She obediently finished the glass, and I handed it to the doctor.

"Then here you shall stay. Shall I ring for some tea? Would you like that? Or perhaps some warm milk?"

"I don't think I could swallow it," she said, her eyes heavy. I glanced at the doctor now, and he frowned, unwilling to leave his patient. But she was bandaged, beginning to feel drowsy, and it was best if she could rest.

"Shall I ask Dr. Harrison to stay?" I asked.

"No. He's missed his dinner. So have I. But I couldn't . . ." Her voice trailed off.

Dr. Harrison stayed a few minutes longer, and then with a nod, turned and left. I sat by Mrs. Travis until she was fully asleep, drew a quilt from the bed over her, then rose and tiptoed to the door.

To my astonishment, Dr. Harrison was waiting just outside it. "You're a good nurse," he said grudgingly, and looked in the room behind me. Satisfied that I hadn't murdered her where she lay, he shut the door quietly and walked with me toward the stair. "A nasty business," he said. "I don't remember the last murder here in Sinclair. Well before the war, at any rate." At the top of the stairs, he paused and looked straight at me. "What part have you had in this business?" he asked. "I couldn't follow what Mrs. Travis was saying when I got here. A muddle of names and murder and heirs to the estate. She blamed you as well."

"I came to the village to ask for help for Captain Travis. He was in a clinic in Wiltshire, and I felt the diagnosis was wrong. As it happens, the Army has just examined him and verified that it was a mistake. Still, Major Davison wants him to have more weeks of attention to the wound in his back. I must return to France shortly. I'm still posted there." Well, it wasn't the whole truth, but it covered what mattered. "For what it's worth, I don't believe Captain Travis killed Mr. Spencer or shot at Mrs. Travis tonight. But that's for the police to determine, isn't it? At the moment, she's more comfortable, and it's best for me to go back to The George."

"Ah." He nodded, as if that explained everything. And we went down the stairs together. "Base Hospital?"

"I was more often assigned to a forward aid unit," I said.

"Were you indeed? Were you telling the truth, that you were shot?"

"I'm afraid so."

We turned in unison to the drawing room as the sound of men's voices carried to us. Mr. Ellis was still there, and Lieutenant Bonham, talking to Simon. They broke off as we came into the room, and stood up.

"She's asleep," Dr. Harrison told them. "I've given her something to settle her nerves and help with any pain. I'll return in the morning. Meanwhile, if she needs anything in the night, you know where to find me."

They wished him good night, and he turned on his heel and left.

"Where is the Inspector?" I asked, noticing that he wasn't there.

"He went out to the tenant cottages," Mr. Ellis said. "I doubt he'll find much in the dark, but he's a good man. Thorough."

"But what happened here? Did you see nothing when you went out to investigate?"

"We had no way of guessing which direction he'd taken. To

the road, most likely, but he could have cut cross-country," Lieutenant Bonham said.

"He doesn't know the countryside well enough for that," I pointed out. "If he came by way of the road, then it's likely he left the same way."

They were about to argue with me—I was a woman, after all, with no experience in such matters. They were being polite but begging to differ. Simon caught my eye and shook his head slightly.

"I think it's best if we go back to The George," I said again. "Good night." Simon followed me, and we'd just reached the door when I heard someone shouting outside.

"They've caught him!" Mr. Ellis exclaimed and started after us. My heart in my throat, I got to the outer door first, throwing it open, and all I could see were the motorcar and the doctor's carriage drawn up by the steps.

"Over here."

It was Dr. Harrison's voice, sharp and worried. It was coming from the corner of the house, and I started in that direction, but Simon caught my arm, pulled me back, and went on ahead.

By the time I reached the corner, Simon was already coming back, moving quickly toward his motorcar. I could see Dr. Harrison kneeling beside someone in a dark coat lying on the ground. I hurried to him, kneeling in my turn as Simon returned with his torch.

But it wasn't Alan Travis. It was Miss Fredericks. I recognized her fair hair, just visible beneath a scarf wrapped round her head. When Simon turned on his torch, we could see that her face was a bloody mask. Dr. Harrison lifted the end of the scarf and used it to wipe away some of the blood. He swore under his breath as he saw the wound. "And she's very cold," he added. "She's been out here for some time."

She had been struck hard across the side of the face. He began to look her over, searching for other signs of injury. I watched. He shook his head finally. "I can't tell here."

The other two men were standing a little distance away, and I could hear Mr. Ellis saying, "That's not Travis. But who is she? What's happened to her?"

I reached for a handkerchief to clean her face, but the doctor pushed my hand away. "No, into my carriage with her. I'll take her to the surgery."

"Her family—" I began.

He turned to Mr. Ellis and said, "Go inside, if you please, and find the staff. Tell them it's Fredericks's girl, and ask them to send for him. Tell him where she'll be."

Lieutenant Bonham said quickly, "It would be best to take her up to a room in the house. Jolting her all the way back to the village—"

Simon cut across his objection. "My motorcar is here. Sister Crawford will drive, Doctor, and you can sit in the rear with Miss Fredericks, to see that she's shielded from the worst of the ruts. I'll bring your carriage."

"Yes, good man. Thank you. Hurry, Ellis, see that her father is told before he hears this from someone else."

"But what does she have to do with Travis?" It was Lieutenant Bonham.

"Not now," Dr. Harrison answered him curtly.

Between the doctor and the two men, we got her into the rear of Simon's motorcar, wrapped in a rug, and Dr. Harrison ensconced beside her. I climbed behind the wheel, and Simon went to turn the crank.

Ellis was gone; I hadn't seen him leave. Lieutenant Bonham shut the door for the doctor and stood back. "He'll want to know. Her father. Will she be all right?"

"It's too soon to say. But for God's sake, don't tell him that and frighten him half to death. Just send him to me."

I was already reversing, heading back toward the village.

Dr. Harrison said warily, "Are you certain you can manage this thing?"

"I've driven larger vehicles than this. In France," I added, because that would make him happier. He didn't need to hear that I had my own motorcar.

He was silent for a time. Then he said, "It appears to me that she's been struck hard across the face, at least twice. If I didn't know better, I'd guess it was a revolver."

"Yes, I saw that," I answered, my eyes on the road.

Miss Fredericks began to moan a little.

"It's all right, Lucy. You're safe now," the doctor murmured, showing a gentle side I hadn't seen before. "Hold on just a little longer."

We were coming into the village. I'd driven as sedately as I could, but with speed, thinking all the while that whoever did this was little short of a monster. She must have got in the way. And that meant she was surely still in danger.

Turning into the lane running up by the church, I saw lights on in the Vicarage. We reached the surgery, and I pulled as close to the door as I could.

Between us we got Lucy Fredericks out of the motorcar, and Dr. Harrison himself carried her inside.

I expected him to send me away now, but he said gruffly, "My assistant has gone home for the night. If you'll lend a hand?"

I opened the door to the room where Mr. Spencer had been taken—and had been killed—but Dr. Harrison said, "Not that one. Over there." And I changed direction.

We got her undressed and covered with a sheet. There was a darkening bruise on her stomach as well. Dr. Harrison, his face grim, worked carefully, examining her. I watched, thinking that she was only a few years younger than I was, but she had seen much less of the cruelty of life. She would find this beating as difficult to understand as Mrs. Travis had with the wound on her arm and the violation of her house.

"Vicious," he said once, and then went on with his examination. Lucy was beginning to regain consciousness, whimpering a little, and then she opened her eyes, struggling wildly before she realized who was standing over her.

She began to weep. I moved forward to take her hands. "It's all right, Lucy," I said gently. "You're safe. Dr. Harrison is here. You're going to be all right."

She clung to me. "I want my father," she pleaded. "Please, will you find him?"

"He's on his way," Dr. Harrison said. "Who did this to you, my dear? Did he kick you?"

There was fear in her eyes now. Her grip was hurting my hand. "Yes," she whispered. "Before I fainted. I thought he was going to kill me."

"Did you see him?" I asked. "Do you know who it was?"

But she shook her head a little. "It was dark."

"What was he wearing? A uniform?" Dr. Harrison asked, glancing up at me.

I steeled myself for her answer, but she said, almost in a whisper, "I don't know."

Relieved, for the only man in uniform they would blame would be Captain Travis, I asked, "Did he say anything to you?"

"I don't remember. I don't think so."

"Let's find you a nightgown before your father arrives," Dr. Harrison said. "But I want you to stay here tonight. I'll need to keep an eye on you." He was still examining the cuts on her face. But I knew what he must be thinking—that she would be safer here.

"Sister Potter could stay with her, don't you think?" I suggested. One didn't tell a doctor what to do.

He said, "Yes, when the Sergeant-Major comes, we'll send him across."

Two minutes later, Simon arrived, and was sent on his errand.

"Is she all right?" he asked me quietly as he turned to go.

"It was a brutal attack. He struck her twice in the face, then kicked her when she went down."

"Did she see him?"

"Sadly, no."

He turned away, but not before I heard him swear under his breath as he set out at a trot across the green.

I knew precisely how he felt.

Back in the room where Lucy Fredericks lay, I saw that Dr. Harrison had covered her with a blanket and turned down the lamp. She jumped when I spoke, before she knew who was there.

"Was that my father?" she asked. "I heard voices."

"He's on his way. It was the Sergeant-Major, asking how you were." I didn't know where Dr. Harrison was, but it was likely that he was seeing to his carriage. And so I said, "Are you sure you didn't see who it was? Even if he came at you out of the dark, you must have seen something?"

"I'm afraid," she said, taking my hand again. "I don't—what if I'm wrong?"

Then she *did* know who had struck her.

"Don't tell anyone," I whispered. "Not even your father. He'll be angry, he'll want to hurt whoever it was. Wait until you're sure."

She nodded. The aftermath of shock was setting in now, and she lay there with her eyes closed.

I heard voices again, and then Dr. Harrison was speaking to someone. I expected it was Simon with Sister Potter, although it was too soon.

The door to the little room opened, and a bear of a man rushed in. I recognized him as Mrs. Travis's driver. Lucy held out her arms to him, crying, "*Papa*."

She might be close on twenty, but just now she was a little girl again, wanting the one adult in her life she truly trusted.

I slipped out and went to wait for Simon and Sister Potter. Behind me, I heard a roar from the examining room, and I knew that Dr. Harrison had begun to describe his patient's injuries.

Mr. Fredericks was large enough and mad enough to do something rash, and I hoped that Lucy had remembered not to tell him everything.

Five minutes later, Simon arrived with Sister Potter, and I could see that he'd told her what had happened. Her face was somber, and she greeted me with a nod. "Does she remember anything helpful?"

"I think she's still in shock," I said. "And more than a little frightened. Her father is with her. But it may come clearer after a while, when she's calmed down."

We could hear Mr. Fredericks's deep voice, angry and frustrated. Sister Potter said, "I'd best go in."

"I'll leave. He doesn't know me. But I'll be at The George. Close by if you need me."

"Good."

I collected my coat from the tree by the door and went out to where Simon had waited.

"I heard you say her father is here? Then I think it's best if we go."

"Yes. But not to The George. Not yet. I'd like to stop in the Vicarage."

"It's late."

"The lights are on. Someone is awake."

We drove there, and I went up to the door. Mrs. Caldwell opened it almost at once, as if she'd been expecting someone. She saw who it was, put her finger to her lips, and opened the door wider.

We stepped inside a very Victorian entry, dark and old-fashioned. I didn't think anything had been changed here since Queen Victoria sat on the throne.

She took us into the front parlor and shut the door.

"My husband has gone up to bed."

I gave her a brief account of what had happened tonight, and she shook her head.

"Poor girl. I'll go over later and see if there is anything I can do. Sister Potter might wish for a cup of tea. Is Mrs. Travis all right? Should I wake Michael and ask him to go out to her?"

"She's sleeping. Dr. Harrison gave her a very strong sedative."

"But who is this officer who came to call on her? Do you have any idea?"

"Only what we've been told. Simon thinks he might be the man who shot at Captain Travis in France. But we can't find any reason for it."

She looked away, then said slowly, "Captain Travis was here earlier tonight. The police didn't find him, thank God. And Michael was in his study, working on his sermon. He had no idea. Alan—Captain Travis—wanted me to tell him about James. He wanted to know." Her voice was a little husky. "He asked about Nigel too. What sort of child he was. I refuse to believe that man killed anyone."

But in the eyes of the police, he had an excellent motive. Because once Mrs. Travis was dead, the way was clear for him to inherit The Hall. After all, no one had *seen* him pull the trigger, and if he could count on Mrs. Caldwell to give him an alibi, there was nothing Inspector Howe could do.

Why had he lost his nerve and run? they would ask. Running was surely proof of guilt. *What had gone wrong? Miss Fredericks in his way, a witness?*

"Simon and I have learned that Mr. Spencer had had death threats from another inquiry he'd conducted in London. His death might not have had anything to do with Captain Travis." I hesitated. "It's also possible he broke into the solicitor's office and saw something there that he shouldn't have. Perhaps that's why he was killed."

"I can't believe that either. I mean to say, who among Mr. Ellis's clients has secrets someone would kill to conceal? This is Suffolk, not the back streets of London. I found Mr. Ellis willing to work with me to free the Captain. He never mentioned a break-in. Surely he would be the first to know if something compromising was stolen. He'd have warned his client and told the police."

"Perhaps it wasn't stolen. But someone might have been afraid it had been seen and made certain Mr. Spencer never did anything about it."

"But how would anyone connect that with Mr. Spencer? The police must not have identified the person who broke in. They've said nothing about that."

I remembered suddenly what I'd seen the night Mr. Spencer was killed. A figure slipping among the barren trees on the green, keeping to the shadows. I'd assumed that was Mr. Spencer, trying to leave the doctor's surgery, and later came to believe it was Captain Travis instead, because I'd stumbled over *him* in the churchyard. I was certain he'd made it there while I was circling around The George, to be less conspicuous as I went to find out what Mr. Spencer was up to.

What if the first figure I'd seen hadn't been Captain Travis, but the killer?

I said, "Where is Captain Travis now?"

She looked away. "I smuggled him out while the police were here asking Michael if we'd seen him. I came in as Michael was talking to that Inspector Howe, and I offered to let them search the premises. But they believed Michael, and didn't bother. I don't know where Alan—the Captain went from here."

"But how long was he here?"

And she told me.

I calculated the timing, when Mrs. Travis was shot, and when the Captain was at the Vicarage. But I couldn't be sure—it was just possible—barely—he'd gone to The Hall first.

And then I caught an expression in Vera Caldwell's eyes that I hadn't seen before. She had lost Nigel. She had lost James. And into the void of loss had come Alan Travis, who was close to the same age.

I wondered if she would lie to protect him. No one had seen him here. There was only her word that he had come at all.

The next thought was so stunning it made me turn toward Simon, so that the woman in front of me couldn't read *my* eyes.

Would Vera Caldwell also kill for Alan Travis? So that he would inherit The Hall and stay in Suffolk where she could watch him through the years, as she'd watched James grow up? Had *she* gone to The Hall while her husband was in his study, working on his sermon? She could have known about that revolver at The George.

I realized I was tired and not thinking rationally. She was the Vicar's wife, and however much she wanted Nigel back, if she had come to know the Captain at all, she would realize that he wanted to go home. Back to Barbados and that house with the wide, cool veranda.

Simon, who had been silent, took my glance his way as a signal, and said, "Your father is still at The George, Bess. If he and the Major are leaving for London tonight, they should start soon."

I smiled gratefully, and turned again to Mrs. Caldwell. "Yes, and we don't want to disturb the Vicar."

She let us out, but at the door, a silhouette against the lamplight behind her, she said, "You'll let me know?"

I promised, and then we were walking across to the churchyard.

Simon put a hand on my arm. "We should look in the church."

"But surely the police went there."

"Still."

And so we crossed the churchyard, wary of the footstones that we could just barely see, and went to the south porch.

I was sure the screech of the door would wake the living if not the dead, it sounded so loud to my ears, but I led the way inside.

The cold struck me, and then the silence. Almost at once it was broken, as the bells over our head struck the hour.

As the echoes died away, I heard something, a scraping sound, hollow and distant. And yet looking around the nave, I couldn't see anyone. I walked as quietly as I could down the aisle toward the pulpit and the altar. Over my head, the dark barrel vaulting of the ceiling high above me seemed to echo each step.

We searched the nave, the aisles, the choir, the altar, behind the only two tombs the church held, and found nothing.

"I was certain he must be hiding here." Simon looked around him. "I thought after talking to Mrs. Caldwell, Travis might have come back to see the brass plaque to James Travis."

With a sigh I said, "For all we know, he might be at The George. With the Colonel Sahib."

"Then let's go back."

But as we walked to the motorcar, Simon warned, "Bess, if we can get Travis clear of this and to the clinic in Surrey that Major Davison recommends, we'll be well out of it. Leave Spencer's murder to the local police. And Ellis as well. The solicitor is too well known for anyone to believe he's somehow involved."

"I know. I know." I looked out at the cottages, many of them already dark. "You don't suppose the Captain is hiding at Sister Potter's?"

"I don't think so. She told me Constable Simpson had looked under her bed and behind the wardrobe."

I smiled in spite of myself at the picture that evoked. "Simon," I said, suddenly, "where is Inspector Howe? He went out to look at the estate cottages, and even with all the noise as we worked with Miss Fredericks, he never appeared."

"He may have been inside one of the cottages."

At The George, Simon stopped to speak to the owner and I went up to my room. My father was pacing the floor, caught in midstride as I opened the door.

"I was worried," he said.

I saw a figure lying on my bed, his back to me, and for an instant I thought it must be the Captain. But it was the Major, sound asleep.

Lowering my voice, I told the Colonel Sahib about events at The Hall.

"Good God," he said, and turned quickly as the door opened again and Simon stepped in.

"He's not in my room."

"Then where the devil is he?" my father demanded. "We need to find him before Inspector Howe does."

"He knew the police were searching for him. They came while he was at the Vicarage. If he had nothing to do with the shooting of Mrs. Travis, he knows he can't prove it. He might have gone to The Swan in Clare, hoping we'll remember and look for him there."

"He will still be a fugitive," the Colonel Sahib pointed out.

We stood there, unable to argue with his logic.

"Mr. Ellis got him out of Bury gaol. He persuaded the police that Captain Travis should return to The George," I said after a moment. "And then Mr. Ellis left him alone here. Was that on purpose, or was it just happenstance that Mrs. Travis was shot then?"

"We're back to Ellis," Simon remarked.

"Yes. I wish Mr. Spencer had trusted someone. I wish we knew what he'd discovered, if he broke into the firm. If he didn't break into the firm, if there's nothing to be found," I went on, "then the Inspector will have to look among the Agency's clients in London."

"That won't solve the shooting at The Hall," my father reminded me.

"No. I see that. On the other hand, if we could clear the Captain of Mr. Spencer's death, that might help us convince Inspector Howe that he had no reason to kill Mrs. Travis. At the moment, it appears that she stands between him and a very large inheritance."

My father glanced at the sleeping form of the Major. "If," he said thoughtfully, "this man Spencer broke into the solicitor's office, why can't we?"

I stared at him, astonished. "But you can't—you'd—we'd be arrested."

"Simon and I have done night reconnaissance before this. And in far more dangerous places than Bury. We can get in and out without being seen. Besides, Howe has half his men here in Sinclair."

"I'm going with you," I said.

"You will not. Your mother would have our heads if we let you try."

"But—" I began, determined to argue.

"Bess. Be reasonable. None of my clothes will fit you, and none of Simon's. You can't very well follow us in that uniform. Even with your coat on, it's bound to be noticed."

He was right. I could get all of us arrested.

"I can't wait here. I'll worry myself to death."

"You'll have to learn a little patience, my dear. Simon? We could use some dark clothing."

"I'll see what I can find."

He went away, and my father began to unbutton his tunic. "I'll leave my clothes in Simon's room. We don't want to rouse anyone's curiosity." He nodded toward the bed, then left as well.

Ten minutes later I heard Simon's footsteps on the stairs, treading lightly. His door opened and closed, and after a very few minutes, opened and closed again. Two sets of footsteps went down the stairs.

I wanted to go down to see them off, but the Colonel Sahib was right, I was conspicuous. Even here in the hotel.

And so I sat down to wait, my stomach a tight knot of worry.

Chapter 22

I finally went to Simon's room, where I could pace the floor without waking the Major. Their uniforms were hanging tidily in the wardrobe, the door still standing wide. Despite my worry, by three o'clock in the morning I could hardly keep my eyes open. It had already been a long and trying day, and a worse evening, and I was exhausted. I sat in the chair by the hearth, slipping in and out of a doze while the room grew colder. I did what I could with the fire, but the scuttle was nearly empty. I dragged a quilt from Simon's bed and wrapped it around me. Listening to the church clock tell the hours had become a torment.

The longer they were gone, the more likely it was that they'd run into trouble. And how was a Colonel of my father's stature going to talk his way out of being caught breaking and entering the office of a firm of solicitors? Especially if that sharp-eyed Constable was on duty tonight.

Four o'clock came. Four fifteen. Four thirty. Sunrise was after seven o'clock. But by that time the hotel staff would be awake and preparing to make our breakfast.

I'd looked in on the Major once or twice, but he was still asleep. How had my father and Simon stayed awake through all these hours?

The adrenaline of the chase?

The two of them had once taken a prisoner out from under the nose of a tribal chieftain—it was a story that had made the rounds of the cantonment afterward. I hadn't known about it, but my mother must have done. My father treated her as an equal, and he would have warned her that he might not come back.

But they had come back.

What would I tell her if they didn't tonight?

I should have talked them out of it, I thought for the sixteenth time. But even as I chastised myself, I knew I couldn't have done it. We were at a standstill, and there was no other way to get the information we needed.

I began to fantasize what it could be. Something that we didn't know about Captain Travis? Something that was to his disadvantage? Something about James Travis and his reasons for leaving his family's estate to a stranger? Or something about James's will that we weren't aware of?

I'd been told that Mrs. Travis had been left a life interest in the house. But what if that wasn't true, and the real reason she was so set against the Captain wasn't the family history, but the fact that there had been no mention of a life interest? What if she had set that about, and Mr. Ellis, as her solicitor, had looked the other way? Then who shot her? Mr. Ellis was *with* her when she was shot.

I heard the clock strike five. And then five thirty.

Where were they? What had happened to them?

I could barely keep my eyes open, and watching the flickering of the fire sent me into a light sleep.

The next thing I knew, the door opened, and Simon said quietly over his shoulder, "She's in here."

And my father's familiar footsteps crossed the passage and he said, "Good morning, love."

From his tone of voice, I knew.

There was an exhilaration, that feeling of having succeeded in a very difficult task that made men make light of dangers past, whether it was a cricket match won by the narrowest of margins or a military action that had gone off flawlessly.

As the Colonel Sahib shut the door, I caught the reek of strong drink, and noticed a slight hilarity in their voices.

I sat up, pushing aside the quilt. "What happened? I was so worried."

Simon grinned. "Someone was still there when we looked up at the windows. We could see his shadow moving about. We went away, gave him a good hour, and when we came back, he was still there. We knocked at the door, and he answered it. The Colonel told him we were from London and demanded to see Ellis, that we'd been hired to do something hush-hush for him. Of course he was still at The Hall. We added that we intended to wait, as Ellis still owed us, and much to the clerk's horror, we sat down and refused to move. He couldn't very well go for the police, he didn't know what we might have done. I looked in a cupboard and found the whisky Ellis keeps for clients, and the clerk nearly had an apoplexy when we began to drink it and complained of Ellis being miserly and too fine to do his own dirty work. Before very long, the clerk took a glass, telling us that Ellis was a shadow of his father before him, and not fit to clean Whitman's boots."

My father said, "He had a much harder head than we'd expected, but he finally passed out. We put the whisky away, cleaned the glasses, and set about finding what we needed to know while the poor man snored in a corner. I daresay he'll be reluctant to mention us to Ellis, and we made certain we left everything as we found it. He'll see no trace of our being there, and neither will Ellis, even if the clerk does talk. I don't think he will. We appeared to be ruffians."

"If there's anything incriminating, how will we explain having such information? It won't be fair to bring the clerk into it."

"That will take care of itself," my father said, divesting himself of an ugly dark coat that looked far too tight on him.

Simon was taking it from him. He had already removed a brown corduroy coat and was on the point of carrying them back where he'd found them. I didn't ask where that was.

My father took the only other chair in the room and pulled it up to the fire. "What Spencer must have learned about Captain Travis was fairly straightforward. Ellis had had to trace Travis to Barbados, then to the Army. That took months. Apparently the Army was reluctant at first to tell a civilian his whereabouts. Ellis was finally given an address to write to, but he didn't do anything about it. Not as far as I could tell. For one thing, Mrs. Travis was against proceeding, and Ellis himself was dragging his feet. Eventually, as the war ended, he was worried enough to discover what had become of Captain Travis. It must have shaken him to learn that Travis was in England, in a clinic—and what sort of clinic it was."

I asked, "Wasn't there anything that might help us now?"

"Ah, that's when we came across Ellis's private files, and those were illuminating. He'd paid several imposters to come to The Hall under various pretenses, to ask for money. But Mrs. Travis is not your usual new widow, easy prey to stories about her son's love child and the like. On the contrary, he had to persuade her not to turn imposters over to the police. Apparently he convinced her it would only encourage others to try their luck."

I was beginning to suspect that my father was saving the best for last, and I felt hope surging. "Why on earth should he have done such a thing?"

Simon came back and sat down on the bed.

"Because, my dear," the Colonel Sahib was saying, "from the

time James Travis enlisted in the Army and wasn't here to keep an eye on matters, Ellis was embezzling funds from the estate. It was there in the private ledgers."

I sat back, stunned.

Ledgers . . .

That single entry under Ellis's name in Mr. Spencer's diary. I'd questioned that, then believed Mrs. Caldwell when she told us the firm was above reproach because she was so certain.

"He must have *encouraged* Mrs. Travis to refuse to deal with her son's heir," I said. "Because if the Captain had appeared, knowing what questions to ask about the estate—he's accustomed to managing his own—Ellis would be caught out."

"Precisely." My father grinned in satisfaction.

"Was it Ellis who killed Mr. Spencer?" I asked.

"I can only imagine it was," Simon replied. "Proving it is another matter. How do we suggest to Mrs. Travis that she should demand an instant accounting?"

That was going to be a challenge.

"And that," my father said, "will be your duty."

I shook my head. "Mr. Ellis must have known that when James came home from the war, he'd discover what had been done."

"It was a gamble," my father agreed. "A gamble that he'd be killed and never know. You need only look at the casualty rate for officers. The odds were in Ellis's favor."

It was slowly fitting together. "What drove him to embezzle? Was the firm not successful?" I asked.

My father looked at Simon, then turned back to me. "He's consumptive. Ellis. He's been in correspondence with doctors in a clinic in Switzerland. As soon as the war ended, he was going there for treatment. Without it he might well die sooner than later. It's his best hope."

I'd thought in the beginning that he looked like a consumptive. And yet he had also looked like a driven man, trying to keep his most important client satisfied. "Such clinics aren't cheap. Did he expect to be in Switzerland before the estate was settled?"

"He was clever enough to keep the money he'd embezzled in a special fund, so that it could be accounted for until the last minute."

Clever indeed! And just how were we going to persuade Mr. Ellis to stand up for Captain Travis, if there was no proof of what he'd been doing? Nothing we could show Mrs. Travis. My spirits sank.

"I wish we could learn more about Lieutenant Bonham," I said. "He's not another of Mr. Ellis's imposters, by any chance?"

"There was nothing about Bonham in the files we looked through. We kept to the Travis boxes, but I can be fairly sure that there wasn't one that was labeled Bonham. We did find that Oliver Masters is dead. Shot by a sniper three weeks before the end of the war."

"Then there truly is no possible heir—except for Alan Travis," I said slowly.

"What will the Captain do, if he's finally cleared and can inherit?" my father asked. "Has he said anything to you, Bess?"

"I wondered—I must admit it—if the Captain had shot at Mrs. Travis. It would have cleared his way, if he wanted the estate badly enough. Or the money it would bring him, if he sold it. But I wouldn't have expected him to miss."

Still, it was one thing to fire at an enemy and another to shoot a defenseless woman in her own parlor.

"You're going to find that Inspector Howe has already convicted Travis in his own mind—the Captain was back in Sinclair, the revolver was here at The George, and Ellis himself was with Mrs. Travis at the time. Howe still believes Travis killed Spencer." My father took out his watch. "I need a few hours' sleep if I'm to drive back to London today. Will you promise to stay out of trouble, Bess, until I can deliver the Major back to his quarters?"

"There's a train from the next village. Or from Bury," Simon told him.

He rose, stretching tired muscles. "I need to look in at the War Office as well. The French are already clamoring for reparations to rebuild the northern provinces of their country. It's getting out of hand. Germany is bankrupt, and it will take them a generation to get out of debt. I know a few men who matter, both in the High Command and in the government. Face-to-face over a good bottle of wine sometimes makes a difference."

I could tell he was worried about the situation here, never mind in France. He didn't want to leave so soon. The fact that he'd been able to break away even this long was amazing. I curled up in the chair again, settling the quilt around me.

"Gentlemen, the bed is all yours."

Long after they were breathing deeply—like most soldiers, they'd learned to sleep anywhere—I sat watching the fire burn down to gray ash, wondering what the day would bring.

It was shortly after a late breakfast that the Colonel Sahib and Major Davison set out for London. I stood in the doorway watching the familiar motorcar disappear around the far bend.

Behind me, Simon put a hand on my shoulder. "It will be all right, Bess."

"Where do we even begin?" I asked as we walked back into The George. "We can't simply tell Inspector Howe what we know. Or Mrs. Travis."

"I don't know," he said. "But I think we should begin with Ellis and see what happens."

"Good advice," I said. "I wish I knew if the Captain was waiting at The Swan. Meanwhile, we ought to see what Miss Fredericks can tell us about last night."

Constables were still searching for Captain Travis. Two of them were just coming out of St. Mary's, and I saw others standing outside Mrs. Horner's tea shop and stepping out the door of the baker's. On our way to the surgery, I waved to Mrs. Caldwell, taking an armful of greenery into the church for the altar vases. That niggling worry came back. Did she know more than she'd told us?

It was just a few minutes past nine when we walked into the surgery. I went straight to the room where we'd taken Miss Fredericks last evening, without speaking to Dr. Harrison's assistant first.

I found Sister Potter feeding her patient from a bowl of porridge. Lucy Fredericks's face was ugly, badly swollen with blotches of darkening bruises running from her jaw to her ear on one side, and under her eye on the other. I'd tapped, calling to Sister Potter before opening the door, and she greeted me with some relief. I was about to ask Simon to wait outside, but Sister Potter shook her head.

"He needs to hear this. Come in, and close the door, please."

Her patient was in a dressing gown too large for her, her hair down her back, looking very young. But she said at once, "I'm so glad you warned me not to say too much. My father was wanting blood, he was so angry. And there's no one at home to see he doesn't do anything rash."

"Are you saying you do remember something?" I asked. "Have you spoken to the police?"

"I haven't. Sister Potter forbade it. But I expect Dr. Harrison has. He told me that Inspector Howe wanted to interview me at a quarter past ten this morning." She looked at me with dread in her eyes. "What will I tell them? Whatever I say, my father will hear of it."

"You must tell me what you saw. Then we'll decide."

She seemed to shrink into the cot. "I never heard a shot being fired," she said quietly. "I didn't know there was one until my father said something about it. I'd walked up to the house to help in the kitchen. There were guests for dinner, I'd been told, and I'd be needed for the washing up afterward. Instead of going directly to the kitchen, I decided to see if there were motorcars in the drive. I like looking at them—my father drives for Mrs. Travis when she needs him. I was nearly to the corner of the house when he came at me so fast, out of the dark, there was no time even to scream."

She paused, her hands trembling. She clasped them together as Sister Potter reached out to pat them. "Go on," she said softly. "Tell them."

"He struck me twice in the face, knocking me to the ground, then he kicked me. I don't know how long I lay there unconscious. I didn't know anything more until I woke up here."

My heart sank. She hadn't recognized her attacker. We were no closer to the truth than we had been last night.

Lucy Fredericks was saying, "But that isn't all. Doctor gave me something to help me with the pain, and I expect I just went to sleep after it wore off. Or perhaps it was the drug. I don't really know. Except that I woke up in the night screaming, and I was so grateful Sister Potter was here, and there was a lamp burning."

"Yes, I'm glad she was here as well."

Then she added uneasily, "I was afraid to say anything before. He spoke to me in the dream—he must have done as he kicked me, but I don't remember that. He said, 'Tell what you saw and I'll finish this.' But what had I seen?"

It was Simon who asked, "Who was it?"

She looked up at him, tears in her eyes still. "He was a soldier in my dream. An officer. Not as tall as you. I couldn't see his face. I tried, but I couldn't. Why should an officer want to hurt me?"

Why indeed, unless he had seen her earlier when he'd shot at Mrs. Travis through the window? And he was afraid she was coming to the house now to tell someone she had been a witness.

"Would you remember his voice? From the dream?" I asked. "And recognize it if you heard it again?"

"Yes. Of course. I always remember what happens in my dreams," she answered simply, as if that was what everyone did.

But how was I to take this to the police? *Miss Fredericks dreamed she heard her attacker . . .*

Inspector Howe would laugh at me. And only intensify his efforts to find Captain Travis.

I said to Simon, "I refuse to believe it's the Captain. The only other officer is Lieutenant Bonham. He claims he came rushing down the stairs when he heard the shot. But he could have come down and gone quietly outside, fired the shot and then raced back. There was time—Mr. Ellis went to Mrs. Travis's aid first. He didn't immediately go to the door. But why should the Lieutenant shoot her?"

Simon answered grimly, "Captain Travis has told both of us that he believed the man who shot him would kill again. And I'm not sure the man isn't Bonham."

"He knew James," I said slowly. "Do you think the problem began there? And both the Captain *and* Mrs. Travis have been his targets. It couldn't have been Mr. Ellis. He was *with* her."

Lucy Fredericks, bewildered, was staring at us.

"What does Mr. Ellis have to do with this shooting?" Sister Potter demanded.

I worded what I had to say next very carefully. "I have wondered, you know. He's dragged his feet so long over this inheritance. What if he's hiding an—well, an irregularity in the Travis accounts?"

I might as well have suggested that Mr. Ellis was another Dr. Crippen, and had buried seven wives in his cellar.

She was appalled, shaking her head vehemently. "That's impossible. I can't believe he would do such a thing. I knew his father, a fine man, above reproach. It's true I don't care for the son, but I can't believe he would betray a trust."

I could see we were worrying Lucy Fredericks. I smiled at her. "You were wise to wait and tell me. Let me see what I can do."

"But what should I tell the Inspector when he comes?"

"It was a dream—" Sister Potter began, but I cut her off.

"Best to say nothing about the dream. For the moment."

Lucy leaned back against her pillows. "My dreams are never wrong," she told me in a small voice. "But no one wants to believe it."

"I do," I said reassuringly. "And so does the Sergeant-Major. But rest now. And try not to worry."

Sister Potter followed us out of the room. "You aren't really going to pursue this wretched business, are you? About the dream?"

I said, keeping my voice low, "The best thing we can do is to prove it wrong."

Satisfied, she nodded. "Poor girl. She's been through a terrible experience. I shouldn't wonder if her dreams are confused."

She went back inside, and I followed Simon out to the motorcar. As he was turning the crank, he said, "Sister Potter is plainspoken and plain thinking. Dreams are beyond her ken."

I saw Mrs. Caldwell coming out of the south porch of the church, and I said, "Let's hurry and catch her up."

But she had no news for us. I thought she hadn't slept any more than we had, and her concern for Captain Travis isolated her from her husband. It was a double burden of caring.

"How is Lucy? Does she know who attacked her?"

"She didn't actually see him."

"Poor child." With a nod, she walked on to the church gate and up the lane to the Vicarage.

Still watching Vera Caldwell, I said, "Perhaps we ought to go back to The Hall."

Mrs. Travis seemed a little feverish to me. Her face was slightly flushed, her eyes bright, and she was wearing a heavy shawl in a room that was as warm as a summer's day. There was a very pretty China tea service on the small table beside the chaise longue, but the cup at her elbow was still full.

I'd left Simon in the drawing room, and I said brightly, "Good morning," as I came in and took her hand. It was too warm. "How are you feeling?"

"Have they caught that madman?" she asked anxiously. "No one will tell me. And Dr. Harrison hasn't come."

"He's got surgery hours this morning. And there's another patient. Lucy Fredericks was attacked last night, after you were shot. She was beaten and left where she lay. It was quite by accident that she was discovered."

She put her good arm across her eyes. "Dear God. Will this never end?"

"Her father is threatening to kill whoever it was."

"I can't blame him. He's always had a short temper, but he was the best there was with horses. He could do anything with them. Is she going to live? Please tell me the truth."

"Yes, I expect she will. There's always the possibility of—"

She put up a hand. "I don't want to know."

"She thinks she remembers her attacker."

"It's Alan Travis. There's no one else who could do such a terrible thing."

"She hasn't told the police anything yet. I think she's afraid to speak up."

"Then you can tell Inspector Howe that I expect him to find the wretched man and put him away where he can't harm anyone else."

I held my tongue. It occurred to me that she'd always been the one to command, the one to set the tone of the village, the one who knew what was best. And now she'd discovered that she was vulnerable, like anyone else. It was a shocking experience. Was it the time to give her another shock?

"The police are still searching the village. What I can't imagine is why Mr. Ellis pleaded the Captain's case and persuaded the police in Bury to set him free last evening. He even drove the Captain back to The George, then left him there alone while he came here to call on you. It was unconscionable." I shook my head in a pretense of dismay.

She stared at me. "That can't be true."

"I'm afraid it is," I told her. "We were having an early dinner in Bury with my father, Colonel Crawford. As we left, we ran into the Inspector. He told my father he couldn't understand why Mr. Ellis had been so certain that the evidence against Captain Travis in the death of Mr. Spencer was circumstantial. But I expect Mr. Ellis felt he was duty bound to represent the Captain, since he's a Travis and heir to your son's estate."

"He is *not*," she said vehemently, showing more spirit now. "He is *not* the heir. And Mr. Ellis is well aware of my views on that subject. I will not have it. Send someone to Bury. I want to speak to him. He cannot serve two masters in this affair."

"Someone in the village asked me—well, I shouldn't be repeating gossip," I said, as if I'd overstepped my bounds.

"What did they ask you?" she demanded suspiciously.

"I—this is only gossip, you understand." I looked away, as if I were answering her against my better judgment. "Someone asked if—well, if Mr. Ellis had something to hide. If he'd been delaying contacting the Captain for reasons of his own, because he feared an accounting of your son's estate."

"Vera Caldwell. That's who it was. That misguided woman acts as if James was *her* son and not mine." She was very angry now, the flush deepening in her face.

"It seems that Mr. Spencer—the man who was killed in Dr. Harrison's surgery—was looking into Mr. Ellis's handling of the Travis estate. I'm told there was an entry in his diary questioning Mr. Ellis's dealings. He was with the Florian Agency, people you've used yourself. There's a suggestion making the rounds that he was killed to prevent him from telling anyone what he'd discovered."

"I don't believe you." She was confused and angry, no longer feeling helpless. "Ring for my maid, if you please. I wish to dress. And send for Mr. Ellis at once." She was trying to sit up and I leaned forward to help her. "No, I've changed my mind. I'm going to Bury myself."

"Is that such a good idea?" I asked. "Before the doctor has looked in on you?"

"He apparently thinks Lucy Fredericks is more important than I am." She stopped, and I thought for a moment that she had heard herself and realized how selfish that must sound. But she went on, frowning. "I can't ask Fredericks to drive me. He won't want to leave his daughter. The Sergeant-Major has his motorcar here, I believe? Yes? Then tell him I will be downstairs presently."

I was beginning to regret my decision to bring up Mr. Ellis. She didn't look well in spite of her burst of energy just now. I persuaded her to let me see to her arm before she rang for her maid. And I didn't like the look of the wound, either. The edges were angry, and there was an unhealthy redness spreading out from it. I cleaned it, added some of the salve that Dr. Harrison had left with her, and then put on a fresh dressing.

Her maid came and brought out a dark blue walking dress. I left to find Simon.

He was in the drive in front of the house, speaking to Fredericks. When I stepped out the door, Fredericks turned to me. "She won't tell me what happened. All I know is what Doctor had to say. But if I lay my hands on that man Travis, he'll wish he'd never set eyes on my daughter." He hadn't raised his voice, but I felt chilled by the power behind his words.

Before I could answer the chauffeur, the door opened and the Lieutenant stood on the threshold. "I thought I heard voices," he said. "Is there any news?" And to me, he asked, "How is Mrs. Travis this morning? I asked the staff, and I was told she was keeping to her room."

"She has business in Bury," I said, as if she were just going in to settle an account with her milliner. "I was afraid she wasn't up to it. But she insists."

His face lit with interest. "I'll go with you, shall I? I haven't been to Bury. I understand it has a famous ruin."

Simon answered for me. "I'm afraid there won't be room in the motorcar. We're taking Fredericks here to the surgery to visit his daughter."

"How is she?" the Lieutenant asked, looking from her father to me.

"Very badly bruised," I told him. "The doctor is keeping her for observation. Fredericks here is anxious to see her."

"Yes. Yes, of course." Lieutenant Bonham glanced up at the sky. The morning's sun had vanished behind clouds, and it looked as if there might be rain before the day was out. "I'll be waiting for her to come back. Will you tell Mrs. Travis that? She was going to show me some photographs last night, but of course that didn't happen." He was covering it well, but I thought he was annoyed by Simon's refusal to accommodate him. With a nod to Fredericks, he turned and went back inside.

"I don't like that man," Fredericks said, looking at the closed door. "The housekeeper caught him in the late Master's bedroom last night. She said it was forward of him, with Mrs. Travis being tended for a gunshot wound." He turned to Simon. "If you meant what you said, I'll take it kindly if you'd drop me at the surgery."

Speaking quickly, I said, "Your daughter still hasn't identified her attacker. Before you do anything rash, speak to her."

"The police haven't found him so far," Simon added. "Something could have happened to him as well."

I had begun to worry about that myself.

Fredericks looked at us. "I'll take that warning to heart, Sister. But if you're proven wrong, I'll do what I think best."

"And wind up in gaol yourself," I told him. "That won't help your daughter. And if *you're* wrong, and it wasn't the Captain after all, who will protect her from the right person, until she can identify him?"

Mrs. Travis came through the house door before he could answer. She was smartly dressed, with a very becoming hat that was the same shade of blue as her clothing. Not quite mourning, but she looked every inch the owner of The Hall, except for the scarf that had been used as a sling for her arm. She greeted Fredericks and asked after Lucy.

Simon told her that we were taking Fredericks in to see his daughter before going on to Bury. I didn't think she quite approved, but there was little she could say without appearing to be heartless.

We dropped Fredericks at the door of the surgery, then went on our way. Mrs. Travis was seated beside Simon, but she was staring straight ahead. Marshaling what she intended to say to Mr. Ellis?

We reached the town just as the sun gave up its struggle against the encroaching clouds and disappeared. Without it, the day's chill increased, and I was grateful when we found a place to leave the motorcar close by the firm's door.

I was surprised when she asked us to accompany her. As witnesses? Or to be abashed by our lies. Mr. Ellis greeted us warily. He must have seen something in Mrs. Travis's expression that warned him. As he ushered us into his private office, he gave me a speculative look. And then he was solicitously inquiring about her wound, and making the right noises of sympathy and consternation.

I thought for a moment that Mrs. Travis had lost her nerve, because here in the inner office, she must have thought it was impossible for an Ellis to be guilty of anything. And then, as I watched, she squared her shoulders and said abruptly, "I should like an accounting of my son's estate, if you please. I wish to bring in someone from London to represent me. I'm no longer convinced that you have my interests at heart."

Whatever Mr. Ellis was expecting, it wasn't this. He stared at her, his mouth open in astonishment. Collecting himself, he managed a smile. "I'm sorry you feel that way. Of course I'll do anything you ask of me. May I know the name of the firm in London?"

But there was no firm. "They will be in touch," she said after a moment. He hadn't put up any defense, and this confused her.

"Why did you persuade Inspector Howe to free Captain Travis? And why did you bring him back to Sinclair? You knew very well that I wanted nothing more to do with him. And then this—" She indicated her sling. "I hold you entirely responsible for what happened to me."

"I didn't think you would care to have the problems over your son's will become public knowledge. My hope was that we could send the Captain back to Wiltshire, where he would cause no more trouble for anyone."

He was clever, I could see that, able to find a suitable answer to each objection she brought up.

"But he wasn't returned to Wiltshire," she told him. "You drove away and left him on his own. That was unforgivable."

"I was told the staff at The George would see to it that he was watched until Sister Crawford returned. I had no idea it would be quite so late before she came back to the inn, or that the staff would be so busy at dinner."

"That's a pathetic excuse," she said, some of her anger coming back. But I thought that all this turmoil and exertion were taking their toll. This man was going to win after all, because she was not as well as she had believed she was.

He saw it too. "You aren't looking yourself. Let me ask my clerk to bring us some tea. You'll feel better, I think."

"I don't wish to have any tea," she said curtly.

"Nevertheless, I think it will do you good." He rose and came around the desk. "You prefer a Ceylon tea, I believe. We always have it on hand for you."

His concern for her welfare brought a frown. But he left the room, and Mrs. Travis turned to me. "He doesn't behave like a man who has something to hide. I'm beginning to wonder if you knew what you were talking about."

"He's kept his secrets for a long time. He won't give them up quickly," Simon replied. "You're doing the right thing."

His answer seemed to lift her spirits. She was accustomed to men looking after her welfare: the solicitor, the doctor, her husband, her son. Simon's encouragement was more effective than mine.

"We'll see," she responded. "I feel a draft coming from somewhere. I wish he would hurry."

But the room was quite warm. I got up and said, "Shall I take your pulse while we're waiting?"

She gave me her hand, and it was dry, hot.

Turning to Simon, I said, "Could you see what's keeping him?"

He knew what I was asking.

Rising, he went out of the room.

"I told him I didn't wish to have any tea," she said querulously.

Simon didn't come back straightaway, and I was beginning to think we'd been tricked. I was right. When he returned, his face was grim. "Ellis was called away on an emergency. So his clerk tells me."

"How impossibly rude," Mrs. Travis said, standing up. But Simon had gone to the shelf behind Mr. Ellis's desk, and he took down a solicitor's box and said, "I believe this is yours, Mrs. Travis. And this one as well. It might be best if you took both home with you and read through them."

"How clever of you," she applauded, unaware that Simon knew precisely where both files could be found.

He carried them for her, and we walked out of the room, down the passage, and met the Ellis clerk in Reception. He stammered an apology, then saw what Simon was carrying. He stared at Simon, then at the boxes. I thought, *Oh dear, he's recognized Simon from last night.*

Mercifully he hadn't.

"Here, you can't take that away with you."

Simon was taller, younger, and stronger. He said only, "Mrs. Travis requested it. I shouldn't try to stop me, if I were you." And the clerk backed away, still protesting.

We got out of there and to the motorcar as quickly as we could. Mrs. Travis was saying, "I feel rather ill."

As we left Bury, she said faintly, "Where do you think he's actually gone?"

"London," I told her. "Or Dover." I was thinking about Switzerland.

"I trusted him," she said, and fell silent for the rest of the journey.

We took her directly to Dr. Harrison's surgery as soon as we reached the village.

He came at once, glancing at me and then putting a hand to her forehead.

"You're running a fever, Mrs. Travis. Not unusual after what happened to you. Go home and lie down. I'll be there to look in on you in half an hour." He turned to Simon. "Fredericks is ready to go home. He's been upsetting his daughter and Sister Potter. I think he will be better off out of here."

Then he said to me, "They've got Captain Travis cornered in the church. There's a room upstairs in the tower. Someone remembered it. I don't know how the man knew, but it seems he's there."

Mrs. Caldwell had told the Captain, I was sure of it. How else could he have known? No one in the village had ever mentioned it. Why should they? It must be as old as the stair tower that ran up beside the main tower, and hardly a topic of conversation with strangers to the village. And then I realized I hadn't thought of it either, after looking at the tower stair.

I said, "Is Inspector Howe here? Is he in charge in the church?"

"Yes, so I understand from one of my patients. I've said nothing to Fredericks. He's very upset over what happened to his daughter."

I turned to Simon. "Take Mrs. Travis home. See that her maid knows what to do. I'm going to the church."

"Bess—"

"I'll be all right," I told him, and set out at a run, lifting my skirts a little so that they wouldn't wind themselves around my ankles and trip me up.

He started after me, but Mrs. Travis called to him, and he stopped.

I heard him say to Dr. Harrison, "Get Fredericks out here. *Now*. There's no time to waste."

CHAPTER 23

I REACHED THE south porch, a stitch in my side from running. Fear had lent wings to my feet, but now I stopped, settling my cap, waiting precious seconds until my breathing returned to near normal. Then I put my hand to the door.

It opened in my face, and Inspector Howe nearly collided with me.

"What the devil are you doing here?" he asked, his anger palpable.

"I was told you'd found the Captain."

"You know damned well I have. Thought you were clever, hiding him up there. And we can't go up, he won't come down." He took my arm, dragged me into the church, and pulled me toward the door to the tower. There were half a dozen men ranged around it, turning as one to stare at me.

"Call to him," Inspector Howe ordered. "Tell him to give himself up before someone is hurt. He's got a revolver up there with him. If we try to go after him, there will be bloodshed."

I wrenched my arm free of his grip. I was about to say the Captain couldn't be armed, but thought better of it in time. "There's been news," I went on. "Miss Fredericks is ready to give a statement about last evening. And Mr. Ellis has disappeared.

Mrs. Travis thinks there has been a problem with his stewardship of her son's estate. Before you do anything drastic here, talk to them."

But he didn't believe me.

"*Call to him*," he ordered me. And I stepped forward, to do as I was told.

"Captain Travis? Are you up there? There have been some new developments. Stay where you are until we've sorted it out."

I thought for an instant that Inspector Howe was going to strike me. He'd lifted his hand, so angry he was red in the face, and if there hadn't been other men present, I was sure he'd have carried through.

I stepped back a pace, just out of reach. "He deserves to know what's happening. Otherwise you'll drag him back to Bury and refuse to listen to anyone."

He said flatly, "If you don't tell that man to come down and give himself up, I refuse to be responsible for what happens next."

"You could try to burn him out," I said, and turning, walked back to the south porch door. He was too angry, and I wanted to find the Vicar, who might calm him down. No one followed me, although I could feel the stares coming my way like daggers between my shoulder blades.

I came face-to-face with Vera Caldwell.

"Betty tells me they've cornered Alan in the tower."

"Don't go in," I warned. "Inspector Howe is in no mood to listen to anything anyone else has to say. He tried to force me to ask the Captain to give himself up. I refused, and it only made the Inspector angrier. Where is the Vicar? He ought to be there."

"He's gone to the Swintons' farm. I don't understand," she said wearily. "It's frightening how they've hunted Alan."

"They don't want to believe him. It's Ellis who is behind this. He's disappeared."

She shook her head. "It can't be—"

"I know," I broke in. "His father was such a nice man. It's very likely he's embezzled from James Travis's estate."

In spite of everything, in spite of her belief in the Captain's innocence, she couldn't believe me. I sighed. Well, when Mrs. Travis looked at her accounts, perhaps everyone would. If it wasn't too late for Captain Travis.

I brushed past her and hurried on toward The George. Someone there would know how to find the Swinton farm. But the staff were busy preparing dinner and claimed they couldn't spare anyone. Angry, I went through the empty dining room toward Reception. I'd find someone on the street I could send.

And I walked straight into the arms of the man coming through the door.

He was rough, spinning me around and forcing me toward the stairs. I fought, but he was surprisingly strong, the strength of desperation, and he half dragged me up the steps, one hand over my mouth. Opening the door to my room, he shoved me hard across the floor and before I could get to my feet, he was on me, tying my hands. The bonds were tight, hurting my wrists.

"Scream," he warned, hauling me upright, "and I'll kill you now. Sit down over there. I don't know what you had against me, but you've made my life a living hell since the day you arrived in Suffolk. If Travis wants the estate, he can have it. I don't give a damn. I've got what I needed."

Mr. Ellis was angry and dangerous. I didn't answer him for fear of making matters worse.

But what was he doing here?

"I have to reach Paris. But the Army still controls passage across the Channel and most likely the trains as well, and I don't have time now to apply for a pass. You have connections. They'll help me, they'll know what permits I need. If you try to stop me, I'll kill you and anyone else in sight. Do you understand? I'm not squeamish."

I believed him. He was cornered, and that made his threats very real.

I hadn't seen his motorcar outside The George. Where had he left it?

I said, "I have only three days left of my leave—there isn't time. The Foot Police will come looking for me if I'm not back soon. They'll find you." It wasn't likely, but perhaps he wouldn't know that. "I have nothing against you. I just wanted to see Captain Travis get what was rightfully his."

"He won't marry you," he said with contempt. "No matter what promises he's made. Once he's got his money, he can wed any woman he wants. There's no title, but there's wealth. I only took a share of it. There's enough left to live well. I wasn't greedy."

"What do you want me to do?" I could hear the patter of rain against the windowpanes. How long would it take Simon to settle Mrs. Travis, return to the church, and find I wasn't there? Would he look in at the surgery, or come here? How much longer?

But he would have no warning either. And I was certain that this man was armed.

"My motorcar is round the back, out of sight. I don't know where the troublesome Sergeant-Major is, but we're leaving before he comes looking for you. We'll go quietly down the back stairs and out to my motorcar. If you call out or give anyone any reason to stop us, I'll kill them. Do you understand?"

"Yes." Before he could touch me, I got to my feet, managing to overturn my chair, as if I'd been clumsy. He picked it up, impatient with me, and shoved it against the foot of the bed, out of his way. "They'll see that my hands are tied."

"No, they won't. They're in the kitchen. We'll go down past the kitchen door and into the yard. I came up that way. No one saw me then."

He was right. The back stairs led directly to the yard door, and we went out without anyone the wiser. He had to help me into the motorcar, and then he went to turn the crank. I was tempted to scream, but thought better of it. The kitchen staff knew Mr. Ellis, they wouldn't be afraid of him, and they would be killed before they realized they were in danger. Even if the shot brought the police running, it would be too late. Instead I tried to ease my shoulders a little, but with my hands behind me, they were beginning to hurt. And my fingers were already swelling from the tightness of the bonds.

Where was Simon?

Mr. Ellis got in beside me, cast a glance toward the kitchen windows, and drove around to the front. There was no sign of Simon, and Inspector Howe was still occupied in the church. I watched the houses we passed, hoping someone was looking out a window. But Mr. Ellis's motorcar must be a fairly familiar sight in Sinclair and wouldn't arouse suspicion.

And then we'd reached the bend, and I tried to twist around to look behind me.

"Sit still, there's no one there," he said harshly, and I believed him. And it was as if the clouds opened at that moment, for the rain increased from a shower to a downpour.

We passed through Clare, where Simon and I had waited in vain at The Swan, expecting Mrs. Caldwell to bring Captain Travis safely to us. I couldn't help but wonder how different everything would have been if they'd arrived.

But the Captain would still be a fugitive. And we'd have had no idea that Mr. Ellis had been behind everything that had happened.

And that reminded me of Lieutenant Bonham.

"Who is Lieutenant Bonham?" I asked.

His attention was on the road as he navigated through the traffic in Clare's High, careful of people with umbrellas obscuring their vision as they tried to cross the street.

I thought perhaps he hadn't heard me. Or didn't know.

But as we left the outskirts of the village behind us, he said, "He's my sister's boy. Takes after his father, not our side, but a good lad at heart. He tried to kill the Captain for me. And when he came home to bury his aunt, he proved useful again. He's fair, like James. Who knows? Mrs. Travis is foolish enough to prefer him to the Captain."

And it all fell into place. Why Lieutenant Bonham had tried to kill Captain Travis before the war ended and he came back to England to learn of his inheritance. Why he'd shot at Mrs. Travis and attacked Lucy Fredericks. And why Lieutenant Bonham was even now worming his charming way into Mrs. Travis's life. With Ellis gone, who was there to tell her that she was taking a veritable viper to her bosom, as the expression went? He would be her rock, the person who stood beside her through this terrible ordeal, while she was unaware that he was no better than the woman with the baby or the other imposters who had come to her door.

"But surely people in Sinclair knew he was your nephew? Mrs. Travis knew your father, she must have known you had a sister."

"She was my half sister, brought up by an aunt in Cornwall. My father had an affair when he was in London. My mother never knew. He told me before he died."

So the father who was above reproach was human after all.

The road along here was tricky. It twisted and turned, blind corners, sharp curves, and with the rain already filling the ruts and disguising them, we were bouncing wildly. My shoulder was bruised from hitting the door, but all I could do was brace my feet against the floor and try to steady myself.

Mr. Ellis was concentrating on the road. And every mile that we gained meant that it would be that much longer before Simon could find us. And if we turned off this road, how would he know?

"I don't have the authority to persuade the Army to allow you to cross to France."

"Your father does. He'll see to it. When he's told the alternative. You'll call him in Dover. Now be quiet, or I'll gag you."

It was a terrible risk, but I had to take a chance. For very soon the road would straighten out for several miles. As we slid into the next curve, hitting a stretch of thick mud, I threw myself toward Mr. Ellis and the wheel.

Startled, he brought up a hand to ward me off—and lost control of the motorcar.

We were going too fast for starters, and the road was uneven. As he fought me and fought the wheel, we crashed through the hedgerow on the other side of the road and plunged into a field. A tree was coming at us, too fast to avoid, although Ellis tried.

We hit it hard, and my head struck the metal frame of the windscreen, and that was all I knew. My last coherent thought was, *We have stopped.*

I came to my senses with rain on my face, my body hurting all over.

For a moment, I couldn't think where I was. And then the crash came back to me, and I slowly began to remember. Mr. Ellis was caught between the wheel and the door, with my body hard against him. I couldn't turn far enough to see what injuries he might have. And trying was too painful.

I lay there, slipping in and out of consciousness, telling myself that I must get out of the rain, that I was cold, it was cold, and I'd be risking pneumonia. But I couldn't move.

I came to again as someone shoved me roughly to one side. I cried out, and a hand struck me in the middle of my back. Suddenly I was falling sideways, and I realized that Mr. Ellis had survived the crash, come to his senses as well, and had opened his door so that he could get out from under me.

I tried to raise myself, to do something to stop him, but without the use of my arms, I was helpless.

I could hear him breathing heavily, as if the effort he'd just made had cost him dearly. And then, with a grunt, he started to move away from the motorcar.

I had to stop him.

In an effort to clear my head, I let it sink against the leather of the driver's seat. It was warm from where he'd been sitting, and I was shivering.

Something had to be done about my hands, I thought hazily. If I could manage to free them I could get out of the motorcar and go after him. Glass from the windscreen, I told myself, ought to be sharp enough. But I couldn't twist around to search for a piece. My vision was blurring, and I realized that the rain was washing blood into my eyes.

I fought against my bonds, but it was useless. I tried to reach the horn—just beyond the door, and it might as well have been on the moon. There was a brightness around me, like a halo, and I realized that at least one of the headlamps was still working.

It wouldn't last long, but it would be a comfort while it lasted.

And then I passed out.

CHAPTER 24

I COULDN'T JUDGE the time. It was fully dark, had been getting close to sunset even as we passed through the last village. I lay there, so cold and wet, and worried about how low the temperature would dip tonight in this rain. I tried to move my legs, in an effort to stay warm, but they were jammed against my own door, and there wasn't much I could do.

And then I heard someone swear. My first thought was that Mr. Ellis had come back and was going to kill me. It would have made sense. It was the best thing he could do.

But the words were in Urdu, not English, and I lifted my head. "Simon?" I called. Or more properly, I croaked.

He was there, in the open driver's door, his hands reaching for me in the glow of the headlamps, and then I realized that he was moving me to one side, getting into the seat and drawing me into his arms.

He was so warm. And I was so cold. He said, "Bess. Can you hear me? Where are you hurt? What did he do to you?"

"I'm all right," I managed to say as he found my bonds and got out his knife to cut them. "A blanket, I just need a blanket and to get out of the rain. Then you must go after him. He can't have got too far, he was hurt too."

"I can't leave you this way. We'll find him, but he's not important now."

"No, listen. You must go. He has to be brought back to the village and turned over—over to Inspector Howe. Before they drag the Captain out of the tower. It won't do if he's caught in London or Dover. Or he gets away for good." My arms and hands were throbbing as the circulation was returning.

Torn, Simon sat there, and then he said, "Are you sure, Bess?" He had a handkerchief in his hand, and he was trying to wipe the blood from my face. "You're bleeding."

"Hurry," I begged. "A blanket, and away from the rain. Then I'll start to feel better."

Afraid to let me walk, for fear that I was hurt worse than he could see there in the dark, he got me out of that motorcar and carried me to his. The rug he brought from the boot was nearly as cold as I was, but he wrapped it around me and said, "It will feel better soon." He started to chafe my hands, to bring back the circulation, but I pulled them away.

"Go. I'll be all right."

But he'd dealt with wounded men, he knew that the wounds you couldn't see could kill as fast as those you could. And then he was fetching his torch from the boot. "I'll kill him when I find him," he said savagely as he came back to me.

I reached for his arm. "No. No, you won't. He has to be taken back to Sinclair."

He stood there for a moment, and I could tell that he wanted to ask one more question. But then he strode away without another word. I could see him casting about for tracks. I doubted there would be any, and facedown in the seat, I hadn't seen which direction Ellis had taken. Suddenly he straightened up, threw one last look toward the motorcar where I was sitting, and took off at a trot.

I sat there, wet through, shivering but slowly warming a little as the blanket kept my own body heat from being lost to the elements. I was out of the rain, although my cap and my hair straggled over my face, and my head hurt. And my greatest fear was that if Ellis offered any resistance at all, Simon wouldn't remember his promise to me.

It seemed like hours had passed, but I thought it must only be half an hour, three quarters at the most, when I saw Simon coming out of the darkness toward me. At first it seemed he was alone, and then I realized that he was dragging something behind him.

"Oh God," I whispered, terrified that he'd killed Ellis. I sat there and watched them come nearer with every stride. And then they were close enough that Simon said, "He's alive. I think there's something wrong with one leg. He didn't get far."

He opened the rear door and managed to shove the unconscious Ellis inside. Then he fumbled in his pocket and took out a revolver. "Hold on to that. I took it from Ellis. It's probably what was used to shoot at Mrs. Travis."

It was an older model, possibly a souvenir from the Boer War . . .

Shutting the door, he went round to turn the crank, and then he got in next to me.

"Are you all right?" he asked again. I could see that he was as wet as I'd been.

"I am now," I said, summoning up a smile. And then he was intent on getting his motorcar out of the field before we became bogged down. We got to the main road with a jolt that made me stifle a cry of pain.

We went back the way I'd come just hours before with Mr. Ellis, only this time Simon drove with caution, for the road was even worse than it had been. We were both relieved to find ourselves in what appeared to be the brightly lit High of Clare. It wasn't really that bright, but it seemed like a beacon after the thick darkness on the road.

Then we were plunged into darkness again as we drove on toward Sinclair. In fits and starts, I'd been telling Simon what had happened. When I'd finished, he said, "When I couldn't find you, when no one seemed to know where you'd got to, I knew something was wrong. Mrs. Caldwell had seen you walking toward the inn, and I went there to look. That's when I saw that your chair seemed to be out of place. Not where you'd normally sit. I guessed then, but which direction? I stopped at the tea shop and asked Mrs. Horner if she'd seen Ellis, that Mrs. Travis was asking for him. She told me he'd passed her shop not quite half an hour before, and I went after him."

I smiled. "I'm very glad you did."

He turned toward me, and for the first time there was a glimmer of a smile. "Your mother would have me shot in the Tower if I hadn't found you."

Simon wanted to take me straight to Dr. Harrison, but I insisted that we go instead to the church, fearful that the standoff was over and someone had got hurt.

But to my surprise, nothing had changed. I found Inspector Howe leaning against the tower wall, staring upward. If looks could kill, Captain Travis would have been dead long since.

Mrs. Caldwell sat in one of the pews, her face haggard. She started up in alarm when she saw me, wet and bloody, a blanket around my shoulders. Inspector Howe turned as he heard my footsteps. "What happened to you?" he demanded, as if I'd put him out by being accosted by a murderer and involved in a crash against a tree.

"I am here to give evidence that Mr. Ellis of the firm of Ellis,

Ellis and Whitman has taken me prisoner under threat of violence, and admitted to me that Lieutenant Bonham is his nephew. You'll find *Bonham* shot at Mrs. Travis to make you think it was the Captain, and attacked Miss Fredericks when he thought she might have seen him. I expect you'll need this." I reached into my apron pocket and pulled out the revolver. "It probably belongs to Mr. Douglas, at the inn. What's more, Lieutenant Bonham tried to kill Captain Travis in France. On the solicitor's orders. The Captain will recognize him. The reason Mr. Spencer was killed has to do with a file now in the possession of Mrs. Travis. He discovered that Mr. Ellis was embezzling from the estate. If you'll step out to the Sergeant-Major's motorcar, you'll see I'm telling the truth."

Inspector Howe was staring at me. I knew what a sight I must look, but it only bore out my story. Mrs. Caldwell, recovering from her shock, was there at my elbow, offering me a clean handkerchief in place of the bloody one I was clutching in my hand.

"Come and sit down," she said, urging me toward the nearest pew. But I stood my ground.

"Not until the Inspector goes out to see for himself."

He beckoned to Constable Simpson, and together they went out to where Simon was waiting on the lane in front of the church.

Mrs. Caldwell was saying, "Are you all right, Bess? You're awfully pale, and there's blood everywhere. You're shivering."

I was still quite wet, and it was cold in the church. I thought of Captain Travis up there in the tower. He'd be cold as well. But at least he was out of the rain.

"I'll be fine," I assured her, as I'd assured Simon. And I thought I probably was, save for the cut on my forehead and bruises everywhere. I suddenly wanted to sit down, and it seemed to take a long time before Inspector Howe was satisfied.

Eventually he came back through the door, his expression grim.

"Simpson and Brandon have taken Ellis to Harrison's surgery. He was just coming to, and he was in pain from his leg. Seems a dog's bite was reopened by the crash. It was just beginning to close."

"Dr. Harrison's dog?" I asked quickly. "We thought he might have bit someone who came after poor Mr. Spencer that first time."

"I'll be looking into that. Meanwhile, Brandon is filling his motorcar with petrol, and then he's driving me out to where Ellis's motorcar was left."

I wanted to object, but who else could take the police there?

I said, "What about Captain Travis? You can't just leave him there in the tower."

"Oh, can't I? He wouldn't come down. He can stay there until he rots, as far as I'm concerned." He beckoned to his men and they trooped out, leaving us in the church alone.

I didn't trust him, and I caught Vera Caldwell's arm as she was about to hurry to the tower door and call to the Captain. We waited a quarter of an hour, in case it was a trick, and then I let her go.

"Alan? You can come down," she called. "It's safe. The police have gone. They have Mr. Ellis in custody now. It's over."

But there was no sound from above.

I got stiffly to my feet. At the foot of the tower, I called, "It's Sister Crawford, Captain. Will you please come down? I'm so cold I can't bear it any longer."

Another minute or two passed, then I could hear his footsteps on the stone staircase. He looked as wretched as I felt, but when he saw me, he said, "Good God."

And I had to explain all over again.

Mrs. Caldwell took him back to the Vicarage, no longer caring what her husband might say. She and the Captain wanted to take me there as well, but I refused. And when they had gone, I walked to the inn in the rain, commanding myself to put one foot in front of the other until I reached the door.

I made it up the stairs, thinking about a hot bath and a cup of reviving tea.

But when Simon came back much later, I'd crawled into bed and fallen fast asleep.

In the morning we went to The Hall. Mrs. Travis was just sitting down to breakfast with Lieutenant Bonham. I could tell that for once, gossip hadn't yet reached her.

We'd agreed, Simon and I, on what to say to him. And with a smile, after inquiring about Mrs. Travis's arm, I said, "Lieutenant? Your uncle, Mr. Ellis, is asking for you. He's been injured, and he's in Dr. Harrison's surgery. Can we drive you there? And Miss Fredericks is there as well. She wants to see if you're the man who hurt her." I turned to Mrs. Travis. "Mr. Ellis had withdrawn the money he took from you. He was carrying it with him when he was caught. I expect he didn't intend to share it with his nephew."

I knew, in an instant, that Mrs. Travis had told the Lieutenant all about Mr. Ellis. She might even have shown him the box of estate deeds and papers. But she hadn't known who the Lieutenant really was. She turned to stare at him.

He tensed, ready to fight his way out. But Simon was between him and the door, and one look at Simon's expression warned him that it was not a wise choice.

Mrs. Travis, horrified, stood there while I went to the door and called to Inspector Howe in the drive. He came in and took the unresisting Lieutenant into custody.

I had the fleeting thought that of the two men, I'd have said the Lieutenant was the more dangerous. And I'd have been wrong.

I followed Inspector Howe, Constable Simpson, and Simon out to the drive, where the motorcars were standing.

We had arranged a final surprise for Lieutenant Bonham. When I was sure he was in custody, I was to alert Captain Travis, whom we'd kept out of sight, to step forward and confront this man, to lay to rest, finally, the nightmare that he'd lived ever since he'd been brought into our forward aid station with a head wound. I'd have liked to have Lucy Fredericks there as well, but she would have her opportunity to identify the Lieutenant when she was stronger. I wasn't quite sure what was going to happen. Simon had been worried about that. But we owed it to the Captain.

We came out into the sunlight, the five of us. The Constable went forward to open the rear door to the Inspector's vehicle, but the Lieutenant stopped just at the edge of the drive, protesting what he called a travesty of justice.

"There's no evidence I was involved in anything here. I can't help it if that man's my uncle. I've done nothing wrong. You can't prove anything against me." He looked from the Constable to Inspector Howe.

"Your own guilty conscience led you to attack Lucy Fredericks—she didn't see you shoot at Mrs. Travis," I said quickly. "She told us, even before you came, that you were trouble. And there's proof that your uncle attacked Mr. Spencer the first time—he's got the dog bite to show for it. If he doesn't want to hang for murder, he'll confess that he sent you the second time to finish his work. And somehow I believe he will, because he's already told me he wanted you to kill Captain Travis in France, if you could find him out there. That was terrible enough, shooting at one of your own side. Killing a man with broken ribs, who couldn't defend himself properly, shooting at a defenseless woman who has welcomed you into her home, and nearly beating Miss Fredericks to death just because you were afraid she might have seen you outside the drawing room window have all the earmarks of a coward's work."

He turned on me then. "You know nothing about me."

"I know all I care to know."

Without waiting for my signal, Captain Travis stepped around the corner of the house, where he'd been impatiently standing. It had taken a good deal of persuasion on my part, and Simon's as well, to keep him from marching into The Hall and confronting Lieutenant Bonham there.

But it had been far more urgent to winkle the Lieutenant out of The Hall without any trouble.

Well before dawn we had been back in Bury, laying out all our evidence for Inspector Howe. Without the boxes of papers from Ellis's office, now in Mrs. Travis's hands, we had been put to some trouble explaining how we knew what the Colonel Sahib and Simon had seen during their midnight carousing with Mr. Ellis's clerk. The man had even been pulled in to give his evidence about the embezzling, but he knew nothing about it. And then there was the connection with Lieutenant Bonham. Inspector Howe had refused to take my word for his relationship with Mr. Ellis, and we had had to send the clerk back to the firm to find those records as well.

Now, as Alan Travis walked out into the sunlight, his head uncovered, I could see that both men were English fair in complexion and coloring. Both men had blue eyes, but Lieutenant Bonham's were not that intense blue of the Captain's, and he was nearly an inch shorter as well, his shoulders less broad, his jawline less firm. And yet for an instant there was a fleeting resemblance, the kind one finds in people sometimes, making one look twice to be sure. I could see as well how much stronger the resemblance was between James and the Captain. Although he was thin and still far from recovered from his back wound, there was something about the expression around the eyes that the Captain shared with his cousin. Lieutenant Bonham was a poor third to both men. All the same, Mr. Ellis had played a very strong hand in sending him to meet Mrs. Travis, still grieving for her son. Who knew what might have come from that?

Something in my face must have alerted the Lieutenant, for he wheeled toward the corner of the house, and the two officers who had twice come face-to-face on the field of battle met again on an English doorstep.

None of us could miss the swift flare of recognition that passed between them. I watched Alan Travis's hands clench at his sides as he came on toward us, and beside me Simon stirred as well, prepared to intervene if need be.

Captain Travis stopped some fifteen feet away. And his eyes swept the man standing there, braced for any attack. Lieutenant Bonham's gaze was cold and angry now, but he waited, saying nothing.

The tension in the air was almost palpable.

Captain Travis said with bitterness, "You look nothing like my great-uncle after all. Nor like the man I met and respected in Paris. I was a fool ever to think you did. Sister Crawford is right. And so was I. You have the instincts of a killer, and someone had to stop you."

Lieutenant Bonham didn't reply.

After a moment, Captain Travis turned to Inspector Howe, adding harshly, "Take him away. He's a disgrace to the uniform he wears."

And then, without waiting, without asking to see Mrs. Travis or mentioning the estate he was heir to, Alan Travis turned and walked away down the drive, back to The George and the room he was sharing once more with Simon.

I was close enough to hear what Lieutenant Bonham was saying under his breath. "If my aim had been better . . ."

But it hadn't been in France, and it hadn't been here in Suffolk, when he shot at Mrs. Travis.

I couldn't stop myself from answering him. "Or perhaps that of the Germans . . ."

And he glared at me, venom in his gaze.

The tension broke then, as the Captain disappeared around the sweep of the drive. And only Simon had heard my words as the men collected themselves and headed for the motorcars.

When Inspector Howe's motorcar drove away with the Lieutenant in handcuffs and guarded by Constable Simpson in the rear seat, I turned to Simon.

"Well," I said, inadequately.

"Well," he answered, understanding.

I left him in the empty drawing room, the sheet still hanging across the shattered window, and went back up the stairs.

It took me some time to comfort Mrs. Travis. First her solicitor had betrayed her, and now the young man she had trusted. She cried a little, then was angry, and finally said, laying her head against the back of the chaise longue in her room, "I've been a stupid woman, but I thought—I believed it was what Hugh would have wanted. He never had anything good to say about that branch of the family. He would have hated seeing them inherit The Hall."

I was sympathetic, but in a way I couldn't feel sorry for her. She had fought the wrong battles. And perhaps had lost the war. I couldn't imagine that Captain Travis would feel kindly toward her.

But I was wrong there. A little later in the morning he borrowed Simon's motorcar to drive out to The Hall while Simon was giving his statement to Inspector Howe. When he arrived, he told me there had been some difficulty with Lucy Fredericks's father, who had wanted to tear the Lieutenant limb from limb. His daughter had finally calmed him down.

When I led the Captain to the drawing room, a sheet still covering the broken window, Mrs. Travis rose from the chair where she'd been sitting and said formally, "Captain Travis? I owe you many apologies. It's my fault this business of the will wasn't settled long ago. It's possible that you would never have been shot, and Mr. Spencer wouldn't have come to Sinclair to die. And Mr. Ellis would have been found out sooner."

He accepted her apology with grace, and she added, "I'm in the process of arranging for a new solicitor. When that's settled, we will come to an agreement about this house and my son's estate. There will be death taxes, of course, but you will still be a wealthy man."

Looking around him at the elegant room in which we stood, he said, "I have a home, Mrs. Travis. In Barbados. I love it with all my heart. You're welcome to stay here as long as you choose. If I marry and have children, perhaps one of them will wish one day to live in England. I won't stand in his or her way."

"That's very gracious of you, Captain." She was fighting to keep her voice from breaking. "And very generous."

"Alan," he said. "That's my name. I believe it was one of your son's names as well."

"It was. The medieval wool merchant who built the church in the village and made a fortune in trade was Alan Travis too. A plain man, the story goes, who refused a title because he didn't want to sit in Parliament when he could live at The Hall. Much as you prefer Barbados. I hope you'll come to Suffolk again. You'll be welcomed. For James's sake and for your own."

We left soon afterward, and I took the Captain back to Mrs. Caldwell. He thanked me profusely for all I'd done. "There's no way I can repay you," he said. "You believed me when no one else did. I'm in your debt, I always will be. Will you come to Barbados one day? And let me show you the island?"

I smiled. "I would like that very much," I said. "We'll see." But even as I said it, I didn't think I would ever be likely to visit Barbados or any other island in the Caribbean Sea.

He came to take my hands and leaned forward to kiss me on the cheek.

"The door is always off the latch," he said quietly.

I walked out to where Simon was waiting in his motorcar. He'd stopped at The George to fetch our luggage while I was giving a formal statement to the police. I was free to go.

I waved to Sister Potter, just walking back to her cottage. Lucy had been allowed to return to The Hall after the Inspector had taken the Lieutenant into custody. And after the doctor had seen him, Mr. Ellis, I'd been told, was taken to Bury. Betty, at The George, informed me that Sister Potter had refused to serve as his nurse.

I didn't know whether to believe her or not.

It was such a pretty village, I thought as we left it behind.

After we'd passed the broken hedgerow where Mr. Ellis's motorcar had come to grief, Simon glanced my way.

"Were you asked to come to Barbados?"

I smiled. "I was. It was kind of him. But Somerset is my home, and I'm used to it."

"Then I'll take you there."

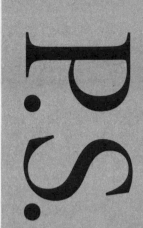

About the author

About the book

Insights,
Interviews
& More . . .

Read on

Meet Charles Todd

Michael Frost Photography

CHARLES TODD is the author of the Bess Crawford mysteries, the Inspector Ian Rutledge mysteries, and two stand-alone novels. A mother-and-son writing team, they live on the East Coast. ～

The Story Behind the Story

As we came closer to the end of the Great War, we were wondering how Bess—and those who'd fought and those who'd been wounded over four long years of bitter fighting—would face it. And whether Bess would consider the war's end the end of her career as a nurse.

As Bess says in *A Casualty of War*, the Armistice was a relief after so much bloodshed, but the wounded don't rise from their beds, shed their bandages, and go home. So many men gave their lives in that conflict. On all sides. And others gave their futures for king and country. They go home not as conquering heroes but as amputees, burn cases, and far worse. Bess is still needed, to see these men through and try to help them return to an England that isn't ready for them.

When we were in Barbados, we saw the memorial to those who had served king and country and never came back to that sunny island in the Caribbean. Many of them had relatives in England, or at least ancestors, and they felt strongly about defending her. It was a tall, white monument in the town square, in a place of pride. Later during that visit, we went to a house that looked much as it had in 1914, and there were photographs of the family who had lived there. It was open and airy, there were guest houses across the spacious, shaded back garden, and tables were set for meals in the cool of the evenings. That house and the memorial in the square stayed with us ▶

when we left, and we began toying with
the idea of a man from that family—now
our family—who might enlist to fight
in the Great War even though he had no
real ties in England, had never met his
cousin there. By a twist of fate, they
encounter each other briefly in a railway
station in Paris where one is just finishing
a short leave and the other is beginning
his. They like each other, but later, when
they meet again on the battlefield, one
tries to kill the other. . . .

That led us to *why*. Bad blood in the
distant past? Or was there something else
that was going on, something the captain
from Barbados wasn't aware of? What did
he really see in the heat of battle? Smeared
with sweat and blood and blackened with
gun powder, men might not be what they
seem.

And, of course, that led to another *why*.
A chance meeting with Bess in the base
hospital canteen wasn't as chance during
the war as it might seem. People in the
same sector were likely to run into one
another. Later, though, when the captain
is brought in to the forward aid station
where she's now posted, she's drawn
into the nightmare he's suffering. Is it
madness? Is he telling the truth? And
if he isn't—

We had our story. And writing it
brought back the sunny afternoon in that
house in Barbados. We also had to decide
if the captain's name would appear on that
white memorial in the square, a casualty
of war, or if he would be one of the lucky
ones who came home. Still, with Bess on
his side, luck might well favor him. ∾

Questions for Discussion

1. *A Casualty of War* takes place in 1918 as the Great War ends, but soldiers and civilians alike are still struggling with unbearable losses and a changed England. Has reading this novel given you a new appreciation of the lasting wounds conflict leaves in its wake on all those involved?

2. Bess encounters many soldiers suffering from post-traumatic stress disorder, a condition that would not be fully acknowledged in the medical community until late in the twentieth century. What is your impression of the attitudes toward "shell shock" during the Great War, and the fates of the soldiers experiencing it?

3. Bess and Simon Brandon have known each other for many years and are very close. Do you think her acceptance of him in the family—she has said he is the son her father never had—has made it difficult for her to see him in any other way? *Should* she? Is a romance between them necessary to the story? Or would it spoil the series?

4. Why do you think Bess feels so much responsibility to help Captain Travis? She feels guilty for mentioning his cousin while he is struggling to identify his assailant. But she also knew him beforehand, knew the man he was. Or was it seeing him ▶

tied to his bed in a windowless room? Perhaps it's a need to find out what is really true?

5. Bess gently refuses Sergeant Lassiter's proposal, insisting there is too much work to be done to consider herself. But as the Great War is ending, what do you think drove her most to decline his offer? She would have to resign from nursing if she said yes. Does that affect her decision? Should she have told him to wait?

6. The Armistice brings the fighting to a close. Why does Bess feel so strongly that her work isn't done? She became a nursing sister to save as many men as she could, and she has done that. Do you think this is true to the nursing profession, to stay on to help those who will never recover fully?

7. Has this series helped you understand the Great War and the sacrifices that were made by so many, both on the battlefield and on the home front? What were your views before you read these books? And after reading them?

8. What is your impression of Mrs. Travis's character? Do you think it is unfair of her to hold the past against the captain? What do you think drives her most to ignore her son's wishes in the will?

9. Do you think Bess and Simon believe the tenant farmer's daughter when she explains the dream she had about James Travis? What do you make of her claim?

10. Did the identity of the killer surprise you? Whom did you most suspect throughout the novel and why?

11. At the end of the novel, the world is on the precipice of massive change, and Bess will eventually have to return to civilian life. What do you think lies in store for her next? What is in her character that you believe will guide her toward the future? ⮍

The Bess Crawford Mysteries

THE SHATTERED TREE

At the foot of a tree shattered by shelling and gunfire, stretcher bearers find an exhausted officer, shivering with cold and a loss of blood from several wounds. The soldier is brought to battlefield nurse Bess Crawford's aid station, where she stabilizes him and treats his injuries before he is sent to a rear hospital. The odd thing is, the officer isn't British— he's French. But in a moment of anger and stress, he shouts at Bess in German. When Bess reports the incident to Matron, her superior offers a ready explanation. The soldier is from Alsace-Lorraine, a province in the west where the tenuous border between France and Germany has continually shifted through history, most recently in the Franco-Prussian War of 1870, won by the Germans. But is the wounded man Alsatian? And if he is, on which side of the war do his sympathies really lie? Bess remains uneasy—and unconvinced. If he was a French soldier, what was he doing so far from his own lines . . . and so close to where the Germans are putting up a fierce, last-ditch fight? When the mysterious officer disappears in Paris, it's up to Bess—a soldier's daughter as well as a nurse—to find out why, even at the risk of her own life.

A DUTY TO THE DEAD

Bess Crawford, a nurse on the doomed hospital ship *Britannic*, grows fond of the young, gravely wounded Lieutenant Arthur Graham. Something rests heavily on his conscience, and to give him a little peace as he dies, she promises to deliver a message to his family. It is some months before she can carry out this duty, and when next she's in England, she herself is recovering from a wound. As she frets over the delay, that simple message takes on sinister meanings. When Bess arrives at the Graham house in Kent, Jonathan Graham listens to his brother's last wishes with surprising indifference. Neither his mother nor his brother Timothy seems to think it has any significance. Unsettled by this, Bess is about to take her leave when sudden tragedy envelops her. She quickly discovers that fulfilling this duty to the dead has thrust her into a maelstrom of intrigue and murder that will endanger her own life and test her courage as not even war has.

AN IMPARTIAL WITNESS

Serving in France during World War I, battlefield nurse Bess Crawford is sent back to England in the early summer of 1917 with a convoy of severely burned men. One of her patients, a young pilot, has clung to a photograph of his wife since he was pulled from the wreckage of his plane, and Bess sees the photo ▶

every time she tends to him. After the patients are transferred to a clinic in Hampshire, Bess is given forty-eight hours of leave, which she plans to spend in her London flat catching up on much-needed sleep. But in the railway station, in a mob of troops leaving for the front, Bess catches a glimpse of a familiar face—that of the same pilot's wife. She is bidding a very emotional farewell to another officer. Back in France days later, Bess picks up an old newspaper with a line drawing of the woman's face on the front page, and a plea from Scotland Yard asking if anyone has seen her. The woman had been murdered the very evening Bess glimpsed her at the terminal. Bess asks for leave to report what she knows to Scotland Yard. And what she learns in England leads her to embark on the search for a devious and very dangerous killer—a search that will put her own life in jeopardy.

A BITTER TRUTH

When battlefield nurse Bess Crawford returns from France for a well-earned Christmas leave, she finds a bruised and shivering woman sheltering in the doorway of her London flat. Realizing that the woman, who eventually reveals that her name is Lydia, has nowhere else to turn, Bess takes her in. Lydia is fleeing from her husband, who struck her after a terrible quarrel, and she refuses to return home unless Bess accompanies her. Concerned, Bess puts aside her visit to her own family and goes with Lydia to Ashdown Forest in Sussex. There are other guests at the Ellis house and the atmosphere is tense, fueled by Lydia's angry husband. Shortly after they arrive, one of the guests, recovering from wounds, is found murdered, and Bess is not only in the center of the hunt for a killer, but is also under suspicion herself.

AN UNMARKED GRAVE

Even deadlier than the bloody engagements on the battle-scarred fields of France, the Spanish influenza epidemic in the spring of 1918 is bringing hundreds of new patients to World War I battlefield nurse Bess Crawford. But war and disease are not the only killers to strike with cold and brutal efficiency. Concealed among the countless dead waiting for burial is the body of an officer whose end was not hastened by a German bullet or an airborne virus. This soldier was murdered, and his death touches Bess deeply, for he was a family friend who once served in her father's regiment. Falling ill herself before she can report the heinous crime, Bess recovers too late to consult with the only other witness, who, by all official accounts, has since hanged himself. Bess refuses to let a killer escape justice, though her persistence turns an assassin's attention in her direction. Or was she already his next target? ▶

A QUESTION OF HONOR

World War I nurse and amateur sleuth Bess Crawford investigates an old murder that occurred during her childhood in India, and begins a search for the truth that will transform her and leave her pondering a troubling question: How can facts lie? In 1908, when a young Bess Crawford lived in India, an unforgettable incident darkened the otherwise happy time. Her father's regiment discovered it had a murderer in its ranks, an officer who killed five people yet was never brought to trial. A decade later, tending to the wounded on the battlefields of France during World War I, Bess learns from a dying man that the alleged murderer, Lieutenant Wade, is alive and serving at the front. According to reliable reports, he'd died years before, so how did Wade escape from India? What drove a good man to murder in cold blood? Bess uses her leave to investigate. But when she stumbles on the horrific truth, she is shaken to her very core. The facts reveal a reality that could have been her own fate.

AN UNWILLING ACCOMPLICE

Bess Crawford has been summoned by the War Office to accompany a wounded soldier to Buckingham Palace, where he's to be decorated for gallantry by King George himself. Heavily bandaged and confined to a wheelchair, Sergeant Jason Wilkins will be in her care for barely a day. But on the morning after the ceremony, when Bess goes to collect her charge for his return journey to his clinic, she finds the room empty. How could such a severely wounded man simply vanish without a trace? Both the Army and the Nursing Service hold Bess to blame for losing the war hero. The Army now considers Wilkins a deserter, and Scotland Yard questions her when Wilkins is suspected of killing a man in cold blood. If Bess is to clear her name and return to duty in France, she must prove that she was never his accomplice. But the sergeant has disappeared again and neither the Army nor the police can find him. Following a trail of clues across England, Bess is drawn into a mystery that seems to grow darker with every discovery. But will uncovering the truth put more innocent people in jeopardy?

A PATTERN OF LIES

An explosion and fire at the Ashton Gunpowder Mill in Kent has killed over a hundred men. It's called an appalling tragedy—until suspicion and rumor raise the specter of murder. While visiting the Ashton family, Bess Crawford finds herself caught up in a venomous show of hostility that doesn't stop with Philip Ashton's arrest. Indeed, someone is out for blood, and the household is all but under siege. The only known witness to the tragedy is now at the Front in war-torn France. Bess is asked to find him. When she does, he refuses to tell her anything that will help the Ashtons. Realizing that he believes the tissue of lies that has nearly destroyed ▶

The Bess Crawford Mysteries *(continued)*

a family, Bess must convince him to tell her what really happened that terrible Sunday morning. But now someone else is also searching for this man. To end the vicious persecution of the Ashtons, Bess must risk her own life to protect her reluctant witness from a clever killer intent on preventing either of them from ever reaching England. ∾